Alias Sherlock Holmes 3:

Showdown

Best wishes

— Russell Baker

Gary Andres

Alias Sherlock Holmes 3:

Showdown

By Rev. Russell Baker

TATE PUBLISHING
AND ENTERPRISES, LLC

Published by Tate Publishing & Enterprises, LLC
127 E. Trade Center Terrace | Mustang, Oklahoma 73064 USA
1.888.361.9473 | www.tatepublishing.com

Tate Publishing is committed to excellence in the publishing industry. The company reflects the philosophy established by the founders, based on Psalm 68:11,
"The Lord gave the word and great was the company of those who published it."

Book design copyright © 2014 by Tate Publishing, LLC. All rights reserved.

Published in the United States of America

ISBN: 978-1-63449-493-9
1. Fiction / Christian / Suspense
2. Fiction / General
14.08.21

Other books by Rev. Russell Baker, available by Tate Publishing

Alias Sherlock Holmes

Alias Sherlock Holmes 2: A Fear of Heights

This book is dedicated to my wife Debbie's parents, Willis and Jean. For your continued support in all ways, I am deeply indebted.

INTRODUCTION

Of all of the parables taught by our Lord, Jesus Christ, one of the most beloved is the parable of the Prodigal Son. At its heart is a beautiful picture of God's willingness to forgive a repentant sinner no matter how badly the sinner had messed up. The prodigal son in Jesus' story seriously messed up his life and received a forgiveness he didn't deserve.

In the *Alias Sherlock Holmes* series, I am attempting to show people living out their faith in the context of mystery stories. In "Showdown", you—the reader—will be meeting a modern day prodigal who wants a second chance, like the prodigal in Jesus' story. It will also mark the first face to face confrontation between Christopher Anderson and the crime boss calling himself Moriarty.

There may be a time throughout your Christian walk that God brings you in contact with real life prodigals. May we, as God's people, share with them that there is always forgiveness to be found in Jesus.

PROLOGUE

Excerpt from THE OKLAHOMA SUN, an online news magazine

Sherlock Holmes Unmasks Moriarty
By Wendy Hughes, staff writer

The nation was stunned as one of the most mysterious figures of Oklahoma's underworld was unmasked by an equally mysterious detective calling himself Sherlock Holmes. Moriarty, the name chosen by the head of Oklahoma City's Crimson Dragons crime syndicate, has finally been identified after years of diligent detective work.

For over 7 years, the Crimson Dragons ruled Oklahoma City's underworld, being involved in every crime from racketeering to murder. The syndicate was under the iron-fisted control of one man: the unknown crime boss calling himself Moriarty.

Moriarty is, of course, the name of the chief villain in the Sherlock Holmes stories. Ironically, it was a detective who calls himself Sherlock Holmes who has successfully unmasked Moriarty. Sherlock Holmes first came under Oklahoma's spotlight nearly six years ago, and has been successfully solving the most complex crimes in recent history.

After a long and complex investigation, Holmes and his partners Crystal Parker and Dr. Watson (yes, Dr. Watson!) revealed that Moriarty is none other than Chase Anderson, the brother of a former Oklahoma City detective. Chase Anderson is known to have a long history of run-ins with the law. As a teenager, he had been convicted of dealing drugs.

After killing a security guard, Chase broke out of the juvenile correction facility. He also murdered a paroled former cellmate, Hugh West, and assumed his identity after murdering his own parents and burning their home. Chase faked his own death by placing West's body in his parents' home before starting the fire.

It was while attending college using Hugh West's identity that he began building his criminal empire. During his college career, he forced fellow students to commit acts of robbery, to sell drugs, and to prostitute themselves. After graduating college, Chase used his Hugh West alias to obtain a job as a scientist at Future Tech, a research facility, and used Future Tech as a front for the Crimson Dragons.

Chase Anderson remains on the run at this time. Although police are watching every possible exit out of Oklahoma, he remains at large. Detective Maria Lorenzo has gone on record as saying...

———————————————

Excerpt from THE OKLAHOMA CITY CHRONICLE, an online news magazine
Oklahoma City Stalker Slays 2 In 1 Night
By Charles Henderson, staff writer

The Oklahoma City Stalker has struck again, striking fear in the hearts of women throughout the city. This time, the Stalker has outdone himself both in the ghastly mutilations he has become known for and in the number of victims he has taken at one time. For the first time, the Stalker has killed two victims in one night.

The victims were Kelly Hawk, age 19, and Amanda Witherspoon, age 22. Both were young prostitutes who advertised their services on *Cyber-Ads*. Miss Hawk's mutilated remains were found behind a dumpster at the Pizza Palace on 5th Street. Sanitation workers found her remains when their trash truck lifted the dumpster to empty the garbage. While police are not releasing the details of the mutilations that were performed on Kelly Hawk and previous victims, they have gone record as saying that whoever is responsible for the killings has some degree of medical knowledge.

Not thirty minutes after the discovery of Miss Hawk, Miss Witherspoon's pitifully mutilated body was discovered in an alley behind *Fantasy Worlds*, a comic book store in downtown Oklahoma City, barely a half mile from where Kelly Hawk's body was discovered. Like the previous victims,

Miss Witherspoon had a history of prostitution. While police are not giving the details of her mutilations, they have gone on record as saying that her death was even more hideous than the other victims.

Detective Jack Chandler, the lead detective on the case, has gone on record as saying...

E-Mail from Chase Anderson [in encrypted code]

To: Mr. Anthony Newkirk,

First, I want to thank you for how well you have been taking care of business while I've been forced into hiding. It's good to know that I still have some loyal employees that I can trust to "mind the store" when I can't be there in person. You will be richly rewarded for your loyalty. I especially like that drug sales are up by 20%.

Second, see what you can do to improve the sale of illegal weapons. Street gangs are good customers, but they don't have the serious cash that we need. Even the Crimson Dragons are hit hard by inflation, my friend.

Finally, there are a few loose ends I need to take care of. Those loose ends will do two things. They will guarantee that I can rebuild the Crimson Dragons and run the operations even though I will be living outside the U.S. You, my friend, will be my general making sure things run smoothly there "on the field" in Oklahoma. Again, your reward will be great. But before I leave the country, I have to settle things once and for all with my brother. By the time I finish with Chris, he won't be able to help anyone, much less himself. He will be utterly destroyed, and he will know who it is that has defeated him.

Regards,
Chase

CHAPTER ONE

"But while he was still a long way off, his father saw him and was filled with compassion for him; he ran to his son, threw his arms around him and kissed him."

--Luke 15:20 (NIV)

Jeremy Winslow's Journal [kept on computer flash drive]

It was the sound of crying that woke me up. I had been having the most wonderful dream of escorting my lovely Shelly on a cruise to the Bahamas when the sound of crying pierced through my mental fog until my eyes snapped open. Bleary-eyed, I looked over at the clock. Gradually my eyes came into focus until I could see the time on the digital display: 3:00 a.m. I looked over at the sleeping form of Shelly. She looked as beautiful as ever and was sleeping very, very peacefully; too peacefully to disturb.

With a sigh, I got up and stumbled into the nursery. Gage lay on his back in his crib, telling anyone within earshot how displeased he was. Smiling, I scooped Gage up in my arms and held him close to my chest. The crying got louder.

Patting his back gently as I held him, I carried him into the kitchen. Setting him in his high chair, I got a bottle ready for him and soon his crying ceased as I sat in a chair and fed him.

Shelly and I had been richly blessed on July 10th, as Gage came into our lives. Gage came crying into the world at six pounds, five ounces, and is just as perfect as he can be. Shelly did great, is doing great, and is the same wonderful mother that she has been with Tim. Her only problem is that she is grieving over her difficulties in losing what she calls her "baby fat". I keep reminding her daily that she is incredibly gorgeous to me, but she still grieves over how hard it is for her to lose that extra weight.

Tim, by the way, is already an incredible big brother; he is forever asking us what he can do to help. He's not in the least jealous about having a new child in the house. On the contrary, he is going above and beyond the call of duty at trying to help us and be a good brother. His German shepherd Rex is going above and beyond to be a good guard dog for Gage. I *almost* pity any stranger that decides to come too close to Gage; almost, but not quite.

My partners Chris and Crystal have been doing great personally as well. After getting engaged on Valentine's Day, they set their wedding date to be November the tenth. Both of them are as happy as can be and seem to glow every time they look at each other. There had been a time when Chris was too afraid for Crystal's safety to commit to marriage; he was afraid that marrying her would make her a target for "Moriarty". However, when Crystal got her P.I. license and was working with us full time, Chris realized that Crystal was already a target for Chris' enemies just by working with us. The bullet that grazed her face in a shootout clinched the deal; Chris realized he could easily have lost her and proposed on Valentine's Day.

One fly in the ointment is that Chris is still in the mental fog of believing he is Sherlock Holmes. As far as he's concerned, I'm still Dr. Watson, and his sister—Jessica Peterson—is "Mrs. Hudson," the landlady of Sherlock Holmes.

When Moriarty was revealed to be his own brother, Chase Anderson, we all had hopes that Chris would start remembering things and regain his sanity. However, while he has had a few brief memory flashes, they haven't amounted to anything. It's like he has a mental block that's as solid as an anvil. A part of me always considered that a blessing. When he does get his memory back, he'll have to come to grips that his own brother had murdered his family, a family that right now he doesn't even remember. That day will come, but it will be far from pleasant. But one thing his delusions haven't hindered is his ability to solve cases. As a matter of fact, Chris is still solving cases as a private consulting detective that baffles the official police.

Speaking of which, the summer has brought the Sherlock Holmes and Company Detective Agency a multitude of cases. While some of them were from the most humble of backgrounds—some of which didn't have two pennies to rub together—other clients brought us substantial financial reward. But, whether the client was as rich as Midas or as poor as the proverbial church mouse, Chris never allowed money to stand in the way of justice.

One of the more interesting cases involved Judge Stanley Rodgers, who stepped out of his office and got into his car, only to vanish from the face of the earth. His car was found abandoned in a field, wiped clean of prints, with no sign of the judge. Two major facts worried his wife: the judge made many enemies by virtue of his profession, and he was incredibly wealthy because of an inheritance. Those two facts alone made him a very tempting target.

With the help of Crystal and me, Chris was able to prove by observing how long it had taken for a dish of the judge's favorite ice cream to melt that he was still alive. From there, he traced some letters that the judge had written in code to Oklahoma City's airport and found the judge boarding a plane in disguise. The Judge's wife was livid when she learned that her husband faked his own death in order to run off with his secretary. Our reward for that paid for Gage's nursery as well as anything needed for Chris and Crystal's wedding.

Gage finished the bottle and seemed satisfied. Gently I burped him, changed his diaper, and carried him back to bed. But the little rascal wasn't quite ready to go back to sleep. So I sat beside his crib and gently massaged him until he was peacefully slumbering. Once I knew he was asleep, I stumbled back to bed and soon *I* was peacefully slumbering. I was slumbering so peacefully that Shelly had a bear of a time getting me to wake up to get to the office on time. However, several cups of coffee helped me to start feeling human enough to greet the day.

By the time I got to the office, Chris and Crystal were already hard at work. She was hard at work on her desktop computer and he was standing behind her, staring at the screen. Looking at them, one would say that their appearance was an interesting study in contrasts. Chris was tall and thin, looking like the very image of the Sherlock

Holmes of literature. The tweed suits he always wore and the deerstalker cap he wore while conducting investigations made him look like he had stepped out of a stage production of the famous detective.

Crystal, on the other hand, was of more average height. The differences in their height under other circumstances would have almost seemed comical. But the depth of their love made any differences in their height totally unimportant. Crystal had long brunette hair and was just slightly overweight. Once she had been so obsessed with losing weight—due to being bullied in high school—that she was tempted to starve herself thin. However, some good counseling from Shelly got Crystal back to eating a healthy diet.

"Right on time as usual, Watson," said Chris, barely giving me a glance, "although I see that Gage kept you and Shelly up half the night again."

I blinked. "Now how on earth could you guess that?"

"I try never to guess, Watson," he said, "it's terribly destructive to logic. I strive to simply observe what is around me and make deductions based on those observations."

I chuckled and closed the door behind me.

"I've barely got in the door," I protested, "What on earth did I give you to observe?"

"Don't get him started," laughed Crystal, "Sherlock has the *longest* way of saying 'good morning' that I've ever seen."

But it was too late. Chris stood stretched and approached me. He looked at me like a scientist studying some new species of bugs under a microscope. It was things like this that made me well aware of how he was able to make suspects nervous when he interrogated them.

"Now," said Chris, "When my friend and partner comes into the office with bloodshot eyes— and I know you never drink anything stronger than coffee—I would be a poor detective if I didn't realize that you had very little sleep. You have mentioned more than once that Gage has his days and nights *very* mixed up."

I nodded ruefully. "We *have* forgotten what a full night's sleep is, thank you very much."

"*Plus*," continued Chris, "You came to the office with your tie not straight and your shirt buttoned wrong. Can you imagine Shelly letting you leave the house dressed like that if she had gotten a full night's sleep?"

I shook my head vigorously.

7

"The fact that you missed half of your whiskers shaving told me that you weren't quite fully awake while shaving," said Chris, "A fact that made me very glad that you use an electric razor instead of an old time straight razor.

"Taking all of these facts into account, I couldn't help but conclude that your baby kept you and Shelly both up half the night. More than likely, Shelly was only half-awake herself and was so focused on getting you up and fed before coming to the office that she didn't notice the shameful state of your shirt and tie."

I laughed and sank down into a chair. You'd think by now I would be used to his reading all of my thoughts and movements from the slightest glances in my direction, but he still managed to astound me every morning. Crystal was still laughing and shaking her head.

"One of these days," said Crystal, "My fiancée is going to simply say 'Good morning' without a long monologue of all my inmost thoughts, and I'm going to have a heart attack and die."

"Then I better never do that," said Chris, "I want you around for years to come."

"You'd better, you bum," snickered Crystal.

8

"So, what are you two love birds up to this morning?" I asked.

"You know my methods, Watson," said Chris, "Apply them."

"Well," I said, "You haven't told me about a new case. And when we don't have a case to work on, you're both either making wedding plans or searching for some clue to the whereabouts of Chase Anderson, AKA Moriarty."

"Perfectly sound reasoning," said Chris, "Now, without looking at our computer screen, which do you believe is the case?"

"The thick file on Crystal's desk doesn't look like bridal magazines," I said, "So I presume it's part of the Moriarty file. Also, we've been keeping the cork board on the fall wall filled with printouts about some of Chase's known underworld contacts. It's got some fresh printouts, which tells me you've been doing some more research on our boy."

"Absolutely correct," said Crystal, "Sherlock is more determined than ever to get Chase before the wedding, especially after what happened to Lestrade."

I frowned. When I first met Chris, he thought that his former partner, Detective Ronald Summers, was the fictional Inspector Lestrade from the Sherlock Holmes stories. Summers had been around in the days when the Organized Crime Task Force was first starting to investigate the Crimson Dragons. Summers had remained Chris' friend and colleague long after Chris' breakdown, and hoped to see the day when Chris regained his memory.

Then another tragedy struck thanks to Chase Anderson. Detective Summers learned that his own father, a retired detective, had owed the Crimson Dragons big time. The Crimson Dragons helped Summers' father get a vital transplant for Mrs. Summers.

The price for the transplant was information. Ron Summers Sr. had to get information from his son on what the task force was doing in their investigation of the Crimson Dragons. That information led to the murders of Jessica Peterson's husband and Chris' family. Our friend found out about his father's deal with the mob, and killed himself rather than testify against him when the truth came out. His death made us even more determined to track Chase down.

"Any luck?" I asked.

"Yes," said Crystal, "And all of it is bad. I'm starting to think that he planned well in advance of where he would go if his identity was discovered."

"I think you're right, darling," said Chris, "Considering how well the man planned his crimes, he *must* have spent some time thinking of an escape if it was necessary."

I switched on my own desktop computer and did some thinking. If Chase had planned in advance on how to get out of town if he had to go on the run, he might have also planned on how to leave town with a lot of cash in his pocket instead of dead broke. Maybe he would have planned on making one more big score before leaving the country for good. I voiced the possibility to Chris.

"That's good thinking," said Chris, "Not only would he be able to leave the country in style, but he would have committed one final crime that the police couldn't solve."

I thought about the possibilities as I went onto the internet. It had been *months* since Moriarty was unmasked as Chase Anderson. In that time, literally hundreds of robberies had occurred in Oklahoma alone. Would there be any clues left after all this time?

"The problem is," I said sadly, "Whatever crime he may have committed, the trail is probably cold by now. Whatever he's done, he's gotten his score and has high tailed it out of Dodge by now. If it were me, I'd be whooping it up in Tahiti and laughing at the cops' failure."

"If it were me," said Crystal, "I'd simply find a safe place to hide right here in town until the heat died down. *Then* I'd pull my big score and flee the country."

Chris and I looked at Crystal in amazement. From the look in Chris' eyes, it looked like the wheels in his mind were seriously turning. He laughed and smote his forehead with the palm of his hand. Then he threw his arms around his fiancée and gave her a big kiss. She didn't mind a bit.

"Crystal, my love," said Chris, "Besides your incredible beauty, you have a wonderful mind to match! You never cease to amaze me!"

"Keep talking," said Crystal, "You're doing great! Feel free to keep on kissing, too!"

"Naturally Chase wouldn't leave town right away," said Chris, "The police are *still* watching all of the bus stations, plane stations, docks, and every possible route out of Oklahoma! How much simpler to simply stay put until the police relax their guard and then leave the country in disguise!"

"If that's true," I said, "He might not have pulled that last big score yet. He may still be planning it as we speak."

"But wouldn't the fact that an enormous robbery occurred make things hot for him again?" asked Crystal.

Chris thought about that for a moment.

"If it were *one big robbery*, yes," said Chris, "But what about a *series* of *small scale robberies*? Maybe even a set of robberies that, on the surface, don't seem to be related to each other. We might find a liquor store robbery here...a jewelry heist there...All of them seemingly unrelated. But, they would all lead back to the doorstep of Case Anderson, AKA Moriarty, as his getaway money."

Crystal and I looked at each other and then dove into our computers. Chris made perfect sense. We weren't looking for a lot of similar robberies, such as a big set of home invasions. We would be looking for a set of *unrelated* robberies, tied together only by the ingenuity with which they were pulled off.

When I first got involved in the Crimson Dragon investigation, I learned that many of Moriarty's agents didn't seem intelligent enough to plan the crimes that they were arrested for. If that pattern still held true, then the one thing the crimes would have in common would be that the crimes would be as well planned as a General's military strategy.

For several minutes, the three of us poured over the internet news pages. Most of the robberies I found consisted of nothing out of the ordinary. Nothing seemed to hold the mark of Moriarty.

"The main thing I'm finding," said Crystal, "Is the latest outrages of the Oklahoma City Stalker. Good grief, the Stalker killed *two* prostitutes last night! He's getting worse, and I wouldn't have thought it possible."

"Tragic," I agreed.

"What's even *more* tragic," continued Crystal, "is that, considering what they did for a living, they probably went into eternity without having ever asked Christ into their lives. That's the thing about murder. Not only are people senselessly robbed of their *physical* lives—which is bad enough—but they are robbed of any more chances to settle things with God if they haven't already."

"I never thought about it that way," I admitted.

I was struck by the point that Crystal had made. As a Christian, I was taught the importance of asking Christ into your life while you had the chance because none of us had a promise about tomorrow. As a detective, I often investigated the aftermath of senseless tragedies. I thought about *who* committed the crimes and *why*. I often advised

14

the families of victims to seek grief counseling. But I had never consciously thought about the state of the victims' souls. If they hadn't already asked Jesus to be their Savior before they ran into their murderers, then they were in for an eternity separate from God in hell. And robbing people of chances to be saved from hell was the ultimate robbery.

"The victims of the Stalker are more than prostitutes," said Crystal, "They're lost souls who needed Jesus. And now they've had any chances they might have had to accept Christ taken away from them. Sherlock honey, why haven't we done anything about this?"

"That's the thing about *consulting* detectives," said Chris, "We go where we're hired to go. No one's hired us to look into this."

Crystal frowned. "The police used to ask for your help when they were stumped, at least when Lestrade was around."

"Sadly," said Chris, "The new chief of detectives—Stanley Hendricks—is allergic to consulting detectives. I offered my help in the Stalker case last week. He made it *very* clear that I was not welcome anywhere near police headquarters."

"You know," said Crystal casually, "We *are* looking into the whereabouts of Chase Anderson without being hired to do it."

"I know where you're going with this," said Chris, "First, Chase ties in with cases we've already been hired to investigate. He's the mastermind behind the scenes of crimes we were commissioned to solve."

"But---" began Crystal.

"Second," continued Chris, "We are looking for any—*any*-- crimes that Moriarty may be involved with. If we just *happen* to discover clues that will lead to justice in the Stalker case, then—as agents of justice--- we would be obligated to follow up on those clues. With no clues to go on, we can't exactly rule out the possibility that Moriarty is behind the Stalker killings."

Crystal smiled, rose to her feet, and crossed over to Chris' desk. Then she threw her arms around his neck and kissed him. As it was a long kiss, I busied myself studying the computer screen, finding myself growing angry for the first time at my partners. For crying out loud, we couldn't solve *every* crime in Oklahoma, and yet Chris had just given Crystal the green light to get sidetracked off what we were supposed to be doing!

"Does anybody here *really* think that Chase would bother killing prostitutes?" I asked, "He's bound to have bigger fish to fry!"

"Hush up, Watson," said Crystal.

"Have you forgotten," I snapped, "that every time that maniac shows his ugly head, I have to send my family into hiding for their protection or rely on police officers following them wherever they go? Forgive me, Crystal, but Shelly and I have a *newborn* at home! I'd love for Gage to grow up without having to look over his shoulder and to be able to leave the house without police protection! And since hookers *make* money for Moriarty, why on earth would he kill them?"

Crystal looked positively crushed. My tirade had come out harsher than I intended, and I instantly regretted it. Perhaps the day would come when I learned to keep my mouth shut whenever I lose sleep. On more occasions than I care to remember, my temper tended to rise when the amount of sleep I got went down. Chris flashed me an angry look and I blushed.

"Watson," said Chris evenly, "at this point we do not know Chase's plans. We are looking for evidence, and are literally grasping at straws. By the same token, I won't know if certain robberies were masterminded by Chase or not until we investigate. While I admit that the murders of the prostitutes won't gain him any money, can you say

17

for certain that these girls hadn't crossed Moriarty in some way and thus earned his wrath?"

I swallowed. "I didn't think about that."

"It's true we can't say for certain that Moriarty is behind the Stalker cases," continued Chris, "But yet we have no evidence to say that he *isn't*. The same is true for any robberies or smuggling operations."

"Then you're saying that the two cases *could* be tied together," said Crystal.

"Until we have something concrete to go on," said Chris, "We have to investigate every possibility, no matter how remote. I'm not saying that Chase *is* the brains behind the Stalker and I'm not saying he's *not*. But, we don't yet have enough evidence to rule anything out. Until we do, we have to consider every possibility."

I sighed. "You're both right. I'm sorry. I shouldn't have gone off like that. Please forgive me."

"That's OK," said Crystal, "Your family *was* threatened by Chase's gang once. The Crimson Dragons case has taken its toll on all of us. It's just that…"

A rap at the door caught our attention. Through the window above the door, we could see the silhouette of a man wearing a fedora. Chris' hand instantly went to his desk drawer, which I knew held a .32 automatic. I nodded and went to the door. Opening it, we found a thin, elderly gentleman with a pencil thin mustache wearing a brown suit and brown fedora. Beside him was a woman in her early thirties. The woman had long blonde hair, wore a dark green dress, and did not look happy to be at our office.

"Is this the Sherlock Holmes and Company Detective Agency?" asked the gentleman.

"It is," called Chris, "I am Sherlock Holmes. This is Dr. Watson and my fiancée, Crystal Parker."

I showed our guests in. The man removed his hat as he sat down across from Chris. The woman sat beside him, looking about as comfortable as a cat in a dog pound.

"Forgive our intrusion," said the elderly man, "But I am simply at my wit's end, and I didn't know where else to turn."

"Grandfather," said the woman, "There's no need to bother them. The police have already laughed at you, and I don't want you to be humiliated any further."

"There's no need to worry about that," said Crystal, "My fiancée never laughs at anyone, and he never judges."

"We only go where the evidence leads," I promised.

"Yes," said Chris, "Very often, our investigations take us in directions that the official police smile at. So you may tell us your story without fear of judgment."

The man relaxed, but his granddaughter still looked worried. The grandfather closed his eyes, as if trying to decide where to begin.

"My name is Dr. Henry Price," said the man, "This is my granddaughter, Glenda. I'm a professor of criminology at Oklahoma Baptist University in Shawnee. I suppose I should have retired long ago, but since my wife went home to be with Jesus a few years back, I'd just as soon spend my time grading papers than going to an empty apartment."

"Perfectly understandable," said Chris, "Although I see that you also like to spend some time watching old time movies and feeding pigeons in the city park."

Dr. Price blinked. "Why that's right! But how did you know?"

"The ticket stub showing from your suit coat pocket bears the name 'Yesterday's Hits,'" began Chris, "Which, if memory serves me, only shows classic old time movies."

20

Dr. Price chuckled. "I went there last night to see the original *TRUE GRIT*. I wouldn't let a dog watch any of the garbage they make today. I was trying to decide what to do when the police laughed at me. I must confess I've been up all night pacing the floor trying to decide what to do. And, yes, I did feed the pigeons this morning after breakfast while I was making up my mind. But how…"

"There are a few pigeon feathers on your shoulders," said Chris, "And, by the way, I was wondering if it's difficult working with your left hand since your right arm was injured?"

Dr. Price gaped at Chris.

"My right arm *was* nearly completely paralyzed in an auto accident," said Price, "The other driver was texting and driving. But I don't see how you knew that."

"You have barely moved your right arm since you came into our office," said Chris, "And yet you don't seem quite comfortable using your left hand, which tells me you're right handed. The only reason I can think of for this would be that your right arm was injured somehow."

Dr. Price chuckled and shook his head. "I think I've come to the right place."

"*Please*, Grandfather," said Glenda, "I still think it's a waste of time!"

Dr. Price smiled and patted his granddaughter's hand.

"You must excuse Glenda," said Dr. Price, "She's very protective of me. She was livid when the Chief of Detectives laughed at... Mr. Holmes, you're choking!"

Chris had been sipping on his coffee while Dr. Price was talking. At the mention of the Chief of Detectives, he choked and coffee splashed on his shirt.

"Chief Hendricks and I have had our differences," admitted Chris.

That was putting it mildly. Since Stanley Hendricks became the chief, he had forbidden anyone on the force to work with us on anything. Stanley Hendricks considered Chris a madman and an amateur who—in his words—solved his cases through luck and guesswork. Chris, on the other hand, considered Hendricks a fool who couldn't solve a crossword puzzle, much less a serious crime. Chris' opinion that Hendricks had earned his promotions through politics rather than through serious police work was right on the money.

I offered our guests some coffee, which they both accepted. As they sipped on their coffee, Chris leaned forward and stared at them intently.

"Now then," said Chris, "Why don't you tell us why you're here?"

Dr. Price frowned and looked into his coffee cup. For several seconds, he was silent. Finally, he looked up at us.

"I'm here," said Price, "Because of the Oklahoma City Stalker case. I have information that could help catch him."

Crystal, Chris, and I looked at each other.

"Go on," said Crystal.

"I told the police a *week* ago that he would strike twice last night," said Price, "And they didn't listen. You read the results in this morning's paper. I know when he's going to strike again, and I know where the body will be found. Will you help me prevent another murder?"

For several seconds, none of us spoke. Slowly, a smile crossed Chris' face.

"You're right, Dr. Price," said Chris, "You *have* come to the right place. Keep talking."

CHAPTER TWO

Detective Maria Lorenzo's Diary

In the three months since I got promoted to detective, I'd had a variety of assignments. I'd worked a few robberies and brought down a few drug dealers. Right now, I'm working the vice detail, and boy is it depressing. It is outright tragic to see the degree to which some people are willing to degrade themselves for money.

Take this morning, for instance. Now, some people start off their day right with a Bible study and a cup of coffee. Other people start off their day with a morning jog. Now me, on the other hand, I start my day off by booking a 20 year old girl for prostitution.

I had barely sat down at my desk and had not even had a sip of my coffee when an officer brought a young brown haired girl in and sat her down in front of me. The officer was short and about ten pounds overweight. His name tag read "Reynolds", and he had brownish gray hair. The girl had too much makeup, nose and lip piercings, and had on clothes that revealed way too much. Her blonde hair was obviously bleached. A string of tattoos went down her left arm. Her figure could be described as attractive, but her expression was full of contempt for everyone and everything.

"Well now," I said with false cheerfulness, "What have we got here, Officer Reynolds?"

"Tina Stewart, AKA Dream Girl," said Reynolds, "She was arrested for prostitution. She was found advertising her 'escort' services on *Cyber-Ads*, and met who she thought was a client wanting sex. The 'client' was an undercover police officer."

"This is entrapment," snapped Tina, "I'll sue this whole city into bankruptcy!"

"You can certainly try," I said, looking at Officer Reynolds' notes.

Tina continued to rant and accuse the entire department of police brutality. I didn't bother to look up as I read Reynolds' arrest report. If I had a nickel for every person who was arrested that complained about entrapment and brutality, I would be independently wealthy. Looking over Reynolds' notes, I saw that Tina had a prostitution record that started when she was just 15 years old. *Crud*! Her record of drug use started when she was 16. I looked up into the face of a girl that had been positively hardened by life. Reynolds tipped his hat and left while I talked to Tina.

"Tina," I said softly, "It says here that you started being arrested for prostitution at the age of 15. Is that right?"

"Look," she snapped, "I got into prostitution when I was thirteen and didn't start getting busted until I was fifteen, all right?"

"No, Tina, it's *not* all right," I said, "Look, between the prostitution and the drug use, girl, you're looking at dying before you're thirty."

"Big deal," snapped Tina, "What's it to you?"

"It matters to me because I care about people," I replied, "You are making a living by renting yourself to strangers. Between that and the drug use, you could die of some very nasty diseases or an overdose. By now, you're bound to have had customers who just love to rough women up..."

Tina laughed. "I can handle myself. I've been beat before, and I'll be beat again. It's no big deal."

"Girl, it *is* a big deal," I countered, "Nobody—I repeat, *nobody*—deserves to be abused. God didn't create you to be anybody's punching bag. And in case you missed the evening news, there's a serial killer out there who preys on women that sells themselves. They also all advertised their services on *Cyber-Ads* like you do.

26

Suppose you're next customer turns out to be the Oklahoma City Stalker?"

Tina shrugged. "I'm careful. He won't mess with me."

"*All* of his victims probably considered themselves to be careful and smart," I countered, "And, besides, you thought you were being careful a while ago and ended up being arrested."

Tina scowled. She knew I was right about her arrest, and didn't like it a bit. If she hadn't been careful enough to avoid being arrested, there was no way she could count on being careful enough to avoid the Stalker.

"Look," she said, "Can we just get on with it? Jail *has* to be better than listening to this. If I wanted a lecture, I never would have run away from home."

That figured. She was a teenage runaway. I wondered what happened in her home that made her run away. Were her parents still looking for her? I made a mental note to check up on that. The world was full of girls who ran away from home only to be swallowed up in the seedy world of prostitution and/or pornography.

But why wasn't she returned home when she began selling herself as a teenager? Was it a case of the parents truly not caring about her, or did she keep running away no matter how many times she was taken back home? It was worth checking out.

"Tina," I began slowly, "Make no mistake; you *will* be booked. However, you need to do some hard thinking about your future. Prostitution will only give you one future: an early grave. It may be the result of all those drugs you take, or it may come through AIDS. It may be at the hands of a violent client or even the Stalker, if we don't get him in time."

Tina snorted. "Who cares?"

I looked at the contempt on her face. She had contempt for everyone, including herself. Before I realized it, I felt dark cold fury swelling up inside of me. I wanted to slap the attitude out of her face and shake her into realizing what she was doing to herself. Without a word, I brought up the crime scene photos of last night's Stalker victims. I spun my laptop around until Tina couldn't miss them. The color drained out of her face.

"All right, Miss I-don't-care-about-myself," I snarled, "*Take a good look!* This is what the Stalker did last night. He took two—count them, *two*—victims last night. They advertised themselves on *Cyber-Ads*, same as you. They thought they could handle anything, same as you. *Now* look at them; they look like they've been through a *slaughterhouse*! Take a hard look at what could easily happen to you if you keep walking down the same road that you're on now!"

Tina swallowed, her eyes wide. "I think I'm going to be *sick*!"

"I hope so," I went on, "I *want* you to be sick. I want you to be so sick that you vow to do whatever it takes to avoid being the next girl that the Stalker sends to the morgue. If you *want* to make the kinds of changes you need, I'll be glad to steer you in the right direction. If you decide to shrug off what I'm saying, you're on your own. Think about it while you cool your heels in jail."

Tina couldn't take her eyes off the photos, even though they were brutal to look at. The pictures were doing what no lecture from me ever could; she was picturing herself as the Stalker's next victim. Before my very eyes, the tough girl act was vanishing. She looked exactly like what she was: a young girl who had gotten herself into something she didn't know how to get out of. Maybe there was hope for her yet.

"But why do you care?" She asked, "I'm nothing but a hooker. I'm *nothing*."

"Yes you are", I thought, *"You're a lost soul that needs Jesus."*

"Everybody has value," I said, "I'm not just about solving crimes after they happen. I got into law enforcement because I wanted to make a difference. I care about people. I would love to help you—and others like you—to prevent you from becoming a victim. In my line of work, *preventing* a crime is a lot better than *solving* one."

Tina looked down at the floor. "Look, even if I wanted to have a different life, it's too late. I made my choices a long time ago. Once a girl goes into my line of work, there's no getting out."

"That's where you're wrong," I said, "As long as you're alive, there's hope for a new start. You just have to want it bad enough to do something about it. If you want to have a real life, there's hope...hope for getting off of drugs, and hope for you to do something with your life besides sell yourself for sex."

"Can we talk later?" Tina asked.

Jeremy Winslow's journal [kept on computer flash drive]

Dr. Price stood and faced us. He stood beside the cork board that held our most recent attempts to find Chase Anderson. For just a moment, I felt like I was back in school watching my teachers. Certainly, he looked like he was settling into his role as a college professor.

"You must realize, Mr. Holmes," he began, "That I specialize in teaching about crimes of the past. I demonstrate to my students the criminal investigations that either solved—or failed to solve—a given case. It is my belief that we have much to learn from the history of our profession."

Chris smiled. "We agree on that, my friend. The past can give us examples to follow...or examples to avoid. Like the man said, if we don't learn from the mistakes of history..."

"We're doomed to repeat them," finished Dr. Price.

Crystal and I looked at each other and grinned. In Dr. Price, it looked like Chris had found a kindred spirit. I could easily imagine the both of them spending *hours* discussing the theory of criminal investigation without letup.

"I also spend considerable time comparing crimes that occur today with similar crimes that have occurred in history, whether they were solved or not," said Dr. Price, "For example, if a major political figure were assassinated today, the assassination might be compared to the murders of Abraham Lincoln or John F. Kennedy."

"I think I see your point," said Chris, "Even if today's crimes had different circumstances, you compare the *natures* of the crimes, and look at lessons learned from the historical crime. In the case of the political assassination, you might look at how the politician's personal security has changed over the course of history and the methods the police use in their investigations."

"There you have me," agreed Dr. Price.

"So what has all this to do with the Stalker?" asked Crystal.

Dr. Price turned and faced Crystal squarely.

"Tell me, Miss Parker," said Dr. Price, "What do the dates August 31, September 8th, and September 30th mean to you?"

Crystal blinked. "Those are the dates that the Oklahoma City Stalker killed those four women."

Dr. Price nodded. "You are absolutely right, young lady. But those are *also* the dates that Jack the Ripper claimed his first four victims back in 1888."

For several seconds, none of us said anything. We stared at Dr. Price as the implication sank in. I didn't know many of the details in the Jack the Ripper case, but I did know that he had killed and mutilated prostitutes back in the 19th century and, as far as I knew, had never been

32

caught. I glanced at Price's granddaughter Glenda, who was simply shaking her head. Whatever Chief Hendricks had said to them at the police station, it had shaken her; she was *most* uncomfortable.

"On August 31, 1888," Price went on, "Jack the Ripper killed Mary Ann Nichols at Buck's Row in Whitechapel. Her throat was cut and there was some slight stomach mutilation. I understand that the press has not been given all the details of the Oklahoma City Stalker mutilations, so I can't compare the types of wounds the Ripper left behind with the Stalker. The press during the Ripper's reign of terror was told that whoever the killer was, he had to have had some degree of medical knowledge."

I blinked. "The papers have been saying that the Oklahoma City Stalker *has* to have medical knowledge to do what he does."

"Eight days after Mary Ann Nichols was slain," Price went on, "Annie Chapman was found murdered on Hanbury Street, on September 8th. Then, on September 30th, Jack the Ripper claimed two victims in one night."

"Just as our boy claimed two victims last night, September 30th," said Chris, "Dr. Price, I do believe that you're on to something."

33

"The Ripper first killed Elizabeth, or 'Long Liz', Stride," said Price, "Her throat was cut, but there was no mutilation."

"The first Stalker victim that was found last night..." began Chris, "She had no mutilation, but her throat was cut."

"Then," went on Price, "The Ripper killed Catherine Eddows. Her throat was cut, and she had mutilations on her face and stomach."

"You noticed the pattern after the second killing," concluded Chris, "And you warned Chief Hendricks that the Stalker would strike again on September 30th and would be claiming two victims."

Price nodded. "I warned him that the Stalker is recreating the crimes of Jack the Ripper and he needed to be prepared."

"The chief laughed in his face," said Glenda, "He even threatened to arrest my grandfather for interfering with a police investigation! He brought information to *help* and the Chief threatened to throw him in jail!"

"Knowing Chief Hendricks as I do," responded Chris, "That does not surprise me. However, Dr. Price, you will find a more attentive ear at *Sherlock Holmes and Company*. What more can you tell us?"

"You have a bit more time to find the killer," said Price, "Jack the Ripper didn't strike again until November 9th, 1888. This gives you some breathing room."

"Thank heavens for that," said Crystal.

"It's widely held that the places where the Ripper's victims were found weren't the places where they died," said Price, "They were dumped where they were found *after* the murders occurred. The lack of blood found at the bodies and the time it would have taken for the mutilations to be performed with surgical precision indicates that they were killed elsewhere."

"Perfectly sound reasoning," said Chris.

"Some believe that the prostitutes were picked up off the street by a coach, murdered, and then dumped," went on Price, "Which indicates that the Ripper didn't work alone."

"So," said Crystal, "The idea that the Ripper just came out of nowhere, killed without fear of discovery, and then vanished back into the London fog is just an urban legend."

"Yes," said Price, "Just like the notion that the Ripper was a random killer. You see, four of the five Ripper victims knew each other."

Chris blinked. "Really? That's news to me. That's interesting…and very intriguing."

35

"Yes," said Price, "Considering that there were over 50,000 prostitutes working in Whitechapel at the time, the odds that four out of five victims would all know each other are pretty slim, wouldn't you say?"

Chris nodded. "It would be stretching the idea of coincidence pretty thin. Of course, I don't believe in coincidence. It also leads one to suspect that the Ripper was targeting *specific* targets. Which one of the five weren't known by the others?"

"Catherine Eddows," answered Price, "She was murdered shortly after being released from jail for public drunkenness. Interestingly, her nickname in the prostitution world was Mary Ann Kelly."

"Why is that interesting?" I wondered.

"The name of the last of the Ripper's victims was *Marie Kelly*," said Price, "Some believe that her nickname got her killed because the Ripper or Rippers intended for Mary Kelly to be their final victim. Poor Catherine Eddows used the last name Kelly because she was living with her boyfriend, John Kelly. She *didn't* know the other victims, but the alias she used as a prostitute may have attracted the attention of the killer or killers. If that's the case, then they thought they were killing the Marie Kelly who was the Ripper's final victim."

"If the Ripper *was* targeting specific prostitutes back in London," said Crystal, "What was his motive?"

"There's been a number of theories," answered Price, "Some have speculated that a mad butcher was the Ripper. Others have tried to say that a member of the Royal family was insane and killed the prostitutes. One theory held that the four victims who knew each other had knowledge about Prince Eddie, the Duke of Clarance and heir to the throne. The theory was that Eddie had married a Catholic girl named Annie Crook, and fathered a child by her before they were married. Because of the political climate of the time, this would have been a scandal if it became public knowledge.

"According to the theory, the Queen's doctor—Dr. William Gull—had Annie Crook declared insane and put in a madhouse after doing brain surgery on her. The child was put in hiding by a young shopkeeper's assistant named Marie Kelly who knew of the scandal and fled for her life into the seedy world of prostitution in Whitechapel.

"According to this theory, Kelly and three of the other victims were desperate for money, so they tried to blackmail the royal family with what they knew. This set into motion the crimes of Jack the Ripper. There are many that believe Dr. Gull himself was the brains behind Jack the Ripper and that he had help carrying out the crimes; a coachman and an artist named Walter Sikertt—the artist frequented the East End and often used prostitutes as models in his paintings. The coachman drove him to and from the crime scenes and Sikertt helped him track down his targets."

Chris' eyes sparkled with interest. "If that theory is true, then the Ripper's crimes were orchestrated to keep what Mary Kelly knew from ever becoming public knowledge."

Price nodded. "Exactly. This theory certainly answers how four of the five victims knew each other, stating that they were specific targets for murder."

Chris rubbed his hands together. "All right. So, Oklahoma City has a killer with medical knowledge copying the crimes of Jack the Ripper— who also had medical knowledge, whether he was Dr. Gull or not—right down to the dates. Four out of five of the Ripper victims knew each other, indicating they were specific targets of the Ripper. Do we know whether the Oklahoma City Stalker victims knew each other in any way?"

"No," I said, "But it's worth checking out."

"Dr. Price," said Chris, "You said that if the Oklahoma City Stalker remained free to claim his next victim, you could predict where the body would be found. Could you explain that?"

"Yes," said Dr. Price, "If you will permit me just a few moments at one of your computers."

I stood up and motioned for Price to use my own computer. He sat down and brought up a map of Oklahoma City. It was difficult for him to do with one hand, but he brushed off our offers to help him. Within seconds, four red dots appeared on the map.

"These dots indicate the places where the victims of the Stalker were found," said Price, "Now, let me open up another window."

A second window opened, showing another map. This time, four blue dots appeared.

"This is a map of Whitechapel, England, as it was in 1888," said Dr. Price, "And these dots show where the first four victims of Jack the Ripper were found."

Dr. Price continued typing with his one good hand. Then the map of Oklahoma City moved to the other side of the computer screen until it was literally on top of the map of Whitechapel.

"Notice anything?" asked Price.

"When you lay the map of Oklahoma City on top of the map of Whitechapel," said Crystal, "The red and blue dots are on top of each other. The places where the Ripper's victims and the Stalker's victims were found line up perfectly!"

"Incredible!" I breathed.

"The Stalker has planned every detail of his crimes to correspond with the crimes of Jack the Ripper," whispered Chris, "Right down to the location of the bodies! Even though Whitechapel and Oklahoma City do not look alike, our Stalker has found places in Oklahoma City to line up with where the Ripper victims were found. Dr. Price, you were quite correct in bringing this most fascinating case to our attention."

"Dr. Price," said Crystal, "Could you tell us where…"

A sudden sharp knock on the door interrupted us. We all jumped as the sharp knocking continued.

"Open up in the name of the law!" called a loud, rather obnoxious voice.

Chris sighed, shaking his head.

"Come in, Hendricks," said Chris, rolling his eyes.

Chris opened the door and a tall, overweight man with a thick mustache stormed into our office. His plaid suit barely fit around his portly waist. His face was so flushed with excitement that I would swear that he was about to burst. Two uniformed

40

officers followed him into the room, along with a medium sized man in a blue suit.

"Aha!" said Hendricks, "I was told I'd find you here, Price."

"Yes," said Dr. Price, "I told my secretary where I'd be in case any of my students needed me."

"Exactly what do you need with our client?" asked Chris.

"That is none of your concern," snapped Hendricks, "This is official police business; nothing to include an *amateur detective* about."

"Well it's *my* business," thundered Glenda, "What do you want with my grandfather?"

"Miss, your grandfather brought to our attention certain details about the Oklahoma City Stalker case," said Hendricks, "He even predicted when and where the Stalker would strike again. It appears to me that your grandfather knows a little *too much* about the Stalker. Detective Chandler, here is your man."

"What do you mean?" asked Glenda anxiously.

"It means," said Chris coldly, "That Chief Hendricks is about to arrest your grandfather on the charge of being the Oklahoma City Stalker."

41

Glenda's jaw dropped. "You must be *joking!*"

"For once, Mr. 'Holmes' is correct," said Hendricks, "Dr. Price, you are under arrest on four counts of murder in the first degree. Detective Chandler, as the lead detective on the case, read this man his rights."

"Dr. Henry Price," began Chandler, "You have the right to remain silent. If you give up your right to remain silent, anything you say can and will be used against you..."

We watched in stunned silence as Dr. Price stood and was handcuffed by Chandler. Glenda sobbed as Chandler recited the Miranda rights that every accused suspect has. Dr. Price looked at Chris helplessly.

"But I was trying to *help you*," protested Dr. Price, trembling.

"Dr. Price," said Chris, "Don't worry. Sherlock Holmes and his colleagues are on the case, and we won't stop until you're cleared and the real killer is behind bars."

Stanley Hendricks laughed. "Don't make any promises you can't keep, Mr. 'Holmes.' No matter how many clever theories you have, Dr. Price is going down in history as the most notorious serial killer in Oklahoma."

The officers led Dr. Price out of our doors in handcuffs. Glenda followed close behind, sobbing and begging them to stop. We watched in disbelief as a man that had to be in his eighties was arrested on the charge of being a serial killer.

"Sherlock, *do something!*" begged Crystal.

Hendricks tipped his hat and walked out of our office. Chris followed close behind and tapped him on the shoulder as Hendricks reached the stairs.

"Chief, may I have a moment of your time?" asked Chris.

"Make it brief," snapped Hendricks, "I've got a killer to book, and a press conference to hold on the arrest of the Oklahoma City Stalker."

"Do you have *anything* on Dr. Price besides what he said in the police station?" asked Chris, "Do you have anything in the way of a motive? Have you checked Dr. Price's whereabouts on the nights of the killings?"

Hendricks looked uncomfortable. "Well, not exactly…"

Chris snorted. "Then you're about to accuse a *senior citizen* of being the man who has terrorized Oklahoma City simply on the grounds that he noticed that the Stalker was imitating Jack the Ripper. A first year law student would tear you to pieces."

43

Hendricks flushed.

Chandler looked at Hendricks. "Sir, begging your pardon, but you may want to think about this. Anybody with a computer could look up facts on the Ripper case and become a copycat. There's also a ton of books on the Ripper. Besides Price's knowledge of Jack the Ripper, we don't really have anything to go on."

Hendricks flushed even more. "Chandler, who signs your paycheck? Think about whether you want to continue *receiving* a paycheck before you say anything else!"

"Listen to your detective," said Chris, "A man comes into your office, and he offers you information to prevent a double killing. You laugh at him, and when he proves right, you arrest him for the crime. If I were a killer, I would avoid telling the police so much *before* the crime…especially if I were standing in the middle of the police station."

"Can you prove he's *not* the killer?" demanded Hendricks.

"Yes," said Chris, "The man here is right handed, but his right arm is nearly totally paralyzed because of an automobile accident. He is physically incapable of pulling off the crimes of the Oklahoma City Stalker. The Stalker knows surgical techniques.

44

Have you even bothered to check whether Dr. Price does or not?"

Hendricks sneered. "I don't need to. A man tells me two murders are going to take place on a certain night. He's proved right. To me, that smacks of knowing a little too much. Maybe he planned the crimes and hired someone to do the deed. But, then again, what do I know? I'm *only* the chief of detectives. Good day, Mr. 'Holmes'."

We watched as Hendricks walked down the steps as fast as his bulk would carry him. Chandler looked back sadly at us, leading Price away. Every step of the way, Price's granddaughter begged for them to let Price go. Glenda looked back at us, heartbroken, as she got into the elevator. Chris pounded the stair railing with the palm of his hands and retreated to our office.

"Lestrade would *never* have done this," thundered Chris, "We had our differences, but Lestrade was *always* a professional!"

"What are we going to do?" asked Crystal, "We can't let Dr. Price rot in jail! I'll never be able to look at myself in the mirror again if we can't help them!"

Chris picked up a shoebox beside his desk and took off the lid. Then he turned to his fiancée.

"Crystal," he said, "You were wanting a reason for us to be working the Stalker case. It's just been handed to us on a silver platter! Any evidence we find pointing to the real killer is in Dr. Price's favor."

"What's the game plan?" I asked.

"First," said Chris, "We need to establish the whereabouts of Dr. Price on the nights of the killings. If we have *one* night where Dr. Price was seen in the presence of witnesses while a murder occurred, then Chief Hendrick's theory goes flying out the window."

"That's right," I said, "I can handle that. What else?"

"We need a copy of Chandler's notes on the killings," said Chris, "Who found the bodies? What physical evidence do we have? I'll check on that. Crystal, I want you to start looking for any links between the victims. There's a ton of prostitutes that advertise themselves on the internet. We have *got* to know how the Stalker chooses his victims."

Crystal smiled. "Consider it done."

"I'm going to see if Detectives Lorenzo and Chandler can get me some information on the Stalker that didn't make the papers," said Chris, "We'll probably all end up going at different ends of this case, especially if—as Crystal speculated—

Chase Anderson really *is* involved. I can't stress enough how important it is that we stay in contact at all times. With that in mind, I've got a little present for both of you."

Reaching into the shoebox, he withdrew two watches. He handed one to Crystal and handed another to me. The watch was a little larger than mine, and thicker as well. There were four buttons on the side.

"Cool looking watch," I said.

"Oh, it's more than a watch," smiled Chris, "See that first button on the side? Press it, if you would."

Crystal and I did as we were told. Pressing the button, the clock display slid to the top of the screen and revealed several computer Aps. I could see one for internet, one for making phone calls, and several others.

"Huh," said Crystal, "There's even a word processing Ap."

"When you call up that one," explained Chris, "You can speak, and anything you say will go to a word processing document. Let us say that you want to file a report on a case while you're driving back to the office after you've interviewed a suspect. All you have to do is call up the word processor, say what you want on the report, and command the watch to send the data to one of our office printers. The printer will receive a signal from the watch, and your notes will be printed in police report format by the time you get back to the office."

"What's *that* button?" asked Crystal.

"It sends out an emergency SOS to anyone else who has one of these watches," said Chris.

"I suppose I can record my interview of witnesses and suspects as well," I commented, "I thought so. Shades of *Dick Tracy!*"

Crystal whistled. "Where on earth did you come up with *this*?"

Chris shrugged. "There are some companies coming out with smart watches now, and I started wondering how they could be modified specifically for detective work. Your watches, naturally enough, have a link directly to the database on my computer system."

"Of course," I said, "But can it tell time?"

"Yes," continued Chris, "Mrs. Watson was *not* to happy a few months back when Watson lost his cell phone just *before* he got into his car and found that someone had placed a rattlesnake into it."

"I wasn't too happy about that, either!" I said.

"Mrs. Watson reminded me that you are always losing your cell phone," said Chris, "And asked me to develop *something* that would help you keep up with your phone. She is not anxious for a repeat performance with the snake, as I'm sure that you're not. Hence, you are now wearing your phone on your wrist. Remember our *compu-pens* that had the recorders and e-mail included? Now you have the *Compu- Watch*."

I chuckled, took off my old watch, and put the new one on. I couldn't help but think back to the old *Dick Tracy* comic strips. Dick Tracy and his team wore watches that also had radios built in. The gadgets were way ahead of their time, and all the kids in my neighborhood pretended that their watches had the built in radios. But having a full *computer* built into a watch was something that even Dick Tracy didn't have!

Chris showed us how to program all of our phone numbers into the phone on our watches. Then he demonstrated how to send e-mails, especially the reports for our cases. What was amazing was how everything on the *Compu-Watch* could be voice activated.

"This button *here*," said Chris, "allows the wearer to pull up a GPS tracking map. If I sent out an emergency SOS to you two, you would be able to pull up a GPS tracking map and it will lead you right to wherever I'm at."

I whistled. "This should be standard issue for *every* detective!"

"Any questions?" asked Chris finally.

"Oh, yes," said Crystal, "I've got an important one."

"What's that?" asked Chris.

"Does it have a button to make you tell me where you're taking me on our honeymoon?" she asked sweetly.

CHAPTER THREE

Crystal Parker's journal [kept on her tablet]

After Jeremy and Chris left, I hurried to my computer and got down to serious business. All of the office computers were outfitted with the software and hardware that Chris had personally designed. His computer system was a hacker's dream. It allowed us to hack into any system without leaving behind the slightest clue that the system had been hacked. True, we would all be outfitted for prison jumpsuits if we were ever discovered, but if our hacking allowed us to prevent more murders it would be worth it.

The first thing I did was to trace as much of the history of each of the victims as possible. If there was *anything* besides their chosen profession that they had in common, I would be able to find it. After all, each of the girls was fairly young. They shouldn't have *that* much history to explore.

As I worked, I couldn't help but wonder at what had driven these girls to become prostitutes. Since they were advertising themselves online, I doubted that they were victims of forced human trafficking. Human trafficking was big business, but usually the victims of sex slavery worked for someone who got the clients for them. These girls were advertising themselves. So what drove them? Did their parents get them started in the business? Did they simply have a rotten home life and they were desperate to escape? Had they gotten into drugs and prostituted themselves to get money for their next fix? Or were they simply willing to do anything for cash?

If Dr. Price was right, then there was one more victim that the Stalker would be claiming. So far, it looked like the killer—or killers---really *were* recreating the crimes of Jack the Ripper as closely as possible. That left one potential victim to find and rescue. I prayed that I *could* find something that linked the victims together; that would certainly narrow the list of potential victims considerably. So far, all they had in common were their profession and the website they used to advertise themselves.

As I sorted through the database, I wondered about what I had said earlier. Was there really a chance that Chase had anything to do with these crimes? Or was I simply looking for any excuse to investigate the Stalker case because crimes against women always infuriated me?

Jeremy's objections did make sense: Chase had every police station in the state looking for him. Why would Chase waste time killing prostitutes when he should be getting enough loot put back to flee the country?   It didn't   make   sense.

Although, there had been many things that Chase and his gang, the Crimson Dragons, did that didn't make sense on the surface. Last year, Chase had been the mastermind behind a number of infant kidnappings. The newborn babies had been kidnapped right out of the hospital nurseries. The kidnappings had masked a truly bizarre smuggling operation that Chase had dreamed up. With Chase Anderson, the normal rules didn't apply. If he *was* behind the murders, it wasn't simply because he enjoyed killing girls. He would have reasons of his own. And the sooner we had him behind bars, the sooner all of us could go on to lead normal lives.

I could sympathize with Jeremy. I really could. His family had been held at gunpoint by the Crimson Dragons on the very first case that he worked with Chris. The threat of a repeat performance hung over his head like a guillotine blade. No wonder the poor man's nerves were frayed, in addition to losing sleep with a newborn in the house. They all had to be desperate to have this case over and done with once and for all. Certainly I would love to have this threat over with before Chris and I got married.

The thought of our approaching wedding never failed to bring a smile to my face. Chris and I had been friends for some time before we started dating seriously. Even when we first met, he was already been suffering for a year from his delusions of being Sherlock Holmes. It often occurred to me that I had never known Chris before his breakdown. His sister, Jessica, and I often talked about that fact in private.

The week after Chris proposed, Jessica and I met for lunch to discuss the wedding. We had met for coffee at a local McDonalds. While discussing wedding plans, Jess also reminded me that there were no guarantees that Chris would *ever* get his memory back, and she asked me how I felt about that.

"Jess," I said, "Do you remember when you told me that Chris' *personality* as Sherlock Holmes is the same one that he had before his breakdown?"

She nodded.

"Well," I said, "Either way, I have a husband that's thoughtful, kind, brave, and treats me with gentleness and respect. He also has a deep abiding love for God. Whether he gets his memory back or not, I still have a wonderful husband and I love him with all my heart."

Jessica smiled at what I said. "Chris fell in love with the right woman."

Looking at the computer screen, I wondered if she was right. After two hours of research, I hadn't found anything. There was *nothing* that I could find that tied any of the four victims together. Sure, they were all prostitutes and they all advertised themselves on *Cyber-Ads*. But that was as far as I could get. A smarter woman might have found more.

There didn't seem to be *any* other links between the victims. Of the Stalker's four victims, Kelly Hawk and Amanda Witherspoon were white, Pamela Carter was Native American, and Sarah Jones was African American. Kelly Hawk had grown up in Oklahoma City, Amanda Witherspoon had been born in North Carolina and had moved to Durant, OK, in her teens. Sarah Jones was born in Fort Worth, TX, and her parents brought her to Edmund when she was ten. Pamela Carter had been born in Norman, where she grew up all her life.

Kelly was born with a silver spoon in her mouth and had gotten kicked out when she turned to drugs. Amanda and Sarah were the daughters of middle class families, and Pamela was born on the poor side of the tracks. They grew up in different cities, they were from a variety of races and

55

economic backgrounds, and they went to different schools. There was nothing to tie them together outside of their profession and the use of *Cyber-Ads* to advertise themselves.

"Maybe it *is* the work of a random killer," I muttered, staring at the screen.

I stood, stretched, and poured myself a cup of coffee. Sipping on it, I looked back at my computer in frustration. It was entirely possible that the Stalker's crimes *were* the work of a random killer. Certainly history was full of them. There'd always been lunatics that were willing to kill anyone just for the sake of killing, and it didn't matter to them who their victims were. Not every crime was the work of a criminal mastermind.

A sudden thought inspired me. Maybe there *was* something else that tied the victims together. Finishing my coffee in one gulp, I returned to my computer. Then I got down to serious business.

Tina Stewart's Diary [written in a Steno pad]

The cell door slammed shut behind me. Busted! Again! The Oklahoma City jail was no better and no worse than any of the other jails I've been in. There was still the same graffiti on the walls, most of it X-rated, as there was in all the other cells I've stayed in. It was as cold and dank as any other cell I've been a guest of. I was grateful that I was in one of their less than fashionable jumpsuits instead of the skimpy clothes I'd been brought in with. It was cold enough as it was. I couldn't begin to identify the sheer filth that was on the floors (and didn't *want* to identify it), but I think the roaches that are eating it are going to be sick later. My cell mate, a middle aged woman with brownish-gray hair and who smelled like a brewery, was snoring in one of the two cots in the cell.

With a sigh, I lay down on the free cot and pulled the blankets up to my chin. Looking up at the dark ceiling, I tried to think. I was six months away from being 21 and had an arrest record as long as my arm. I was hooked on morphine and made a lifestyle of prostituting myself in order to feed my habit. I had no friends, and the only people I was acquainted with were my dealers and other prostitutes. *What a life!*

That cop that booked me was right. Any of my clients could carry a deadly disease or be a killer like that Stalker that was killing prostitutes in the city. Good grief, those pictures the detective showed me were sick! I couldn't get them out of my head. I closed my eyes, but when I did, the images of what that wacko did to those girls kept flashing before my eyes. Nobody deserved a death like that; nobody.

And yet it was happening. Girls like me were easy targets for people that liked to inflict pain and suffering. I mean, who cares if a hooker gets knifed? No big loss, right? Girls like me know the risks when they go into the business, so who cares?

And yet the detective seems to care. She told me that I was worth something. It's been a long time since I've heard that. I think the last time I heard that was when I was a child. Now, people only care about what they can get from me.

When does it end? I don't *want* to end up like the girls in those pictures! The mere thought of it sent a shiver down my back. What those girls must have gone through when they realized what was about to happen!

But how can I get off the crazy cycle? How can I stop what I'm doing and get a real job? How can I get off the drugs and *stay* off? The thought of the drugs filled me with a cold dread. Soon my body would be craving my next fix. I didn't want it, but I couldn't help it. The withdraw pains are *bad*. Anyone that thinks it's easy has never gone through it! The last time I went through withdraw, I ended up in a hospital. They helped me through it, but it was only temporary. I need someone to help me *stay* off the junk once I *get* off it.

If I can get clean and stay clean, then I can think about getting a normal line of work. I wanted it so bad! I didn't want to end up dead at a young age, lying in a gutter or trash dumpster somewhere. But that's where I was headed if I didn't change things. But where could I start?

I closed my eyes. Tears were running down my cheeks. I wanted a new start so badly I could taste it! I wanted a new life, a regular job, and someone that loved me for myself and not just someone who wanted to use me. Was it even *possible* that a girl with my past could start over?

"God," I cried out, "Please, if you're out there, help me! I want to change but don't know how! Please help me!"

The only answer I heard was the snore of the woman in the next cot. The darkness of the cell was as black as my soul felt. Opening my eyes, I wiped my tears on the sheets. Gradually, my eyes cleared and focused. I saw something small in the far corner of the cell. I couldn't tell what it was, but for some reason I was curious about it. I walked over and picked it up.

It was a small Gideon New Testament. It was small enough to fit in a shirt pocket, but big enough to read. The cover was faded and it was covered in grime. But, the pages were very readable.

"A Bible," I muttered, "I guess it's a start."

I carried it over to my cot, wiped the gunk off the cover with the sheets, and opened it. I saw from the table of contents that it had the entire New Testament, the book of Psalms, and the Book of Proverbs. There was a blank page beside the table of contents, and I noted that someone had written in pen: *"This New Testament changed my life. I came into this cell lost, on drugs, and with no future. I left this cell with hope and purpose. May you find that same hope."*

"Well," I said softly, "Whoever you are, I'm with you on the being lost, on drugs, and having no future. Maybe I can be like you in finding hope."

It was time to see if God can help me find what I'm looking for.

Jeremy Winslow's journal [kept on flash drive]

Oklahoma Baptist University is in Shawnee, Oklahoma. It's a prestigious college with a high graduation rate, and has a high percentage of students that go on summer mission trips. In short, over the years it has earned a reputation as a highly respected college.

Chris, Crystal, and I had been to the college once before. A while back, a lunatic had attacked several of the female students. The man was an employee at a local retail store who was so obsessed with vampires that he actually came to believe he was Count Dracula. We had managed to track the man down and stopped the attacks, and the papers had a field day with the idea of Sherlock Holmes capturing Dracula. The good news was that our little visit to the college would be remembered and it could open some doors to get some information, especially since we were acting on behalf of one of their professors.

It was about an hour's drive from Oklahoma City to Shawnee, so I picked up a sandwich and a thermos of coffee from home before hitting the road. Shelly was more than used to these sudden trips, so when I called her from the office she had my lunch and coffee ready and waiting for me. Before I left the house, I kissed Gage and then Shelly threw her arms around me and gave me the smooch of a lifetime.

"I love you," she whispered.

"I love you, too," I said.

"But I'm not going to tell you to be careful," said Shelly, "One time I told you to be careful, and then you were in one of the twin towers when it collapsed on 9/11. Another time I told you to be careful, and you and Chris nearly fell off a speeding train while fighting a criminal. A few months back, I told you to be careful and somebody put a rattlesnake in your car. I'm almost afraid if I tell you to be careful again, you're going to get thrown out of an airplane without a parachute or something."

I frowned. She hadn't asked me the details of the case, and she seemed to be afraid to. Since the birth of Gage, she has gotten even more protective of me then she was before. She had always known that the life of a detective was dangerous, but the Crimson Dragon case was the first case that had ever endangered the entire family. Now, with Chase on the run, she was even more worried. No animal was as dangerous as a cornered animal, and Chase had to be feeling desperate.

I showed her the *Compu-Watch* Chris had designed. She was greatly relieved to see the phone Ap on the watch, as well as the SOS button.

"Dick Tracy would be proud," chuckled Shelly, "Now *there's* an invention I'm proud to see! No more having a cell phone fall out of your pouch just before climbing into your car and finding a snake for you! Hey, maybe Chris' next invention could be a robot maid like on *The Jetsons*!

"You used to *always* lose your phone when you were outside playing with Tim! I always knew that someday you'd lose it when you were in a dangerous situation on a case. You have no idea how glad I am that I don't have to worry about *that* anymore!"

"You and the boys are my life," I said, "I'm hoping that what we're investigating will lead back to Chase and we'll be leading him away in handcuffs."

"Do you think it will?" she asked hopefully.

I sighed. "We're not sure. We believe that Chase has some things to do before he tries to leave the country. We need some evidence before we know for sure that Chase is involved. But one thing we do know for certain is that an innocent old man is sitting in jail for some horrible crimes he didn't commit."

"Tell me what you can," she said, "I'll worry whether I know the details or not, but I need to know how to pray."

Briefly, I told her what we knew. Her eyes widened when she learned of Hendricks' arrest of

Dr. Price. When I finished, she looked at me pride in her eyes.

"Darling," she said, "I know I worry about you...maybe a little too much...but I'm proud of all you're accomplishing. Don't ever forget how proud I am of you. Forgive me if I ever sound like I'm worrying too much."

I smiled. "When you worry about me, I've only rejoiced at how much you care. I love you, Shelly. You and the boys are everything to me!"

Shelly and I walked hand in hand to the car. We had another lingering kiss before I left. As I pulled out of the driveway, I glanced in my rearview mirror. Shelly stood in the driveway looking at me as I drove away.

If there's one thing I like about long drives, it's that they give me time to think and pray. I thought about everything we knew about the case and everything we speculated. Whoever was behind the crimes knew a lot about the original Ripper murder case. Yes, Dr. Price knew a lot about it, but anyone with a computer could look up the details of the Ripper case and find out enough information to be a pretty good copycat killer.

The kicker was in how far the Stalker had gone. How many people would think to compare the layout of nineteenth century Whitechapel with that of Oklahoma City in order to find similar places to dump the bodies? Who thought like that? Even though 19th century Whitechapel didn't look like Oklahoma City, our killer found a way to make the dumping grounds line up. This was *not* the style of a purely random killer.

Could Chase be behind the murders? Certainly he was clever enough to pull it off. But did he have a *reason* to do it? The man had every police officer in the state looking for him. He was a fiend, but he wouldn't risk disaster unless he had something to gain by it.

"But *are* there any connections between the victims and Chase?" I asked aloud.

I took a nibble of my sandwich as I pondered on this. There were literally thousands of girls advertising their services on *Cyber Ads*. A large percentage of them worked for the Crimson Dragons, at least before Chase was unmasked as Moriarty, but not *all* of them did. We needed to know whether the victims were working for the Dragons or not. Then we would know whether Chase was behind the crimes or whether we needed to look elsewhere. But how could we find out for sure?

By the time I reached Shawnee, I still had no idea on that. Hopefully, Chris and Crystal would have a productive time on their ends of the investigation. I turned onto Macarthur from I-40, drove past the hospital, and reached the Oklahoma Baptist University campus. I drove past the dorms and student center, and made my way to the business offices.

From the business offices, some aids escorted me to the criminology area on campus. It was on the top floor of a three-story building close to the campus library. I found the dean of law studies in a little cubical in one corner of the third floor. The dean was a forty-something year old man who only had hair on the sides and back of his head. He had thick glasses and wore a blue striped suit. His name plate read, "*Dr. Forbes.*" Smiling warmly, he rose and gave my hand a firm handshake.

"Do have a seat, Mr. Winslow," said Dr. Forbes, "Or would you prefer Dr. Watson?"

I chuckled. "Either would be fine. I've certainly been called a lot worse than that, especially by the people I've arrested."

Dr. Forbes laughed. "Of that, I'm sure! We're still talking about how you and your associates apprehended that lunatic who thought he was Dracula. It's become a favorite case study among the students. Somehow, the notion of

Sherlock Holmes capturing Dracula on our very own campus fascinates the students. As horrible as the crimes were, the students can't help but be intrigued by it."

"I'm sure," I responded, "How are the students that our so-called vampire attacked?"

"They're all doing fine," said Dr. Forbes, "They had some counseling for a while, but they are all doing well, both emotionally and academically. The campus *has* upgraded our security so that there's no chance of any more nut cases sneaking on and off campus to do something stupid. I admit that I've been curious about Mr. Anderson. Does he still..."

I shrugged. "He still believes he's Sherlock Holmes, but he's still solving cases."

"Remarkable!"

"He and Crystal Parker are getting married, by the way," I said, "And she's become a full partner in our agency."

"I knew it," he laughed, "I knew that those two were in love! A blind man could tell it by the way they looked at each other! You have no idea how many of my female students have asked whether those two were romantically involved! They'll be *delighted* at the news! Have some coffee and tell me all about it."

67

"I won't insult you by turning you down on the coffee," I said, "My newborn son stays awake all night. And when he doesn't sleep, *nobody* sleeps!"

Dr. Forbes laughed as he poured me a cup of coffee in a mug with an OBU logo. The coffee was as weak as a kitten, but—hey—it had a good flavor and had caffeine. I told him a bit about Chris and Crystal's romance and the fears that made Chris hesitate to propose to her for a time. By that time, I had finished the coffee and gratefully accepted a second cup. By the time I gulped it down, I was starting to finally feel like a human being.

"I've raised five children whose days and nights were mixed up," said Dr. Forbes, "Believe me, I feel your pain at losing sleep! Now, what can I do for you?"

With a sigh, I replied, "It's more along the lines of what you can do for Dr. Price."

"Henry?" blinked Dr. Forbes, "He's one of my oldest friends. What's wrong with him?"

As quickly as I could, I told Dr. Forbes about our meeting with Dr. Price. When I got to the part of Price being arrested for murder, Forbes' face grew purple with rage. He pounded his desk in frustration.

"That's idiotic! The only thing Henry is guilty of is caring about people and justice!"

"That's what we believe," I said, "But, as the dean of the criminal law department, you're well aware that there's a difference between *knowing* someone's guilt or innocence and *proving* it in a court of law."

"You're preaching to the choir, detective," said Forbes grimly, "I love the justice system, but sometimes justice doesn't prevail. I've seen innocent people get convicted and guilty people go free based on evidence or lack of it."

"So have I," I replied, "We'd love to prevent a miscarriage of justice here!"

"Does the chief *really* think that Henry would hire someone to carry out some mad scheme to recreate the crimes of Jack the Ripper?"

I nodded. "He's only seeing what fits his preconceived theory."

Forbes shook his head. "The chief ignored what Henry said until he was proved right. It sounds like he's trying to save face by arresting *anybody* that has knowledge of the crimes."

"What can you tell about Dr. Price?" I asked, "Anything you say could possibly help him."

Forbes sighed, rose to his feet, and looked out his window. He frowned, looking like he was thinking of things that were painful to remember. I activated the audio-record Ap on my watch, which fascinated Dr. Forbes. With a deep breath, he started to speak.

"Henry Price is one of the most honest, loyal, and dedicated men I know," began Forbes, "He also carries with him a lot of baggage that he has spent a lifetime trying to overcome."

"What do you mean?"

"His father was a career criminal that died in prison," said Forbes, "Wilson Price was an enforcer for Al Capone back in the nineteen-twenties in Chicago. The man had forty kills to his credit before Eliot Ness and his Untouchables broke up Capone's mob. The only reason that Henry's father avoided execution was because he gave state's evidence against the mob in exchange for a lighter sentence. However, he got stabbed to death in a prison shower a few months later. It was interesting---Wilson Price was killed in the shower in front of ten other guys, none of whom saw anything."

"Right," I said knowingly.

"Henry grew up with the stigma of being the son of a gangster," continued Forbes, "And you can imagine the time he had with his peers. Henry kept hearing, 'The apple doesn't fall far from the tree.' He became determined to not only avoid repeating

70

his father's mistakes, but he also wanted to put lawbreakers away."

I blinked. "Wait a minute...are you saying that Henry Price used to be a *police officer*?"

Forbes nodded. "He was an officer on the beat at the same time that he was working on his PhD. Look up his record...the man has a chest full of awards he won for bravery. He could have made detective, but he wanted to teach police investigation techniques to the next generation."

I thought about that. Hendricks not only arrested an innocent man, but he arrested a former police officer with no evidence to back up his theory.

"Tell me," I said, "What is Henry's financial status?"

"I'm sad to say that the man is living hand to mouth," said Forbes, "The past couple of years has given him a good idea of what it was like for Job. First his wife developed cancer, which his insurance didn't cover, by the way. Poor Henry was up to his neck in debt before his wife died. He's still paying for cancer treatments that didn't work and he's also still paying for the funeral."

"What about life insurance?"

Forbes looked at me sadly. "They owed so much money on Mrs. Price's treatments that they had no choice but to cancel the life insurance to cover expenses. Then there was the accident that crippled his arm."

"But it was the other driver's fault, right? Wasn't the other driver texting and driving?"

"Yes," said Forbes, "But he was *uninsured*. Henry didn't get a dime from that accident. You've heard about how when it rains, it pours?"

I nodded.

"He's living with his granddaughter," said Forbes, "He sold and pawned everything he owns except his own name. Really, the man reached mandatory retirement age a while back, but no one has the heart to make him retire. Even though the school and his church have had fund raisers for him, Henry still owes his shirt."

"So, if you were testifying in court," I said, "I think you could safely say that it's unlikely that he could afford to hire a hit man to carry out some lunatic serial killing scheme."

"The man can't afford a hamburger at *McDonalds*," said Forbes, "He certainly couldn't afford to hire an assassin."

Forbes offered me some more coffee, which I cheerfully accepted. As I sipped on it, I started thinking about some possibilities.

"What you've told me could work one of two ways," I said, "It could show that Dr. Price couldn't possibly have anything to do with this. *Or* Hendricks could continue playing the stupidity game and say that Price is having these killings done out of desperation…hoping to find a way to profit from it."

"You have to be *kidding!*" snarled Forbes.

"Chief Hendricks is ridiculously stubborn," I said, "We need *hard* evidence."

Forbes sighed. "How can I help?"

"My associates and I are looking into a few possibilities," I said, "Right now, we're doing a process of elimination. I need everything you can give me on Dr. Price, his friends, and all contacts, even his students."

"Give me a couple of hours and I'll have everything you need," said Forbes, "Is there anything else I can do to help?"

"Yes," I said, "We can use all the prayer we can get."

"Believe me," said Forbes, "I'll be doing a lot of that, and so will the rest of the campus."

CHAPTER FOUR

Detective Maria Lorenzo's diary

Yesteryear is a quaint little restaurant in Bricktown. The food is good, and they have prices even a detective can afford. The main attraction of *Yesteryear* is the atmosphere. The whole play is decorated with movie stars and comedians of the past. The walls were covered in posters from old time movies, like *Gone with the Wind* and *Some Like it Hot*. Elvis and Marilyn Monroe posters covered several other places on the wall. Waiters and waitresses dressed in clothes of the jazz age. There was also live entertainment. When I arrived at the restaurant, two comedians were doing their own version of Abbott and Costello's *"Who's on first?"* routine.

Slipping into a booth, I listened to the comedians and waited. If there was one thing I hated, it was going behind my superior's back. I had been brought up to respect those in authority— as long as they were honest—and to do what they asked. The problem was, Hendricks was honest...but he was incompetent. The man was the politician's politician, and knew absolutely nothing about detective work. Word around the station had it that Hendricks viewed his position as merely a stepping stone to higher offices. Most thought he had an eye on, first, the DA's office and then the Governor's mansion. A quick solution to big crimes like the Oklahoma City Stalker case would be a big feather in Hendricks' cap.

Now I didn't give a tinker's cuss whether Hendricks advanced in politics or not. But, political ambition is no excuse for sloppy police work. There was a maniac on the streets that was carving up women, and I wanted him caught yesterday. I certainly didn't want an innocent person going to prison just to advance a man's political career.

I was grateful for Chris' call. It took no time to contact Detective Chandler, and it was a relief to find that Chris was right. Chandler was no happier about Dr. Price's arrest than Chris was, and he was livid about Hendricks stepping in to arrest a man Chandler didn't believe was guilty. I mean, Chandler was the detective Hendricks assigned to the case and Hendricks was ignoring what he had to say! And Chandler was a highly respected and seasoned detective.

The comedians finished their act and received a thunderous applause from the audience. Then a woman dressed as Marilyn Monroe in a

75

green gown began singing "Diamonds Are a Girl's Best Friend". She did a good job. I liked the song, too. Maybe if I sang it to my boyfriend, he'd start thinking about diamond engagement rings.

Looking up, I saw Detective Chandler entering the restaurant. I waved to him, and he walked over to me. Chandler is a medium sized man in a blue suit with brownish-gray hair, about fifty years old. As a detective, he was considered brilliant and had a ninety percent conviction rate on his cases. He was also known as a friendly guy, quick to give out compliments and slow to take praise. At the moment, he looked mad enough to chew nails in half. Hendricks can do that to a person. Sitting across from me, Chandler's frown deepened.

"I hope your day is going better than mine," said Chandler, "I don't know whether to ask for a transfer or retire."

"Let me guess," I said, "You've got a headache with Hendricks' name on it."

"Right on the first try," said Chandler, "That guy must have been sick at home the day brains were passed out."

"The arrest of Dr. Price isn't exactly Hendricks' shining hour," I commented, "Hopefully Chris will be able to help us."

Chandler sighed. "Do you really think so?"

"Hey," I said, "Working with Detective Anderson and his team helped me get promoted to detective! I was a uniformed cop the first time I met him. Anderson and his team handed me evidence on a silver platter that led to discovering the real identity of Moriarty."

Chandler snorted. "It's crazy! Detective Anderson is going after his own brother and doesn't even know it! I feel like *I'm* crazy going to someone that is legally insane for help!"

I smiled. "Detective Anderson has his mental issues, but he's still a *very* brilliant detective."

"I hope so," said Chandler, "Dr. Price is no more the Oklahoma City Stalker than you are. I don't like going to a madman, but if there's the slightest chance this will help…"

"See for yourself," I said, "Here he comes now."

Chandler turned just in time to see Chris enter the restaurant. Chris was clad in his familiar tweed suit, cape-covered overcoat, and deerstalker cap. In other places, his appearance would have stuck out like a sore thumb. However, with all of the workers and performers in the restaurant

77

wearing costumes from bygone days, Chris fit right in.

I waved and Chris walked over to us. Chris removed his coat and slung it over the chair beside Chandler. Sitting down, Chris removed his cap and sat in in the chair beside him.

"Good day, detectives," said Chris, "I trust you enjoyed your walk at the Midwest City dog walking park, Detective Lorenzo. And you were walking a poodle, too! And Chandler, I see you're suffering from an ulcer. I trust you'll be careful about what you order from the menu."

Chandler looked at me, his mouth hanging open. I smiled.

Shelly Winslow's journal

After Jeremy left, I spent considerable time cuddling with Gage. The baby is all smiles. He loves his toys and especially loves crawling after Rex, our German shepherd. Poor Rex...he's as lost as a goose without his good buddy, Tim. We knew that he'd miss Tim once Tim was back in school, and we were right. The poor dog spent the first week of school holding a lonely vigil on Tim's bed until it was time to pick him up from school. He

78

still spends a good portion of the morning on Tim's bed.

It's still strange looking out the window and knowing that detectives are stationed in the house next door. They had been hand-picked for our protection detail, and we have that protection 24/7. Once Chase had been unmasked as Moriarty and was able to go on the run, Jeremy had insisted on round-the-clock protection, for which I was grateful.

My phone rang. Wouldn't you know it? Telephones are nice, but there were times when I just know that Alexander Graham Bell should have kept his ideas to himself. How is it that a phone always seems to know when a person is getting into the shower, is setting down to a meal, or—in this case—is nice and comfortable with a baby and dog on the couch? And then, nine times out of ten it's a telemarketer or something.

I got up, much to Rex's dismay, with Gage in my arms and managed to get the fool phone on the third ring. Rex whimpered, letting me know that he had just been getting comfortable. For a German shepherd who had once been a police dog, Rex could sure be a baby when he chose!

"Hello," I said, listening to Rex whine.

"Shelly, it's Jess."

I smiled. "Oh, hi Jess. How are you doing?"

Jessica and I had gotten real close since we had met last year, just like I had gotten close with Crystal. We were the female version of the three musketeers. In almost a year's time, we had gotten to be spiritual sisters, and shared everything together. Jessica, for one, needed that. She had really been struggling with everything that had happened in her family.

First, her husband gets murdered by the same people that had killed Chris' wife and daughter. Then Chris not only has a breakdown, thinking he is Sherlock Holmes, but he doesn't even realize that Jessica is his own sister. He thinks that she's Mrs. Hudson, the landlady of Sherlock Holmes.

Jessica had moved into another house since the murders, and let Chris move in with her. For a time, he had used his rooms as his office for his detective work. It had been a good thing when Jeremy and Crystal had led Chris to move the detective office to downtown Oklahoma City. It gave Jessica a much needed break when Chris was out of the house. With everything she's gone through, she *needs* a break!

"Shelly," said Jessica in an odd sounding voice, "can you come over? I know you're probably busy, but I really need to show you something."

Her voice sounded hollow, like she was trying to make sense of something that made no sense. Whatever was going on, it was worrying her plenty.

"Jess, I'm never too busy for you," I assured her, "Gage always loves seeing you. Can I bring Rex? He's as restless as everything and could stand some time out of the house."

"Rex is always welcome," she answered, "In fact, I think I have some dog treats with his name on them."

"Jess, is something bothering you? You don't sound like yourself."

"I'll show you when you get over here," said Jessica, "I want to show you something, and you tell me if I'm going nuts."

"Should I call Jeremy or Crystal?"

"No," said Jessica, "Not yet. I just want your opinion on something…something important."

"I'm on my way," I said.

It only took me fifteen minutes to pack up Gage's diaper bag and to get him in the car seat. A quick call to the detectives in the house next door, and they were alerted that I was going out for a while. I was told to watch for a black sedan that would be a few cars behind me in traffic. They, in turn, alerted the detectives that were across the street from Jessica's house. Once I got Gage in the car seat, Rex climbed in beside him. Then we were off.

I couldn't help but wonder what was bothering Jessica. There were a lot of things that she let roll off her like water off a duck's back. She was certainly handling enough drama in her life to fill ten soap operas. Whatever it was, it had her worried plenty even though she didn't like to show it. Whatever it was, it had to be big. And that scared me.

Detective Lorenzo's diary

"What is this?" demanded Chandler, "Some sort of parlor trick? Holmes, maybe you should be on that stage doing a mind reading act after the next singer finishes."

"Hardly a parlor trick," answered Chris, "Simply an exercise in observation and deduction. I observed Detective Lorenzo's shoes as I approached the table. There's some red clay on the toes of her shoes that are common to the Midwest City dog walking park. Some fur on her sleeve looks like the fur from a poodle."

"Someone's been swiping dogs at the dog park," I said, "I was undercover. And the dog I used *was* a poodle."

"What about my ulcer?" asked Chandler.

"I observed the top of a medicine bottle sticking out of your shirt pocket," said Chris, "True, it could be a bottle of *anything*. However, I *have* seen you rubbing your stomach several times since I entered the room. I took that to mean that you have an ulcer and your prescription bottle was treatment for it. I take it from your reaction that I was correct in my deduction."

Chandler blinked. "Right on every count."

"I want to thank you both for meeting me here on such short notice," said Chris seriously, "I know you do so at great risk to your careers, considering how Chief Hendricks feels about consulting detectives."

"We just want to see justice done," I said, "Justice is more important than careers any day."

Chris smiled. "Capital! You're detectives after my own heart! Hopefully we can achieve justice *without* hindering your careers."

Chandler shrugged. "Hey, there's no guarantees in life except for death and plenty of taxes. Here's a copy of the notes from the crime scene."

Chandler handed Chris a flash drive. I, in turn, handed a flash drive to him. He stuffed both into his suit coat pocket.

"Those were the ME's autopsy reports," I said, "They've got every gruesome detail."

"Great," said Chris, "Every detail, no matter how trivial, is of the utmost importance."

"One thing you can do for us," I began, "is to…"

"Excuse me," said a voice, "Are you ready to order?"

We looked up. Before us was a waiter dressed like a character from *Star Trek*. He had one of those red shirts with the *Enterprise* emblem on it. In his hands was a waiter's notebook and pen. His hair was jet black and he had a neatly trimmed beard.

"Well, well," said Chris, "Do join us, Professor Moriarty. Or would you prefer I call you *Chase Anderson*?"

Chandler and I looked up at the waiter, our mouths hanging open. With a shrug, Chase sat down…right beside me. In an instant, he pulled a wig and phony beard off and sat them on the table.

84

Chase's face totally resembled his wanted photo: brown hair and the coldest blue eyes I had ever seen. His expression was totally ruthless, without a trace of humanity.

"I must say I'm surprised to see you," said Chris.

"You have a gift for understatement, Holmes," I exclaimed.

I couldn't believe it! The man who topped Oklahoma's most wanted list was sitting here beside me—an Oklahoma City detective—and two other detectives as calmly as if he didn't have a care in the world! He even managed to crack a smile.

"I'm sure you *are* surprised, Holmes," said Chase, "But, I *do* like a surprise every now and then. I'm sure your friends are planning right now on taking me into custody."

"Feel free to stop talking about us as if we weren't here," snapped Chandler, "And, yes, we *do* have handcuffs with your name engraved on them."

"But you won't use them," said Chase, "As a matter of fact, I'll be walking out of here in a few minutes and none of you will be doing a *thing* to stop me."

"By what stretch of the imagination do you think we're letting you just waltz out of here?" I snapped.

In response, Chase reached into his pocket. When the rest of us began to reach for our weapons, he grinned at us and pulled out a cell phone.

"Easy now," said Chase, "I only get into gunfights I believe I can win. And I'm sure none of you wishes a shootout in a crowded restaurant where lots of innocent people can get caught in the crossfire. I only want to show you a picture."

Chase pulled up a photo and handed it to Chris. Chris glanced at it and handed it to Chandler, who looked at it and handed it to me. The picture showed two senior citizens—an old man in a flannel shirt and ball cap and an elderly woman in a red pants suit. They were both sitting in chairs, with a white building behind them. On the wall behind them were the words, "ce Retirement Hom". Whatever else had been on the sign, it didn't make it into the picture.

"Tell me," said Chase, "What do you see?"

"It looks like a nursing home," said Chandler, "So?"

"What about it?" I asked, "What does a retirement home have to do with you?"

"Tell me, Holmes," said Chase, "Can you tell me where this nursing home is?"

"As you know," said Chris, "I would need to blow up the picture and examine it with my equipment before I can do that."

Chase smiled. "At least you're honest."

Chris shrugged. "Why bother lying to someone who already knows the answer?"

"Of course, of course," laughed Chase, "Then maybe you wouldn't mind sharing how you saw through my disguise? Where did I go wrong there?"

Chris shrugged. "One who is trained in the art of disguise learns how to recognize others who are using them. Now, it is your turn. What's the point in the nursing home picture?"

"If I fail to walk out of here at the right time," began Chase, "Then I won't be able to call my associates and give them the proper signal. If I don't give them the proper signal—and you'll never guess what it is—there won't be anyone to stop them from *detonating the explosives* they've placed throughout the nursing home."

The words hit my gut with the force of a sledgehammer. Either he was bluffing, or he had ordered his goons to wire a nursing home to explode! There was no telling how many elderly patients plus the staff in that place! Chris looked as horrified as I was; his face was as white as a glass of milk. Chandler looked at Chase with his mouth hanging open.

87

"Think of it," said Chase, "There are a hundred residents in that facility. Many of them are bedridden or in wheelchairs. There's also an Alzheimer's unit in there. That's not even counting the workers in that place. Picture all of them going up in one huge fireball! Of course, if you agree to allow me to walk out of here after our little talk, I'll be more inclined to give my associates the proper signal to prevent the big boom."

For several seconds, none of us spoke. We looked at each other, grim faced.

"You're bluffing," muttered Chandler, "Even *you* wouldn't do that!"

"Do you really want to take a chance?" asked Chase.

Our silence told him everything he wanted to know. He had us and he knew it. Chase laughed and clapped his hands.

"Oh, this is beautiful!" exclaimed Chase, "The great Sherlock Holmes and two of Oklahoma's finest are sitting at the same table as me, and they can't lift a finger to arrest me! I have literally *dreamed* of this moment!"

"Get to the point, Chase," growled Chris, "Or should I call you Moriarty?"

Chase shrugged. "I've been called a lot worse."

88

"I'm sure," I added, "*I'm* one of the ones who called you worse! Now, would you kindly *GET TO THE POINT?!*"

"Of course, of course," said Chase, "Holmes, you and I have been at each other's throats for years. I don't think you even remember *how* our little duel began. But even though we're enemies, I've come to respect your intelligence. Out of my respect for your powers, I come to give you a little warning."

Chris raised his eyebrows. "A warning?"

Chase nodded. "Drop it, Holmes. I've only got one more crime to commit, and then I'm out of the U.S. for good. If you persist in this persecution of my organization, I promise you that the only thing you'll gain from it is an early grave."

"I've faced death before," said Chris with a shrug, "It goes with the job."

"Fair warning," said Chase, "the next time you face death at the hands of my men, it will be the last time you do so. That's a promise."

Surprisingly, Chris smiled. "Allow me to make you a promise as well. No matter where you go, you can tell yourself that Sherlock Holmes and his associates are trailing you. And if I fall in my endeavor, I won't be going down alone. You'll be going down with me."

I looked at both men, mortal enemies locked in a combat in which neither would give an inch. I had once read the story *The Final Problem*, which detailed Sherlock Holmes' final confrontation with Professor Moriarty. Moriarty, whose gang had been arrested, came out of hiding to try to threaten Holmes into abandoning the chase. Talk about life imitating art! Chase was doing the same thing as the fictional Moriarty, and it looked like Chris wasn't giving in any more than the fictional Sherlock Holmes.

But why would Chase go to all this trouble? He had to know that Chris would never abandon his investigation, so why go to all the risk of coming out into the open like this? This gamble was so reckless it was insane! With a shrug, Chase stood up. His hands on his hips, he faced us squarely.

"Well, I can see there's no convincing you," said Chase, "You've made your choice. Let the chips fall where they may. But don't say I didn't warn you."

"What *I'm* more concerned with," said Chris, "Are those patients at the nursing home along with the workers at that facility."

"Don't worry," smiled Chase, "As long as I walk out of here a free man, I've no reason to harm them. You all may congratulate yourselves. There's a number of people that you've given a gift to…the gift of their lives. Good day, all."

We watched him go, our blood boiling. Chase waved at us and walked out of the restaurant. For several seconds, we all stared at each other. Then Chris sprang to his feet.

"Come on!" ordered Chris.

"But…" began Chandler.

"We allowed him to go," said Chris, "He didn't say we couldn't write down his license plate number. Move it!"

Donning his cap, Chris bolted for the door. I was right behind him, followed by Chandler. We found the parking lot was as full as a used car lot. Chris frowned, scanning the parking lot for Chase. I was coming up a few feet behind him, with Chandler bringing up the rear.

"Blast it!" fumed Chris, "How could he disappear so…*DOWN!*"

Chris whirled around and pushed me to the ground. As I hit the asphalt, there was a loud *KA-BLAM!* Chris cried out in agony, and then he fell to the ground beside me. I rose to my knees and saw, to my horror, a trail of blood seeping from Chris' head. He had been shot in the head!

Chandler was already running in the direction of the gunshots, screaming into his phone.

91

I pulled a handkerchief out of my back pocket and applied it to Chris' head. In seconds, it was saturated with blood. Chris moaned in pain.

"Holmes! Stay with me," I cried.

I looked beside Chris. His deerstalker cap lay on the asphalt beside him, a hole in the crown. Chris was still moaning.

"Holmes," I said, half sobbing, "You stay with me! Crystal needs you, and you're going to be a fine husband to her. You're going to be a great father to her children! You stay with me, Holmes!"

In the distance, I could hear a siren screaming.

CHAPTER FIVE

Crystal Parker's Journal [kept on her tablet]

One of the wonderful things about Chris' computer system was just how sneaky it could be. Between the software he had designed and the hardware that went with it, Chris' computer knew every way there was to get around firewalls and into the most sensitive of systems.

I had personally seen Chris hack into defense department computers when he had been looking for a traitor who was selling secrets to other countries. However, the best thing about Chris' software was that it could cover all traces that a system had been hacked. I don't know how Chris managed it, but his system managed to fool the system being hacked to the extent that the hacked systems didn't even know that anyone had accessed it.

I figured that any computer system that could fool the IRS computers would have no problem accessing the arrest records of a few prostitutes. One thing that most prostitutes had in common was that sooner or later, they usually get arrested. Since every one of the Stalker's victims had different backgrounds—both from where they grew up as well as their ethnicity—it was possible that their arrest records might shed some light on the matter. If that didn't pan out, I would be at a loss to explain whether they had ever met each other at all. And if they had never *met* each other, how was the Stalker selecting his victims? Was it truly a random killer after all?

It only took a few minutes to get into the Oklahoma City Police database. And in five minutes, I got a red flag on each victim's record. The records were sealed.

"Sealed? Since when are a prostitute's records *sealed*?" I wondered.

For a half hour, I tried every way there was to worm my way into the records. Nothing. Whatever had happened, the records of the victims were off limits to everyone. With a sigh, I switched tactics and tried my luck at their juvenile records. After all, it was probable that the victims had started work as hookers while they were in their teens.

A few minutes later, I pounded the desk in frustration. The victims' juvenile records had been totally erased. Whatever these girls had gotten themselves into, it was big enough to have someone in very high places get their records sealed so tightly that no one could ever find them.

"Girls," I muttered, "Who in the *world* did you get mad at you?"

Whatever these girls had blundered into, it was more than a random serial killer. At least one, possibly all, of the victims had seen or heard something worth killing for. And somebody with an incredible amount of influence was using their pull to keep anyone from finding out what. Whatever it was, they were doing an incredible job at cover-up. That made it all the more unlikely that anyone, even Chris, would figure out how these girls had met each other.

"Who in the world has that kind of influence?" I wondered.

The thought that Chase, AKA Moriarty, was behind it was starting to look like a real possibility. OK, so killing a bunch of hookers wasn't going to get him any money. It was possible that they knew something that could help Chris track him down, or had some info on a job he was trying to pull off before fleeing the country. It wouldn't be the first time people had been killed to keep them quiet.

I had used the possibility that Chase was behind the crimes simply as an excuse to investigate the Stalker. I realized that now. I had been so outraged that women were being butchered in the streets that I had been looking for an excuse to get involved in the investigation. It struck me that I was actually surprised that Chase could truly be behind the crimes.

"OK," I thought, "I might know *who* is behind this. But how do we use that to prevent another murder and track that maniac back to his lair?"

The phone rang, interrupting my train of thought. I got it on the second ring and recognized Detective Lorenzo's voice.

"Crystal," said Lorenzo, "*Thank heavens!*"

"Hi, Maria," I replied, "What's up?"

"We just had an encounter with Chris' brother," said Lorenzo.

My jaw dropped. "*Chase?* Where is he? Do you have him in custody?"

"I'll tell you everything later," said Lorenzo, "We need to get ahold of Jeremy and Chris' sister. Meet me at the *Christ's Church Hospital.*"

My heart leaped to my throat. "Hospital? What's wrong? Is Chris hurt?"

For several seconds, there was silence. That silence terrified me.

"Maria? Maria, are you there?"

"Chris is in the hospital," said Lorenzo slowly, "Somebody took a shot at him. Crystal, he...he's got a head wound."

"*WHAT?!*"

A head wound! Chris had been shot in the head! My darling could be dead before I even got to the hospital! Dear heaven, my sweetheart could *already* be dead!

"It's just a graze," said Lorenzo quickly, "He's going to be fine. But, he's unconscious. He's being admitted at *Christ's Church Hospital.*"

"I'm on my way."

Trembling, I shut down the computer, grabbed my purse, and ran for the door. I took the steps two at a time as I made my way to the lobby and out into the parking lot. I was speed dialing Jeremy on my *Compu-Watch* as I ran.

Jeremy Winslow's journal [kept on flash drive]

Driving back to Oklahoma City, I thought about everything that Forbes had told me. I had a lot of mixed feelings, let me tell you. According to Forbes, Price was bending over backwards to prove that the old saying, "Like father, like son," didn't apply to him. Having a gangster for a father could do that to a guy.

But the sad fact was, the man was desperate for cash. I had investigated several crimes where people who were desperate did things they would never have done under normal circumstances. I had

97

once arrested a woman who once had been a pillar of her community for welfare fraud. She had been desperate and driven to commit fraud because she hadn't been able to get a job. I hated to admit it, but Hendricks *could* make a neat circumstantial case for the theory that Price's desperation had led him to have the Stalker murders committed in order to profit by them.

I didn't for one moment believe that Price truly *was* guilty, but innocent people have been convicted before. Stranger things have happened. I just didn't want it to happen *here*. If Price went to trial, the stress alone would probably kill him.

We needed hard evidence to show that Hendricks was a buffoon with sawdust for brains when it came to arresting Price. We needed to show that Hendricks never did a real investigation, and that he had arrested a man whose only crime was trying to help.

My *Compu-Watch* suddenly beeped, showing a call coming in, interrupting my thoughts. I glanced at the watch and saw that it was Crystal's number. Right about now, I was grateful that the watch worked on voice commands.

"Answer call," I commanded the watch.

"Jeremy," said Crystal, "It's Crystal."

"Hi, Crystal," I said, "I was just driving back, and…"

"Jeremy," sobbed Crystal, "Chris just had a run-in with his brother. Chris is in *Christ's Church Hospital*."

"Hospital?! What happened?"

"He's got a head injury," said Crystal, "Somebody shot at him. It's just a graze, but he's still unconscious."

"I'm on the way," I said, "Does Jessica know?"

"Not yet," said Crystal, "Can you call her and Shelly? I'm on my way to the hospital and plan on having a serious talk with the doctors when I get there. And, Jeremy, get here quick, OK?"

"As quick as I can."

"Thanks, and Jeremy?"

"Yes?"

"I think Chase really *is* behind the Stalker killings. I'll tell you what I found later."

"You have no idea how glad I am to hear that," I said, "We'll pool our information when we see how Chris is."

Shelly Winslow's journal

Jessica Peterson lived in a magnificent Victorian house that she had owned for the last five

99

years. She had bought the house after the murders of her husband and Chris' family. For six years, she had cared for Chris since his breakdown and had allowed Chris to set up the den as an office to conduct his investigations.

The whole setup had been an incredible strain on Jessica. That was especially true since Chris believed that Jessica was his landlady, Mrs. Hudson. It had been heartbreaking to see that Chris had no idea that Jessica was actually his sister! Although Jessica never complained, it had been sweet relief for her when Crystal and Jeremy talked Chris into moving the office to downtown Oklahoma City. This gets Chris out of the house more, giving Jessica a much needed break. She needed it, poor thing.

After I pulled into the driveway, I scooped Gage out of the car seat. He voiced his disapproval at being waken up as I walked up the front walk. Jessica met me at the door, and relieved me of Gage. He squirmed as he curled up in her arms, and she grinned at him as she led me into the house. Rex obediently followed us into the house.

She offered me some coffee, which I gladly accepted. It had been a bear to get used to being off of regular coffee curing my pregnancy. I was a three-cups-a-day person when it came to coffee, and being away from it for months had made me an absolute bear at times.

Once I poured my coffee, we retreated to the living room. Jessica sat on the couch, cuddling Gage in her arms. Rex sat down at my feet, chewing on a rawhide bone Jess had given him.

"How are you doing, Jess?" I asked, sipping on my coffee.

"It's been a horror," sighed Jessica, "So much has happened that I don't know where to begin. But, at least I've had some time to think with Chris out of the house. I know it sounds awful, but it's been a blessing to just have some time to myself. I mean, I love Chris to death, but it's been nice to have some time to think."

I smiled. "It's not awful at all. Look how drastically your world changed in a moment! You lose your husband, Chris loses his family, and he loses his mind all in one night! You've devoted every waking moment since then taking care of Chris."

Jessica nodded. "You know, it didn't hit me until recently that in spending all my time taking care of Chris, I never took time to grieve my own loss."

"That's very normal with caregivers," I said, "It's very common for caregivers to be so focused on caring for a loved one that they don't consider their own needs."

"Yes," sighed Jessica, "And I was just starting to come to grips with some things when Chris unmasked Moriarty. To think that Chase not only was still alive, but he was the maniac behind the very mob Chris was trying to bring down! Our little brother murdered my husband, Chris' family, and so many others!"

Jessica held Gage tightly to her chest as silent tears flowed down her face. Jeremy and I had often wondered how Jess was coping with everything, but until now she had refused to say anything. All she could think of was helping Chris. Now that the tears were coming, they were flowing like a river. I sat my cup on the coffee table and sat beside her. I put my hand on her shoulder, and for several minutes I prayed for her. When we finished praying, Jess looked at me sternly.

"You know how I told you I have something to show you?" asked Jessica.
I nodded.

"Come with me," she said sternly.

She handed Gage to me, and I followed her down the hall. Rex trotted obediently behind us. She led me to the den that once served as her brother's office. When Jeremy and I first met Chris, he showed us his office. Back then it had been both an office and a workroom for his electronic experiments. It had also been wall to wall clutter. Now, Jeremy had never been the most organized of men, but Chris had needed to stick a CONDEMNED sign on his office door.

But as Jess opened the door, I noticed a big difference. The former disaster area was neat. There were no stacks of file folders on the floor. The electronic workbench was free of clutter. It actually looked like a person could walk in the room without tripping over something.

"Wow," I said, "I can see the floor. Did you find the lost continent of Atlantis somewhere down there?"

"No," quipped Jessica, "But I did find that lost ark that Indiana Jones was always looking for. Come here a minute."

She led me to one corner of the room and pointed. There, beside a steel filing cabinet, was a small black file box. I recognized the box at once. It was the box that Chris had put a huge stack of documents in; documents that contained everything from his birth certificate to his wedding license, and several other documents and photographs from his life before his family's murders.

Chris had put all those documents in that file box on the night of his family's murders. In his wild imagination, he thought the documents were actually notes on unpublished case files; cases that he said would remain unpublished until Moriarty was behind bars.

"The file box? What about it, Jess?"

"I had been sweeping the floor and had to move the box," said Jess, "I had expected it to be heavy. But feel for yourself."

I handed Gage to Jess and picked up the file box. It was unbelievably light.

"That's strange," I said, "I've picked up file boxes like this before. It should be heavy enough to require two hands to lift it."

"I know," said Jess, "I personally watched Chris cram that fireproof box as full as it could possibly be filled. You should be risking a backache lifting it up. I got to wondering about that. Open it up."

I blinked. "*Open it*? Jess, you know Chris' rules. He would have ten cows if anyone nosed into that box before he gave the nod! He's *adamant* that this file box stay closed until Chase is behind bars!"

"I'll take full responsibility," said Jess, "Open it, girl."

With trembling hands, I opened the lid and gasped at what I saw. I was expecting to find the file box stuffed to the max with photographs, a marriage license, and birth certificates. But there was nothing. The file box was totally empty!

"Jess," I said, "Did Chris…"

"He hasn't opened that box since the night he filled it while suffering his breakdown," said Jessica, "Believe me, I know that for a fact. Shelly, someone's been in this house! Somebody has broken in just to steal the documents from that box!"

"But who…"

My cell phone rang, cutting off my train of thought. Unlike a lot of girls, I carried my phone in a pouch on my belt instead of in my purse. It made things handy if I was away from my purse. Hearing the theme from *Love Story* as the ring tone, I knew at once that it was Jeremy.

"Hi, handsome," I said, answering it.

"Shelly," said Jeremy, "something's happened to Chris. You need to get to *Christ's Church Hospital*. Call Jessica."

"I'm with her at her house," I said, "Honey, what is it?"

"Chase just tried to kill him," said Jeremy, "Chris has a head injury. Crystal's on her way. Just

105

get here quick, darling!"

My hands were shaking as I hung up the phone. Pale and wide-eyed I looked at Jessica. She swallowed as she saw the look of fear on my face.

"Jess," I whispered softly, "We need to go. It's about Chris."

Tina Stewart's diary (Kept on a Steno pad)

I've spent the last few hours doing nothing by reading the Gideon New Testament that I found. My cell mate made bail, so I didn't have her snoring to disturb me. Hopefully I can make bail soon. It'd be nice to talk to someone who can explain to me what I'm reading.

The Bible is interesting, but man is it hard to understand! I had never read the Bible before. I've heard about it, and I know it talks about Jesus. But I didn't know beans about it. The main time I heard the name of God or Jesus when I was growing up was when my mother was swearing. She swore a lot and drank a lot more. The only thing she ever taught me was to follow in her footsteps as a prostitute.

One thing Detective Lorenzo is right about is that I need to *change*. I do not want to end up like those girls that are getting sliced up! And I don't want to catch AIDS. I have no idea how I've avoided AIDS so far, but I don't want to press my luck. A lot of people say that the Bible can show a person how to turn their lives around, but I sure need some help to get it.

Four guys—Matthew, Mark, Luke, and John—wrote about the life of Jesus. Some of it was giving all of Jesus' family tree, and John even said that Jesus helped God create the world. I wonder how on earth Jesus went from creating the world to going to that manger in Bethlehem. Why would the Son of God leave heaven to come down to earth as a human baby and live in poverty? I couldn't figure it.

"Well, well, well," said a voice.

I looked up from the Bible and saw the face of my mother standing outside the cell. Her black hair had just a few streaks of gray. She had on too much makeup, as usual. Her eyes were bloodshot from too much alcohol. Her faded red dress was stained with food and I don't to think about what all. Her face was older than her years, thanks to all of her hard living.

"Take a good, hard look, Tina," I told myself, *"that's what you're going to look like in a few years if you don't make some better choices."*

"Hi, Mom," I said weakly.

107

Mom looked at me with contempt. For several seconds, she just looked at me and said nothing.

"I taught you better," she said finally, "I taught you how to know when a cop is setting you up to bust you. You should have been able to smell a cop a mile away."

"I messed up," I agreed, "I've messed up in a lot of ways."

"I *told* you that those ads on the internet weren't the right way to go," said Mom, "In *my* day we didn't need all these fancy computers to advertise ourselves. But all you could think of was how the computer was the way of the future."

"Mom, I---,"

"You've always been stupid and nothing but trouble," said Mom, "I could go for months and months without getting busted. You've already got an arrest record as long as your arm. I always knew you were an idiot; an idiot who *ruined* my life. I tried to teach you the best ways to survive as a hooker, but you thought you knew more you're your mother. You're too stupid to even make a good prostitute. It was a blessed day when you left home!"

My stomach began churning. I could feel the cramps coming. I knew it was only a matter of time until the withdraw hit. My nice little homecoming with Mom only brought it on faster. I doubled over in pain, groaning. Mom kept right on ranting. I could see her mouth moving, but I couldn't hear her. All I could do was moan in agony.

"*Guards*," I muttered, "Get a guard!"

"And *now* it's the drugs," sneered Mom without an ounce of mercy, "Alcohol wasn't good enough for you, like it was for me. You had to go to the hard stuff. You always knew best, didn't you?"

"*WILL YOU GET THE COTTON PICKING GUARDS?!*"

She threw up her hands, muttered something I didn't care to hear, and buzzed for the guards. I rolled off the cot onto the floor. I was lying on a cold, damp floor that was covered in something I didn't want to identify. I found myself in a fetal position, groaning and clutching my Gideon New Testament. After an eternity, I heard footsteps approaching the cell and heard the turning of a key.

Then I heard the guards talking. I couldn't make out what they were saying; it all sounded like gibberish, even though they were right in front of me. All I knew was that the withdraw pains were getting fierce. I could hear screaming as if from far away and barely aware that it was *me* who was screaming. Then the world went dark.

CHAPTER SIX

Crystal Parker's journal [kept on her tablet]

I sped towards *Christ's Church Hospital* as fast as I could, praying harder than I'd ever prayed in my life. Ever since it had been discovered that Chase was still alive and was actually the brains behind the Crimson Dragons, we had feared an assassination attempt on one of us. While we all took precautions, the danger was still there.

And now it had happened! Chris was in the hospital! A bullet had grazed his skull. I praised God that it was *only* a graze, but he was still hurt. A head wound was a head wound. And now Chris was unconscious and helpless. Suppose Chase trailed him to the hospital and made another attempt on his life?

Not on my watch!! Gripping the steering wheel tightly, I vowed that I would be with Chris every second that he was in the hospital. I would move all my computers to the hospital room and run the investigation from Chris' room if I had to. But there was no way on earth that Chase was going to get at my darling while he was unconscious and helpless!

I pulled into the hospital parking lot and ran for the emergency room entrance. Detective

Lorenzo met me in the waiting room and gave me a hug. I was crying as she led me to a chair and told me everything that happened at the restaurant. She told me that Detective Chandler was conducting the crime scene investigation personally.

"I don't get it," she said when she had finished, "Chase *had* to know that his brother would never drop the investigation! Your fiancée has been after him for over six years, and has put his life on the line every day. He knew he was making a threat that Chris would ignore, so why reveal himself like that? It was an incredible risk, and there were less risky ways to make an attempt on Chris' life."

I thought about that one. Chase Anderson had every cop in the state watching for him. It *was* an incredibly dangerous move on his part to reveal himself. He could have just sent one of his assassins to do the job while Chase remained in hiding. Why come out in the open and make a threat on the lives of innocents at a nursing home? Then it hit me.

"There's a couple of reasons he might do that," I said.

"I'm listening," said Maria.

"Up until now," I continued, "Chris didn't know *who* Moriarty was. The only time he had seen

111

Moriarty was on Skype, and he was wearing a mask and disguising his voice at the time. Chase may have been curious as to whether discovering Moriarty's true identity had triggered Chris' memory."

Maria nodded. "That's one thing I've been considering. *We* knew that Chris' memory hadn't improved a lick since then, but Chase had no way of knowing that."

"And," I continued, "We now have reason to believe that Chase is the mastermind behind the Oklahoma City Stalker murders. He was probably waiting to see if Chris would make a slip on how much he really knew."

I quickly brought her up to speed on what I had learned that morning. She was all attention. I could practically see the wheels turning in her head as she listened.

"I couldn't even get the arrest records of the victims using Chris' computer system," I said, "Somebody way up the chain of command had their records sealed tighter than a drum or had them purged from every database."

"Only Moriarty and his Crimson Dragons have that kind of pull," mused Lorenzo, "But knowing that and getting the evidence to prove it is two different things."

"I'm sure Chris will have an idea once he wakes up," I said, "If there *is* another victim on the hit list, we only have so long to find out who it is and prevent it."

"What I would love to know..." began Maria.

The waiting room doors slid open. Shelly hurried in with Gage in her arms. Jessica was close behind her. They hurried over to us. Jessica gave me a hug. Shelly looked at me, worried.

"Any word?" asked Jessica, anxiously.

"Not yet," I answered, "Thank heavens it's just a graze! I just wish he wasn't still out cold."

"He saved my life," mused Lorenzo, "He shoved me out of the way just in time. Judging from the trajectory of the bullet, if he hadn't pushed me down, it would have taken my head off."

I blinked. *What* had she just said? A bullet from a professional sniper nearly killed *her*? The color slowly drained from my face. I started to speak, but saw Jeremy walking towards us. He kissed Shelly and Gage, and then we got down to business. We brought him up to speed on Chris. He told us everything he had learned at OBU, and I told him about my end of the investigation.

"Detective Lorenzo," I began slowly, "Think about what you just said a minute ago. A professional assassin doesn't usually miss. He carries a sniper rifle with a state-of-the-art scope. He would have killed *you* if Chris hadn't pushed you down. Could *you* have been the intended target?"

Detective Lorenzo looked at me. "But it's *Chris* that Chase has a grudge against. Wouldn't it make more sense to get rid of the detective that has come closer to nailing him than anybody? And Chase has a grudge against Chris that goes back to their teenage years, with Chris testifying against him at his trial in juvenile court."

"How close where you and Chris standing together?" asked Jeremy.

"About four feet," said Lorenzo.

Jeremy and I exchanged glances. Four feet; that's more than enough room to rule out a blunder on the part of the sniper. A true professional would have been able to hit his target with half that amount of space.

"I hate to say it," said Jeremy, "But Crystal has a point. We may not be able to say for *sure*, but I've seen Moriarty's snipers in action. They're true professionals and usually don't make those kinds of mistakes. I once saw one of his snipers assassinate an informant standing just *inches* from Chris and me."

"But why *me*?" asked Maria, "I just became a detective a few months ago, and I'm hardly breaking any conviction records right now. I'm the new kid on the block! What would Chase have against *me*?"

"That's a good question," said Jessica, "But with my brother Chase, it's not a good idea to take chances."

Lorenzo opened her mouth to speak, but was interrupted as a doctor walked up towards us. The doctor, wearing surgical scrubs, looked to be in his sixties, was thin as a rail, and had a very serious look on his face. I could feel my heart leap to my throat. My hands were shaking as the doctor approached us.

"Hello," said the doctor, "My name is Dr. McIntyre."

"Doctor," I said, my voice barely a whisper, "I'm Crystal Parker, Chris' fiancée. How is my darling doing?"

Dr. McIntyre sat down beside in a chair beside us. He looked at us with true compassion written all over his face.

"Miss Parker, we need to talk," said Dr. McIntyre.

Chase Anderson's journal [in encrypted code]

If there's one thing I like about rural farming communities, it's that they're isolated. The *Shady Rest Cemetery* is deep in the back roads of Earlsboro, and it is *super* isolated. It is so overgrown with weeds and tall grass that I don't think anyone has been in the place since JFK was President. The tombstones are ancient and fading, and in the center of the graveyard is an ancient crypt. The bricks on the crypt were cracked with age, but the building is still solid enough. A rusted padlock was on the single door.

The boys were already waiting on me when I arrived. Good. I like people that are on time. There was Johnny Wilson; he's young, about 24, and a great marksman. He wears a ton of gel in his hair, and likes leather jackets and that black Camaro of his. Then there's Tony Dobbs, my best forger. He never wears anything but gray suits and is more into minivans. And, of course, there's Winston Hawk; he's the world's most ruthless drug smuggler. He's more into the western culture; always wearing a cowboy hat and driving a pickup truck. They all waved as I parked my van beside the crypt.

"Hi, boss," said Dobbs as I walked towards them.

"Ready and waiting," I said, "I like that. It shows loyalty."

"So, what's up?" asked Wilson, "This isn't exactly the top party spot in the state."

"I've got some merchandise I need moved," I replied, "It's in here."

"In *there*?" asked Wilson, "What, are we into stealing bodies now?"

I chuckled. "Not quite. Hawk, you do the honors."

Hawk nodded, grabbed some bolt cutters from out of the back of his pickup, and cut the padlock on the door of the crypt. I opened the door and motioned for everyone to follow me in. Inside the crypt was years full of dust, at least four or five inches thick. There wasn't an inch on any of the coffins that wasn't covered in dust and cobwebs. Anyone who might have mourned the loss of the people inside this crypt was long dead themselves.

"OK," asked Wilson, "Where's the merchandise?"

"Right *here*," I answered.

As I spoke, I punched Wilson in the stomach with all my might. Wilson grunted in surprise and doubled over. A second punch, this time to the face, sent him to the floor. He let out a moan as he struck the hard concrete floor. He looked up just in time to see Dobbs and Hawk aiming their firearms right at him. His eyes were twin saucers as he looked at me, puzzled and terrified.

"Boss, *what…*?"

"Mr. Wilson," I said evenly, "When I give you a direct order, it is to be carried out exactly as I give it. Have I not made that clear to you since you joined my little organization?"

"Yes," cried Wilson, "And I have!"

"Oh, *no*," I corrected, "You have botched your last orders royally! What were my explicit instructions back at the restaurant?"

Wilson swallowed. "You said to shoot…you said to shoot…."

"I told you to shoot *Detective Lorenzo*," I said, "Those were your orders! Instead, you nearly killed my brother and detective Lorenzo is still breathing."

"But you were going to kill your brother anyway!" protested Wilson, "Besides, what's a lousy OKC detective to you? It's your *brother* that's hounded you over the years. He's the one that caused your identity to be revealed!"

It's a good thing that Wilson was still kneeling on the floor. It made it easier for me to kick him in the jaw with all my might. He fell

118

backwards, blood pouring from his mouth.

"My brother *will* die," I said, "But on *my* timetable, not yours! He is going to know exactly *who* beat him and destroyed him before he dies. That will be at a time and place of my choosing, and will be my magnum opus in Oklahoma before retiring to the tropics. Your task was simply to remove an immediate threat to my operations; namely, Detective Lorenzo."

"But what's this girl to you?" protested Wilson, rubbing his jaw.

I sighed, and looked down at Wilson with all the disappointment that was in my soul.

"Mr. Wilson, Mr. Wilson," I said sadly, "Haven't you learned by now that I don't like to tell my aids too much? One thing that helped me to remain anonymous over the years was giving my workers only what they needed to know. I gave you an order. All you had to do was obey it."

"But I tried!" cried Wilson, "I had the shot perfectly lined up! Your brother suspected something and pushed her out of the way!"

"What prevented you from taking a second shot?" I asked, "You could have. She was in the ground right out in the open! You could have done that. But instead, you packed up your gear and ran like a scared rabbit."

119

My foot shot out again. This time it collided with his nose. He cried out in pain and held his hands to his face. Dobbs took the initiative and pulled a pair of handcuffs from out of his suit jacket. While Wilson was holding his hands to his face, eyes clenched shut in pain, Dobbs fastened the handcuffs to his wrists.

"Hey!" cried Wilson.

"Sorry, Mr. Wilson," I said, "You had a most promising future in my organization. I had hoped you would be my best assassin when I rebuilt and reorganized the Crimson Dragons. However, I have no use for failures who question my decisions."

"Wait! Boss, please!"

Hawk had retreated to his pickup. He returned with a set of leg irons, just like the kind that prisoners wear when being escorted from the courthouse to prison. In seconds, Hawk had Wilson's legs securely chained. A third chain was quickly run from around his waist to a handle on one of the caskets. The man was going nowhere.

"Boss!" cried Wilson, "Please, don't!"

"Don't call me 'boss'," I said grimly, "You are now among the ranks of the unemployed."

Wilson opened his mouth to protest. At that moment, however, I pulled my handkerchief from my pocket and stuffed it into his mouth. Wilson's eyes were panic stricken. He looked at me, silently pleading.

"Goodbye, Mr. Wilson," I said, "I hope you enjoy your new home. You're going to be here for a looooooonnnnnngggggg time!"

I led Dobbs and Hawk out of the crypt, ignoring Wilson's muffled voice. Hawk got a fresh padlock from inside his pickup and locked the door shut. None of us gave Wilson another thought as we drove our separate ways.

Jeremy Winslow's journal

Crystal and Jessica's faces with contorted with fear as Dr. McIntyre came towards us. I wondered just how bad it could be. After all, the bullet wasn't lodged in Chris' skull. It had been a graze. He should wake up and return home…shouldn't he?

"In a lot of ways," began Dr. McIntyre, "Mr. Anderson is fine. Physically, anyway. The bullet grazed his skull, and it doesn't look like there's going to be any permanent damage."

"So my brother is going to be all right," breathed Jessica.

121

Crystal breathed a deep sigh of relief. "Thank you, Jesus!"

"He should wake up soon," said Dr. McIntyre, "But there is one thing that puzzles me."

"What's that?" asked Jessica.

"When we were working on him," said Dr. McIntyre, "We found something very, very odd. Inside his skull, close to where the bullet grazed him, we found a microchip."

All of us looked at the doctor, our eyebrows narrowed. It was several seconds before he continued.

"I don't know what it's for," he continued, "But we removed the chip for the lab to analyze. I can tell you one thing, however. It's got a date stamped on it; May 2nd, 2005."

"Wait a minute," said Jessica, "May 2nd, 2005?"

The doctor nodded.

"That was around the time he started on the organized crime task force," said Jessica, excited, "It was long before everything went sour. He had been taken a bullet in the shoulder while taking down a drug dealer, and had to have surgery."

I blinked several times. "Jessica, is that the last time your brother had surgery?"

Jessica nodded. "And it was only a shoulder wound."

I stood up and faced everyone. Their faces showed that they were thinking along the same lines as I was.

"He was investigating the Crimson Dragons back then," I said, "And he had to have surgery."

"Whoever took *out* the bullet," said Crystal slowly, "also put a microchip *into* his skull."

"Doctor," said Lorenzo, "I am going to need that microchip. It is going to have direct bearing into this investigation."

Dr. McIntyre nodded. "I can speculate as to what it's for, but there's no way I can tell you for certain until it's examined by experts. It's out of my field of expertise."

"That's OK," said Lorenzo, "You've been more of a help than you know."

"I'll tell you when he wakes up," said Dr. McIntyre, "And then you can go see him."

Crystal stood and stretched. Judging from her face, she was both relieved and worried. Chris was going to recover, but we didn't know what to make of that microchip. Chase was still out there, and whoever had fired that shot. We didn't even know if Chris was the target or if Detective Lorenzo was.

123

"We need to know who did the surgery on Chris back in 2005," said Lorenzo, "I am going to want to have a *serious* talk with that doctor."

"I'll lay you odds that our little microchip was a tracking device," I said, "A lot of pet owners put them into their pets so the owners can find them if their pets get lost."

"If we're right," said Crystal, "Then Chase used Chris' injury to have that microchip implanted so that he could keep track of Chris' movements during the investigation of the Crimson Dragons."

"But why go to all that trouble?" asked Shelly, "I mean, I'm glad that he never killed Chris, but from Chase's point of view, killing Chris would have been a lot simpler."

Crystal thought about that for several seconds. Then she looked at us, her eyes wide with fear.

"This is a *game* to Chase," said Crystal, "He has a serious grudge against Chris and wants his suffering to be as bad as possible."

"But he already killed Chris' wife and daughter," protested Jessica, "How much more does Chris have to suffer?"

"He's dragging this out," said Crystal, "Because he wants Chris to *know* who it is that finally beats him."

Shelly thought about that and looked at me. She looked like something she had forgotten just popped into her mind.

"I bet *Chase* is the one that stole all of the things out of Chris' special file box," she said.

Crystal and I looked at each other and then back at Shelly. Jessica nodded.

"You're right, Shelly," said Jessica, "I hadn't thought about that."

"What do you mean?" asked Crystal, "What was stolen from Chris?"

"*Everything* was stolen out of the file box Chris was going to open once he put Moriarty away," said Jessica, "The things he kept saying were his unpublished cases."

A sickening feeling was gnawing at my gut. That box contained all kinds of documents verifying Chris' identity. We had all put our hope in the idea that seeing those documents and pictures would bring Chris back to reality. Instantly I pressed the Internet Explorer Ap on my watch. My news screen appeared, showing the latest Hollywood star that had checked into rehab. A touchscreen keyboard appeared under the picture and I began typing.

"What are you doing?" asked Crystal.

"I'm looking up Chris' records in the OKC police department," I answered.

Crystal looked at her watch and pressed the Internet Explorer Ap on hers as well.

"I'll check his birth records," said Crystal.

"What are you two doing?" asked Shelly.

"There's a reason why Chase bothered to have Chris' records stolen," I explained, "And I hope…"

My screen beeped and I looked at the results. Nothing.

"What is it?" asked Jessica.

"Chris' record has been erased from the police department," I said, "There's no record that he was ever on the force."

"That can't be!" exclaimed Lorenzo.

"You've got to be kidding!" said Crystal, "There's no birth certificate for Chris on file *anywhere*! I'm going to check his banking records."

"You can get into someone else's bank records with your watch?" asked Lorenzo.

"The computer in this watch has a direct link to Chris' computer system in our office," said Crystal.

"But—"

I smiled. "Chris has a very…unique computer system. The less you know, the happier you'll be."

"This is *not* good," said Crystal frantically, "*All* of Chris' banking records have been erased!"

Jessica sat up straight. "Have you checked under both Christopher Anderson *and* Sherlock Holmes?"

Crystal nodded. "Now I'm hacking into his tax records at the IRS."

"Oh," said Lorenzo, "You hack into the IRS computers, too?"

Shelly and I looked at each other and smiled. I couldn't help but think back to when I first partnered with Chris, one the things that was *very* hard to get used to was how Chris could hack into top secret computer systems without leaving a trace of evidence. As a detective, I had never even bent *any* of the rules before, especially when it came to collecting evidence. If anyone had asked me, I would have insisted that there was *never* any justification for breaking the rules of police procedure.

But then Shelly and Tim had been kidnapped by Moriarty's men. Their lives had been on the line, and time was far from on our side. We had been ordered to drop our investigation in exchange for the release of my family. The only thing was, we knew that once Moriarty had what he wanted, he would kill my family anyway. Chris used his hacking techniques and equipment to get the evidence we needed while we tracked my family down to where they were being held. The result was my family was rescued unharmed and we solved the case Moriarty had been trying to get us to drop.

That was when I learned the lesson that Lorenzo was just starting to learn. Sometimes a rule had to be bent in order to save lives. I didn't like it, but there were times it was necessary.

Crystal looked up, pale and shaking. "Either Chris has never paid income taxes in his life, or someone has erased every record of the taxes he filed."

"My brother has *always* paid his taxes on time," insisted Jessica.

"I've heard of peoples' identities being stolen," breathed Lorenzo, "But I've never seen a person's identity being *erased*!"

Shelly stared at me. "Every record showing Chris' identity has been erased. *Why?*"

I swallowed. "I wish I had an answer."

CHAPTER SEVEN

Crystal Parker's journal [kept on her tablet]

Chris' room was dark when the orderly showed us to it. After we showed our badges to the police officers stationed outside the door, they showed us in. The lights were off and the shades were drawn. The top of Chris' head was wrapped in bandages. His breathing was slow, labored. I walked to his side and placed my hand on his shoulder gently. He stirred, but didn't waken. I felt numb as I watched my darling breathing.

"He's going to be OK," said Jeremy, "The doctor said…"

"It's not just the wound," I interrupted, "I know that it's just a graze. But that microchip! And *all* of his personal records are missing! You know, after all his other records turned up missing, I checked for his school records. There's not even a record of Chris ever attending school!"

Jeremy sat on the sofa beside Shelly and Jessica. All of them looked as worried as I felt. Jeremy toyed with his fedora as he thought. My own thoughts were whirling also. We had an innocent old man sitting in jail. We had a killer on the loose that we believed was working for Chase. Vital records of the victims were sealed tighter than a drum, and Chase was going to great lengths to wipe out *all* of Chris' records.

I used to think that life was stacked against me before. First there were the stinkers in high school. For some reason, the girls in my high school just plain loved to make themselves look superior by making other people feel small.

I had been a favorite target of the other girls because I struggled with my weight. While I had never been obese, I was forever just enough overweight were people could notice. And once they found a weakness in a person, they would exploit that weakness to the max.

Even though I was just a *little* overweight, the girls nicknamed me The Blimp. From the day I sat foot in high school until the day I graduated, the only people at school who called me by my name were the teachers. Being bullied tends to stay with a person. While Chris and I were dating, I knew that he was postponing marriage simply because he was afraid that I would become a target for Moriarty. That was back in the day before we knew who Moriarty really was.

I understood Chris' reasons, but a part of me was secretly afraid that he was putting off marriage because he didn't think I was pretty enough to be his wife. For a time, I also secretly struggled with an eating disorder of my own making. I had put myself on a starvation diet in a desperate attempt to lose weight. Thanks to the help of Shelly and Jeremy, I had gotten past all that. Shelly gave me wise counseling. Jeremy managed to secretly record a conversation he had with Chris, in which Chris told Jeremy that he considered me to be stunningly beautiful. My favorite part of the recording was when Chris said that Jennifer Lopez was jealous of my beauty in the same breath that he said my kisses are to die for. That wonderful recording now rests in a safe place where it will *never* be erased!

Then there were the issues with my parents. Dad had been a fourth generation career soldier, and he expected all of us kids to follow in his footsteps, no exceptions. Of all of us children, I was the only one to break that cardinal rule. The day I announced I would be working as a secretary for the police, Dad announced that I was no longer his daughter. He hadn't spoken to me since, and has forbidden Mom and all of my brothers and sisters from speaking to me either.

I had hoped that when I got my PI license and announced my engagement, things would improve. They hadn't. All of my letters returned unopened. None of my phone calls have ever been returned. The only family I've got is here with me in the hospital room, and right about now I sure could use some advice from Mom. As it stands now, they don't even know I'm about to be married because they wont take my calls. I would give anything—*anything*—for Dad to hug me, tell me he loves me, and walk me down the aisle. But it looks like they won't even *be* at the wedding.

None of that, however, could hold a candle to how I felt right about now. Seeing someone you loved helpless in the hospital had a way of making you feel weaker than a sick kitten. You couldn't do anything to make the situation any better, and you were utterly at the mercy of the doctors. Squeezing Chris' hand gently, I silently prayed for him.

"Detective Lorenzo is having a little chat with the officers watching Jessica and Chris' house," said Jeremy, "There's no excuse for *anyone* being able to break in under their noses and emptying out Chris' personal files."

"I've been wondering about that as well," said Jessica, "I don't feel safe in there right now."

"You're staying with us," said Shelly, "We've got a spare room. No, no arguments. The boys both adore you. And you better believe that Jeremy is having our home protected!"

"You can't do that indefinitely," protested Jessica, "You've both got your own lives!"

132

"We'd never forgive ourselves if anything happened to you," said Jeremy, "And that goes for you, too, Crystal."

"I'm a detective," I answered, "and I just hope the people responsible for all this *does* try to mess with me! I scored *very* well on the gun range! And the more I see Chris like this, the more I'm looking forward to meeting up with the morons doing all this!"

"What *I'm* looking forward to," said Jeremy, "Is having Chris wake up and sharing all this with him. He's got a way of making sense of things that leaves me scratching my head. I just wish he'd wake up."

Detective Maria Lorenzo's journal

The four officers stood at strict attention before me, hardly daring to breathe. There were two men and two women, all of whom had spectacular records. Until today. After leaving the hospital, I sped directly to where they were stationed; right across the street from Jessica and Chis' Victorian house. From there, I spent a full thirty minutes making them wish they had chosen another career to go into.

"There were four of you," I ranted, "*Four* of you! Two outside and two inside. You had security cameras covering every entrance. A *mouse* shouldn't have been able to sneak into that house, much less a bunch of thieves."

I glared at the officers, who were looking down at the floor miserably. They were blushing, as well they should. There was just plain no excuse for this blunder.

"You were assigned to protect people that are targets of the *mob*," I continued, "People who courageously choose to stay in their own homes to help the police smoke them out. Think about that. I know that some of them are seasoned detectives, but Jessica Peterson isn't. She's a civilian.

"Now then," I continued, "As bad as this blunder was, consider yourselves lucky. All the burglars did was steal some documents. If they had succeeded in murdering Mrs. Peterson right under your nose, then this conversation would be a whole lot worse."

One of the female officers stiffened. Her name tag read "Officer Rollins". She was having a lot of trouble listening to my tongue lashing, and she looked fit to bust.

"Yes, Officer Rollins," I said, "Do you have something to say?"

"Yes," she said, "You're acting as if you *know* that the thieves responsible were the Crimson

Dragons. How do you know that it wasn't just some run of the mill petty thief? It could have been some junkie looking for some quick cash to pay for his next fix."

I smiled and raised my eyebrows. Sometimes in my line of work, there is an officer that just plain asks for it and I was always glad to give it to him or her.

"Officer Rollins," I began, "Are you trying to tell me that you four experienced officers allowed some dope addict sneak past you *and* your high-tech security equipment and break into a house that you were *supposed* to be guarding?"

Officer Rollins blushed and shook her head.

"If you officers are staking out a house that you know is a target of the mob," I continued, "and you can't stop some spaced-out drug addict from breaking in, then you must not have been paying attention while you were in the police academy."

"I didn't mean--," began Rollins.

"Oh yes you did," I countered, "I've got a widow visiting her brother in the hospital; a detective who just personally saved me from an assassin's bullet. Besides wondering about her brother's recovery, she's also wondering why her police protection wasn't able to protect her!"

135

The more I ranted, the more red my face was becoming. *Easy, Lorenzo. You need to watch the blood pressure. All the blood pressure medicine in the world won't help if you don't bother to try controlling yourself.* I took a deep breath before I continued.

"Now then," I continued, "In light of your records, I'm going to give you a chance to redeem yourselves. We are going to march across the street and go over that house and yard with the finest of fine-toothed combs. And we are not leaving until we find whatever evidence our burglars left behind. We work together. No one goes off on his or her own. What one sees, everybody sees."

Officer Rollins shook her head. "I guess that means you totally don't trust us."

I smiled. "I trusted you when I assigned you to this detail. Work with me now to regain that trust."

My phone beeped. I flipped open the phone and saw a text message from the lab. I quickly opened the text.

"This microchip is pretty sophisticated," read the message, "We need more time to examine it to see what it was for."

I frowned and quickly texted a thank-you to the lab. Just what we needed: another mystery. If it *wasn't* for tracking purposes, what was it for? We desperately needed the records from Chris' operation. *Somebody* had put that microchip in, probably the doctor that operated on Chris, and at the service of Chase Anderson, AKA Moriarty. I knew it, but needed proof. An officer or detective can *know* someone's guilty, but has to have proof beyond a reasonable doubt to take to a jury.

"Let's go," I ordered.

The officers followed me as I led them across the street. Crime scene tape was already set up. Neighbors were looking at the tape curiously. As I reached the front door, my phone beeped again. This time the message was from Officer Trent. Trent and I had worked together several times before my promotion. We had fought gang wars together, and we had trusted each other with our lives more times than I could count.

"Thought you would like to know," read the text, "One of the prisoners you booked, a prostitute named Tina Stewart, was taken to *Christ's Church Hospital* suffering from withdraw. She was asking for you."

I swallowed. I had promised to look in on her while she was in jail and never had. I had let myself get busy getting those records for Chris and his team, all the while hoping that Chief Hendricks didn't catch me. Visiting Tina had fallen between the cracks. *"Maria Lorenzo,"* I thought, *"you're no better than the officers you just chewed out."*

"Thanks," I texted back, "Let her know that I will be visiting her this evening."

Hopefully, this would be a promise I could keep.

Crystal Parker's Journal [kept on her tablet]

Chris was still out cold when the others had to leave. Shelly had to pick up Tim from school and help Jessica get some of her things to her and Jeremy's house. Jeremy had to continue with the investigation.

Me, I was torn about what to do. A part of me wanted to help Jeremy, and a part of me wanted to stay with Chris. Jeremy made the decision for me by telling me to stay with Chris. He promised to keep me in the loop every step of the way.

I sat in a chair beside Chris, holding his hand. I couldn't help but think about that had happened since I woke up this morning. It wasn't enough that my fiancé had nearly been killed. But now I find out that his brother was systematically wiping out all traces of Chris' existence! What was the *point* of it?

"Sherlock," I whispered to him, "It's Crystal. I'm here for you, darling. I love you."

His breathing remained labored. I don't know whether he heard me or not, but a lot of doctors believed that people *could* hear other people talking even when in a deep sleep or coma. I didn't know whether it was true or not, but it sure couldn't hurt.

"Sherlock," I whispered, "I need you to wake up, darling. I want to hold you and kiss you and tell you how much you mean to me! I want to tell you that, after Christ, you're the best thing that ever happened to me. You're going to be such a wonderful husband, darling, because you're such a wonderful man!"

Chris continued to breathe hard.

"Please, honey," I continued, "I need you. We *all* need you! We think Moriarty—or Chase, or whoever you want to call him--is behind the Stalker murders. There's a lot of other things he's doing, too. We were right. There's a lot of things he's trying to pull before he leaves the country. We're trying, but we need you—Sherlock Holmes—to put it all together. He's covering his tracks well and we can't do it without you."

"Can I have those kisses you promised first?"

I looked up and saw Chris' eyes were opened and he was smiling down at me. I threw my arms around his neck and kissed him. His lips were warm and wonderful. Several kisses later, I pulled from him and looked at him sternly.

"The next time you need a break," I said, "Just let us know you need a day off. Don't scare me like that again!"

"I'll try," he whispered, "Water."

I poured some water from the picture into a cup and held it to his lips. He took several swallows greedily.

"What *happened* out there?" I asked Chris, "Detective Lorenzo told us about your meeting with Chase and about you shoving her out of the way of a bullet. What told you there was a sniper?"

"I would be very slow of wit indeed if I saw the glint of the sun reflecting off metal and failed to recognize a sniper's rifle," said Chris, "I'm just glad Detective Lorenzo is all right. What about Detective Chandler? He was out there, too."

"He's fine," I said, "Everybody's been so worried, I need to let them know you're awake. Then I have so much to tell *you*."

Chris swallowed and took my hand in his.

"Sweetheart," he said, "Before you do, I have something to tell you."

I looked at him. "What is it, darling?"

"Crystal, my love," he whispered, "I...I...need to tell you..."

My watch beeped. I mentally cursed as I saw an incoming call. I saw it was Jeremy and hit the phone Ap on the watch.

"Watson," I said, "Great news. Sherlock's awake."

"Great," said Jeremy, "I've been talking to Dr. Price."

"How is he doing?" asked Chris.

"Not too good," said Jeremy, "he's still being held without bail. But he told me some more things about his research into the original Ripper killings. We need to see if it matches our Stalker."

"Go ahead," said Chris.

"The victims of the original Ripper were dead *before* their throats were cut and before they were mutilated," continued Jeremy, "First, they were incapacitated by being fed poisoned grapes, which acted as a sedative. Then they were strangled to death. Then their throats were cut and they were mutilated."

I whistled. "It sounds like overkill to me. We'll need to see if this matches the ME's report on the Stalker's victims."

Chris' eyebrows narrowed. "Lorenzo and Chandler gave me flash drives with police reports and the ME's reports on the Stalker's victims. They should be in my coat pocket."

"Did you catch that?" I asked.

"Yeah," said Jeremy.

"Sherlock and I need to talk," I said quickly, "Why don't you touch base with Detective Lorenzo on those *other matters*, Watson?"

"Gotcha," said Jeremy.

I silently thanked God that Jeremy caught on that I didn't want him to mention about the microchip and the theft of Chris' personal documents. I had no idea how we were going to explain that, and desperately wanted time to think. One aspect of this entire situation that was a bear to get around was Chris' delusions.

He had absolutely no idea that Chase was his brother or that Jessica was his sister. He thought those documents in that battered file box were accounts of his unpublished cases. Every doctor that Jessica and I had talked to had stressed the importance of allowing Chris to recover in his own time.

Forcing him to face facts he wasn't prepared to deal with might only serve to drive him even further over the edge. If he tried to deal with it all at once, he would have to face the notion that he had spent the last six years in the grips of insanity, that a brother he didn't remember having—and who was supposed to be dead--was actually alive and was the criminal mastermind he had been chasing for years; that the woman he thought was his landlady was actually a sister he didn't know he had; and that he had lost a wife and child that he didn't even remember. I could see how having to deal with all that at once could unhinge someone permanently.

But there was one huge question that was staring me in the face. What if Chase was about to back Chris into a corner where he was forced to deal with issues he wasn't prepared to deal with? Was that it? Would his final revenge be to drive Chris so far over the cliff of madness that there could never be any hope of recovery?

My *Compu-Watch* beeped, signaling the end of the call. I glanced over at Chris, who was staring at me. His expression was a mixture of love and sadness. Something besides the obvious horrors of this case was bugging him, and I had no idea what.

"Now then," I said, "You wanted to talk, Sherlock?"

He took my hand in his again, and looked at me in all seriousness.

"Sweetheart," he said, "You know I love you with all my heart."

"You better," I smiled, "After all, we're getting married soon."

"I know," he said, "And I need to be totally honest with you."

Chris sighed and closed his eyes. For several seconds, he said nothing.

"If this is too much for you," I said quickly, "This can wait. You may need to rest."

"No," said Chris, "This is just hard, that's all. I *need* to get this off my chest."

I squeezed his hand affectionately. For several seconds, we just sat there in silence holding hands. Under other circumstances, it would have been romantic. Right now, however, my man needed my support and I wanted him to know he had it.

"For some time," Chris said softly, "I've been aware that there were some...gaps in my memory. There were things I couldn't remember. I gradually came to realize that I could remember nothing earlier than six years ago. I could

144

remember my name and certain details of some of my cases, but much of my earlier life was a solid blank.

I blinked several times. A few months back, it seemed like he was on the verge of remembering a few details from his past, but it all came to nothing. If he was starting to realize that he *has* a huge gap in his memory, that would be an *incredible* first step to recovery!

"How long have you known this?" I asked.

"For the past few weeks," said Chris, "I told myself it didn't matter, and busied myself in my cases, especially in the pursuit of Moriarty."

"Darling, why didn't you tell me?" I asked.

Chris shrugged. "I didn't want you to worry about me."

"Honey," I said sternly, "We put our lives on the line for a living! We go into gun battles and face gangsters on a daily basis! How can you even *talk* about not wanting to worry me?"

Looking up at the ceiling, Chris said, "I didn't want you to think there was something *wrong* with me. Mentally, I mean. I was afraid that you would think that I was losing it. No woman wants to be married to a madman."

I stared at him, thinking about the irony of what he had just said. He was delusional and didn't even realize it. Yet he was afraid of me *thinking* he had mental problems. *My poor Chris! If you only knew...*

Then the full meaning of what he was saying hit me with the force of a sledgehammer. *No woman wants to be married to a madman...*could he be saying what I *thought* he was saying?

"Sherlock," I said, "were you afraid that if I thought you had mental problems, you would *lose* me? Were you afraid it would drive me away?"

Chris blushed and nodded. "You're the girl of my dreams, Crystal. It would *kill* me to lose you. I could bear almost anything, but I couldn't survive losing you."

My jaw dropped. For years I had been afraid that no man would ever be able to love me because I didn't have a cheerleader's body, and here Chris was saying that it would *kill* him to lose me! Tears flowed down my face and I threw my arms around him. I practically smothered him in hugs and kisses. When I finally pulled away from him, I looked at him with all the love in my heart that I felt for him. I wiped my tears with a tissue as I stared at the man I love.

"You listen to me, Sherlock Holmes," I said, my voice choked with emotion, "There is *nothing* you can tell me that would drive me away! I love you with all my heart and I will be the proudest woman in the world when I can say that I'm your wife!"

Chris visibly relaxed. He pulled me close and held me tightly against his chest. I was afraid of hurting him, but he didn't seem to care.

"Thank you," he whispered, "That means a lot. You see, Crystal, there's more I need to tell you."

CHAPTER EIGHT

Jeremy Winslow's journal [kept on flash drive]
After talking to Crystal, I called Shelly. She and Jessica were greatly relieved to hear that Chris was awake. She told me that Jessica was *very* reluctantly settling into our guest room. Jessica still thought she would be a bother, but we were adamant. Until we knew that the danger was over, Jessica was not going to be out of our sights. I tried reaching Chandler, but my call went straight to voicemail. I left a message, urging him to call me back.

I found Detective Lorenzo still leading an investigation at Jessica and Chris' house. She and the officers on duty were studying the front yard thoroughly. The officers on the scene were examining the scene as if their lives depended on it. As angry as Lorenzo was when she stormed out of the hospital, the officers' lives probably *did* depend on their investigation! Lorenzo was *most* displeased to hear that a break-in happened right under those officers' noses!

"Hey, detective," I said, greeting her, "Can you use a spare hand?"

"Sure," she sighed, "And a spare *head*. Whoever broke into Jessica and Chris' house knew

148

what he was doing. We've examined the inside of the house, and came up with a big fat zero. He somehow approached the house without any of my officers being aware of it, and then got in and out without leaving so much as a shoe print behind. I'm close to checking for tunnels under the city, Watson...I mean, Winslow. Sorry."

I chuckled. "Don't worry. I'm close to believing that my legal name really *is* Watson. By the way, Chris is awake. He and Crystal are talking."

"And probably kissing, too," smiled Lorenzo, "Detective Anderson sure is more romantic than the Sherlock Holmes in the stories."

I nodded. "His personality seems to be a combination of his own and that of Sherlock Holmes. The way I understand it, when his breakdown happened, he began thinking of himself as Holmes simply because Chase was using the name Moriarty for a code name. Because Chris was already a brilliant detective, the Sherlock Holmes personality fit him nicely."

"Well, we could sure use Sherlock Holmes on this one," mused Lorenzo, "I'm not exactly an idiot, but this is about to be beyond me."

"Have you examined the security camera footage?" I asked.

"Not yet," confessed Lorenzo, "I wanted to secure the crime scene first. But that was going to be my next item of business."

Lorenzo motioned for one of the female officers, an officer Rollins, and she led us across the street to the empty house that the officers had used for a base. There were several desktop computers set up on the dining room table. Each computer monitor showed a different angle to the house.

"Officer Rollins," said Lorenzo, "We need to start going through the camera footage; all of it."

Officer Rollins swallowed. Then the color drained out of her face. I could see from her eyes that she was trying to think of a response.

"Uh, detective," said Rollins, "are you sure? There's still a lot of ground left to cover outside."

Lorenzo blinked. "You've been given a direct order, officer. I'm only going to say it once more. We need to see that camera footage."

Rollins looked down at the floor. She had the look of a person that had just been backed into a corner and knew that there was no way out. She whispered something that we couldn't hear.

"What was that, officer?" demanded Lorenzo.

"There *is* no security camera footage," confessed Rollins.

"WHAT?!" demanded Lorenzo.

"We had orders from above," said Rollins, "we were ordered not to record anything."

Crystal Parker's journal [kept on her tablet]

Chris sat up in bed. I cautioned him against moving too quickly, but he brushed aside my concerns. He blinked several times and then took a deep breath.

"Honey," I said quickly, "Are you sure you need to…"

"I've got to get my strength back," said Chris, "I have a feeling I'm going to need all the strength I can get to bring this case to a close. Right now, I just have to be a little cautious, that's all."

"Is there anything I can do to help?"

"Just hear me out," said Chris, "because I have the sickening feeling that whatever part of my life I can't remember from my past has a direct bearing on the case we're investigating now."

My poor darling, I thought, *If you only knew!* I patted him on the shoulder affectionately.

"Since I've woke up," continued Chris, "I've been seeing….flashes in my mind."

I swallowed. "What kinds of flashes?"

151

Closing his eyes, Chris said, "Faces…there's some people's faces. There's a woman, a little girl, and then a man. I see them just for a few seconds, and then they're gone."

I nodded. A woman, young girl, and a guy. That could only be Tabitha, Grace, and Jessica's late husband Jack. Chris had had a few slips of the tongue before, moments when it seemed like he had been on the verge of remembering. There had been a time when he thought my late boss Ronald Summers was the fictional Inspector Lestrade. Yet on one occasion he came frustratingly close to calling him by his real name.

Why was he starting to remember now? Could his head injury be causing a few memories to return? If so, how *much* of his memory would he regain?

"I feel," continued Chris, "Like I should *know* these people. Yet, when I try to remember, the faces go away."

"It's all right, darling," I whispered, "You'll remember when it's time."

"That's just it," said Chris, "Whoever these people are, I have the feeling that Moriarty has something to do with them. And if so, it could be the key to tracking him down and putting a stop to the Stalker killings. Remembering my past *could* be the key to preventing any further murders."

My mind was reeling. Everything the doctors had told Jessica came crashing through my consciousness, especially an incident that happened shortly after Chris' breakdown.

After Chris and I had gotten engaged, Jessica told me of a horrifying incident that happened the day after Tabitha, Grace, and Jack were murdered. I had been pressuring Jessica to allow me to tell Chris the truth, to stop waiting for Moriarty to be captured before leading Chris back to sanity. One day, Jessica came over to my apartment and we sat down to discuss it over coffee.

"Believe me, Crystal," said Jessica, "I would love nothing better than to just tell Chris the truth. But, you see, I've already tried that once."

My eyes grew larger when she told me that. "*What*? What happened?"

"It was the day after the murders," said Jessica, "Chris had been sedated and rushed to the hospital after he saw the bodies. When he woke up, he introduced himself there in the hospital room as Sherlock Holmes."

"That had to be *so* incredibly hard," I breathed.

"You can't imagine," said Jessica, "And you better believe that my first instinct was to gently tell him the truth about himself and his family!"

"How did he take it?" I asked.

Jessica stared down into her coffee cup. "Worse than you can possibly believe. The moment I told him the truth, he passed out. He became catatonic for nearly two weeks."

My jaw dropped. "You're *kidding!*"

Jessica shook her head. "No. For two weeks, he stared straight ahead in a trance without knowing anything. I was buying the house I live in now, and brought Chris home to care for him. After a couple of weeks he came out of it.

"But the doctors warned me that under no circumstances could we try to force him to remember his past; he could possibly go back into a catatonic trance that he wouldn't come out of. By that time, I got him his Sherlock Holmes outfit and I've gone along with his delusions ever since. Every step of the way, I've prayed that something would bring him back to reality *safely.*"

I couldn't blame her. Listening to Chris now, I was terrified that he would try to force himself to remember things he wasn't near ready for. But, yet what if he was right? What if his past *was* the key to stopping Moriarty now?

"Now," muttered Chris, "There's one thing I'd love to know right off the bat."

"What's that, darling?"

"What could possibly have happened that *caused* me to have such a big gap in my memory?"

Jeremy Winslow's journal [kept on flash drive]
Detective Maria Lorenzo stared speechless at Officer Rollins for several seconds. She had been furious before, but she was several degrees *beyond* outraged now. Her face had turned several shades of purple, and it was a full minute before she trusted herself to speak.

"Let me get this straight," said Lorenzo was a forced calm, "You all were *ordered from above to do sloppy police work?!*

Sheepishly, Rollins nodded.

"Who ordered this?" demanded Lorenzo.

"I can't say," mumbled Rollins.

Lorenzo gaped at Rollins, not believing what she was hearing. I was starting to sense the fine hand of Chase Anderson behind this, but I said nothing. This was Lorenzo's call and she needed to hear what Rollins had to say before I said a word.

"What do you mean you can't say who initiated the order?" demanded Lorenzo, "Nobody

155

orders an officer to foul up an investigation or a stakeout, *especially* where lives may be at stake, without answering for it. I am asking you one last time, Rollins. You will tell me who initiated that order, and the full extent of those orders, or you will surrender your shield and gun pending a full investigation!"

Rollins took a deep breath and looked from Lorenzo to me, and then back to Lorenzo again. She was backed into a corner with no way out and she knew it. It suddenly occurred to me that this would be a good conversation to record. I turned my back on Lorenzo and Rollins, and tapped the "Audio Record" Ap on my watch. Turning back towards them, I saw that Rollins was sitting in a chair, looking very exhausted.

"Right after we got assigned to this detail," said Rollins, "Each of us got a text message telling us not to record anything on the security cameras. We were to ignore anything that happened on our watch."

"And who, pray tell, gave you such an order?" demanded Lorenzo, "And why on earth would you obey it?"

"I can't tell you *who*," said Rollins, "But I can tell you *why* we obeyed it. In addition to the orders, each of our text messages came with a photograph. We all got pictures of our loved ones. Smith got a picture of his wife and daughter. Cooper got a picture of his girlfriend. Linda Maloy got a picture of her sister. And I got a picture of my husband and the twins."

"So whoever sent those texts threatened your families," finished Lorenzo.

"They knew where we lived!" cried Rollins, "Those texts promised our families would die nasty deaths if we didn't do as we were told."

"I see," said Lorenzo, in a tone of voice that told she really didn't.

"We had no choice," insisted Rollins, "You have to understand."

Lorenzo stood over Rollins, eyes glaring. Rollins seemed to shrink under the detective's gaze.

"You had clear evidence that somebody in the department, who knew your assignment, was working for the mob," said Lorenzo, "You could have gone to someone higher up the chain of command. You could have asked for *help*."

"We didn't know who to trust! We couldn't risk it," protested Rollins.

"Excuse me," I said, "Forgive me, Detective, but I just have to respond to this one. The very first time that I got involved in a case involving the Crimson Dragons, I got the same kind of text messages as these officers did. They had kidnapped my wife and first born son. *And* my wife was pregnant with our second child. They demanded that me and Detective Anderson drop our investigation in exchange for my family's safe return."

Lorenzo nodded. "I remember hearing about that. And would you please enlighten Officer Rollins on how you handled that situation?"

"I'll be glad to," I said, "Detective Anderson and I used every resource at our disposal to track down my family, rescue them, and set up a sting operation. We tricked the culprits into believing that my family were still being held hostage when they were actually at a safe house. From there, we were able to track down the culprits and arrest them, freeing several other kidnap victims at the same time."

"Well, not all of us are that brilliant," snapped Rollins.

"You should have been smart enough to seek out some help!" snapped Lorenzo, "Maybe you didn't know who to trust on the force, but it's common knowledge at police headquarters that Detective Anderson has done more to bring this mob down than anyone else you can think of."

"Detective Anderson is a *nut,*" snapped Rollins, "He thinks he's a fictional character!"

"He's also a very, *very* brilliant detective," said Lorenzo, "And he would gladly have helped you. Even now he's solving cases that leave other detectives baffled."

I sighed. "Were there any other orders that they gave you?"

"We can answer that," said a voice from behind us.

Lorenzo and I turned around. Officers Smith, Cooper, and Maloy stood in the doorway. Their guns were drawn, and they were aimed right at us. Rollins quickly stood and drew her own firearm. Reluctantly, we raised our hands.

"I was wondering how long it would be before you guys showed up," said Rollins, "You guys are slower than Christmas."

"Was any of what you just told us for real?" asked Lorenzo.

"Oh, yes," said Rollins, "But there's one thing I left out. We also got orders on how to handle anyone that asked too many questions."

Before we knew what was happening, we were relieved of our weapons. Our pockets were emptied. Maria's purse was emptied out onto the floor.

"Where is it?" demanded Rollins.

"Where is *what*?" asked Lorenzo.

"The boss' merchandise," demanded Cooper, "We know you've got it, Lorenzo. Where is it?"

Lorenzo and I glanced at each other. She looked as puzzled as I was and was trying to think of how to handle the situation.

"If you'll just tell me what it is I'm supposed to have..."

"Don't mess with us, Lorenzo," said Cooper, "The boss is already in a foul mood."

"I guess having your picture all over the television will do that to a person," I said.

Cooper suddenly introduced his fist to my stomach. The wind went out of me, and I fell to the floor. But I didn't stay down. I came up swinging, giving Cooper's mouth a close encounter with my right hook. I felt two of his teeth loosen. Good. Cooper wrapped his arms around my waist and shoved me backwards against the wall. Hot pain shot through my back as I hit the wall.

I responded by pushing forward with all my might. Cooper fell backwards, taking me with him. He hit the floor, and before he could move, I punched him square in the nose. He bellowed in pain, and I followed up my punch with a second one.

While I was giving Cooper a face full of fist, Lorenzo decided to get in a few hits of her own. While the other officers were watching me and Cooper fight, Lorenzo whirled around and punched Rollins in the jaw. Rollins flew backwards, stunned at the suddenness of her attack. She hit the wall, and rushed forwards at Lorenzo. Lorenzo, however, greeted Rollins with a sudden kick to the stomach.

Lorenzo and I both were giving our opponents a battle while their partners watched. Their guns were drawn and were looking for an opening. Smith and Maloy looked on, watching. Then, Smith raised his weapon and fired once at the ceiling.

The blast from the gun sounded like a canon. And, just like that, the battle was over. Cooper gave me one final punch to the jaw. Then my hands were cuffed behind my back. Rollins, likewise, took delight in handcuffing Lorenzo.

"Looks like they're going to need some persuasion to loosen their tongues," snarled Cooper.

Rollins nodded. "Let's go."

CHAPTER NINE

Crystal Parker's journal [kept on her tablet]
Chris closed his eyes and sighed. His confession of having such a huge memory loss had taken a lot out of him. My heart broke for him. He was trying to deal with knowing there was a lot in his life that he couldn't remember *plus* trying to track down notorious killers at the same time.

Mentally, I tried to figure out what to do. Chase was his *brother;* it was possible that something from their past could give us a clue on how to track him and the Stalker down. That would allow us to not only *solve* a string of crimes, but it would help us *prevent* a murder. It would also help us clear our client of a murder charge.

I gently ran my fingers through his hair as he lay there resting. I had come *so* close to losing Chris! My blood ran cold as I thought about it. If that bullet had been just another inch lower...

But God had been merciful, and I silently praised Him. I also silently prayed that He would give me the answer of how to handle this situation. I needed a plan before I was backed into a corner of being *forced* to tell Chris everything at once. He had already shown that he couldn't take the whole story at once. If I was forced to go that route, I could end up helping to bring Chase to justice, but losing Chris forever to a worse insanity than he was already in.

"*Lord*," I silently prayed, "*help me through this. Show me what to do.*"

"Sweetheart," said Chris softly, "Let's review what we've got."

"Darling," I said sternly, "You need to rest."

"We've got an innocent client rotting in jail," countered Chris, "We've got a murder to prevent, and I have good reason to believe that Moriarty has sent a sniper after us. I don't have time to rest."

Chris sat up quickly, and instantly regretted it. The color drained from his face and he closed his eyes tightly.

"Are you all right?" I asked anxiously.

"I will be when the room stops spinning," said Chris, "Anyway, have you gotten any closer to discovering what the link is between the Stalker and Moriarty, or how the Stalker chooses his victims?"

"At the moment," I said, "this detective is clueless. I know that the records of all of the Stalker's victims have either been sealed tighter than a drum or they've been totally erased. The law doesn't go to that kind of trouble for a few prostitutes, so I believe that the order came from Moriarty for some reason."

"Sound reasoning, Crystal. Go on."

"I don't have enough evidence to show whether Moriarty himself is the Stalker, or one of his underlings," I continued, "I also don't have proof of the motive. Maybe the prostitutes crossed him somehow, or they learned something that they shouldn't have. But as for *how* he's choosing what prostitutes to kill, I'm still out at sea. There are literally *thousands* of prostitutes advertising themselves on that *Cyber-Ads* websites. I've yet to find out what links these particular women besides their job and that website."

Chris sighed. "Maybe when we go through the evidence I was given we'll find something."

"Maybe."

Chris looked at me. "I've been meaning to tell you and Watson about a lot of research I've been doing into the background of Chase Anderson."

I blinked. "Really? What have you discovered?"

"Even before he faked his death," said Chris, "He had an arrest record as long as your arm, especially in regard to dealing drugs. It's believed he killed a former cell mate, Hugh West."

164

"I see," I commented cautiously, "Is there anything else?"

Chris nodded. "It's also believed that he killed his parents and torched their house. The thing was, Chase has a sister named Jessica and a brother named Chris. Chris and Jessica barely got out before the house imploded in flames."

I swallowed, fighting back tears. He was describing his own family and didn't even know it! I had long known that the guilt he felt at being unable to save his parents from the fire and—he thought—being unable to save Chase from the fire had *started* Chris' mental problems.

Survivor's guilt—the guilt people feel at surviving some horrible experience that leaves loved ones dead—can take a hard toll on people. That guilt had only intensified when Chris' family was murdered. Knowing that the murders had been retaliation for Chris' undercover investigation had driven him so far over the edge that he was reading his own background and didn't even know it!

"Maybe you better rest," I begged him, my lip trembling.

"I can't," insisted Chris, "Moriarty—or Chase, if you prefer—is sending hit men after everyone investigating him. It's going to take *everybody* working together to bring him to justice."

165

"But—"

"There's more," continued Chris, "After Chase firmly established the Crimson Dragons under the guise of Hugh West, his brother Chris became part of an organized crime task force set up to bring down Chase's mob."

"Oh, no. Don't go there. Please!" I silently begged.

"Chris Anderson had no idea that he was investigating his own brother," Chris went on, "but somehow Chase found out about his involvement. He retaliated by having Chris' family and Jessica's husband murdered. Poor Chris suffered a nervous breakdown from which he still hasn't recovered, and—"

I couldn't take anymore. I let go of Chris' hand and rushed out of the room. I barely made it out the door before the flood gates opened. I sank to the floor and buried my face in my hands, sobbing.

Jeremy Winslow's journal [kept on flash drive]

Within five minutes, Lorenzo and I were relieved of our weapons. That included our weapons that we had strapped to our ankles under our pants legs. We were handcuffed and led to the basement

166

of the house. The basement was cluttered with a workbench, power tools, and gardening tools. We were shoved into a couple of folding chairs while our captors calmly looked for something to force us to talk.

"Unlike other prisoners," said Rollins, "You *don't* have the right to remain silent. Anything you say *can* and *will* mean the difference between death and survival."

"Cut the comedy," snapped Lorenzo, "We all know that you guys don't intend to let us walk away alive. You intend to kill us no matter what."

"True," agreed Cooper, "You really *should* use what time you've got saying whatever prayers you know. But, if you cooperate, you'll get a quick death. Maybe you'll get a simple overdose of sleeping pills or a quick bullet. But, if you disappoint the boss, you'll suffer an *incredibly* slow and miserable death. He's been known to drag an execution out for *days*."

Lorenzo and I looked at each other. The other officers returned to the crime scene, leaving Rollins and Cooper to get the information Chase wanted. The problem was that neither of us knew what in the world Chase was after. It could be blackmail information on some wealthy citizens. It

167

could be a biological weapon. It could be forged documents...it could be anything. And we were clueless. Clueless and handcuffed; what a combination.

A few months back, Chris had been a prisoner in the back of a van with his hands handcuffed behind his back. He had managed to pick the locks without his captors figuring out what he was doing and had somehow managed to turn the tables on his kidnappers.

I must have been absent on the day the police academy had taught the finer techniques of picking the locks on police handcuffs. I didn't have the foggiest idea of how to do it. And even if I *did* know how to do it, these "police officers" had taken everything I could have used to pick the locks. They hadn't left me so much as a ball point pen.

But they *had* left me my watch. And my watch had all kinds of security devices on it. My hands were behind my back, making this a true challenge, but maybe that was for the best. Neither Rollins nor Cooper would be able to see what I was doing.

Cautiously, my fingers felt around for the buttons on my watch. This was harder than it sounds. I had to move without looking like I was moving. Plus, I had only gotten the watch this

168

morning and had to remember which button was the one I was looking for.

There were four buttons besides the various Aps that were on the watch. There was no way I would be able to find any particular Ap by feeling around behind my back. But that was Ok. Of the four buttons, one activated the camera in the watch. One button was for audio record. One button sent information from the watch's word processor to a printer. Then there was the button I needed: it sent out an electronic SOS to my partners' watches.

If I remembered right, it was the third button from the top. The thing was, I knew that I wouldn't be able to know if I had pressed the right one. If it worked the way Chris had said, it wouldn't make a sound on my watch. I pressed the third button and prayed.

I prayed I had pressed the right button. Otherwise, we were dead.

Crystal Parker's journal [kept on her tablet]

I'll never know how long I was out in the hall crying. It could have been five minutes; it could have been an hour. But eventually I wiped my eyes and went back into Chris' room. He stared at me, his face clouded with worry.

"Are you all right, honey?" he asked anxiously.

Wouldn't you know it? *He* was worried about *me*! I took his hand in my and gently caressed it.

"I'm just worried about you," I answered, "I just came close to losing you and it scared me."

Well, it wasn't *exactly* a lie. I had been several steps *beyond* terrified when I heard about how close he had come to dying. But I still felt guilty about keeping this kind of a secret from the man I love. And judging from the look on his face, he wasn't exactly buying what I was saying. Yet, he drew me close and kissed me gently.

"Are you *sure* you're not scared at the thought of marrying a guy who can't remember beyond a few years ago?" He wondered.

My jaw dropped in astonishment. Then I threw my arms around him and held him close. After smothering him with kisses, I looked at him.

"The only things that scares me," I whispered, "Is the thought of losing you."

My watch beeped. Glancing down at my watch, I noticed a red blip showing underneath the time. My heart leaped to my throat. It was an emergency SOS!

"Sherlock," I said, "It's an emergency signal from Watson!"

Instantly, Chris was alert.

"There's an Ap to pull up a map of the city," he said, "It'll show where he's at."

I hit the Ap with the map of the world on it. Instantly, a detailed map of Oklahoma City appeared. A small red dot appeared on the map, blinking rapidly.

"He's still at the house next to Mrs. Hudson's," I said.

"Throw me my clothes and wait for me outside," ordered Chris.

I nodded and found his clothes in the closet while he stood up. I had brought him a fresh suit, coat, and deerstalker to replace the ones that had been torn and bloodied in the attack. Chris was moving slowly, but with great determination. Setting his clothes on the bed, I retreated outside the door. For five long minutes, I waited. What in the world could have happened to him? He had simply gone to touch base with Detective Lorenzo at Jessica and Chris' house. What kind of trouble could he have gotten into there?

Lord, please let Jeremy be all right!

Chris emerged from the hospital room, looking pale but determined. We had brought him a fresh suit and spare deerstalker cap to replace what had been ruined at the restaurant. He dismissed the guards and allowed me to lead him to the elevator.

"Sherlock, I…"

"Go get the car," ordered Chris, "I'm springing myself from this place.

I nodded. I hurried for the exit and was back with the car within five minutes. Chris didn't waste any time in checking himself out. Oh, the receptionist was furious! Chris ignored her and we were on our way. I led him to my car and offered to help him in, but he brushed my hand away as he climbed into the passenger seat.

"If I can't climb into a car," he said, "I'm worse than useless to Watson."

I nodded and climbed into the driver's seat. Then I gunned the engine and pulled out onto the highway. Chris studied his own *Compu-Watch* as I drove.

"He's still at the house," said Chris, "Whatever's going on, he hasn't moved."

"Good," I said, "Hang on, Watson, we're coming to get you!"

"And probably Detective Lorenzo, too," added Chris, "He was on his way to see her. Whatever happened probably involves the both of them."

"We've been toying with the possibility that the sniper at the restaurant was after *her* rather than you," I said.

"Good, Crystal! That's an astute observation," said Chris, "There were several feet between the two of us when the sniper fired that shot. Any assassin worth his salt would *not* make that kind of mistake."

"That's what I thought," I said, pleased at his compliment.

"We'll play it cool when we get there," said Chris, "Don't assume anything until we know what we're getting into."

I nodded. The light was just turning red when we approached it. I groaned. This was a time when seconds counted. The amount of time we spent at the traffic light could mean the difference between life and death.

"Easy," said Chris, patting my leg, "He's not going anywhere. He's still at the house if that's any consolation."

"Right now," I said, "The only thing that would make me feel better is having the car that Batman drove in the *Dark Knight* movies. That bad boy was a jet propelled tank that could go *up* and *over* other cars."

"I know what you mean," said Chris grimly.

"We have no idea what we're getting into," I muttered, "We need some backup."

"That's why I'm calling Chief Hendricks," said Chris, pressing buttons on his watch.

"*Hendricks*?!" I replied, "I thought you were going to call for *help*!"

"Chief Hendricks is stubborn, egotistical, and foolish," said Chris, "But, judging from the background check I did on him, he *is* honest and cares for his personnel. He *has* to be informed about what's going on."

"When did you do a background check on him?"

"The moment he was promoted to chief of detectives," said Chris, "Come *on*! Pick up."

The light turned green. Traffic started moving, but with painful slowness. We were moving, but an inch at a time. *Good grief,* I thought. Here we were only a few miles from where we needed to go, and we were stuck in gridlock traffic! We'd *never* get through at this rate!

"He's picking up," said Chris, putting the phone on speaker. "Hello, chief."

"Who is this?" demanded Hendricks.

"It's Sherlock Holmes," said Chris, "And we need to tell—"

"I don't have time to mess with *amateurs*," snarled Hendricks, "I've got a police department to run."

"Look," said Chris, "I just got an urgent call for help from Watson. I have reason to believe that he and Detective Lorenzo are in deadly danger. You need to…"

"I need to put *you* behind *bars* for interfering in police investigations," snapped Hendricks.

"Chief," said Chris with a forced calm, "No matter what you think of me personally, I got a *call for help!* They're at…"

"I'm *not* getting involved in one of your wild goose chases!" yelled Hendricks.

"Chief," said Chris, "We're stuck in traffic. We can't get there in time. We need squad cars to go to 704 Martin Luther King Blvd. and…"

"Nothing doing."

"If I'm *wrong*," said Chris, "You can blast my name in every newspaper in the country! But if I'm *right* and you do nothing, you'll have the deaths of two detectives on your conscience. What you need is…"

There was a loud click as Hendricks slammed the phone down. Chris and I looked at each other in disbelief. The traffic was practically at a standstill. For several seconds, we were both silent. The only sound we could hear was the blare of angry motorists honking their horns, accomplishing nothing but honking their horns.

"I never would have believed it," growled Chris, "I knew Hendricks was stubborn beyond belief and that he's the politician's politician, but I never would have thought he'd ignore a call for help!"

"Try Detective Chandler," I suggested.

"Good idea," said Chris.

He brought up the touch screen on his watch and punched Chandler's phone number. Seconds later he groaned in frustration.

"It went straight to voicemail," said Chris.

The blaring of the horns grew louder. In five minutes, we hadn't moved an inch. Jeremy and Lorenzo desperately needed our help, but we couldn't get to them. They were totally on their own.

CHAPTER TEN

Jeremy Winslow's journal [kept on flash drive]

Rollins looked on calmly while Cooper threw tools left and right from the workbench. Cooper was clearly enjoying what he was doing; he whistled merrily while looking for something to torture us with. Finally he stood up and faced us, grinning wickedly.

He was holding a butane torch. Cooper fished a lighter out of his pocket, turned on the gas jet on the torch and watched as the flame ignited. Instantly, he adjusted the flame. The torch let out an angry hiss and the torch burned.

"Your choice," said Cooper, "talk and save yourselves some pain, or I see how loud you can scream."

"He means it," said Rollins, "Believe me, he has a thing for hurting people."

Lorenzo snorted. "Tell me how I can tell you what you want to know if I'm too busy screaming?"

Lorenzo tried to sound brave. But, believe me, she was as pale as I felt. Mentally, I was begging God to let my partners get that SOS that I had sent and to come find us. They could feel free to bring an army of SWAT officers with them. I wouldn't mind a bit.

"She's right, Cooper," said Rollins, "We *do* need her to talk."

If anything, Cooper's smile got wider. His eyes had a crazy look to them. He was the kind of guy that enjoyed inflicting pain on others for any and all reasons. He held up the torch in front of him, making sure we could see it. If it was the last thing I did in this life—and it very well could be—I wanted the chance to wipe that smile off his face.

"She doesn't get it," said Cooper, his voice giggling with joy, "It won't be *her* that I burn. Either she talks or I start burning her partner's face off right now."

Lorenzo looked at me helplessly. She hadn't a clue as to what these jokers wanted and didn't know how on earth to respond. How could you run a bluff if you didn't know what your enemy wanted?

Cooper advanced towards me. The torch was held directly in front of him. He brought it down until it was inches from my face. He turned the gas jet up full blast, making the flame larger. I was getting a good, close-up view of the flame. The heat from the torch was horrible.

"*All right*," said Lorenzo, "I'll tell you what you want to know."

Tina Stewart's Journal [kept on Steno pad]

If there was one thing I could say about going through withdraw in a hospital, it was that it beat going through withdraw in jail. Yes, the pain was still agonizing—first I was afraid I would die and then I was afraid that I *wouldn't*—but at least I had a bed and nurses.

I lay curled up in a fetal position in the bed. My hands still clutched the battered New Testament that I had found in the cell. Occasionally I had doctors and nurses looking in on me, checking my IV and my charts. They asked questions I couldn't understand—I was in too much pain to truly comprehend what they were saying—and I couldn't remember what I said to them if my life depended on it.

After an eternity, the pain started subsiding. I knew better than to relax. The agony could come back at any moment with a vengeance. However, I appreciated any relief that I could get.

My lunch was some red Jell-O. Hurray. If there was one thing I could count on with withdraw, it was that I would have absolutely zero appetite. I mean, withdraw is *intense.* That's why drugs are such a hard thing to get off of. The body absolutely craves the poison that is killing you, and makes you hunger for your next fix. Then the body does everything in the world to punish you when you don't get your next dose of drugs on time. That's why an addict like me is willing to do anything in the world just to get another fix. But if there was one thing a junky going through withdraw *doesn't* feel like doing, it's eating.

However, even though I sure didn't feel like it, I started picking at my Jell-O. I did, after all, need my strength. After a time, I shoved the tray away. It was strange. While I picked at the Jell-O, I felt a bit of appetite. But, while I ate, I didn't feel like eating. Was it possible to be hungry and yet not hungry at the same time?

I looked at the wall and saw my New Testament on a stand beside the bed. With a sigh, I picked it up. At least there was one source of comfort in this place. Opening up the Testament, I started to read.

Crystal Parker's journal [kept on her tablet]

The traffic couldn't have moved any slower if it tried. I *swear* I could see cobwebs forming on the cars! The only good news was that Jeremy hadn't gone anywhere. It wasn't much, but it was something. On television, the heroes *never* got this stuck in gridlock traffic. Even in high speed chases, the traffic was always conveniently light and the heroes never got stopped by a train. Real life, however, did not resemble television in the slightest.

"Maybe we'll get through by this time tomorrow," I muttered.

"It may encourage you to know," said Chris, "They still haven't left the house."

"You *know* that doesn't mean anything," I replied, "They could be being tortured right this second."

"True," sighed Chris.

"I still can't believe the *gall* of the man," I cried, "It's one thing to disagree with another detective's methods. But it's *unforgivable* to ignore a cry for help!"

"I know," snarled Chris, "I swear, if Watson and Lorenzo die because Hendricks refused to help us, I will personally take great delight in shouting what just happened from the rooftops. Hendricks will be hounded out of the country for this."

I looked helplessly at Chris. He looked as outraged as I felt.

"Now what?" I asked, "Does that watch have a gadget that will let this car fly like a helicopter?"

181

Chris shook his head sadly. "I'm afraid not. Right now we need a lot of prayers. Unless this traffic suddenly starts moving faster, we're going to be too late to help Watson and Lorenzo with *anything*."

Chase Anderson's journal [in encrypted code]
Disguise is a wonderful thing. It allows one to move about through public without the threat of attracting undue attention. Sometimes celebrities will don a disguise so they can go about in public without attracting attention. I do know my brother is fond of wearing disguises to track down criminals. And, as they say, two can play at that game. And in my motel bathroom, I played that game to the hilt.

Take wigs, for example. A different hairstyle and hair color can do a lot to alter a person's appearance. My own hair is a light brown and is kept in a crew cut. However, a dark red wig in a different style than my own did wonders for my appearance.

Some decent stage makeup gave my face a different complexion. With my picture being plastered all over television and the internet, everything I can do to give myself a different look is a plus. It took some doing to get the makeup perfect where anyone close by wouldn't be able to tell that I was wearing makeup, but my hours of practice paid off.

Finally, I applied the coup-de-grace. Some colored contact lenses did what no amount of makeup could do: change the color of my eyes. I gave my own brown eyes the appearance of being green eyes thanks to modern contact lenses.

Once my disguise was complete, I donned a blue suit and drove to a little out of the way spot at a strip mall just twenty minutes from my motel. Al's Photography Studio is a charming little place that specializes in photographing weddings, baby pictures, graduations, and forged documents. The later, of course, was what I was most interested in. Some forged credentials and a nice new passport would be just what the doctor ordered.

I entered the studio, which was decorated in portraits, wedding pictures, and graduation shots. Camera equipment complemented the decorations. A young couple was looking through a photo album of pictures while a cashier talked to them. Judging from how excited the couple was and the way they held hands, I would say they were about to walk down the aisle.

"And *here* is an example of some pictures that were taken in the gazebo in Central Park," said the cashier.

"Oh, honey," exclaimed the woman, "That would look beautiful for our wedding pictures!"

"Any picture that *you're* in would be beautiful," said the man.

I rolled my eyes as the couple kissed. Ah, young love. It was so sweet. It was so sentimental. And it made me want to puke.

Looking around, I saw the man I was looking for. Some young parents came out of one of several studio rooms carrying a young toddler dressed as a Disney princess. Behind them came good old Al Martin. Al was short and had black-gray hair. He was a thin, nervous man who always looked like he was guilty of *something*. That was good. It made him easy to intimidate.

He saw me, tensed, and resumed his conversation with the parents. Obviously he had made them happy. He shook hands with the father, gave the daughter a lollypop, and the parents went to check out.

Al motioned for me and I followed him into the studio. Once we were inside, he shut the door.

"Hi, boss," stammered Al, "How's things?"

184

"I'm surprised you recognized me," I said, "How is my disguise faulty?"

"Oh, the makeup is great," answered Al, "But you wore a similar disguise once before. Remember? The only thing different is the color of your eyes. I might not have noticed, but I *am* a photographer. A photographer has to pay close attention to detail."

"Thank you, Al," I said, "I'm glad *you* noticed this instead of the police. I need good employees like you to keep me straight."

Al grinned. "Always glad to help."

I patted him on the back. "Good! Right now, help is what I need."

Al sat back in his chair and motioned for me to sit down.

"Tell me what you need, my good friend," said Al.

"The usual, plus some extra," I responded, "I need a set of phony doctors credentials, as well as police I.D. I will also need a fresh passport out of the country. I'll pay the usual fee, plus thirty percent."

Al whistled. "That's pretty generous, my good friend."

I shrugged. "I can afford to be. You do great work, and with every police officer in the state

185

looking for me, I need some loyal friends."

"I assume you will want to alter your disguise before we do the pictures."

My smile was without a trace of humor. "I hate to, but I have to. When would be a good time to come back?"

"Come back in the morning, eight sharp," said Al, "That will give me time to have everything set up. We'll be finished well before I open up at nine."

I stood and shook his hand. Pausing at the doorway, I turned back to face Al.

"Al," I said, "You have been a good, trusted friend. However, from time to time I have encountered employees who have tried to take advantage of little difficulties that I have found myself in. Usually, they get greedy and threaten to go to the police unless I pay them more money than we agreed upon. When those unfortunate events occur, I always make sure that the guilty party is never found, at least in one piece. Remember that, *my good friend!*"

Jeremy Winslow's journal [kept on flash drive]
"I'll tell you whatever you want to know," said Lorenzo.

Cooper paused. The butane torch was five inches from my face. The angry hiss of the flame was evil to hear. He looked almost irritated that Lorenzo was giving in. Of course, having known the Hispanic detective for several months, I knew she wasn't really giving in. She flashed me a knowing look. The girl was totally trying to buy time and was praying that her story was believable.

"We're waiting," said Rollins.

"First," said Lorenzo, "Turn that blasted torch off! If Winslow gets so much as a blister from that thing, your boss will be in for a big disappointment. And that, 'officers', will fall back on *you*."

Rollins looked at Cooper and nodded. Cooper sighed, turned off the torch, and sat it back on the workbench.

"Now then, smart mouth," said Rollins, "Start talking."

Lorenzo snickered. "Right. I talk and then you ice the both of us. I'm not stupid."

"You became stupid when you crossed the boss," snarled Cooper, "People that do that have a way of ending up dead."

"So do people that work for him," I countered, "I can tell you of a number of his employees who got killed just because Chase didn't

187

need them anymore. What do you think he's going to do once this is over and leaves the country?"

"That's right," said Lorenzo, "He won't need the likes of you anymore."

"Shut up!" yelled Cooper.

"You wanted us to talk," said Lorenzo, "So, we're talking. When Chase goes to flee the country, he's going to tie up some loose ends. He's got to decide who in his organization he can trust."

"That's right," I agreed, "Why should he trust a bunch of cops who betrayed the oath they took to protect and serve? You crossed your fellow officers. Why should he think you won't cross him?"

Cooper reached into a tool box and produced a claw hammer. He held it high and advanced towards us.

"Last chance, Lorenzo," said Cooper, "For both you and Winslow."

"I'll have to take you there," said Lorenzo quickly, "I'll have to show you where it is."

I glanced at Lorenzo. She was handling herself well, especially when you consider that she had no idea what she was supposed to be handing over to these clowns.

Cooper sat down the hammer and jerked me to my feet. Rollins was equally rough with

Lorenzo. Lorenzo glared at Rollins, obviously wishing for a chance to get her hands around Rollins' throat.

"Let's go," snapped Rollins, "And just remember, this better *not* be some kind of stupid trick."

Collins gave me a look that was pure evil. He obviously hoped it was scaring me. However, all I wanted was a moment to remove the sneer from his face once and for all.

"Rollins is right," snarled Collins, "If you're pulling a fast one, you'll spend a *very* long time dying. Let's go!"

CHAPTER ELEVEN

Jeremy Winslow's journal [Continued]

"Let's go," repeated Collins.

Reluctantly, Lorenzo and I walked up the stairs, side by side. Our hands were still handcuffed securely behind our backs. Rollins and Cooper were bringing up the rear, their guns aimed squarely at our backs. When we moved too slowly for their tastes, a not-so-gentle nudging in the backs from their weapons get us moving quicker.

Every step I took, I was thinking hard. I had sent out an SOS. If the gadget worked—and Chris' gadgets usually did—then Crystal and Chris would be doing everything possible to get to us in time. The problem was, there was no guarantee that they *would* get to us in time, even if the SOS got through. What if Chris was still too weak to leave the hospital? Sure, they could call the official police, but Chief Hendricks hated Chris and might not listen to him.

Then there were a number of other things that could go wrong. A tire could blow out at the worst possible time. There could be an accident on the freeway. In the movies, the hero always managed a nick of time rescue. But, real life wasn't a movie. In real life, sometimes the hero got delayed a little too long.

So…even though I was hoping that rescue was about to be at hand, I had to plan as if no help was coming. As we marched up the stairs, I began considering our options. Cooper and Rollins were behind us with guns and our hands were cuffed behind our backs. The only good news was that the other "police officers" were in the yard across the street. If we could make a move now, Lorenzo could make a move against Rollins and I could take out Cooper. Even one on one, the odds weren't in our favor. Our chances were slim, but it beat playing the game by Moriarty's rules.

My eyes caught Lorenzo's. I motioned with my head. She blinked and then nodded. She understood. We were two steps from the top of the landing. If we were going to make a move, it would have to be now.

"Now," my lips mouthed.

She nodded. Without warning, she and I both turned on our heels and whirled around. Rollins and Cooper were standing directly behind us, their guns raised chest high. Both of them were too surprised to move.

Their moment's hesitation was all we needed. Lorenzo and I both lifted a foot and kicked. My foot kicked Cooper in the gut. Lorenzo's likewise collided with Rollins' stomach. Cooper

191

and Rollins flew backwards, gasping as they fell. Their guns fired straight up in the air. Our assailants went rolling backwards down the stairs. They screamed and cursed as they fell, until their heads hit the concrete floor of the basement ten steps below. Both of them lay still.

Lorenzo and I lost no time. We hurried back down the steps, knowing that at any minute the other officers could be back. We knelt down beside our captors and started feeling our way around their gun belts. It wasn't easy, let me tell you, finding the keys with our hands cuffed behind our backs. But we managed. In seconds, my hands felt inside the pouch containing the keys, and I began working the key into the lock. Looking up, I saw Lorenzo was having the same luck as I was.

I breathed a sigh of relief as I felt the locks open. Lorenzo, likewise, got her cuffs open. Both of us together whipped the handcuffs off, rolled our kidnappers over on their backs. Then we put their cuffs to good use—handcuffing *their* hands behind their backs.

"When those two wake up," said Lorenzo, "they're going to have *awful* headaches."

"Boy, that's a shame," I said, "Let's see if we can round up some backup."

Crystal Parker's journal [kept on her tablet]

"Come *on!*" I fumed at the traffic.

Chris was more frustrated than I was. In the five minutes since his call with the intrepid Chief Hendricks, Chris had placed four different calls for reinforcements and had gotten absolutely nowhere. We would find out later that Hendricks had advised all of his detectives that they were under no circumstances to take any calls of any type from us whatsoever. Chris swore several oaths under his breath. I won't repeat what he said, but I agreed wholeheartedly with him.

Chris' watch beeped suddenly. He glanced at it and his face brightened.

"It's Watson!" he said excitedly, "Watson, are you all right?"

"It's been interesting around here," said Jeremy's voice through the speaker, "Any chance you and Crystal are going to be in the neighborhood anytime soon?"

"We're stuck in traffic on the interstate," said Chris, "We got your SOS, by the way. We've been trying to get to you, but it's absolutely bumper to bumper here. What's happening?"

We listened intently as Jeremy told us how the officers assigned to watch Chris and Jessica's house were actually working with the Crimson

193

Dragons. We were even more amazed at how Jeremy and Lorenzo managed to escape.

"Lorenzo has been talking to police HQ," said Jeremy, "And some legitimate officers are loading everyone up in a paddy wagon. Lorenzo found out about Sherlock's call to Hendricks, and right now she's having a long talk with the police commissioner about Hendricks' conduct. She's spelling out how Hendricks ignored your call and it nearly led to our deaths."

"Good for her," I said.

"Offhand," chuckled Jeremy, "I'd say that Hendricks is in for a *very* uncomfortable hour on the commissioner's carpet. Cooper and Rollins were carried unconscious into an ambulance, and they probably won't wake up until they're in a jail cell. The other two dirty cops are in custody and we're checking out the crime scene for evidence."

"As soon as traffic lets us," said Chris, "We'll be there."

It was another twenty minutes before traffic started moving, and another fifteen minutes after that before we could get to Jessica's house. Needless to say, we covered every square inch of those houses with a fine toothed comb. We photographed everything as we went, getting extra-close-up pictures.

In the end, we simply verified what we already knew. The only thing missing from Jessica's house was the contents of Chris' file box. And not a thing was ever recorded on the police security cameras. The only good thing to come from all of it was the arrest of several corrupt officers; that and the fact that Jeremy and Lorenzo came out of it all alive and well.

Jeremy Winslow's journal [kept on flash drive]
Before we left Jessica and Chris' house, we all compared notes. We asked Lorenzo several questions about her case files. She told us she couldn't think of any reason why Moriarty would think she had anything he wanted. Of course, we had just been through an ordeal and she may have needed time to think. She promised us that she would go through every one of her case files from the last week and call us when she had something.

It was dark by the time I got home. My house was a modest three bedroom home, but no mansion ever looked finer as I pulled into the driveway. Glancing around, I saw several vehicles parked by the curb up and down the street. A few of them were official police. But, I later learned that Chris also had his own "security detail" guarding my home. The unofficial security was made up of the parents and guardians of the Baker Street Irregulars. The Baker Street Irregulars were made up of teenagers that had at one time been a part of a street gang.

Chris had been instrumental in getting them out of the gang and turning them into law-abiding citizens, and they became Chris' eyes and ears around Oklahoma City. The youths' parents and guardians were so grateful to Chris that they always jumped at the chance to do him a favor. Considering that Shelly and Crystal had in recent months helped the Baker Street Irregulars get back into church, they were especially grateful

The parents of the Irregulars, I later learned, had agreed to watch my home in shifts and kept in constant communication with Chris. After finding an entire group of police officers that were supposed to be guarding Jessica's house was actually under Moriarty's command, I was grateful that Chris had his own watchdogs guarding my home.

Walking up the front steps, I felt myself torn about what I should be doing. I knew that Chris and Crystal weren't about to just go to sleep. A part of me thought that if *they* were still working on the case, I should be as well. But there's something

196

about being kidnapped and nearly getting my face burned off with a blowtorch that just plain drains a person of their strength. It also makes a man want to give his family a hug, so I didn't argue when Chris said that I needed to go home for the night.

Shelly and Tim welcomed me with open arms. Rex nearly knocked me over, barking and wagging his tail. I held Gage close as Shelly reheated my supper; one of Shelly's famous homemade stews. It might as well have been a seven course banquet; it was awesome.

While I greedily gulped down the stew, Shelly told me about their day. Jessica had very reluctantly agreed to move into the bedroom until we knew that she would be safe in her home. She still protested about disrupting our lives, but her protests fell on deaf ears. She still protested, but we could tell that she was secretly pleased to have friends that cared about her.

After Gage was asleep in bed, Shelly and I got ready for bed ourselves. Climbing under the covers, Shelly asked me about the details of the case. Shelly was all ears when I told her about the kidnaping. I left out the part about the torture that I had narrowly avoided, but I was honest about it being dangerous.

"Shelly," I said, "I owe my survival all to you."

My wife blinked. "To me? What did I do?"

"You challenged Chris to design something that would help if I lost my cell phone," I answered, "No one suspected that my watch could do anything but tell time. They certainly didn't suspect that it could send out an SOS."

Shelly wrapped her arms around me and drew me close. Having her close to me never felt so wonderful, especially considering that for a time I didn't think I would ever see her again.

"Are you getting anywhere *near* close to finding Chase?"

"I don't know," I confessed, "We're getting some leads, but there's still a few pieces of the puzzle that's missing."

"It'll come together," insisted Shelly, "Hey, Crystal texted me a little while ago. Chris *knows* that he's missing a lot of years in his memory. He knows he can't remember beyond six or seven years ago."

"*Really*?! Since when?"

"He's realized for a few months," said Shelly, "But he kept it to himself. You won't believe it, but Chris was afraid that if he said

198

anything to Crystal, she'd be afraid he was losing his mind and wouldn't want to marry him."

I stared at my wife. "You're pulling my leg."

"No," said Shelly, "The man was afraid that Crystal would think he had mental problems and that he would lose her."

I closed my eyes and shook my head. Shelly snuggled up close to me. It felt *wonderful*.

"I'll be glad when this is over," I said, "I am *so* ready to snap the handcuffs on Chase and put him away for good."

"Me too," said Shelly, "Crystal's just afraid that she's going to be backed into a corner and be forced to tell Chris the entire truth about his memory."

Briefly, Shelly told me everything Crystal told her. For the first time, I truly understood why everyone was afraid to just tell Chris everything. No wonder everyone walked on eggshells and played along with Chris' delusions! The truth could put him into a catatonic trance that he might *never* come out of! It had to have been a bear for her to hear Chris talk about his own past without even knowing he was talking about himself!

"So far," continued Shelly, "Crystal's been able to work around Chris' delusions."

199

"That's good," I said, "I would truly *hate* to arrest Chase but lose Chris along the way."

"So would I," said Shelly, "So would I."

Crystal Parker's journal [kept on her tablet]

Chris insisted on treating me to supper after our rescue of Jeremy and Lorenzo. Once we took Jeremy home, Chris insisted on taking me to *Vinnie's*, the most expensive steakhouse in the city. *Vinnie's* had everything; great food, candlelight, and—to my delight—a violinist that knew how to play all of my favorite romantic songs.

The waiter showed us to our table. Chris insisted on pulling the chair out for me, and we began looking over our menu. I tried not to worry about Chris' head, but it was impossible; one look at his face told me that he was still fighting pain.

"Are you *sure* you don't want any pain killer?" I wondered.

"All they'll do is knock me out," he insisted, "Then I won't be any good to anyone, including myself."

"Is there anything I can do?" I asked.

"Sure," he said, "It's been a few hours since I last got to kiss your delicious lips, and I think I'm starting to go through withdraw because of it."

200

We corrected that with a smooch as our violinist began to play *Unchained Memory*. As the violinist played on, we talked through some wedding plans. But, try as I might, Chris would give no details as to our honeymoon. My detective fiancée was leaving that little detail a mystery.

"Come on," I begged, "At least give me a hint. Do I need to pack clothes for warm weather or cold?"

"Yes."

I swatted him playfully. Our steaks and baked potatoes arrived. Pausing just long enough for us to say grace, the violinist continued to play the most romantic songs ever written. The steaks were so tender they practically fell apart if you looked at them. The baked potatoes weren't shabby either. Cutting into his steak, Chris' watch beeped. He looked at it and turned serious.

"I just got a text from Detective Lorenzo," said Chris, "It's about her case files."

"*And...?*"

"After doing the paperwork on the dirty cops who ambushed her and Watson," said Chris, "She looked through her case files for the last few weeks. At first there wasn't anything out of the ordinary; a few minor robberies and a cyber-bully. Certainly there was nothing to bring on the attempted murder of two detectives. However, there was one item of interest."

"Well, don't keep me in suspense, Sherlock."

"Yesterday," continued Chris, "She did the paperwork booking a young woman arrested for prostitution."

My fork paused midway to my mouth.

"Tell me about it," I demanded.

"She's a young woman named Tina Stewart," continued Chris, "She's young but is *very* experienced as a prostitute, unfortunately. She's well known by the police for advertising her services on a website known as..."

"*Cyber-Ads*! Sherlock, that's got to be it!"

"I agree," said Chris, "At the same time that the Stalker is murdering prostitutes, Detective Lorenzo does the paperwork on a prostitute who advertises on the *same* website as all of the victims. Shortly thereafter, a sniper takes a shot at Lorenzo and then she's kidnapped by people working for Moriarty. Said kidnappers believe that she has some merchandise that Moriarty very desperately wants."

Between bites of my steak, I said, "This has to be it! Sherlock, I think we've got the motive for the murders. One of those prostitutes had something

202

that Moriarty wants. He's trying to get it back and is killing anyone who disappoints him."

"It would be worthwhile to find out if Miss Stewart remembers meeting the Stalker's victims at any time," said Chris, "There's a reason why all of the arrest records for the victims have been sealed or erased. Our killers are making sure no one makes the connection between them."

"Where's Miss Stewart now?" I asked.

"She's in the hospital, suffering through withdraw," said Chris, "She's heavily addicted to drugs, and she's suffering from missing a badly needed fix. Detective Lorenzo is personally supervising the security detail guarding her."

"That's good," I said, "But what about Dr. Price? Surely *this* should persuade Hendricks that Price is innocent."

"You would think," said Chris, "But Hendricks is nothing if not stubborn. He's convinced that Price himself masterminded the killings and is bound and determined not to face the evidence staring him in the face. After the dressing down he's gotten from the commissioner for ignoring our call for help, the man's more determined than ever to prove his theory on the Stalker killings is correct."

We chatted about some other aspects of the case as we ate. We talked at length about the disappearance of the documents from his file box and the forms that had been erased from every known database.

"He's having every trace of your existence deleted from every government website there is," I fumed.

Chris smiled. "You can guess why that is. Chase will *have* to flee the country after he gets whatever he's after, and by that time, he'll want *me* to have been erased as thoroughly as those documents were."

"You need a safe place to stay," I said quickly, "Jessica was told to stay at the Watsons' home. Don't get the wrong idea, but you could stay on the couch at *my* place. I promise you that the apartment complex has great security."

Chris smiled. "I appreciate your concern, but it wouldn't look right for me to stay overnight at my fiancée's apartment."

"I'm more concerned about *your* safety than *my* reputation," I insisted.

"Nonetheless," said Chris, "*Neither* of us are staying in our homes tonight."

I blinked. "We're not? Then where are we staying?"

"We're going to visit the King of Atlantis."

"*HUH?!*" I exclaimed.

Chris smiled but would say no more about the matter while we ate. Every time I asked him what he was talking about, he just grinned. That was one thing about Chris: when he didn't want to talk about something, it would be easier to turn straw into gold than to get him to talk. It was so infuriating; he reminded me of me.

After we finished supper, Chris took me to a nearby house where the homeowner allowed us to borrow his car. We parked my car in his garage and borrowed the man's Chevy Malibu. I later learned that the homeowner was a judge that Chris had once helped when the judge's daughter was missing. Before leaving the judge's house, Chris pulled a laptop case out of the back seat of my car. He opened the passenger door of the Chevy for me, and then settled down into the driver's seat. Once we were on the road, Chris relaxed visibly.

"How's your head?" I asked him.

"It's doing remarkably well," he answered, "The pain has eased up considerably. The kisses you gave me are the best therapy in the world."

"Oh, that's good," I said, "Because if you don't start telling me who this 'King of Atlantis' is,

I'm going to wallop you right on *top* of your pointy head!"

Chris chuckled. "His real name is Justin Drake. His code name in the world of computer hacking is the King of Atlantis. I once proved he was innocent of the charges of hacking into the Federal Reserve."

"That's good."

Chris shrugged. "It's also bad. I proved he was innocent of hacking into the Federal Reserve by proving that, at the time the Federal Reserve was hacked, Justin was hacking into NASA."

I smiled and shook my head. Only Chris could prove that a man was innocent of one crime because he was committing another crime at the time!

"So he gets jailed for another crime instead of the one he was charged with," I said, "Why should he do you any favors?"

"Because of one important fact that I pointed out to NASA," said Chris, "When Justin hacked into their system, he corrected a flaw in the programming of a satellite that they were about to launch into space. Had the programming not been corrected, the satellite would *not* have made it into space. Instead, it would have crashed into downtown Dallas."

206

"Wow," I breathed, "I don't remember hearing *that* on the news!"

"NASA was very particular about not letting that little bit of information become public knowledge," said Chris, "If there's one thing every government agency is fond of, it's secrets. That's a topic that Justin is *very* vocal about."

I grinned. "He's fond of conspiracy theories, huh?"

"More like obsessed," answered Chris, "If you ever get the man started on the Kennedy assassination, Hanger 18, or the Men in Black, he'll be talking to you until doomsday."

"'Hanger 18'? The 'Men in Black'?"

Chris smiled. "Hanger 18 and the Men in Black are urban legends about UFO's. According to legend, the government has a UFO that crash landed years ago and it's stashed away in their top secret Hanger 18. The Men in Black are supposed to be government agents that intimidate people that have seen UFO's into keeping silent."

"I see. And this conspiracy-theory fanatic is supposed to help us *how*?"

"You'll see. Now settle back, Gorgeous. We have a long drive ahead of us."

207

CHAPTER TWELVE

Detective Maria Lorenzo's Journal

After checking my case files and connecting the dots between Tina Stewart and my kidnapping, it was time for a little chat with Officer Cooper. I had the joy of interrogating Cooper, while the rest were interrogated by other detectives.

Oh, at first Cooper was defiant, especially after he lawyered up. However, after I enlightened him on what life was like for a cop in prison, it didn't take long for the sneer to leave his face. Before long, the man was begging for mercy, but I was not in a merciful mood. What I wanted to do was to strap him to a table and threaten to burn *him* alive with a torch unless he talked. Hey, fair's fair.

Sometimes, justice happens. Cooper's lawyer was a court appointed attorney with the interesting name of Walter Walters. And Walters was fresh out of law school. I mean, this lawyer was greener than grass. He had a horrendous case of acne, was as thin as a toothpick, and wore his hair in—so help me-- a mullet. He had never worked on any cases more serious than traffic court, and certainly wasn't well versed on the fine art of getting sweetheart deals for mad dog criminals. In short, I had Cooper in my power and I was playing it for all it was worth. Two hours into the interrogation, Cooper was sweating like he was in a steam bath. I was loving every second of it.

"Now then," I said, glaring daggers at Cooper, "I am sure that by this time, your partners are ready to throw you under a bus and leave you holding the bag on everything."

Actually, I knew no such thing. But Cooper didn't have to know that. And his pimply faced lawyer was too busy scratching his head to do Cooper any good. I loved it!

"You're crazy," said Cooper, "Rollins is as loyal as they come. Smith and Maloy aren't ones to turn on their partners either!"

I snickered. "None of you were loyal to your *oath* to protect and serve. You oafs have bound yourself to a crime boss who uses people and then throws them away when they're no longer useful to him. Haven't you ever read his file? He killed his *parents* when he was a teenager. He murdered his sister's husband. He murdered his brother's wife and little daughter. And you think he's going to do anything to help *you*? He'll toss you away like an empty soda can."

Cooper shook his head, terrified. "No. No, he protects the people that are loyal to him!"

"Guess again, goofball," I said, "I can show you case file after case file in the investigation of the Crimson Dragons in which people that have served Moriarty well were murdered just to keep them quiet. Haven't you ever noticed that most people who join the mob don't die of old age?"

Cooper looked helplessly at his lawyer. He was silently pleading with Walters to do something to help him. Walters frowned.

"You know something," said Walters, "The detective does have a point. Most people who join the mob die untimely deaths, I'm afraid. Those that do live to old age usually live out their days in prison until they're carried to the grave."

"Whose side are you on?" growled Cooper.

"But she's got a point," insisted Walters, "I studied law back in Chicago. Once while I was in law school, there was a case where a police officer was caught taking bribes from the mob. He wouldn't cooperate with the police when he was caught and got sent up the river. The funny thing was, his cell mate happened to be someone that was part of the same mob. He and some fellow inmates made this former cop drink battery acid."

Cooper was about as green as I'd ever seen a man. Cooper was the perfect example of a person who was great at inflicting pain on others, but who thought the world was unfair if others inflicted pain on him. He stared open mouthed at Walters, not believing what Walters had just said. I was starting to like Walters by this time. I made a mental note to personally request that Walters be the court appointed attorney for every lowlife I had to interrogate.

"How about saying something to *help* me?!" demanded Cooper.

"The only thing that will remotely help you is to give us something," I said, "Give us some names and dates. I can't get you immunity, but I can get you a reduced sentence. Who knows? You might actually get out of prison before your five year old daughter gets married and has children. But, what you say has to be the Gospel truth. In the mood that I'm in right now, you *don't* want to be found lying to me!"

Cooper considered this. He looked over at Walters, who simply shrugged. Actually, I probably *could* have gotten Cooper immunity in exchange for his testimony, but there was no way that I was offering that crumb immunity! The man was going to do some hard time.

"I'm going to advise my client to accept your offer," said Walters, "Provided it is put in writing."

211

I grinned. As I said, sometimes justice does happen. After the interrogation was over, I clocked out and headed towards *Christ's Church Hospital.* I had yet to fulfill my promise to visit with Tina. Not only did she need help starting a new life, but—after talking with Anderson—I realized that she could be a key to cracking the Stalker case.

It was dark by the time I pulled into the parking lot, and I realized that I hadn't eaten since breakfast. The nurse on duty directed me too Room 207. Along the way, I grabbed a protein bar out of the vending machine. I was grateful to see three security guards on duty. Showing my badge to them, I entered the room.

I saw that Tina was curled up in a fetal position, snoring peacefully. Her hands clutched a small, grime covered New Testament, gripping it like children would grip a security blanket.

"How are you doing, Tina?" I silently wondered, *"Are you making it through the withdraw pain? Are you finding answers in the Scriptures?"*

I made a vow that I wasn't going to leave until I found out. If Chris was right, then my talking to Tina was what made me a target for Chase, or Moriarty, or whatever his name was. That also meant that Tina herself was a target on

Chase's list. And I had no intention of letting that maniac claim another victim.

I gulped down my protein bar, which my hunger laughed at. Thankfully, the cafeteria was still open, so I could order a burger, some fries, and a piece of apple pie with some coffee. I set a new speed record for eating my meal, and then retreated to the sofa beside Tina's bed.

Within ten minutes I was sleeping soundly.

Crystal Parker's journal [kept on her tablet]

In most fantasy stories, a king lives in a royal palace. The palace is usually surrounded by a moat, and you'll find knights having jousting tournaments. You might even find King Arthur and his Knights of the Round Table talking about the best way to find the Holy Grail while Merlin the Magician advised him.

The King of Atlantis, however, lived in a gray, dingy apartment in a drug infested neighborhood. From the moment I stepped out of the car to the time we approached the front steps of the complex, I saw no fewer than five drug deals go down. You'd think a king would live in better surroundings than this. Of course, when you're the king of a place that doesn't even exist, you probably won't live on the better side of town.

Justin Drake greeted us at the door. Justin was in his mid-thirties, had a scraggly brownish gray beard that made me think of a hermit living in a cave at some remote mountain, and his long hair was pulled back in a ponytail. He had on old, torn jeans that looked like their patches were the only thing holding them together. He was barefoot, and had on a filthy tee-shirt with a picture of a flying saucer. Above the flying saucer was the legend: *"This Ship Last Seen in Hanger 18"*.

"Hey, Holmes," exclaimed Justin, holding out a hand that was stained from cheese puffs, "Good to see you again, dude."

Chris smiled and shook his hand. "Good to see you, Justin. This is my fiancée, Crystal Parker."

Justin grinned and shook my hand. "Good to finally meet you, Miss Parker. Sherlock's told me so much about you."

"Call me Crystal," I said, "And I hope Sherlock's said a few *nice* things about me."

"Not really," said Justin.

I raised my eyebrows and looked at Chris.

"Actually," grinned Justin, "He said some *wonderful* things about you. The man can talk for *hours* about how awesome and beautiful you are."

I smiled. "Thanks. You just saved Sherlock's life."

Justin laughed and showed us into his apartment. It was like stepping into *The Twilight Zone.* Now, I'd seen Chris' first office before Jeremy and I had talked him into moving the office to a downtown office complex. Chris had done everything possible to recreate the fictional Sherlock Holmes' office with a modern twist, substituting electronic experiments for the fictional Holmes' chemical experiments. In Chris' office, computer circuits and relics from his cases could end up in the most interesting of places, including in our chairs and in the teapot.

If Chris' office had been eccentric, Justin's apartment was truly insane. Scale model replicas of spaceships from *STAR TREK, STAR WARS,* and *BATTLESTAR GALACTICA* hung from the ceiling. There were two windows in the living room, both covered with newspaper clippings taped over the window. One window had a newspaper story bearing the headline *"Air Force Shoots Down UFO in Twenty Minute Dogfight".* The other window held a news article with the headline: *"Second Shooter Identified in Kennedy Assassination".* Music from the television series *"The X-Files"* played on a CD.

215

The living room itself was a replica of the bridge of the Starship Enterprise. Computers filled every wall. The furniture was designed after the fabled spaceship. In the center of one wall was a flat-screen TV with a computer keyboard connected to it. Over the TV was a large portrait of the original cast of *Star Trek*. The floor was covered from wall to wall with popcorn kernels and potato chips.

"Hey, guys, you're just in time," said Justin, "I was just about to reenact that time on *Star Trek* when the crew of the *Enterprise* was on the planet where everyone acted like gangsters from Chicago in the 1920's. I'll be Captain Kirk, Sherlock here can be Mr. Spock, and Crystal can be Lt. Uhura."

"Perhaps some other time," said Chris pleasantly.

"And if we ever do," I said, "I *will not* be wearing that mini-skirt that all the girls on *Star Trek* seem to wear! Those are the shortest skirts in existence!"

"Awwww," said Chris, "I was looking forward to seeing you in one of those skirts! I was going to special order one for you online."

"Not on your life," I said, "You don't get to see *that* much of my legs until *after* we're married! One look at my legs will scare you off."

"Actually," said Chris, "One look at *your* legs would remind me of what a gorgeous woman you are and how lucky I am to be engaged to you."

"Have a seat, lovebirds," said Justin, "I was hoping to get the chance to tell Sherlock about the newest video game I'm programming."

"Oh, so you're a video game programmer," I said.

"Yeah," said Justin proudly, "*Warlords of Atlantis*. I just finished the seventh in the series. It's insanely popular with the college crowd."

"I'll be glad to hear about it," said Chris, toying with his deerstalker, "But there's this case where we need a person of your...computer talents."

Justin smiled. "You mean the kind of talents that the law frowns on."

Chris nodded. "We understand each other."

Raising his eyebrows, Justin said, "You know, you're not too shabby in the computer hacking business yourself, especially with that equipment you developed a couple of years ago."

"Ordinarily I would take care of it myself," agreed Chris, "However, time is of the essence. There are lives at stake, and I have a ton of evidence to go through in addition to the hacking work I need done. My associate, Dr. Watson, was nearly killed

217

today and so I ordered him to take the night off to be with his family. If I could persuade you to assist me with the hacking I need done while Crystal and I look at our evidence…"

While Chris talked, he unzipped a compartment in his laptop bag, pulled out his personal laptop, and sat it in a chair marked "Captain Kirk's chair". Unzipping a second compartment, he pulled out a small black box and plugged the wire into a USB port on the laptop.

Justin was positively drooling. Judging from the way his eyes lit up like a Christmas tree, he had heard all about Chris' homemade computer system and was just dying to try it out.

"Is that the hardware I've heard you use in all your cases, Holmes?"

"It is," said Chris, "But if you're too busy recreating old *Star Trek* episodes…"

"Not to worry," said Justin eagerly, "I just parked the *Enterprise* in the nearest starbase."

Chris flashed me a knowing smiled as Justin sat down at Chris' laptop. As the computer warmed up, a picture of Chris' detective badge filled the screen. Chris turned the screen away from Justin momentarily as Chris typed in the User Name and Password. I pulled out a list from my purse and handed it to Justin.

"Somebody has been erasing important data from a lot of high security databases," said Chris grimly.

"They've investigated the arrest records of several murder victims," I explained, "And they've erased every bit of information on Sherlock."

"You're kidding," said Justin.

"At this moment," I said, "Sherlock has no record of his birth, no school records, no record of his time on the police force, and he doesn't even have any records in the IRS database. Officially, Sherlock doesn't exist."

Justin whistled. "Man somebody has some high-tech equipment and a *lot* of know-how."

"Agreed," said Chris, "And we're hoping you can help us with *this* end of the investigation while we pursue some police files that were secured for us."

"Whoever has been erasing files," I said, "is probably the same people who implanted a computer microchip in Sherlock's shoulder without his knowledge when he was undergoing emergency."

Justin's eyes widened in horror at the news of the microchip. He looked from Chris to me and back to Chris again.

"These cats implanted a secret *microchip* in you?" asked Justin, "It's got to be the shadow government. It has to be! They killed JFK, they covered up the Philadelphia experiment, they…"

"*'The Philadelphia Experiment'*?" I exclaimed in spite of myself.

"The Philadelphia experiment," explained Justin, "Was a top secret naval experiment back in the 1943, where they tried to make a battleship invisible."

I looked at Chris, giving him my best "is this guy for real?" look. Chris shrugged.

"See," continued Justin, "the navy wanted a way to make their ships invisible to enemy radar, using Einstein's Unified Field Theory to figure out how to do it. The navy figured they could use several generators on a ship to bend light around the ship and make it so that their ships couldn't be picked up on radar. They got a battleship—the *USS Eldridge*—in the Philadelphia Naval shipyard in October of 1943. They got the crew on board, turned on the generators, when it happened."

I started to tell him that we had other things to be concerned about than some old naval experiment, but Justin was getting warmed up. No wonder Chris cautioned me against bringing up any of Justin's pet theories!

"The first time they turned on the juice," continued Justin, "the ship was engulfed in a green fog and the ship became nearly totally invisible. When the ship reappeared and the fog was gone, the navy found that some of the sailors on board were mad. Others had parts of their body fused to the bulkheads of the *Eldridge*.

"The *second* time they did the experiment a few weeks later, things really got interesting. This time, the ship not only became invisible, it totally vanished for a time after being surrounded by a blue light. It then reappeared in Norfolk, Virginia. That's over *two-hundred miles away*, my friend. When it reappeared back in Philadelphia, there were some more sailors who went mad, and others who had parts of their bodies fused to the hull of the ship. Then there were others…who just plain vanished."

Although I didn't really believe this story, a chill went down my spine. I looked back at Chris helplessly. Seriously now, when you know that the mob has you in their gun-sights, the last thing you want is to hear ghost stories!

"We believe this is mob related," said Chris quickly, "You've heard me talk about the Crimson Dragons, Justin?"

"*Endlessly*," said Justin wearily.

I smiled. Justin knew Chris well.

221

"We have reason to believe that our current case is tied to them," said Chris, "And we believe they're raising the stakes as we get closer and closer to the truth. What we need you to do is to hack into the computer systems that Crystal has written down. We need evidence that the systems have been hacked."

"How do you know that they don't have a similar setup to yours?" asked Justin, "Your system doesn't leave any evidence of your hacking. *And,* some hackers know how to leave a different IP address than your own, a sort of ghost IP address. You can make it look like a different computer has done the hacking, you know."

Chris shrugged. "We have to start somewhere. All we can ask you to do is to do your best."

"OK," said Justin, "So how do I use this bad boy?"

"You just do what you always do," said Chris, "And my little black box will do the rest."

"Will do," said Justin, typing away.

"We need to use one of *your* computers to examine a couple of computer flash drives," I told him.

"Use any of them," said Justin, "Anything for the man that helped me track my sister's killer."

222

I blinked and looked at Chris.

"I thought Sherlock saved you from going to prison," I said, "Something about you hacking into NASA."

Typing away on the laptop, Justin grinned. He looked over at Chris, who was turning on one of Justin's computers. Soon, Chris inserted the flash drive into the computer and brought up the disk's main menu.

"I guess he didn't tell you *why* I hacked into NASA," said Justin, "My sister was an engineer developing new satellite technology. The girl was an absolute genius, and she had it all. She had a brilliant career, her marriage was rock solid, and they were expecting their first child.

"Anyway, Lisa—that was my sister—was on her way home from work one night when her car flipped going around a sharp turn. She went straight down a cliff and the car exploded. Everybody wrote the whole thing down to an accident caused by trying to go around a curve too fast. It was all tragic, and NASA sent official condolences.

"At first we all believed it. Then, a couple of weeks after the funeral, Lisa's husband—his name's Harold—came across Lisa's diary. She kept the thing on a flash drive and it was hidden in a desk drawer. He started reading Lisa's diary, and

223

some of it was the usual stuff---her feelings about Harold and the baby, love poems, anything you would expect from a gal's diary. But, some of it was work related."

"Sherlock told me that there were flaws in the satellite's programming," I said.

Justin frowned. His typing became erratic, and he was nearly pounding the computer keyboard. Obviously, remembering the past was stressful for the man.

"Lisa knew about the flaws," said Justin, "She was an *engineer* and an excellent one. She noticed the flaws and went to her supervisor. The problem was, the supervisor was getting kickbacks from some of the computer programmers. If the truth about the system came out, said supervisor's corruption would become known.

"Lisa's diary revealed the steps she had taken to try to warn NASA about the flawed system. On her own, she tried to see how far the satellite's system was corrupted. But, her investigation became discovered before she could go farther up the chain of command."

"That's when the 'accident' was arranged," I concluded.

Justin nodded. "To honor my sister, I picked up the investigation where she left off. I soon realized that Lisa was trying to save lives by launching her investigation, and did as much as I could to get the evidence Lisa was looking for.

"But," continued Justin, "I wasn't as careful at covering my tracks as I should have been. I guess I let my emotions get carried away and got careless. I got found out and arrested. I hired Sherlock to find the truth. He not only proved what Lisa was trying to prove, but he brought in the people who tampered with Lisa's car. Too bad NASA was able to keep the full story from hitting the press, but at least there was justice for Lisa and her unborn child. I owe your fiancée a lot, my friend."

I glanced over at Chris. He was absorbed in examining the computer disk that Lorenzo had given him. Justin looked at Chris and then at me.

"Miss Parker," whispered Justin, "Is he anywhere *close* to remembering who he really is?"

"He's had a very few memory flashes," I whispered, "He also knows he has gaps in his memory. But he's got so very far to go. I was hoping that once we shut down the Crimson Dragons for good, he would be able to see some of his records and be brought back to reality. But whoever erased his identity from the databases stole a lot of personal documents from his house."

225

Justin frowned. "What about you? What if he *never* gets his memory back?"

"I didn't know him *before* he began thinking he's Sherlock Holmes," I whispered, "But I've always known him to be a wonderful man. Whatever happens, I intend to do everything possible to be a good wife for him."

Justin smiled. "He's getting a good woman. He deserves one. You're a lot like my own girlfriend, Ruth. She…"

"Hello," said Chris excitedly, "*What have we here?*"

Jeremy Winslow's journal [kept on flash drive]

As exhausted and drained as I felt, I still couldn't sleep. For over two hours I lay still in bed listening to Shelly's breathing. I tried hard to be still; just because I couldn't sleep was no reason that *Shelly* needed to be disturbed.

With a sigh, I slid out of bed and pulled on my robe over my pajamas. I tiptoed out of our room and walked down the hall to the living room. Staring out of the front window, I could see our security force driving up and down the road.

I smiled. The parents of the Baker Street Irregulars were still doing their thing. I'll say one thing about Chris: he has inspired intense loyalty

226

among his friends. In the last year, I'd met several people he had helped since his breakdown, and all of them were incredibly dedicated to helping him in any way they could.

Chris had told me that the parents of the Baker Street Irregulars were a sort of neighborhood watch group. If they saw anything suspicious, they were to contact the police immediately. Chris never allowed his civilian assistants to endanger themselves whenever they helped him.

A part of me couldn't help but feel guilty. That's what was nagging at me like a dog gnawing on a bone. Here I was, safe and secure in my own home while my partners were still on the case. Sure, I knew Chris said I needed some down time after my ordeal and I was grateful for it. Still…

"Having trouble sleeping?"

I jumped at the sound of Shelly's voice. Turning around, I was treated to the sight of my wife approaching me. Her face radiated the love in her heart.

"You know me too well," I responded.

"I should, after all this time," she said, "Want to talk about it?"

I shrugged. "Not much to tell. It's just hard to sleep knowing my partners are staying up and

227

working on the case. I mean, I'm torn between being grateful to be home and feeling guilty that my partners have a long night ahead of them without me."

Shelly smiled and, throwing her arms around me, drew me close. She felt warm and wonderful.

"Honey," she began slowly, "I love you. And one of the things I love about you is your heart. You care about others. It's just that sometimes your concern leads you to feel guilty when you shouldn't. Do you remember how, after 9/11, you felt guilty about surviving when some many other first responders got killed?"

"I'll carry those memories with me for the rest of my life."

"But you finally realized that you had nothing to feel guilty about, right?"

I nodded.

"Feelings and emotions are funny things," she continued, "They can be good. We can enjoy the feelings we have when we do something fun as a family or have some romance as a couple. But, our emotions can also take us to dark places for no reason."

"True," I said.

"Now," she continued, "If it had been Chris or Crystal that had just been through an ordeal, wouldn't you have advised them to take some down time?"

"Yes," I said, "I guess a part of it is that I'm concerned that they're going to need me while I'm here safe at home."

Shelly kissed me and grinned at me. A mischievous twinkle was in her eyes.

"Well," she said, "You took their advice and came home. What you do with your time here at home is up to you."

"What do you mean?"

"The internet is up and running 24/7," said Shelly, "What's preventing us from doing our part here at the house?"

"'Us'?"

Shelly tugged at me and led me back to our bedroom. There on the bed, she already had my laptop set up, and a steaming cup of coffee on the nightstand on my side of the bed.

"Yes," she said, "us. Gage will probably be awake and asking for a feeding in the very near future. To put it bluntly, we're both awake. Let's put our time to good use."

I smiled and sat down on the bed. In seconds, I plugged the black box that Chris had

229

made for me into my computer. Then, typing in my access ID and PIN number, I logged onto Chris' database. Shelly was right. I *did* have some leads that I hadn't had time to investigate.

"So what's our first step, Watson?," asked Shelly.

"I guess our first step is to have my last name legally changed from Winslow to Watson."

Shelly giggled and swatted my arm playfully.

"Seriously," I said, "I've got a list of names from Dr. Price's classes. Our first step is to see if there's anything interesting about his students."

It was a long, tedious process. Contrary to what television leads people to believe, detectives seldom get what they need on the first, second, or even third try. It often takes *hours*, even when you have the most up to date, state of the art equipment. Dr. Price had a long list of students, and I had to go through the list one at a time.

There were a lot of records to go through. There was the students' banking information, for example. Were there any mysterious deposits or withdraws? Did they have a Swiss Bank Account? Were there any police records? The list went on. I had to go through the whole ordeal for every student on the list.

It wasn't long before Gage was crying for a feeding. Shelly got him and brought him back into the bedroom while she nursed him. I had thought that she would be bored by the sheer drudgery of the details I had to look up. But, on the contrary, she was fascinated by the details that went into detective work. Every step of the way, she was asking questions and listening closely to my answers.

Shelly had a lot of experience doing corporate research before we got married. It had been a mutual decision for her to be a stay at home mom when Tim came along, but she had never lost her touch with computer work. She had been instrumental in aiding Crystal in investigating some of the police officers that were suspected of being in league with the Crimson Dragons. This, in turn, had led to finding the ones responsible for betraying Chris to his brother; thus, paving the way for the murder of his family and Jessica's husband.

Since that time, I could tell she was batting around the idea of getting back into the game. She had never said anything, but a husband learns to read his wife the same way a wife learns to read her husband. If I were a gambling man, I would bet that she was tempted by the idea of getting back into research but felt like a heel for even

231

considering that with a baby at home and Tim being home in the afternoon.

"You're still fascinated by this kind of stuff, aren't you?" I asked.

"Always," she said, "Of course, I was in the corporate world before we got married. But, research is research, whether it's for the business world or for detective work."

"You certainly did well helping Crystal a few months back," I said.

"I enjoyed it," she said, "I enjoy it the way you enjoy detective work."

I stood and stretched. Shelly held Gage close to her, cuddling him and looking at the computer at the same time. Gage had been nursed, burped, his diaper was changed, and now he was sound asleep.

"Here," I said, "Let me put Gage back to bed. I was just about to key into the personal e-mails for Hector Crane. He's in Dr. Price's nine o' clock Tuesday and Thursday class."

I cradled Gage in my arms and carried him gently back to his bed. Covering him with his Snoopy blanket, I watched him for a few minutes as he slept. I could almost believe that a halo was shining over his head.

"*Gage,*" I thought, "*We're going to end this case. You're never going to be threatened the way your mother and brother was. I swear it!*"

Gage stirred and started to cry. This was nothing new. A lot of times he could be sound asleep in either mine or Shelly's arms. Then, when we start to lay him down, he would wake up. With a sigh, I pulled the rocking chair over beside Gage's crib and sat down. Gently, I rubbed his arm, letting his hand touch mine. Gradually, his crying stopped. His breathing became more relaxed. Soon, he was asleep.

But I didn't move from my spot. I didn't want him to wake up the second I moved my arm. So, I sat there with one arm cradling Gage. It was soothing watching the gentle rhythm of his breathing. From my experience with Tim when he was a baby, I knew that it could take several minutes for a baby to get into a deep sleep. So I figured that, within ten minutes or so, it would be safe to move.

As I sat in the rocking chair watching Gage breathe, I felt my eyelids growing heavy. The gentle breathing of Gage was certainly relaxing. Gradually, Gage and his crib were growing blurry. Then I was asleep.

CHAPTER THIRTEEN

E-mail from Chase Anderson to Hector Crane [written in encrypted code]

Mr. Crane,

Greetings. I want to thank you for your assistance in our little arrangement. Things are progressing well. However, there are a few items of business left to attend to.

The police aren't quite as sure about Dr. Price as they once were. Until now, Dr. Price's own personal problems made it seem like he had the perfect motive for the Stalker's crimes. Sadly, they are now being forced to look at the lack of evidence tying him to the crimes. That simply will not do. I am counting on you to assist me in correcting the situation. As one of Dr. Price's students, you are in the perfect position to help me. With Dr. Price's background in criminology, he is the perfect fall guy.

FIRST, I want you to continue giving your "undying support" of your college professor. Let him think you are his most loyal student. You've played your part great thus far. Keep it up. That should place you above suspicion. SECOND, you will soon be receiving a package with some instructions on what to do with the package. Unless

I am very much mistaken, this package will be the final nail in poor Dr. Price's coffin.

It is absolutely essential that you follow the instructions to the letter, and don't ask any questions. REMEMBER: THE LIFE OF YOUR SISTER DEPENDS ON YOUR OBEDIENCE!

Regards,
The Boss

Crystal Parker's journal [kept on her tablet]

Chris looked up from his computer terminal, excited. He motioned for me to join him, and I was at his side instantly. Before me were crime scene photos of one of the Stalker's victims. They were, quite simply, ghastly. The victim had been so badly mutilated that it was hard to believe that I was looking at a human.

"That's *obscene!*" I cried, "How can anybody do that to another human being?"

"When we find the killer, we'll ask him," said Chris, "But, besides the obvious, what do you see in this picture?"

"All I see is some poor soul that looks like she's been through a slaughter house," I said, "What she must have gone through when she was killed!"

"Interestingly enough," said Chris, "All of those mutilations were performed *after* she was already dead."

I blinked. "Really? But I thought Moriarty was recreating the crimes of Jack the Ripper. Why would he do the mutilations *after* the victims died?"

"Jack the Ripper also mutilated his victims *after* they died," commented Chris, "Some of Dr. Price's notes confirmed this. The Ripper fed his victims poisoned grapes, which acted as a sedative, and lessened the chance of the victim fighting. Then he strangled his victims to death. *Then* he performed his ghastly mutilations."

"Oh yes," I replied, "Watson said that earlier when you were in the hospital."

"Yes," said Chris, "Now, I've read the ME's autopsy notes. In each case, the Stalker's victims had a mild sedative in their blood streams. Believe it or not, the victims were strangled to death."

My jaw dropped. "*Really?*"

"Really. Like Jack the Ripper, he sedated his victims and strangled them. The mutilations were done postmortem."

"I wouldn't have guessed that in a million years."

Chris grinned. "But that's not the best part. Besides the body, do you notice anything else in this crime scene picture?"

"I'll have to confess that it's hard to notice anything *except* the body."

"Look beside her neck," instructed Chris.

I looked. There beside the victim's neck was a small white piece of cloth stained red with blood. "It looks like a handkerchief."

"Exactly," said Chris, "Usually its *men* who carry handkerchiefs, right?"

I nodded.

"So it isn't the victim's," said Chris, "Which leaves one conclusion."

My eyes widened. "It's the killer's handkerchief!"

"Exactly, my gorgeous fiancée," said Chris, "I do believe it's time to place a call to Detective Lorenzo. We need to see what's happened to said handkerchief since this photo was taken."

Chris stood and stretched. I glanced over at Justin, who was still crouched over the laptop, looking very frustrated. As Chris punched numbers into his watch, I walked over to Justin.

"How's it going, O King of Atlantis?" I asked.

"The king is losing his crown," he said glumly, "No wonder no one's been able to nail these goons for years! These jokers are better at covering their tracks than a politician."

"Don't give up," I said, "Sherlock has confidence in you. So do I."

Justin flashed a goofy grin. "Your fiancée didn't give up on solving my sister's murder. I'm not giving up either. Hey, did Captain Kirk give up when..."

"Probably not," I interrupted, "And I don't see you as a quitter, either."

He nodded and got back to work. I was just as glad. I didn't really care to hear a long monologue about how none of the heroes of science fiction shows gave up when the odds were against them. It wasn't that I hated science fiction shows, because I don't. In fact, I watch a lot of them myself. But right now we had some answers to find, and relieving old television shows wasn't going to get the job done.

"Detective Lorenzo," I heard Chris say into the watch, "I've been reviewing some of the notes from the Stalker's victims. A bloody handkerchief was found at the scene of Amanda Witherspoon's murder, but---interestingly enough—I find no mention of it in Detective Chandler's notes when he processed the crime scene. Yes, I'll text you everything I find. You will? Great! Make sure you stick with Ms. Stewart like glue; she may be the link between the Stalker and what happened to you and Watson earlier. Awesome!"

I stared at Chris' computer screen. He had pulled up the notes that Detective Jack Chandler had written at the crime scene. Sure enough, no mention of the bloody handkerchief had been made. Chandler had written the details of the mutilations, the items found in Witherspoon's purse, the fact that no cell phone was found, and...there was mention of handwriting found on a nearby wall. I was just pulling up the notes on it when Chris was at my side.

"I've e-mailed what I found on the handkerchief," said Chris, "Lorenzo is with Tina Stewart now and is going to stay with her. Lorenzo intends to find out about the handkerchief."

"Great," I said, "Have you looked at this about some handwriting found on a wall?"

Chris shook his head. "I was about to, but I wanted Lorenzo to have that handkerchief tracked down ASAP. But here's another case where history is repeating itself. When Jack the Ripper committed his 'double event', there was handwriting found on a nearby wall. It was no doubt left by the killer or killers, giving the police a sample of the killer's handwriting."

"What happened?"

"The Commissioner of Scotland Yard—Sir Charles Warren—personally came to the crime scene and wiped the handwriting off the wall."

"You're kidding!" I exclaimed, "The commissioner wiped out their best evidence?"

"Yes," said Chris, "The writing said, 'The Juews are the men who wont be blamed for nothing.' Sir Charles said that the writer was blaming the Jews and that he was trying to prevent Jews from being murdered in the streets in retaliation. But it doesn't explain why he wouldn't let the writing be at least photographed or the area blocked off until the writing could be investigated."

I clicked on the link. "Let's see what our friend the Stalker left for us on the wall."

A window popped up on the screen. A scanned copy of Detective Chandler's notes in his own handwriting appeared on the screen. Chris and I read it and looked at each other in disbelief.

"Some ten yards from where the body of Ms. Witherspoon was found," read the note, "A single sentence was found written on the wall of a warehouse. The note was every bit as ludicrous as some of the notes that were sent to police headquarters, so I felt it wasn't to be taken seriously. I therefore ordered the writing to be washed off."

Chris pounded the coffee table in frustration. I sighed in exasperation. Just like the historical Jack the Ripper—some of the best evidence that would be a direct link to the killer was obliterated! The whole thing stank of cover-up. Somehow, Chase still had a few police officers on his payroll in the department. That's the only way I can think of that would lead seasoned detectives to literally throw vital evidence away without a thought.

"At least we've got two vital pieces of evidence from this fiasco," said Chris.

"Really? All I can see is that a detective threw his best evidence away."

"Clue number *one*," said Chris, "Now we have a detective to investigate. Is there evidence to be found that would indicate that Chandler is something besides an idiot? Clue number *two*: Police headquarters is receiving a number of letters concerning the Stalker."

"And clue number *three*," whooped Justin, "We have a winner over here!"

Instantly, we were at Justin's side.

"What have you got?" asked Chris anxiously.

"Proof that the king is regaining his crown," said Justin proudly, "And also a little wedding present to you two."

241

"What is it?" I asked.

"Only an IP address to show who hacked into Sherlock's elementary school and erased all of his school records," said Justin, "Odds are, the same person erased *all* of his records and was in on that break-in to steal his files from out of his house."

"Was it Chief Hendricks?" I asked.

Justin shook his head. "I traced it to a computer used by one of the detectives on the force, a detective Jack Chandler."

Chandler! The lead detective on the Stalker case! If Justin was right, Chandler's mistakes were more than incompetence. The lead detective on the case was working for the Crimson Dragons.

Detective Maria Lorenzo's journal

Daylight was filtering through the window when Chris called me about the handkerchief. I instantly called in some favors from some detectives I trusted. How in the *world* could a vital piece of evidence like a bloody handkerchief be overlooked? No sooner did I make my calls when a text message came in from Crystal.

"Do NOT trust Detective Chandler," read the text, "Chandler's computer was used to get rid of a lot of Sherlock's personal records. He also wiped out evidence that needed investing in the Stalker case. He needs some SERIOUS investigation! Sherlock and I are going to trail Chandler. You need to keep Tina Stewart safe."

Chandler! The lead detective on the Stalker case...and his computer was used to erase Chris' personal records? He destroyed evidence in the Stalker case? That was impossible. Chandler was a seasoned veteran. He had made more collars on the force than most detectives dream of. He also had the respect of all his peers. Could he truly be working for Chase Anderson?

Maybe. Maybe not. I'd certainly seen some things in the past few months that I had never thought I would see. After all I'd been through, I couldn't afford to ignore any possibility until I personally investigated any and all evidence.

As for his computer, there was one of two explanations. Either Chandler did the hacking or someone *using* his computer did. All we knew for sure right now was that his computer was used to commit some serious crimes. That didn't mean that Chandler was the one who committed the crimes.

Destroying evidence in a criminal investigation, however, is something else altogether. If Chandler wasn't a criminal, he—at the very

243

least—had some serious explaining to do. Whether the man was criminal or simply guilty of incompetence, it would be a sad footnote to an otherwise stellar career.

A low moaning caught my attention. Tina was tossing, turning, and groaning. She was drenched with sweat, and was suffering through a serious case of drug withdraw. My heart went out to her. Even though she had made some seriously poor choices and was suffering the consequences of those choices, it was heartbreaking to see anyone suffering so badly. Gradually, she opened her eyes and blinked several times.

"Detective Lorenzo," she whispered.

"I'm here," I answered, "And I'm not going anywhere."

Tina smiled and licked her lips. "I'm thirsty."

I nodded and poured a cup of water for her from the picture on the night stand. She gulped the water greedily.

"I've messed up bad," she whispered, "Real bad."

"You'll get through it," I answered, "I'll help you. You'll get through this, and you'll have a new life once you do."

244

"I want that," she whispered, "More than you possibly know. I...was reading...I found a Bible in jail and started reading it."

"That's good," I said, "That's real good."

Tina smiled. "I guess it's dumb...a girl like me...reading a Bible. As if God would want anyone...that's done as many things...as I've done!"

I wiped her forehead with a damp cloth. She was literally drenched in sweat. Her entire pillow was sopping wet.

"The thing about God," I said, "Is that He loves everybody. Have you read *John 3:16*?"

Tina nodded. "Yes. It was something about how God loved the world so much that He gave His only begotten son so that everyone who believes in Him would not perish..."

"But have everlasting life," I finished, "That's good! And it's true! God sent Jesus so that everyone who believes in Him will have the chance to go to heaven."

Tina swallowed and looked scared. "But what about someone who's wrecked their life on drugs and prostitution?"

I thought about that. "Once there was a man who slept with the wife of one of his best friends. The wife became pregnant. To cover it up, he had

245

his friend set up to be killed. Would you say that's pretty bad?"

"I'd say it's pretty horrible," said Tina, "I've done a lot, but I haven't murdered anyone."

"The guy who did that was King David," I said, "The same man who killed Goliath when he was a teenager. And God forgave him when he repented."

Tina was amazed. "*Really?*"

I nodded.

"I read one of Jesus' stories," whispered Tina, "It was called the Prodigal Son."

"That's one of my favorites," I said, "A boy royally screwed up his life, burned a lot of bridges with his family, and ended up in the gutter. But, the boy woke up, humbled himself before his father, and his father forgave him."

Tina smiled sadly. "My Mom is no better than me, but she's totally washed her hands of me."

"The father in Jesus' parable," I said, "Represents God. Any and all of us are prodigals. Every one of us has sinned. The Bible says that all have sinned and fall short of the glory of God."

"Really?"

"A person doesn't have to be a thief, murderer, or prostitute to be a sinner," I said, "A person who gossips or lies is just as much a sinner as someone who cheats on their spouse or steals. In God's eyes, all sin is equally evil. That's why God sent Jesus to die for our sins. He wants all people to have their sins forgiven through Jesus."

Tina licked her lips. "I would like that. And someone…who has sinned…as much as me can be…forgiven?"

"Yes," I said, "You can be forgiven and changed into the type of person God wants you to be. And it's simple to do. All any of us have to do is confess our sin to God, ask Jesus to forgive us, and ask Him to be our Lord and Savior."

"That's *all*?"

"Yes," I answered.

Tina swallowed. "I so want that. Would…would you pray with me? Please?"

I smiled. "I'll be glad to."

There, in the middle of Tina's hospital room, we prayed for several minutes. I prayed for Tina, and then she prayed. Tina sobbed aloud as she confessed her drug use and years of prostitution. She begged Jesus to forgive her, to help her have a new life, and to be her Lord and Savior. When she had begun praying, she was a terrified prostitute. Now she was a new creation in Christ. The angels in heaven sang.

CHAPTER FOURTEEN

Jeremy Winslow's journal [kept on flash drive]
It was Shelly gently rubbing my shoulders that woke me up. I blinked and realized that I had fallen asleep in the rocking chair with one hand in Gage's crib. I blinked again and tried to stand. Instantly, my back protested as I stood. I found myself barely able to stand up straight.

"I *hate* growing older," I growled.

"Look at it this way," said Shelly, "There's only one alternative to growing older...and I'm not ready to be a widow."

"I hope you're *never* ready to be a widow!"

"Never fear," she assured me, "What I *am* ready to do is give you some breakfast so you can get back on the case. I just got a call from Crystal."

"*And...?*"

"I'll bring you up to date while you're eating."

I quickly donned some fresh clothes while Shelly fixed me an omelet, toast, and coffee. While I gulped down my breakfast, Shelly sat a stack of e-mails on the table.

"I got some interesting things in the personal e-mails of one Hector Crane," said Shelly, "I have no idea what it means, but it does look interesting. It looks like some sort of code."

248

"Thanks, sweetheart," I said, "You're a life-saver."

I started to pick the top one off the top of the stack, but Shelly swatted my hand.

"Eat now," said Shelly, "You can look at these with your team once you get to the office. From what Crystal said, you've all got some notes to compare. We weren't the only ones who stayed up late doing some serious investigating."

"Sounds good."

"I'm going to finish up going through Dr. Price's class roster. I've got students from two other class periods to investigate."

I smiled. "Keep up *this* kind of good work and you'll have to become a permanent part of the team. And I'm not joking."

Shelly grinned. "You think I could?"

"You're great at it," I said, "Why not?"

She leaned over and kissed me on the cheek.

"That would have been on your lips," she said, "but your mouth is full of food and I don't want to taste it."

"Awww," I said, "What's a little food sharing between husband and wife?"

She swatted me playfully. One omelet and two cups of coffee later, I was on the road and made record time in getting to the office. Chris and

Crystal were setting out stacks of paper on every surface available, and from the bleary looks in their eyes, they hadn't had much more sleep than I had. They had an interesting system of organizing their papers. Chris tossed the papers carelessly on the floor, and Crystal separated them into neat stacks. They were nursing a couple of cups of coffee themselves, and another pot was brewing.

"Good morning, Watson," said Chris, "I see from the redness in your eyes that you've had about as much sleep as we have."

"After a few hours of tossing and turning," I said, "I gave up the ghost. Shelly and I spent the night investigating Dr. Price's students. Shelly hit pay dirt after I fell asleep while getting Gage asleep."

"We've had a productive night as well," said Crystal.

Chris wheeled a dry erase board to the center of the office. Interestingly, Chris had drawn a huge spider on the dry erase board in the center of a spider web that filled up the rest of the board. The spider was labeled "*Moriarty/Hugh West/Chase Anderson*".

"Here we have the leader of the Crimson Dragons and all of his aliases," said Chris, "For years, he has ruled Oklahoma City's underworld in the shadows, like some huge spider sitting motionless in his web. Although he has stayed in the background, he has been aware of every criminal act occurring in the city the same way that a spider is aware of anything brushing against its web. And what a laundry list of events that have been brushing against the web of Moriarty!

"First, Watson, we have the Oklahoma City Stalker murders. We have a group of prostitutes who advertised themselves on *Cyber-Ads*, and whose arrest records have been mysteriously erased and/or sealed. Tied closely to that is another prostitute---named Tina Stewart—who also advertised her services on *Cyber-Ads*. This same prostitute was booked and processed by Detective Maria Lorenzo."

"Chase thought that Detective Lorenzo had something he wanted," I said, "That's why he had someone shoot at Detective Lorenzo. When that didn't work, she and I were ambushed by dirty cops."

Chris was writing this information along the spider-web. He circled it in bright red dry-erase marker. He then circled Tina Stewart's name in blue marker.

"Obviously," said Chris, "At some point, Tina's path crossed with the victims of the Stalker.

251

Moriarty believes that Tina either *has* something that he wants or knows where it is."

"The only thing I can think of," said Crystal, "Is that Tina and the Stalker's victims met in jail, possibly during a police crackdown on prostitutes."

"Five prostitutes that may or may not have knowledge of what Moriarty is after," said Chris, "And Jack the Ripper killed five prostitutes in 1888; hence, Moriarty recreates the crimes of Jack the Ripper in order to get his 'merchandise'."

"He has someone on the inside erase all records of the victims," I said, "Has anyone checked the arrest records for Tina Stewart?"

"According to police and juvenile records," said Crystal, "Tina Stewart doesn't exist. Even the information that Detective Lorenzo entered into official police records *yesterday* has been erased."

"Sounds to me," I said, "That Tina Stewart would benefit from one of your safe houses, Sherlock."

"I've already made arrangements," said Chris, "We'll let Lorenzo know she needs to take her there."

"Good," I said, "Any luck on *who* is erasing all of these computer files, including yours, Holmes?"

"That would be Detective Jack Chandler," said Chris, "At least it was *his* computer who was used. At this point, we don't know whether it was Chandler himself who used his computer for illegal purposes or someone else using it and trying to frame him."

"Speaking of frame-ups," I said, "I have here some e-mails from one of Dr. Price's students, one Hector Crane. They're in some sort of wild code, but maybe we can get something that can prove that Dr. Price is innocent."

I handed Chris the stack of e-mails. He handed some to Crystal and I took a few. We looked at them, blinked, and looked blankly at each other. The e-mails were obviously in code, but it was a code I had never seen before.

"Shelly managed to get these e-mails after I fell asleep with Gage," I said, "She said they were in code, but this is something else."

The e-mails consisted of a series of diagrams with writing on them. I looked at a drawing of a large plant with a few short sentences written in another language.

"I must say," commented Chris, "If this *is* a coded message from Chase Anderson, AK Moriarty, it's different from any other code I've seen."

"Different is right," muttered Crystal.

"Agreed," I said, "I don't know about you, but I'm finding every e-mail has a different picture. So, it's a code. How do we decipher it?"

Chris opened his mouth to speak when a sharp knock on the door interrupted him. Crystal and I quickly turned over the e-mails.

Chris sighed. "Come in, Chief Hendricks. The door's unlocked."

The door opened. Chief Hendricks walked in, looking as smug as ever. He was wearing a loud, bright yellow and green striped suit that made me want to wear sunglasses and looked like he wanted to burst out laughing. I know that seeing that suit on him made *me* want to laugh.

"Good morning Miss Parker," said Hendricks, "And same to you, Mr. *Holmes* and *Dr. Watson.* I don't know how you knew it was me, but…"

"That college ring you wear makes a very distinct sound when you're knocking on the door," said Chris, "But I doubt that you came here this morning simply to pass the time talking."

"You are so right," said Hendricks, "I wanted to personally pay you a courtesy call. Just to let you know, we've got all the evidence we need

254

to officially charge Dr. Price with masterminding the Oklahoma City Stalker murders."

I exchanged glances with Chris and Crystal. Both of them looked as horrified as I felt.

"And what do you regard as positive evidence?" demanded Chris.

Hendricks chuckled. "Oh, it's not much, I admit. We've only got the knife used to do all of those horrible mutilations. That's all. And it was found in Dr. Price's home. I grant you, that physical evidence is nothing compared to all those fancy theories of yours, but it's enough for me. Good day, all."

Chris followed Hendricks out to the elevator. Crystal and I were right behind him.

"One moment, Chief," said Chris.

Hendricks stopped just as he reached the elevator. He turned to Chris with a grin that covered most of his face.

"Yes, Mr. Holmes?" said Hendricks.

"Didn't you search Dr. Price's home when you first arrested him?" asked Chris anxiously.

"Yes, we did," said Hendricks.

"And you didn't find it then, right?" continued Chris.

"True enough," admitted Hendricks.

"What made you search his home a second time?"

Hendricks shrugged. "An anonymous tip."

Chris snorted. "And how do you explain the fact that you *didn't* find the murder weapon the *first* time you searched the house, only to conveniently find it the *second* time on the advice of an anonymous tip?"

"I suppose we just happened to miss it the first time around," snapped Hendricks, "But that's neither here nor there."

"That won't do and you know it," insisted Chris, "Your theory is that Dr. Price planned the crimes and had someone else do the dirty work because he isn't physically able to do the deed himself. *Why* in the world would Dr. Price have the knife if he is only *planning* the crimes? I would have thought that the knife would be in the *killer's* possession. Also, how did the person who made the tip know the knife was in Price's house?"

Hendricks was turning red. "I admit we don't know everything, but it's enough to go before a grand jury."

"Any lawyer worth his salt would see the knife for what it is," said Chris, "Someone working for the real killer planted the evidence. Is Dr. Price's fingerprints on the knife?"

"There are *no* prints on the knife, but---,"

"Were there any sedatives in Dr. Price's house?" continued Chris.

"'Sedatives'?"

Chris sighed. "Have you even bothered to read the autopsy reports?"

Hendricks' eyebrows narrowed. "How did *you* manage to read the autopsy reports?"

"And how did you manage *not* to?" snapped Chris.

Hendricks shifted his weight from one foot to another. He hated Chris, but he knew Chris was right. That made Hendricks hate him all the more.

"It was *Detective Chandler* who searched the house and made the collar," mumbled Hendricks.

"But he's under *your* authority," countered Chris, "Chandler should have known that a knife was used to perform the mutilations *after* the victims were already dead! As the Chief of Detectives, you should know how solid a case is before it goes before a DA!"

Hendricks looked fit to explode. He was growing increasingly red in the face, which clashed like you wouldn't believe with his bright suit.

"Just where do you get off telling me how to do my job, Mr. Consulting Detective?"

"And where do you get off," shouted Chris, "*Not* doing the job you were hired to do? So help me, if you go through with this, you're going to ruin an innocent man's name! You'll end up looking like a fool as well, but at Dr. Price's age and poor health, the stress of the trial alone will *kill* him!"

Hendricks turned and pressed the elevator button. The doors opened and Hendricks stepped in. But then he paused and held the doors open.

"I'll read the autopsy reports," said Hendricks, "As well as Detective Chandler's notes. I don't think you're right, mind you, but it never hurts for a detective to have all his ducks in a row."

"Thank you," said Chris, "While you're at it, why don't you look up the arrest records of the Stalker's victims?"

Hendricks blinked. "Why do I need to do that?"

"Just say it's in the interest of having all your ducks in a row," said Chris, "Prostitutes always have arrest records, sometimes going back to their teenage years. Maybe you'll find out why the killer chose those particular victims. Consider that suggestion a present, Chief. Our methods may be different, but we do both serve the cause of justice."

Hendricks shrugged. "I'll do that."

The elevator closed. Chris shook his head and led us back to the office. Once we were inside, Chris fairly slammed the door shut.

"See what happens when promotions are made through good-ol' boy politics rather than efficient work?" asked Chris, "Being a consulting detective rather than an official one does have its advantages!"

"At least you've gotten him to agree to do some true detective work," I muttered, "It buys us a little time."

"A little, but not much," said Crystal, "We've got truly bizarre code to decipher, a witness to protect, and a detective who is either incompetent or corrupt."

I looked again at the coded e-mails, thinking. It would take a massive effort to get to the root of these codes. From the looks of things, it would be a full time job just getting pointed in the right direction on deciphering the code. And our case was going in too many different directions to be devoted full time to code breaking.

"Shelly was the one who successfully hacked into Hector's e-mail account," I said, "I'm sure she wouldn't mind taking a crack at this, if she had something to go on. She enjoys this kind of thing."

"She certainly did a great job helping *me* a few months back," agreed Crystal.

For several seconds, Chris considered this. He muttered something about cyphers and research. Then he pulled a flash drive out of his desk drawer. "It reminds me a lot of the Voynich Manuscript," said Chris finally.

"I hope *you* know what you're talking about," said Crystal, "I've never heard of the thing."

"The Voynich Manuscript is a fifteenth century book named for the antique book dealer who discovered it," said Chris, "You might say it's the Holy Grail of mysterious codes. The entire book is made up of diagrams ranging from botany and medicine to the solar system. There *is* writing with the diagrams, but the meaning of the book is a mystery. The prevailing theory is that the book is a sophisticated code, and—to date—no one has been able to decipher it."

"That's encouraging," said Crystal dryly.

"*However*," said Chris, "We have something in this case that the people working on the Voynich Manuscript don't—we have a good idea of what this code is referring to. See the times that those e-mails were generated? They were sent *before* the knife was planted in Dr. Price's house. If we go from the theory that the code is referring to the crimes in question, this will give Shelly a starting point. This flash drive has a full encyclopedia on cyphers and code-breaking."

A quick call to Shelly confirmed what I had been saying. She jumped at the chance to contribute to the investigation.

"I'll bring everything we've got by the house shortly," I told her, "Love you."

"Love you, too," she said.

When I hung the phone up, I turned to Chris and Crystal.

"It's all set," I told them, "Shelly's more than happy to help."

"Capital!" said Chris, "Watson, you and I are going to pay a visit to Detective Chandler's apartment."

"But he's at work," I protested.

"No doubt you will be surprised to know that I'm aware of that," said Chris.

"We're going to break into the apartment of an Oklahoma City detective?" I asked.

"Only if you have no objections," said Chris.

I sighed. "Holmes, if we get caught, Hendricks will throw away the key to our cell after he stops laughing!"

"That *would* be interesting, wouldn't it, Watson?"

"*Interesting* is not the word I would choose," I growled, "But, if it will help us clear an innocent man and arrest the guilty parties…"

"Great! I knew I could count on you, Watson!"

"And what am I supposed to do?" asked Crystal.

"I want you to go to talk to Tina and Lorenzo," said Chris, "You and Lorenzo can question Tina about her past. Does she remember a specific time she met the Stalker's victims? Did any of them mention having something that Moriarty is interested in? Call me greedy, but I want anything she might remember."

"Great!" said Crystal, "Hopefully she can clear up this mystery."

"I hope so," said Chris, "Otherwise before we're done, the stress of his ordeal will kill poor Dr. Price."

CHAPTER FIFTEEN

Jeremy Winslow's journal [kept on flash drive]
    Chris and I made two stops before going to Detective Chandler's apartment. First, we took the e-mails and flash drive to Shelly. She had transformed the living room into a kind of mini-office. She had confiscated my laptop desk so she could sit on the sofa in comfort while using the laptop. The printer was connected to it and was sitting on the coffee table, filled to the max with paper.

    Gage's playpen was right beside the sofa. Jessica was helping Shelly with Gage and playing with Rex. Rex was playful, but kept a wary eye on Gage. His look said, "Anyone who messes with my family will be missing some hide!" Shelly gave me a lingering kiss after I handed her the e-mails and flash drive, and promised that she would do everything possible to crack the code.

    Our second stop was at the county jail to visit Dr. Price. He was brought to a holding cell and we talked to him through a telephone. It was strange seeing him in an orange jumpsuit. We found him to be looking haggard and drained. For several minutes we assured him that we were doing everything possible to clear his name and urged him to keep his faith up.

"Glenda has been great about visiting me and praying with me," he said, "She has been a boon of encouragement."

"Your granddaughter loves you very much," I said.

"At the same time," continued Dr. Price, "It is great to know that the team of Sherlock Holmes and Dr. Watson are on the case. I know you're doing everything you can."

"As we speak," said Chris, "Our associates are helping us on other avenues of your case. But I must ask you, have you noticed anything strange with any of your students?"

Dr. Price blinked. "My students? Nothing more than usual. I have been blessed with highly dedicated students. Some of them struggle more than others, but that is to be expected at any campus."

"Have you noticed," pressed Chris, "Whether any of them seemed bothered by anything? Any bad news or personal problems?"

Dr. Price chuckled. "All of us have personal problems, Mr. Holmes. Sadly, it is a part of life. Are there any students in particular that you have in mind?"

"Hector Crane," I said, "What do you know about him?"

Dr. Price blinked and thought hard for several moments. Then he picked up the phone again and looked at us.

"Hector Crane is a good man," said Dr. Price, "He has a sister, Lola, who is a receptionist somewhere in Edmund. I know this because I am Hector's counselor. Hector is one of those individuals who had to grow up very fast, my friends. His father died when Hector was two. His mother worked two jobs to make ends meet. When the mother *was* home, she was usually drinking. You might say that Hector raised Lola and managed to keep his grades high enough to get into college on a full scholarship. I have high hopes for that young man. He's not in trouble, is he?"

"We hope not," said Chris, "We sincerely hope not."

After leaving Dr. Price, we went to the police impound yard and checked out a van. The van had belonged to a plumber that also used the van as a place to deal drugs. The guard at the impound yard knew Chris well, owed him some favors, and so he loaned us the van.

It had taken Chris a total of five minutes to find Detective Chandler's address at Palm Trees Apartments online. That was the thing about the internet: even without sophisticated equipment like

265

Chris', anybody with a computer can find anything about anybody. I didn't know how to feel about that. On one hand, the technology was very useful to detectives.

But on the other hand, it showed that privacy truly is a thing of the past in our country. A friend of mine on the force told me about a case where a woman kept moving from state to state to escape a stalker. Each time the stalker found her, he used the internet to find her again. The last time it happened, the stalker brutally raped her, and she ended up in an asylum because of it. Perhaps someday a way will be found to balance the need for being able to obtain information with the need for people to have safety and privacy. But it will take somebody smarter than me to find the best way.

Chris had brought along some old jeans and shirts with the logo "Ken's Plumbing", and—after a quick change of clothes in the back of the van—we made our way to the apartment. I carried a large tool box that must have weighed as much as an anvil while Chris carried a couple of lightweight lengths of pipe.

Somehow or other, whenever I'm carrying something heavy, the place I'm going to is never on the first floor. Sure enough, I had to lug that heavy toolbox up three flights of stairs before reaching Chandler's apartment.

Looking down over the railing, I saw there wasn't a soul in sight. That was good, considering that Chris was picking the lock with his Swiss Army Knife. The knife was one of those thick models that had everything, even a pair of pliers. Chris carried it in a pouch on his belt rather than in his pocket. While Chris worked on the lock, I stood directly behind him. I hoped that I was blocking any view that others would have of Chris picking the lock.

"I must say," whispered Chris, "Crystal got me a good replacement knife for the one I lost when we fought that militia group who wanted to start a revolution a few months back. This one has better tools for breaking and entering."

"Hopefully it has a file on it to cut our way out of jail if we get caught," I whispered back.

"As a matter of fact, it does. The metal file is right beside the pliers."

I sighed. "That was *sarcasm*, Holmes!"

The door opened and we quickly went inside. In all, it took less than a minute for Chris to get us inside. I had to say, Chandler had one nice apartment. There was a wall mounted, flat-screen television, expensive paintings on the wall, and

267

furniture that I wouldn't be able to afford if I lived three lifetimes.

"Interesting, Watson," said Chris, looking at a painting.

"What?"

"Have you ever known a detective to be able to afford an original Van Gogh?"

I chuckled. "The only detectives I've ever known to have an expensive *anything* inherited it from a rich relative."

"Exactly, Watson. Unless the intrepid Detective Chandler has a rich relative we don't know about, he's getting some extra money from *somewhere*. That somewhere couldn't have been through legal channels."

I thought about that. "Why would anyone get enough illegal loot to buy expensive paintings and still live in a cheap apartment instead of a penthouse?"

"To keep up appearances, Watson! The man can afford to buy expensive things for the *inside* of his home with his ill-gotten gain and—unless he has friends over to visit—no one would ever know. But to move into a plush penthouse that no honest cop could afford would take *some* explaining!"

I pulled a digital camera out of my coat pocket and started snapping pictures. I got good close-ups of the paintings and the autographs of them. Chris took his investigation to Chandler's bedroom while I continued to take pictures.

"Watson, look here!"

I hurried to Chandler's room and saw Chris sorting through the man's closet. He pulled out a navy blue suit.

"I've been in the store this suit came from, and quickly walked out," said Chris, "These suits cost a thousand dollars apiece."

I whistled. And to think I cringed at the thought of paying a *hundred* dollars for a suit! A few pictures of the labels on those suits later, we turned our attention to the laptop on Chandler's dresser. Chris switched the computer on and waited.

"Now to figure out the password," muttered Chris.

He began typing furiously. Judging from his oaths, he was getting nowhere. I turned my attention to Chandler's bookshelf. Most of the titles on his shelf were pornographic in nature, complete with pictures. I blushed and decided to turn my attention elsewhere.

Turning from the bookshelf, I began moving the pictures on the wall. In the old detective movies, the criminals often hid a wall safe behind a painting.

There was nothing behind these paintings except bare wall. There weren't even any convenient documents taped to the backs of the paintings themselves. So much for old movies being as realistic as real life.

"Bingo!" exclaimed Chris.

"What?" I responded, at his side instantly.

"The password," said Chris, "I simply went down the list of the most common passwords that people use on their computers, and—sure enough—Chandler's was on that list."

"What *was* his password?"

Chris smiled. "The word 'Password' *is* his password!"

I rolled my eyes. "You have just *got* to be kidding me!"

"If we had time, I'd log off and let you try it for yourself. But, in the interests of not spending more time here than necessary, I think I should download the contents of his hard drive onto this flash drive."

I nodded. "I'll keep watch while you do."

We had a good system for this undercover operation. Since we were disguised as plumbers on assignment, I made a show of carrying a length of pipe to the van and coming back with a longer section of pipe. A few minutes later, I carried a sink faucet—which had been in my tool box—to the van and returned with another style of faucet. Anyone looking out their windows would think we were truly plumbers at work.

As I came back into the apartment with the faucet, something caught my eye on the coffee table. It was a common sight in many people's homes; so common that anyone could see it without noticing it. It was a thick, family Bible.

The Bible struck me as odd. Why would a corrupt cop, working with gangsters and with pornographic books on his shelf, want a Bible? It made no sense. I picked up the Bible and quickly slid the dust jacket off of the book. Instantly I saw it wasn't a Bible. It was an artist's sketchbook.

I opened the sketchbook and my jaw was hanging open. Before me was the same type of drawings that I had seen earlier, on the e-mails that Shelly had found in Hector's e-mail account. I snapped a picture of the drawing and turned the page. Then a third.

The entire sketch book was filled with the bizarre drawings and odd bits of writing on the pictures. How I wished I had time to copy the entire book! But, knowing that was impossible, I prayed that I could get enough on my camera to at

271

least get Lorenzo to launch a more official investigation.

Snapping pictures of the pages, I couldn't help but smile. In Edgar Allen Poe's *The Purloined Letter*, a stolen document was hidden in plain sight. But it was so well camouflaged that it took a professional detective to find it. This sketchbook containing code for the mob was out in plain sight, disguised as—of all things—the Holy Bible.

"Holmes," I called out, "I've got something here!"

"So do I, Watson," said Chris grimly.

I hurried back into the bedroom. Chris sat before the computer screen, looking as grim as I've ever seen him look. Instantly, I saw why. The screen had two pictures showing. Both were of the same young girl, a red-haired woman that couldn't have been more than 21 or 22. The first picture showed her slumped over in a vehicle, her hands tied up in front of her, terrified. The second picture showed what was left of her, dumped in an alleyway, horribly mutilated. The implications of what we were seeing were both obvious and bone chilling.

"Detective Chandler isn't just *investigating* the Stalker murders," said Chris, "He *is* the Stalker!"

Shelly Winslow's journal

Well, I wanted a way to help Jeremy with the case and I got it. But boy did I get more than I bargained for! Looking through the e-mails I had gotten from Hector's account, I agreed with everyone that it had to be some kind of encrypted code. But how in the *world* could I crack the code? It was overwhelming just trying to figure out where to start.

I compared the diagrams to every code that Chris provided on the flash drive. It didn't bear the slightest resemblance to any of the encrypted codes that Chris had given as an example. I compared it to military codes, cypher substitutions, everything. At Jeremy's suggestion, I compared it to something called the "Voynich Manuscript"; some 15th century book believed to be an unsolved code that's in the Yale museum. These documents looked similar, but I still couldn't make heads or tails of it. Whatever kind of code it was, it was something unknown and we didn't have the cypher key.

After four hours of comparing the diagrams to every known code, I rubbed my eyes and sighed in frustration. Rex whimpered and, trotting over to the couch, laid his head down on my legs. I scratched his ears.

"Hey, boy," I said, "I want to whimper too. This is harder than my college algebra class, and I didn't think that *anything* was harder than that."

Jessica came into the living room from the kitchen, carrying a tray of coffee and donuts. Manna from heaven! During my pregnancy, I had to give up any and all caffeine. That was pitiful enough. But I also tried to limit junk foods, since I was eating for two. Now I was free, and made up for lost coffee drinking time. I tried to limit myself with sweets; after all, I had just recently given birth and I had a tummy to get back into shape. However, my newborn was keeping me up at night. This momma seriously needed a caffeine fix!

"I hope I remembered to fix this as you like it," said Jessica, pouring me a cup.

"Thanks, Jess," I said, "I like it any way, except as strong as Jeremy takes it. He likes *his* coffee strong enough to lift weights."

Jessica laughed as she handed me my cup.

"Your husband and my late husband Jack would have gotten along great," she said, "I'm just sorry you guys didn't get to meet him."

"I'm sure he was quite a guy."

274

"He was," she smiled, "I know I'm probably bothering you when you're busy, but..."

"You're fine," I said quickly, "I was just needing a break anyway. I'm trying to break a code for the team, but the code is about to break *me*."

Jessica chuckled. "When my Jack got frustrated with a problem, he would go away from it for a little while and then, when he got back to it, he would see the solution staring him in the face."

"It's often like that for me," I said, "It works out like that a lot for Jeremy also."

A soft cry from the playpen caught my attention. Sure enough, Gage was waking up from his nap and was telling me that he needed changing. I scooped up my little darling and placed him on a changing pad on the floor. Jessica smiled at him while I changed him.

"Shelly," said Jessica, "I've been doing some thinking."

"Yes?"

"Crystal told me something a few weeks ago," continued Jess, "She said that she and Chris decided that after they get married, they're going to move into a new place instead of moving in with me."

"Really?"

275

"Yes," said Jess, "It was Crystal's idea. I think she wants to get Chris out of *my* house where I don't have to feel responsible for taking care of him anymore."

I raised my eyebrows. "How do you feel about that?"

Jess frowned. "I've got mixed feelings, I guess. He *is* my brother and I love him dearly. But, a part of me is looking forward to not being a caregiver anymore. I guess I feel a little guilty about that."

"Jess," I said, "You have no reason to feel guilty. You've been taking care of Chris for six *years*. You've been so busy taking care of him that you've barely had time to grieve for your own loss. You lost a *husband*, girl! I think Crystal is right. Once they get married, you can relax and take some time for yourself, knowing that Chris is in good hands."

Jessica smiled. "Yes. I admit it *will* be nice. Who knows? Maybe there *is* still a chance that Crystal can help my brother recover once they get Chase behind bars for good."

Sipping my coffee, I said, "Maybe. Since Chris' injury, he *has* remembered a couple of things."

I quickly brought Jess up to speed on Chris' memory. Her eyes widened when she learned that he was having memory flashes of people that could only be Tabitha, Grace, and Jack.

"I guess we'll have to proceed very, very carefully," said Jessica, "But there is one other item I want you to advise me on."

"What's that?"

Jess frowned. "I've been thinking. After the wedding and things settle down, I'm going to have some time on my hands. Maybe I'm being foolish, but I've thought about enrolling on one of those Christian dating websites that I've seen advertised on television. Maybe I'm being silly, but it *has* been six years since my husband died and with Chris marrying Crystal..."

I smiled. "Jessica, that's not silly at all! I'd *love* for you to find some happiness, girl! Heaven knows, you deserve it."

"I'd love to, Shelly, but who am I kidding? I'm...never mind how many years old!"

I smiled. "Jess, don't you dare think of yourself as being too old for happiness!"

She considered this. "You really think I'm not being foolish? You really think someone would like me?"

"Any man would be nuts *not* to, Jess," I responded, "You're a woman who loves the Lord, you're pretty, you're smart, and you've got a *great* sense of humor. You're also willing to sacrifice for the people you care about. You, girl, have a lot to offer some lucky man."

Jess grinned. "Shelly, you've talked me into it! Once the wedding is over and things settle down, I'll take the plunge and try."

I sat my coffee cup down and gave her a hug. Life had thrown everything, including the kitchen sink, and Jess these last six years. Jeremy and I had spent many an evening praying that the door would open for her to get to enjoy life again. How I would love to see her have a reason to smile again!

"Now about this code...," said Jessica, picking Gage up off the floor.

I sighed. "I love doing computer research for the team, but I would give *anything* to have a starting point! I've tried every code I could think of, and I've just been spinning my wheels."

"What have you tried?"

"Every established code I can find," I said, "I've even compared it to some old manuscript Chris referred me to."

"*And...?*"

"It's similar, but different," I said, "Look here at what I've got."

I sat some of the e-mails out on the coffee table. She looked at them, as puzzled as I was. While she was looking at them, I opened a window on Chris' flash drive. I clicked on a page from the Voynich Manuscript. It showed a bizarre diagram of the galaxy and had some writing on it that had yet to be identified.

"It looks a lot like *this* picture here," said Jess, "But the writing appears different. What is that book, anyway?"

"A book called *The Voynich Manuscript* that no one's been able to figure out," I said, "It's got pages on botany, medicine, astronomy, and other things. At least that's what the pictures look like. The writing is a mystery, as well as the meaning of the book. That's why a lot of people think it's an ancient code for something, but no one knows what."

Jess considered that. "If no one else has been able to figure it out, it stands to reason that *Chase* hasn't either. It looks like he's invented a code system that was inspired by this old book, but he's got his own meaning for it."

"So how do I figure out the meaning of it?" I wondered, "We know the obvious---the code is for

279

criminal intent. But how do we go beyond that?"

Jess frowned, deep in thought. Rex nudged up against me, and I scratched his ear again.

"Let me tell you a bit about Chase as a *person*," said Jess, "Maybe knowing more about who he is will give you a starting point on all this."

Detective Maria Lorenzo's journal

When Chris and Jeremy suggested that I take Tina to a safe house, I was at first concerned. The girl still needed some medical treatment big time. She was starting to hold her own through the withdraw, but wasn't making a whole lot of progress.

Then they told me what this "safe house" was. After they explained themselves, I realized that it made perfect sense and readily agreed. Tina didn't understand what I was doing, but she trusted me while I checked her out of the hospital.

After taking care of checking her out, I found her dressed in jeans and a sweater. She was weak, but eager to leave. I helped her out to my car and, while she buckled herself in, I did a quick check of everything. The brake line was intact, as were the tires. Looking under the hood, I found

280

nothing suspicious wired to the ignition. So far, so good. There's something about nearly getting shot at by a sniper, kidnapped, and threatened with a slow death that will make a person extra cautious!

"So where are we going?" asked Tina as I pulled out of the parking lot.

"There's an outfit that some friends of mine helped out a few months ago," I said, "You'll be safe there."

"These friends," she said weakly, "Are they cops?"

"Private detectives," I answered, "Although, they prefer to call themselves 'consulting detectives.'"

"Oh. Is one of them the guy you told me about, the one who thinks he's Sherlock Holmes?"

"Yes," I answered, "But, you can trust him with your life."

While I drove, I kept looking in my rearview mirror. So far, it didn't look like I was being tailed. But I was going to keep a careful eye out, just in case.

"The place I'm taking you," I continued, "is called the New Hope Rehab clinic. They're good, and they offer you Christian love and friendship as well as medical treatment. They'll also work to help you find a future once you finish your rehab. You couldn't be in finer hands. Detective Anderson helped them out tremendously a few months ago, and they haven't forgotten."

"A future," muttered Tina, "Something other than the life of a prostitute. That would be wonderful!"

"You're not going back into *that* dark world if I can help it," I said firmly, "You're a new creation in Christ, and you're going to have a new life as well! Now, have you thought about any of the things I asked you last night?"

Tina sipped on a water bottle and nodded. "I can think of several times that I was booked into Oklahoma County jail at the same time some of the other girls were busted. A girl gets used to it."

"And…?"

Tina frowned. "I *may* have been arrested at the same time as the Stalker's victims, but I can't be sure. I've been arrested so many times that everything sort of blurs together."

It made sense. It just didn't make my job any easier, especially with arrest records being erased. Who does that sort of thing? I glanced again in the rearview mirror. Still no sign of being followed. Good. Maybe everything would go smoothly.

"OK," I said, "Of the times you were arrested, did any of the other girls say anything about knowing something or someone that would help her?"

For several seconds, Tina said nothing. I could tell she was trying to think, but it was hard because she was weak. That didn't make life easier, but I knew she was trying so I didn't push.

"There was a time a couple of months ago," Tina said finally, "There were five of us girls that the law arrested at once. It may have been the other girls the Stalker killed, but I don't know."

"OK," I said, "Go on. Tell me what you *do* know."

"We were all hired from the web," she said, "We were supposed to entertain some guys at this big party at a mansion over in Oklahoma City. Only the party got raided and we were loaded up into a police van. I didn't know the real names of the other girls—that's one thing that makes this so hard—and since we didn't know each other, we really didn't pay attention."

"So you knew the trade names of the other girls?"

Tina nodded. "That's the only way we knew each other. Anyway, there was this one girl—her

283

trade name was Sweet Dreams---that boasted that no one would ever put her away. She said she had the *trigger*, and if anyone messed with her she'd let everyone know about it."

I raised my eyebrows. This was getting very, very interesting. If I could find out who used the name "Sweet Dreams", then this could blow the case wide open.

"Did she say what this 'trigger' was?"

Tina shook her head. "All she said was that it was her insurance."

Insurance. Right. Getting ahold of this "trigger" probably signed her death warrant. So, this prostitute manages to get a "trigger" that is of high value to Chase Anderson. She mouths off about it when she's busted at a party, and there happens to be five prostitutes arrested together. If I was right, then the victims of the Stalker were the other prostitutes in the police van that hauled Tina off to jail that night.

"Nothing else was said about it?"

"No," said Tina, "One of the guards in the van whispered something to Sweet Dreams. Don't ask me what his name was; I don't know. Anyway, she turned as pale as a ghost and hushed up mighty quick."

"All right," I said, "What about the mansion? Do you remember anything about it? If you know where it was at, that could *really* help."

Tina laughed. "As if I could forget! The mansion belonged to some dude named Philip Rice. He's the king of internet porn movies. All of us girls who were arrested that night were even in a few of his films."

I frowned. Philip Rice was a lowlife that had a long history with the law. He made a fortune filming porno movies for the internet. The only thing was, some of the people in his filthy films were minors. He should have been put away to do hard time long ago, but he kept getting off on technicalities. Rumor had it that he had powerful friends, but nothing had ever been proved.

I sat back. We had another hour's drive to the clinic. I kept glancing into the rearview mirror every few seconds. After a few minutes, my cell phone rang, startling me. I was grateful for Bluetooth. It sure made answering the phone while driving safer. I glanced at the phone, saw Crystal's number, and put the phone on speaker.

"Hi, Crystal," I said, "How's everything?"

"Where are you guys at?" asked Crystal, "I was just at the hospital and they said you checked Tina out."

"I wanted to get Tina to the rehab," I said, "She needs it bad. We're on the road now."

"I'm in the hospital parking lot, but I'm about to be on the way," she said, "Don't leave the rehab until I get there."

"All right," I answered, "But tell me…"

"*OH MY STARS!!*" cried Crystal.

Crystal screamed. Tina looked over at me, horrified.

"*Crystal, are you all right?*"

A loud POP filled the speaker. Then another. I could hear glass shattering. Crystal screamed again, and my heart leaped to my throat. Tina looked at me, looking as terrified as I felt.

"Crystal, *ANSWER ME!*"

A third explosion came through the speaker, sounding like a canon. It was the sound of gunfire.

I was already looking for a turnoff. Why in heaven's name are interstates built with so few places to turn around?! Traffic was heavy and not a turnoff was in sight.

"Crystal!" I shrieked, "*What's going on?*"

She didn't say anything. There was the sound of someone moving. Then there was the muffled sounds of voices saying things I couldn't make out. Then there was silence.

"Crystal, are you there? *Speak to me!*"

My only answer was static.

"Crystal," I repeated, "Please talk to me, girl!"

Still nothing. Then I lost the connection.

"*SPEED-DIAL ONE!*" I shouted into the phone.

Up ahead I could see an overpass approaching. I turned on my turn signal and eased over into the far right lane.

"Police dispatch," said a voice.

"This is Detective Maria Lorenzo," I said, "Badge number eight-oh-four. I want to report gunshots fired in the parking lot of *Christ's Church Hospital*. Repeat, gunshots fired at the *Christ's Church Hospital* parking lot. There is at least one possible victim, Crystal Parker. Gunshots were fired on her car. I am on I-40 about to be en-route to the scene. Crystal Parker is a detective; repeat, she is a detective."

"Acknowledged," said the dispatcher, "I am dispatching other units and phoning the hospital as we speak. Over."

"Thank you, dispatch," I said, "Over and out. End call. Speed-dial three."

I made the overpass and navigated my turn. I was now fifteen minutes away from the hospital.

Please, please, please let her be all right!

"Hello, Detective Lorenzo," I heard Chris say, "Has Crystal…"

"Holmes," I interrupted, "Whatever you're doing, you need to drop it. Crystal called me from the hospital parking lot. I was already transporting Tina to New Hope, and I guess I missed her by a few minutes. I heard what sounded like gunfire over the phone, and then Crystal screamed. Holmes, *I can't reach Crystal!*"

There was dead silence on the phone for several seconds.

"We're on our way," said Chris grimly.

"I've already called police dispatch," I said.

"Thanks," he said weakly.

The connection ended. Tina was crying as we turned back to the hospital. Traffic was heavy and, while not exactly moving at a snail's pace, it still wasn't moving fast enough. The traffic was literally bumper to bumper.

"Come *on*," I begged the traffic.

"This Crystal," said Tina, "Is she a friend of yours?"

"Yes," I said weakly, "She's one of my *best* friends, as nice as they come. She's getting married soon…to the detective I just called."

288

Tina swallowed hard. For several seconds she said nothing. Then she turned to me again.

"Maybe she's OK," said Tina, "The police are on their way."

"Maybe," I said, not believing it myself.

After an eternity, we made our way to our exit. Within a couple of minutes, we could see the hospital approaching. I was terrified of what we would find.

CHAPTER SIXTEEN

Shelly Winslow's journal

Jess stood, holding Gage in her arms, thinking hard. She had only known Chase in his early years, before he faked his death and torched their parents' home. The odds that whatever he had used to invent his code was from his childhood years was probably slim. But we had to start somewhere.

"You'll find this ironic, Shelly," she said, "But when Chase and Chris were children, they were as close as they could possibly be."

"That *is* ironic," I agreed.

"They were always playing adventure games they made up," she continued, "They played soldiers, cowboys and Indians, cops and robbers...they even had their own on-going Sherlock Holmes game."

I smiled sadly. "Why do I have the feeling that Chase played Moriarty while Chris was Sherlock Holmes?"

"You've got it," said Jess, "Ever since I found out that Chase was alive and was the crime boss calling himself Moriarty, I figured that all those childhood games inspired him when he decided to become a criminal."

"You're probably right," I said, "Did he ever do things with secret codes when you were kids?"

Jess nodded. "He liked to paint pictures. A lot of times when he and Chris were designing their detective games, Chase would paint pictures and put codes into the paintings."

Chase Anderson an *artist*? That was news to me. I knew he was a criminal scientist, but who would have figured that he had an artistic flair? But still, the thought got me to thinking...

"Jess," I said, "Look at these pictures. See if you recognize any of the kinds of codes that Chase used in the past."

Jess came over to the table and started looking. Handing me Gage, she picked up the pictures, studying them one at a time.

"I don't know, Shelly...it's been years."

"Take your time, Jess."

Jess studied the pictures hard, frowning over the details. I've got to hand it to her; she hadn't seen any of his paintings since they were teenagers, but she was trying with everything she had.

"I'm trying, Shelly," she said finally, "But it's hard. Chase designed so *many* different codes. You see, he was trying so hard to defeat his brother when they played their games that he would invent

291

different codes to make it harder for him. It was always a competition between those two."

"It still is," I said grimly, "Only Chris doesn't know it's with his own brother."

"The thing is," said Jess, "He carried those codes over to the real crimes he committed. You see, Shelly, when he became a drug dealer as a teenager, he used his paintings to cover it up. He told us that he was starting to sell his paintings for extra money.

"What he was really doing was putting the times and locations for the drug sales into those paintings using a code he had designed, just like in *these* pictures. It was when Chris spotted the clues in the pictures and figured out the code for what it was that he took what he knew to the police and Chase was arrested."

"Wow!" I said, "No wonder Chase is so bound and determined to outsmart Chris on this! He's tried his entire life to outsmart Chris, and he's determined to finally succeed before leaving the country."

"Crazy, huh?" asked Jessica.

A new thought struck me and I stared at the pictures again.

"Jessica," I said quickly, "I think I've got it! You've just given me the key to it all!"

Jeremy Winslow's journal [kept on flash drive]
We had just finished up with Chandler's apartment when the call came in. We had shut down the computer, planted hidden cameras throughout the apartment, and were loading up the equipment in the van when Chris' *Compu-Watch* signaled an incoming call. Thirty seconds later we were speeding through traffic. When I say speeding, I mean *speeding*. Chris was driving, and he had both feet flat on the floor. He went from one lane to another, darting in front of oncoming cars and earning angry honks from people he cut off.

"Fool that I am, Watson," growled Chris, "I make Hendricks look like a genius by comparison! I should *never* have let her go off on her own!"

"You sent her to team up with Lorenzo," I pointed out, "You didn't think Crystal *would* be alone!"

We darted in front of a semi with barely four seconds to spare. I looked through the back window and saw nothing except the grill of the truck. I heard it squeal on its brakes, and my stomach melted through the floor.

"Holmes," I said slowly, "We're not going to do Crystal any good if you get us both killed in a car crash!"

"We won't crash," he said firmly.

A new sound greeted my ears. I looked and saw flashing red lights coming up behind us. Yes, sure enough, a patrol car was right behind us. Chris kept on driving.

"Uh, Holmes," I said gently, "You may want to pull over."

"No I don't!"

The police car got into the opposite lane and pulled up behind us. The officers were motioning for us to pull over. Chris ignored them and kept on driving.

"Sherlock, my man," I said, "They're telling us to pull over!"

"Here's our exit," said Chris.

So help me, Chris made the exit, ignoring the police, and the police pulled in right behind us. Staring out the back window, I could see one of the police officers calling for backup on the radio. This day was just getting better and better.

Our van shot left the interstate and pulled onto Main Street. The hospital was just a hundred yards ahead. The problem was, there were two other police cars *seventy* yards ahead of us, and they had spike strips out on the street. That was when Chris sped up.

"Have mercy," I said, "You're not going to…"

He did. He hit the spike strips and we felt all four tires go flat. Chris kept going. Soon we had all three patrol cars behind us—lights flashing and sirens blaring---and Chris led them into the hospital parking lot. Up ahead, we could see several other patrol cars with their lights flashing. Chris led the officers chasing us right up to them. We came to a screeching halt right in front of six other patrol cars. An officer from one of the cars behind us came running up to us on Chris' side, gun drawn. Another officer came on my side.

"Get out with your hands up!" shouted the officer on Chris' side.

Chris shrugged and stepped out of the van. I did likewise. Our hands were high in the air. Two other officers were patting us down, and withdrew our firearms from our holsters.

"Do you have permits for these?" demanded an officer, whose badge read "Tanner".

"Yes," said Chris, "We're detectives."

"That may be," said Officer Tanner, "But right now you're under arrest for---,"

At that moment, I caught a glimpse of Detective Lorenzo pushing her way through the mob of officers. She glared at Tanner angrily.

295

"If you're through trying to arrest honest detectives," she said, "We have a crime scene up here to investigate."

Tanner blinked. "But do you know what these jokers…"

"A fellow detective has been ambushed in this parking lot," snapped Lorenzo, "These detectives are here at my request. One of them is the fiancée of the victim. And do you *really* want to go down in history as the policeman who arrested Sherlock Holmes?"

Tanner looked very, very puzzled. "Sherlock…Holmes?"

"Return their weapons this second and help us with a *real* investigation," snapped Lorenzo.

Meekly, Tanner ordered our guns returned. Chris led the way through the line of officers and we came to Crystal's car…or, to be precise…what was left of it. The car was riddled with bullets. The passenger side of the car was caved in from the impact of the rounds. Officers were gathering spent shells and bagging them. Other officers were taking pictures while still others dusted for prints. Over in the distance, we could see other officers interviewing witnesses.

Chris' face was pale as he observed the progress. For the first time since I've known him, he was totally frozen in place. I swallowed, thinking of everything I had ever heard about the deaths of his family.

Lord, I prayed, *Chris has lost so much. Don't let this be happening a second time! Please!*

"Crystal…," he whispered hoarsely.

For another second Chris just stood there. Then he burst forward towards the car. I tried to hold him back, but he was a wild man. He shook me off and looked into the driver's seat.

The car was empty. There was no blood. No signs that anyone had been hit by bullets or shattered glass. Crystal was just gone.

"They didn't kill her," said Chris, "They *kidnapped* her, just like they did me a few months back. She must have dove on the floorboards the second she was ambushed. They figured she would, and were able to snatch her."

"Then she's alive," I said, "Thank God!"

"I was en-route to New Hope with Tina when Crystal called," said Lorenzo, "I'm so sorry. I had no idea she was coming to meet me!"

"She must have assumed you were still there and didn't call ahead," said Chris, "Where's Tina now? We have to keep her safe at all costs."

Lorenzo nodded. "She's waiting in my car. There's no need for her to see any of this stuff.

297

From what we've gathered from witnesses and the shells we've gathered, they weren't looking to kill her. They wanted to kidnap her. Witnesses say that Crystal had just gotten back into her car when a van blocked her exit. Four masked gunmen started shooting at her car with AK assault rifles. Then they forced her out of her car and into the van. They had snatched her and got away in all of thirty seconds."

Chris exhaled. The man had been holding his breath the entire time he was looking in the car.

"If they took her alive," said Chris, "Then they intend to use her to their advantage. We can expect a call or text message soon. That gives us a little time. The witnesses are great, but we also need security camera footage. Those spent shells look like they were from AK 37's. Am I right? I thought so."

"Tina's remembered a few things," said Lorenzo, "And everything you thought is right on the button. She was arrested with four other prostitutes a few months back. One of them said something about having something called 'the trigger' that guaranteed her safety. Then one of the arresting officers whispered something to this prostitute that scared her into shutting up. This was not long before the Stalker murders began."

"Who was this prostitute?" demanded Chris.

Lorenzo shrugged. "I don't know…yet. Her trade name was 'Sweet Dreams.' If we identify her, we'll be able to prove what we suspect."

"The other four prostitutes arrested that night *have* to be the victims claimed by the Stalker," I said.

"*And* the motive is to retrieve this 'trigger', whatever it is," muttered Chris, "They think we have information about it. That's why they snatched Crystal…to force us to turn over this 'trigger'."

"I can say one thing," said Lorenzo, "Tina doesn't know what it is. Believe me, she's scared enough to talk if she had anything to say. I just wish we had a quick way to *prove* that the other four prostitutes that were arrested along with Tina are the girls that the Stalker already killed."

Chris dug into his pocket and pulled out his flash drive. Then he calmly dropped it into Lorenzo's hands.

"A present for you, Lorenzo," said Chris, "Here is hard evidence of the Stalker's identity. He kept a library of pictures on his personal computer showing before and after pictures of the Stalker's victims. This flash drive has the entire hard drive downloaded on it."

299

Lorenzo's eyes went wide. "You *know* who the Stalker is?"

"That's right," I said, "And we have proof of his ties with the Crimson Dragons. The man had a book of codes that we know has ties to Chase Anderson."

"The thing is," said Chris, "You're not going to like who it is."

"There's very little about this case that I *do* like, Holmes," snapped Lorenzo.

Lorenzo's face went grim when we told her the Stalker's identity. She hung her head and said several things I could never say in mixed company. It was always discouraging to discover a fellow detective is dirty. I could remember the heartache we had gone through when we thought Summers was corrupt.

"We need to bring Chandler in," said Lorenzo, "Bring him in and make him talk. He's *got* to know where they've taken Crystal."

"My sentiments exactly," said Chris, "And may I talk to Miss Stewart? There's some questions I'd dearly love to ask her."

Lorenzo nodded. She led us past the crime scene to her Ford Explorer. Chris' face was a mask of grim determination. On the first case I had worked with him, there was a time when Crystal

300

had apparently been shot in the chest. At first we thought she was died, not realizing that she had been wearing a bullet-proof vest fitted with phony blood capsules to give the illusion of actually being shot.

When Chris realized that she was still alive, he had said one thing to the shooter: "*If you succeeded in killing her, I would have personally put you in a body bag in small pieces. And I wouldn't have cared what the police did to me afterwards!!*"

I could easily imagine the turmoil he was going through now. He had seen pictures of what the Stalker did to his victims and we had hard proof that he was in league with Chris' mortal enemy. Now his fiancée was totally at their mercy. My heart broke for the man.

"Tina," called Lorenzo, "We need to…"

Lorenzo stopped suddenly as she came to her car. She stood speechless with her jaw hanging open. In a flash we could see why.

Lorenzo's car was empty. The passenger door was open. The passenger side seatbelt was cut, and Tina Stewart was gone. She had been kidnapped not thirty yards from right under the very nose of over twenty police officers.

CHAPTER SEVENTEEN

Shelly Winslow's journal

"You've just given me the key to the code!" I told Jessica again.

Jess looked at me blankly. "What did I do?"

"Chris cracked Chase's codes when Chase was dealing drugs," I said, "Was the cypher to the code ever published?"

Jess blinked. "I don't know. I know it was reported that Chris broke the code, but whether the key to the code itself was ever made public, I have no earthly idea."

I quickly began web searching for everything available about Chase Anderson. It didn't take long. Just like with Chris and the Stalker's victims, everything had been erased. Even his trial information was nowhere to be found.

"I'll say this for him," I said quickly, "the man's thorough. Jessica, do you have *anything* from those days in a scrapbook or something? Did your parents save anything?"

Jessica thought for a moment. Then her eyes flew open wide.

"Yes! Mom was *forever* keeping diaries and scrapbooks," said Jess.

"Do you still have any of them?" I asked.

"*Maybe*," she answered, "There was a tiny metal safe that survived the house fire. It was filled with papers, not money. I've kept it in my garage for years."

I stood up. "Let's go check it out! Maybe…"

The phone rang. I recognized the Caller-Id number as Jeremy's *Compu-Watch* number. I quickly answered it and put it on speaker phone.

"Hi, Gorgeous," said Jeremy, sounding as exhausted as I felt.

"Hi yourself, handsome," I answered, "How's everything?"

"Do you want the good news or the bad news first?" answered Jeremy.

I swallowed. This did not sound good. "What's the good news?"

"We know who the Stalker is and can prove he's in league with Chase," said Jeremy.

"That's great, darling!" I said, "But what's the bad news?"

"They've got our only living witness," said Jeremy, "and honey… I…I don't know how to say this."

I swallowed, terrified of what he was trying to say.

"Jeremy, what is it?"

"Honey," whispered Jeremy, "They've taken Crystal!"

"Oh no!" I cried, "Oh dear heavens, no!"

Jeremy Winslow's journal [kept on flash drive]
Chris studied Lorenz's car with a fine toothed comb. Looking through the magnifying glass on his Swiss Army Knife, he first examined the area surrounding the car. He literally crawled on the ground peering through the lens.

"There were two of them," he said, "one of them I would say is five-foot-seven and a chain smoker; you can tell from the number of times he flicked his ashes. He wore sneakers. Watson, get some pictures. The second one wore dress shoes, and—by Jove, look at this! There's grease-paint on the door handle. Our second man was in disguise!"

"Disguise," I said, "Then it was someone that Tina knew?"

"Or someone that the police are looking for," said Chris, "Perhaps Moriarty himself."

"That's insane!" said Lorenzo, "This place is crawling with police officers!"

"As I said," answered Chris, "He's in disguise. Perhaps he's disguised as a doctor…or even a police officer. Look here, Lorenzo, at the length of the second man's stride as he walked. I would place this man at being the exact same height as Moriarty. He couldn't show his true face, but who would look twice at a doctor at a hospital or a policeman at a crime scene?"

"True…" said Lorenzo.

"We know for sure that Moriarty wanted Tina Stewart," said Chris, "He's looking for something called 'the trigger.' Picture Moriarty coming to the hospital hoping to snatch her disguised as a doctor. But, you prevented that by checking Tina out of the hospital.

"Before Moriarty can think of what to do next, Crystal arrives at the hospital to talk to both you and Tina. Moriarty has Crystal kidnapped while you are talking to her on the phone. When you returned to the hospital to oversee the crime scene, Moriarty had the perfect opportunity to snatch Tina while you were with the other officers."

"But how could he *know* that he would need all that extra manpower to pull off Crystal's kidnapping?" demanded Lorenzo.

"One of the reasons Moriarty has been so difficult to track down is because he always brings a backup plan in case something goes wrong," explained Chris.

"I'll have the security cameras checked," said Lorenzo, "This was out in plain public sight. The cameras *had* to have picked up some pretty good footage."

"You do that, detective," said Chris, "What I...,"

Chris swallowed. He had been leaning over into the car when he bent over further. When he stood up, he was holding two large objects in in hands. One was a cell phone. One was a large watch.

"I take it that this is Tina's cell phone?" asked Chris.

Lorenzo nodded.

"And this is Crystal's *Compu-Watch*," said Chris, "I had hoped we could track them by the GPS chips either in Crystal's watch or Tina's cell phone. So much for that."

A gloom fell over us. Chris took samples of the grease paint in dead silence while I took pictures. Crystal's car was still being processed by a team of officers. No one had to say the obvious: Chase had two hostages. Once he had what he wanted, their lives were worth nothing. Lorenzo's cell phone beeped. She instantly looked at it and frowned.

"I've got a text message," she said, "And the number it's from is withheld."

"What's it say?" asked Chris anxiously.

"'They're both alive for now,'" read Lorenzo, "'Find the trigger. Instructions for delivery will be coming shortly.'"

"Alive," I said, "Thank heavens!"

"Note the operative words, '*for now*,'" snarled Chris, "Detective, did Tina say *anything* about what this 'trigger' could be?"

"She didn't know," insisted Lorenzo, "It could be anything."

Chris continued investigating the car. His face was flushed, eyes alert, looking for all the world like a bloodhound on the scent. He covered the car inch by inch through the magnifying lens on his knife. Then he returned to the ground surrounding Lorenzo's car.

"Aha! Moriarty approaches the car with our chain smoking friend," muttered Chris, "Moriarty opens the car door. Tina unbuckled her belt herself. No signs of a struggle. Of course, with Moriarty and friend in disguise—probably as policemen—it would have been easy to set Tina's mind at ease. Tina stops, again no sign of a struggle.

"Look at the motor oil on the ground here! She simply got into the car with them! Then they drove away. It probably took all of about a minute."

Chris stood, pocketed his knife, and faced us. He faced us grimly.

"Detective," said Chris, "Unless we learn what this 'trigger' is that Moriarty wants so badly, we're going to have to pull off the best bluff in history to get Crystal and Tina back safely. I believe it's time to encourage Detective Chandler to enlighten us."

Lorenzo nodded and reached for her radio.

Shelly Winslow's journal [kept in shorthand]

Jessica's garage reminded me of my own. It was filled to the max with boxes and crates that hadn't been looked at in ages. Officially, it was a two car garage. However, Jess would be doing good to fit one car in it.

The enormity of the task we were facing overwhelmed me. So did the importance of what we were doing. It had been of vital importance that we find a key to this code before, and now it was even more so. Fortunately, our security task force—the parents of the Baker Street Irregulars—were assisting us. From the second we told them of the kidnapping, wild horses wouldn't have been able to keep them from helping us. More than a few of them reminded us of things that Crystal had done to help their sons go from being street toughs to getting back into church.

Just hearing of all the nice things she had done for these people made me all the more determined to help find her. My best friend and the only living witness that Jeremy and Chris had were in the hands of killers. One of those killers was the Stalker himself. I had read enough of the Stalker case to know that what he did to his victims was incredibly obscene. The thought that they could end up like those poor women we had read about in the papers...

Any lead we could get was vital. Chris and Jeremy no doubt were processing the crime scene with a fine toothed comb. I still had the task of breaking the code. If we could find the key to it, *maybe* it could help us figure out what this 'trigger' is that Chase wanted so badly. If I was right and this code was tied to past codes that Chase had invented, *maybe* some papers that Jess had saved from her childhood would help. That was a lot of maybes. But, it was all I had.

"All right," I said, "Where do we start?"
"Far wall, close to the bottom," said Jessica.
"Of course, of course," I agreed.

Jessica led me to the back wall. Gage was asleep in his carrier. I sat him down close by, and I started lifting boxes. All of us opened the lids to various boxes and handed them to Jessica. She would glance threw them and set them to the side. With every box she sat aside, my mood worsened. After the first hour, I started losing patience. The lives of two people, one of whom was my best friend, could depend on us finding the elusive needle in the haystack, and we were getting nowhere!

"If we don't find it soon," I said, "I'm going to have to stop long enough for me to get Tim from school."

"Some of us will go with you to school if we need to," said one of the parents, "while the rest continues to help Mrs. Peterson."

Jess nodded and frowned as I handed her another box. She opened it up and smiled.

"Here we go," said Jess, "Here's some things of my mother's. It's just what we need!"

A loud cheer erupted from all of the parents. I looked in anxiously. There inside were some photo albums, scrapbooks, and diaries. Bingo!

"This is it," said Jess, "If Mom kept anything from the Chase's trial years ago, it would be in here."

I picked up Gage while Jess carried the box to the car. She selected some diaries while I strapped Gage into his car seat, and then she put the box in the back seat beside Gage. She started looking through a diary while I climbed into the driver's seat.

"We need to get Tim from school," I said, starting the engine, "We'll go through all this when we get back to the house."

"I'll start with these diaries," said Jess, "You just drive."

Crystal Parker's journal [kept in a memo pad]

I was alive. I don't know *how*, but I was still alive. I had just got to my car after finding out that Maria Lorenzo had checked Tina out of the hospital, was talking to Lorenzo on the phone, and was starting the car when it happened.

A blue van pulled up in front of my car, and men in ski masks jumped out, guns blazing. I instinctively ducked, thanking God that I hadn't yet buckled my seat belt. The windshield exploded and a shower of glass came down on top of me. Before I knew what was happening, the door opened and a masked man yanked me to my feet.

I offered no resistance. What could I do? There were two men beside me holding AK assault rifles! Both of them wore ski masks; one red and the other green. They pushed me into the van. Another masked man was behind the wheel of the van. He had on a black ski mask. There was no way I would ever be able to identify them. That was a point in my favor. If I couldn't identify them, there was a chance that I might get out of this alive. I was pushed towards the back seat, where I buckled my seat belt.

"One minute," said the driver, "Check her out. We don't want her bringing along any weapons or tracking devices."

He gunned the engine and we were off. My kidnappers found my gun and proceeded to tear through my purse.

"No cell phone," said the man, "Since when does anyone leave home without a cell phone these days?"

"Keep searching," said the driver, "She has to have one *somewhere*. Look good; cell phones have GPS tracking chips."

"I must have dropped it," I said weakly.

"Keep searching," growled the driver.

I prayed they were stupid. When they didn't find a phone, maybe they really would believe that I dropped it. I had been using the *Compu-Watch* to call Lorenzo when I was attacked. I knew there was a tracking system in the watch—that was how we had been able to trail Jeremy yesterday. If they didn't figure out that my watch could do more than tell time, Chris and Jeremy would be able to track me easily.

The goon brothers dumped my purse on the floor. Then they looked at me. One of them grabbed my wrist and looked at my arm.

"Well, well," said one of them, "Looks like those fancy Dick Tracy watches have been invented after all."

My heart sank as the watch was yanked off my wrist. Whatever they intended to do, I was truly on my own. Red Ski Mask showed the watch to the driver. The driver parked the van, took my watch from Red Ski Mask, and stepped out of the van. A few seconds later, he got back behind the wheel and we took off.

We drove forever in total silence. No one said a word, and I was afraid to. I found a memo pad on the floorboard and scribbled a few quick notes and prayed it would be found if the worst happened. I didn't know how they knew I would be at the hospital or what would happen once we got to wherever we were going. I just knew I was going to have to look for an opening to get the upper hand. My life depended on it.

Mentally, I was praying and thinking. I knew there would be no reasoning with these clowns. They had their orders, and they knew the penalty for disobedience. But, there were a few things in my favor.

The crime had been pulled off in broad daylight. There would be witnesses and security camera footage. Maybe the cameras would have a good clear image of the make of the van and the license plate.

Certainly, Chris and Jeremy would be assisting the police and find enough clues to find me. There would be road blocks set up, and a BOLO—Be On the Look Out—would be put out for the van. They'd find me in no time. All I had to do was stay calm and not anger these jokers and trust that God would send some help in time.

I couldn't say how long we drove, but it seemed like it was forever and a day. But eventually, the van slowed to a stop. Everyone started unbuckling their seatbelts.

"OK," said the Driver, "Let's go."

We were on a deserted gravel road. Around us were bushes, trees, and absolutely no houses. I was starting to feel incredibly lonely. I heard the sound of an approaching vehicle and rejoiced to see another van approaching. It was a green Nissan and came to a screeching halt right beside us. Behind the wheel was a man in a blue ski mask.

"Let's go," said Red Ski Mask, "Time to switch vans."

My heart sank. A different van! Any security camera footage showing me being forced into a van would be useless now! Even if Chris figured out we'd changed vehicles, there's no way that he'd know *which* vehicle I'd been put in!

"Let's go!" snarled Red Ski Mask.

Reluctantly, I climbed into the van.

Jeremy Winslow's journal [kept on flash drive]

Detective Chandler sat before us, a defiant look on his face. We had found him doing paperwork at police headquarters, and had been amused when he had been dragged into the interrogation room. His hands were handcuffed behind his back, making him most uncomfortable. Not that we cared about his comfort, mind you.

"All right," said Lorenzo, "Let's try it again."

"I've got nothing to say," said Chandler, "You've got *nothing*."

"Really?" asked Chris, "You've got a computer hard drive full of pictures of each of the

315

Stalker's victims, taken *before* the murders while the victims were bound and helpless. As we speak, every computer file you've got is being examined by good, honest detectives. It didn't take long of looking up your records to know that you had a year of pre-med before you decided to become a police officer, and we've known for a while that the Stalker has a certain amount of medical knowledge."

Chandler's smile faded a little.

"A Bible I found on your coffee table wasn't a Bible at all," I said, "It was actually a book of what we suspect to be codes that Moriarty is using to contact his people."

"Then," said Chris, "There is the little matter of your computer being used to hack into computers and erasing official records...even income tax records at the IRS."

"My IP address was supposed to be...I mean..." stammered Chandler.

Lorenzo smiled. "Keep going, Chandler. You're doing fine. As we speak, a warrant is being issued to examine all of your phone records and banking information. Your case files are being examined line by line.

"We're especially interested in why you destroyed evidence on the Stalker case...but then, since we suspect that you *are* the Stalker, the 'why' of your destroying evidence is pretty obvious. I'm pretty sure that DNA found on a handkerchief at one of the crime scenes will be a match to yours, and then you'll be up before a grand jury."

Chandler was starting to sweat furiously. He pulled out a handkerchief and wiped his brow.

"Those girls were *nothing*," insisted Chandler, "Just a bunch of hookers! They're nothing!"

"What those poor girls did for a living doesn't matter," said Chris evenly, "What matters is that they were murdered. They were still *people*; people who had as much right to life, liberty, and the pursuit of happiness as you.

"You don't get a free pass to hunt down people and kill them just because of their chosen profession. However, we all know that you didn't kill them simply because you like to kill. Moriarty thought they knew something, didn't he?"

Chandler's eyes were wide. "I don't know what you're talking about!"

Chris stood over Chandler, his face a mask of stone. A part of me was worried about Chris being in the interrogation room with Chandler. It was normal police procedure to *never* allow a detective to be on a case where family or friends

317

were involved. There were way too many emotions that could get in the way. The love of his life was in the hands of his mortal enemy, and he had seen what Chase could do to his enemies. Could Chris *possibly* hope to control his emotions right now?

"Allow me to enlighten you," whispered Chris softly, "Moriarty is trying to pull off one final score before fleeing the country, and taking revenge on me in the process. He had something in his possession that he calls 'the trigger'. This so-called trigger was stolen by a prostitute working for him."

The color began to drain from Chandler's face. Sweat was pouring off of him in rivers.

"The prostitute who stole it was arrested along with a few other prostitutes as a result of a raid where they were entertaining at a party," continued Chris, "The prostitute who stole it mentioned that she had it and it was her insurance."

We had his attention now. Chandler had to be wondering how much more we knew and how he could wrangle any kind of a deal from us.

"When she talked about having it," continued Chris, "She signed her death warrant. She and all of the other girls in that police vans instantly became targets of Moriarty's gang. There were five altogether. Someone observed that there were five targets, just as Jack the Ripper claimed five victims in 1888. Moriarty decided to disguise the murders as the work of a lone maniac copying Jack the Ripper's work. He had two goals—to silence the talk about the trigger and to recover it."

"That's where you came in, Chandler," added Lorenzo, "You became his assassin in this filthy business. You used your resources as a detective to track the victims down. As the detective on the case, you were in the perfect position to cover up any and all evidence that would lead to the truth."

"The photo album on your hard drive alone frees the innocent man you allowed to take the fall for your crimes," I put in, "He became a handy fall guy because his knowledge of the Ripper murders led him to offer his assistance to the police."

"Once the money trail is followed," said Chris, "I am positive that it will explain your willingness to throw away an honored career to throw your lot in with Moriarty. I've yet to meet an honest detective who can afford the kinds of things I saw in your apartment."

Chandler looked at each of us hard. We had him dead to rights and he knew it. There was no explaining away the sheer magnitude of evidence that we had against him. No matter what he had accomplished as a detective before he went corrupt,

319

he would go down in history only as the Oklahoma City Stalker, and as a crooked cop who worked for the mob. Unlike the father of Detective Summers—who had sold out to get a life-saving transplant for his wife—Chandler sold out his honor for the almighty dollar. Sad.

"What is it you want?" demanded Chandler, "You must want something, or else you would have just booked me and tossed the key."

"There's two things you're going to tell us," said Lorenzo, "We need to know what the trigger is, and we need to know where they've taken Miss Stewart and Miss Parker."

Chandler shook his head. "You have no idea what they'll do to me if I talk."

"Yes we do," said Chris, "That's why we're prepared to spread the word that you fed us every bit of that evidence you just heard us speak."

Chandler nearly flew out of his chair. "*WHAT?!* That's crazy!"

"Is it?" asked Lorenzo, "We had to get the evidence from somewhere. All it will take is a few well-placed hints and Moriarty will get the impression that you had been working undercover all along and was about to turn on him."

"No," stammered Chandler, "You can't!"

Chris grabbed Chandler by the collar and jerked him to his feet. Then he pushed back until he had Palmer up against the wall. Chris' eyes were blazing crimson fury.

"Police brutality," muttered Chandler.

"I'm not official police," said Chris, "I'm a consulting detective. The rules of police brutality don't apply here."

Lorenzo smiled at me and motioned for me to follow her. I nodded and started to walk.

"WAIT!" called Chandler, "Where are you two going?"

"It's been a long day," said Lorenzo, "I need some coffee."

"Me, too," I said, "We'll be back in, say, a half hour or so. Anything you need, Holmes?"

Chris' eyes were terrible to behold. "Just be sure we're not disturbed for the next thirty minutes, Watson. I'm simply going to ask this gentleman real nicely where I can find Crystal Parker and Tina Stewart."

"Oh," said Lorenzo, "And just to let you know, Chandler, Crystal Parker is Mr. Holmes' fiancée. Have a nice chat with Mr. Holmes, Chandler. You two play nice now, you hear?"

Lorenzo opened the door. All of Chandler's protests didn't stop Lorenzo from walking out of the room. I followed. I was just starting to shut the door when Chandler caved in.

"WAIT!" shrieked Chandler, "COME BACK!!!!"

Lorenzo led the way back into the room, all smiles. Chris was holding Chandler by his collar some three inches off the floor. Chris' face reminded me of the shark from *JAWS* looking at its next victim. Chandler's face, however, was the most interesting shade of green that I'd ever seen.

"You were saying...?" began Lorenzo.

"First," said Chandler, "Tell this guy to let me go."

"You heard the man," I said, "Let him go."

Chris shrugged and loosened his grip on Chandler. He fell to the floor and rolled over on his side. Chris continued to stand over him.

"Where are they?" demanded Chris, "And what is the trigger? Answer the questions in that order, and do it now."

Lorenzo helped Chandler back to his chair. He glared at us with a look of sheer contempt. So he hated us. I could live with that. We weren't the ones that had the lives of four girls on our conscience. We weren't the ones that sold out to the mob. Whatever happened to Chandler in the future was bound to be better than he deserved.

"I don't know where he's taken them," said Chandler, "I swear I don't. He only tells us what we need to know. All he told me was which girls to kill and to get the trigger back. He only tells each of us people what we need to know to complete the job we're assigned to do. That way, if anything goes wrong, no one knows all the details of his plans. We can't tell what we don't know."

Chris pounded the wall in frustration. I hated to admit it, but what Chandler said made perfect sense. That was one of the reasons why it had taken so long just to unmask who Moriarty really is.

"The trigger," continued Chandler, "is a computer flash drive. It's called the trigger because of what it does."

"And what, pray tell, does it do?" demanded Lorenzo, "Or is that something *else* you don't know?"

"Oh, I know all right," said Chandler, "My cousin was in on designing it. *He* told me even though Moriarty didn't. The trigger is a computer virus that Moriarty designed."

"What does it do?" asked Chris.

"It's designed to get into everything computerized," said Chandler, "And shut every computer down. Remember back at the turn of the

323

century when so many people were afraid that all the computers would stop working?"

Lorenzo snorted. "The so-called Y2K bug. But all that turned out to be a lot of hooey."

Chandler nodded. "But this is an *intentional* virus designed to get into everything: hospital computers, defense computers, businesses, personal computers, the works. It's designed to so thoroughly corrupt computers that they'll never work again."

We looked at each other, puzzled and horrified. One of the things about modern life was that so much of *everything* was tied to computers. Whether people liked it or not, everything operated through computers and the internet these days.

If every computer suddenly crashed with no warning, society would be in absolute chaos. People in the hospital could conceivably die because hospital equipment was computerized. Businesses could fail. The list could go on endlessly. There would be rioting in the streets, and there was no telling how many people would die as a result.

"Why would he do this?" asked Chris, "Moriarty never does anything unless he could profit from it. Why would he go to so much effort just to crash the nation's computers?"

Chandler sighed. "There's an interesting side effect in this computer virus. When it hits the computers in our nation's banks, the virus will do more than shut the computers down. The computers will wire every dollar in the banks to Moriarty's Swiss Bank account."

The full enormity of what Chandler had just said hit us with the force of a brick. If this so-called "trigger" actually worked, it would cripple the entire country. Not only would the nation's computers be useless, but our society would be bankrupt. Moriarty would walk away from all this with a king's fortune and America would lie in ashes.

CHAPTER EIGHTEEN

Shelly Winslow's journal [kept in shorthand]

After Jess and I picked Tim up from school, we hurried home. Jeremy and I always allowed Tim a half hour of play time with Rex before starting homework. The two best friends chased each other around the house while Jess and I got back to serious business.

We went through the diaries of Jess' mother line by line. None of them gave us a clue to the code. We read about the heartache of an abusive marriage and how it turned her mean herself. We also read about how devastated she was to have one son testifying against the other. But about the code Chris had deciphered, there wasn't a word. The scrapbooks, however, revealed everything. The second scrapbook we picked up had article after article about the trial of Chase Anderson. There were articles and pictures of Chase's initial arrest, the grand-jury indictment, and of Chris' testimony.

Then we saw it. Towards the center of the scrapbook were lengthy articles devoted entirely to Chase's unique codes. Diagram after diagram detailed how Chris broke the codes and gave the translations.

"Look at this!" I exclaimed to Jess, "According to this, the pictures were just basically decorations to throw the police off if they got too close. The real message is the little markings on each painting."

"I never would have guessed this," added Jess, "Those letters in the messages are from the Hebrew alphabet, written backwards like they were written in a mirror!"

I nodded. "Even if someone started plugging in different languages, they wouldn't have got it right with Hebrew because the letters are the mirror image of each Hebrew letter. Amazing!"

I quickly reached for the phone and speed-dialed Jeremy.

Jeremy Winslow's journal [kept on flash drive]

"We want the key to the code," said Chris.

Chandler glared at Chris. Then, incredibly, a smile slowly etched its way across Chandler's face.

"Having a bit of trouble figuring out the code, Mr. Holmes?" asked Chandler sarcastically.

"There are two lives at stake," said Chris, "We don't have much time. We need that cypher key."

For several seconds, Chandler stared at us. Then he started to laugh. We glared down at him,

327

and he laughed some more.

"Sherlock, my friend," chuckled Chandler, "I think I just heard the sound of a deal being offered. What is that deal, you ask? All right, I'll tell you. For starters, I get full immunity from prosecution."

"Forget it!" snapped Lorenzo, "There's no way you're getting immunity."

"My copy of the cypher key is nowhere in my house," said Chandler, "By now, you've figured that out. I put it in a secret place just in case I came under suspicion. If you want it, I get full immunity."

Chris opened his mouth to speak, but was cut off when I heard a ringing coming from my watch. Chandler looked at me, fascinated, when I pressed a button on the watch to answer the phone.

"Hi, handsome," I heard Shelly's voice say, "How would you like some good news?"

"I'll take it," I answered.

"We've got the key to the code," said Shelly.

"What's that, you say?" I said loudly, "You've figured out the code?"

"Impossible!" snarled Chandler.

"It's a code that Moriarty used years ago, just before he was arrested the first time," continued Shelly, "Ignore all the pictures. The key is that the

328

writing is Hebrew words written backwards, like in a mirror."

"It's Hebrew written backwards," I repeated to Chris, "Like in a mirror."

Chris raised his eyebrows. He had the look of a man who had just heard something familiar and was trying to recall where he'd heard it before. Lorenzo, however, had a look of pure happiness on her face.

"Hebrew written backwards," said Lorenzo, "How interesting. What you are now seeing, Chandler, is the sight of your demands for immunity waving bye-bye."

Chandler hung his head in utter defeat. He was facing the reality of being a cop in prison. It was entirely possible that he would encounter some of the convicts he had personally put away, and probably wasn't going to last more than a month.

I tried to find it in my heart to find some sort of pity for the man, but it was totally impossible. He had put his lot in with gangsters for money, and now the consequences for those actions were knocking on his door.

"Shelly, my gorgeous wife," I said, "Remind me to tell you about how wonderful your sense of timing is, as well as everything else about you."

329

"I'll be *sure* to remind you," said Shelly, "Just get Crystal and that witness back. Love you!"

Things started moving quickly after that. Chandler was escorted back to his cell, cursing to himself. Armed with evidence, Lorenzo secured Dr. Price's immediate release. After we told him about the language code, Price was able to recommend two language professors at the university to tackle the monumental task of deciphering the code book.

While Lorenzo studied the security camera footage frame by frame, Chris and I set about the task of finding Chase's long lost "trigger". Chandler finally confessed to us that Amanda Witherspoon was the prostitute who had stolen it from Chase. That meant finding her personal effects and going through them piece by piece.

Our first step was studying the personal effects that were found with her body at the crime scene. Some friends of ours in the department made sure we could get into the evidence locker undisturbed and soon we found a cardboard box with everything found at the crime scene. Wearing rubber gloves, we sat the box on a table outside the evidence locker and opened the box. There wasn't much: a purse, bloodstained clothing, and a single shoe. What a pitiful inventory to testify to a person's life---a few items in a cardboard box.

"Interesting," said Chris, "Only one shoe. The last time I checked, most people with two legs wear *two* shoes."

"Which proves...?"

"Only that we were correct in surmising that the victims were killed elsewhere and dumped where they were found."

Chris opened the purse. Inside where items you might find in any woman's purse—keys with a penknife hooked to the keychain, a checkbook, a wallet, a hairbrush, makeup, and lipstick. Chris got out his Swiss Army Knife and selected the magnifying glass.

"Car keys," muttered Chris, "Here we have an apartment key. Nothing of interest...typical penknife, Watson, with toothpick and tweezers...by Jove, what have we here? The tweezers don't seem to match up with its slot on the penknife. See how there's a tiny gap between the head of the tweezers and the slot for the tweezers in the knife's handle?"

I looked through the magnifying glass. Sure enough, there was the tiniest of gaps between the plastic head of the tweezers and the knife handle.

"So, it's a factory defect," I said.

"Maybe, maybe not," mused Chris.

Chris sat down his own knife and gently tugged on the tweezers on the penknife. But instead of finding a small pair of tweezers, we found a tiny key. The key was incredibly small and firmly attached to the head of what we took to be a tweezers.

"Ingenious," mused Chris, "Who would have guessed to look inside a penknife for a key?"

"That's great, Holmes," I said, "But what does it go to?"

"Hopefully, Watson, Miss Witherspoon has left us some other clues behind."

The wallet was a big nothing. Two hundred dollars in cash, some pictures of Amanda and her parents during happier times, a credit card, and debit card, and seventy-five cents change. Her checkbook was a typical checkbook, no surprises there. Chris examined her compact and found nothing but makeup.

With a sigh, I picked up Amanda's lipstick tube. I could probably bet my next paycheck that there was nothing in it but lipstick, but Chris' cardinal rule was to assume nothing where evidence was concerned. As I pulled the cap off it, the lipstick fell out and rolled to the floor. Then a piece of paper fell out of the tube and floated down to the floor.

"Watson," exclaimed Chris, "You've done it again!"

Chris bent over and retrieved the paper. It was a small piece of unlined paper, rolled into a small tube. Unrolling the paper, he examined it under the magnifier on his knife.

"Common copy machine paper," muttered Chris, "You could find it anywhere. It was cut from a larger sheet with tiny scissors, probably the scissors on her penknife."

I waved impatiently. "That's all well and good. But what's written *on* the blasted thing?"

"Four numbers and letters, written in black ink with a ball point pen," continued Chris, "We've got forty-three L, sixty-one R, twelve L, and twenty-four R."

"Well," I said, "It sounds like a combination lock. But a combination lock to *what*?"

"Find the answer to that," said Chris, "and we'll also have an answer to what that key goes to…as well as finding the flash drive that Moriarty is killing to find."

Crystal Parker's journal [kept on a memo pad]
I couldn't begin to say how long we drove. It seemed like eternity. If only they hadn't thought

to check my watch! It would have been so easy to send out an SOS like Jeremy had done.

But they were smart, doggone it! They were smart enough to check my watch and smart enough to have a second van waiting to switch into.

Eventually, the van stopped. My kidnappers stepped out and drug me out by my left arm. I saw that we were in the Arbuckle mountains. Before me were beautiful mountain ranges, lush green meadows, and the enormous Turner Falls. The roar of the falls was broken only by the sound of the cascading water hitting the rocks below. A log cabbin was ten yards behind me. About forty yards away was the edge of a steep cliff.

"Don't try nothing," said Red Ski Mask, "Beyond the cliff is a thousand foot drop straight down to the rocks below. Mess with us, and we'll see how fast you can flap your arms, if you know what I mean."

I said nothing as they forced me towards the cabin. Inside the cabin were a fireplace, a table, and a few chairs. Once inside the men pulled off their ski-masks. The man in the red ski-mask was revealed to be a man with blonde hair and a thin mustache. The man in the green ski mask had no hair on top and gray hair on the sides. The driver

334

had curly red hair. All of them kept their guns at their sides, ready in case I tried anything.

"OK," said Curly Red, "We got her like the boss said. What now?"

"First," said Mustache, "She can cook us some grub. Then she can join the other one."

Other one! That had to be Tina Stewart. Somewhere in the cabin, Tina was being held prisoner. Probably she was sick. According to Lorenzo, she was suffering greatly from narcotic withdraw. She probably offered no resistance; she would be too weak to misbehave. My mind started going in several directions at once.

Gray Hair led me to the kitchen. It was larger than the one in my own pitiful apartment. The stove and refrigerator were state of the art, and a there was a huge pantry full of everything a person could want out in the wilderness.

"Get to it, girl," ordered Gray Hair, "We're hungry."

"What's the matter?" I wondered, "Didn't your mother ever teach you to cook?"

"Why should I cook? That's *woman's* work," said Gray Hair.

I clenched my fists, wishing I had a cast iron skillet to sling. Of course, as hard as Gray Hair's head was, I would probably end up denting the skillet on his skull! But, oh, the fun I could have denting it!

"We want to be eating in the next thirty minutes," said Gray Hair, "Better get to it. We're starved. If it's good, *maybe* we won't rape you. Maybe."

I glared daggers at him as the other men laughed. With a final grin, he left me to my "woman's work." I opened the cabinets, searching for inspiration; anything I could use to buy some time.

I knew that Chris and Jeremy would literally move mountains to try to find us. But, Chase was no dummy. He had planned this very, very well. Obviously, Chase was planning to use us to get what he wants, whatever that was. Even if the boys figured out where we were in the next few minutes, their options would be limited as long as Tina and I were being held hostage. With Tina being weak from withdraw, it was up to me to even the odds in our favor. The question was, how?

If I *did* manage to turn the odds in my favor, I still had a very sick girl to rescue. Whatever I did, I would need something that would give me the time to find Tina, get out of that cabin, and make a run for it. The wonderful thing about the Arbuckle Mountains was the many campgrounds. It was very possible that we would find help just a few miles down a trail. The key was to get Tina, get out of the cabin, and to *find* other people along the trail. It would have been wonderful if I just happened to have a bottle of sleeping pills in my pockets to dump into their supper. But, since I didn't, I would have to improvise. I found some rice, canned vegetables, and some canned chicken. It wouldn't take long to make a nice simple casserole or soup. Hopefully by then I would have a plan.

Otherwise, Tina and I were dead.

CHAPTER NINETEEN

Jeremy Winslow's journal [kept on flash drive]

Chris and I learned that while we were looking through Amanda Witherspoon's personal effects, Chief Hendricks was giving Hector Crane a *very* thorough interrogation. Dr. Price's student confessed that the Crimson Dragons had stalked Hector's sister long enough to learn her day to day habits. They threatened her life if Hector didn't do what Moriarty wanted.

I had to hand it to Hendricks. Once the man had definite proof that everything we had said about Price was true, Hendricks let him go with a *very* humble apology. He also decided that Chris just might have something to offer after all.

While Hector Crane was being raked over the coals, Chris and I were on our way to Durant. Amanda Witherspoon's family had moved from North Carolina to Durant, Oklahoma, when Amanda was a teenager. We were hoping that her parents might know what the key went to and how to find it.

Chris' face was beyond grim as I drove us to Durant. He had barely said two words since we left the police station. He sat back, his face framed between the earflaps of his deerstalker, staring at a picture taken of him and Crystal on a picnic.

"We're going to find them," I said, "I know we will."

Chris said nothing.

"Look, Holmes," I continued, "I know what it's like. I've been where you're at, remember? I still have dreams about when they kidnapped Shelly and Tim. I was as scared as you are now. But, with God's help, we managed to find them."

"The thing is," said Chris, "Moriarty is a desperate man now. He's got every hand against him, and he's looking for payback. He's looking to flee the country with more money than he could spend in ten lifetimes. But, he wants to pay back everybody who uncovered his secrets first. And, in case you missed it, Watson, I top the list of people he's got a score to settle with."

"I know, Holmes," I responded, "But I want to give you the same advice that you…"

Chris' watch beeped, cutting off my thoughts. Chris looked at his watch, frowned, and pressed a button. He instantly put the call on speaker.

"Sherlock Holmes here," began Chris.

"Well, hello there, Mr. Holmes," said a mocking voice with a giggle, "It's good to hear your voice again. I was a little concerned about your welfare since our last conversation."

Chase! Chris' face was absolutely purple with rage. I could see him clenching and unclenching his fists. I could see from the look in his eyes that he wanted with every fiber of his being to reach through the phone lines and throttle Chase. I know. That's what I wanted to do to the people who had kidnapped Shelly and Tim. I prayed that God would give me wisdom to help my friend now.

"Where are they, Moriarty?" demanded Chris, "So help me, if you've harmed one hair on their heads…"

"You'll *what*? Oh, Mr. Holmes, the last time I checked, you still don't know where to find me."

"That will change," vowed Chris.

"But not before Ms. Stewart and your dear little fiancée pay a dreadful price for your investigation. Really, Holmes, haven't you learned by now what happens to people who cross me?

Chris slammed the palm of his hand against the dash board. His face was growing redder by the minute. My poor friend was trying with everything that was in him to keep cool, but he was being driven closer and closer to the edge.

340

"What do you want?" snarled Chris through clenched teeth.

"Only what I've been after all along," answered Chase, "The trigger. Give me the trigger and they walk free."

"Where and when?" demanded Chris.

"You have until noon tomorrow," said Chase, "Meet me at noon to do the exchange. You can meet us at the cabin tomorrow at noon."

Chris blinked. "Cabin? What cabin?"

Chase laughed. "Think about it and you'll figure it out, detective. After all, what happened at the cabin was a life changing event."

"Do you *really* expect me to trust you to let them go?"

Chase laughed again. "Offhand, I'd say you have no choice. Oh, and if you're not alone, I'll shoot both girls personally. And you better think hard, now. Poor Ms. Stewart is suffering from a bad case of withdraw from missing her daily fix. If you're late, I won't have to shoot her; the narcotic withdraw alone will kill her. Bye, now."

Chris stared at the watch for several seconds after the call ended. He breathed deeply and exhaled several times, calming himself down. It was six p.m. and we had until noon tomorrow to have a workable plan. Not a whole lot of time.

"Holmes," I said, "What can we do? Even if we find that blasted flash drive, we can't just hand it over."

"No doubt it will surprise you that I'm aware of that," said Chris dryly, "But we need to at least have a good forgery. To begin with, you can get flash drives in a multitude of colors. We need to know what the flash drive looked like. We also need time to come up with some fake files that will fool Moriarty just long enough for us to get the girls away from him. After that, all bets are off."

"I had Shelly call Amanda Witherspoon's parents," I told Chris, "They promised they would be looking through all of Amanda's personal effects. Maybe they will have found the location to the flash drive by the time we get there."

"I hope so," said Chris, "Time is certainly not on our side."

For nearly a minute, we drove in silence.

"Holmes," I said, "What is this cabin that Moriarty mentioned?"

"That's what I'm wondering," said Chris, "I don't remember *anything* about a cabin. Of course, as you're well aware, I'm having trouble remembering anything that happened beyond a few years ago."

I frowned. "I know. I'm sorry."

"What I need to know," said Chris, "is what I've forgotten. According to Moriarty, something important concerning a cabin occurred. I need to know what it is."

"You're assuming he's telling the truth," I said, "He may be toying with you, trying to get you to remember a special cabin that doesn't exist. He could be setting you up to fail, my friend. If you don't find them in the time limit, he'll kill the girls and you'll spend the rest of your days blaming yourself. He could be sending you on a wild goose chase just for you to fail as his final revenge."

For several seconds, Chris stared at me. He was considering my words very carefully, and finally he sat back in his seat.

"Watson," said Chris quietly, "You may very well be right. But I need to know for sure. I need to know whether this cabin really does exist and why it's so special. I need someone who can fill in the gaps I have in my memory."

"Holmes…"

"I'm not going to regain my memory on time just by wishing for it, Watson. If I could find someone who knew me from years past…someone who would *know* if I had a cabin and where it would be if I did… That would be half our battle."

343

I thought about this. Ever since I'd known Chris, all of us had been very careful to go along with his delusions. We'd all been banking on him regaining his memory with the help of the contents of his file box once he nailed Moriarty.

But we might not have that luxury anymore. Our hand was being forced. The contents of his file box were gone, probably destroyed. Every possible record of Chris' existence had been totally erased. And now we had a time limit to save two lives, one of which was the life of Chris' fiancée. If he couldn't remember his past, those girls could very well be dead tomorrow.

I might just not have a choice now. I might have to take a huge gamble with my best friend's sanity in order to save the lives of Crystal and Tina. I might have to tell him the whole truth.

Crystal Parker's journal [kept on a memo pad]

There was one thing about my mom that always amazed me. She had the ability to create a perfect meal with whatever she had at hand. You might say she was a *MacGyver* in the kitchen. I've seen her take a bit of hamburger, rice, and canned vegetables and fix a feast fit for a king.

I did not inherit my mother's cooking skills. If I don't have a recipe right in front of me, forget it.

Knowing this did not make me feel comfortable right now. I had armed gunmen in the other room expecting a decent supper and a weak hostage somewhere in the house. I needed to buy time for Chris and Jeremy to find us, and I couldn't think of how to fix supper much less how to stage a decent escape.

But there was one lesson that I do remember Mom teaching me. If you couldn't fix a banquet, you could at least fix a soup. I sat about pulling cans of vegetables and tomato sauce from the cabinet and sat a pot of water on the stove to boil. I turned the gas jet up high, and it wasn't long before the water started bubbling.

While it boiled away, I started mentally reviewing my options. How in the *world* was I going to disarm the gunmen, find Tina Stewart, and get out of the cabin? There was no question that, no matter what Chase promised Chris for our safe release, he had no intention of letting us walk out of here alive. Chase wanted revenge as much as he wanted money.

Watching the water come to a boil, it hit me what I had to do. There was a trash can next to the stove, filled with empty pizza and TV dinner boxes. Sheesh, no wonder they wanted someone to cook them a full meal! I filled the rest of the trash can

345

full of paper towels, and kept one paper towel for myself. I moved the pot over to another burner and held one end of the paper towel to the flame. Instantly, it caught fire and I tossed it into the trash can.

Instantly, the inside of the trash can burst into flames. Fire and smoke belched upwards, and in a few seconds, the smoke alarm was going off.

"Fire!" I shouted, "*The kitchen's on fire!*"

Well, I wasn't lying. Smoke and flames were shooting upwards from the trash can. In seconds, Mustache came running into the kitchen. First he saw the trash can. Then he saw me. Then he saw the boiling water I threw into his face. He screamed and clawed at his face, which was already a mass of blisters and boils. That gave me all the time I needed to follow through by hitting him on the head with the pot as hard as I possibly could. Mustache sank down to the floor, out cold. The pot had a good dent in the bottom of it. Beautiful!

I picked up a fire extinguisher, quickly doused the flames, and picked up Mustache's AK assault rifle. Peering into the other room, I saw the other two men sitting on the couch watching television. They were absorbed in some monster truck rally. For the first time in my life, I was grateful for monster truck shows.

"Hey," said the balding man, "What's taking so long to put out a kitchen fire?"

"Yeah," said Gray Hair, "Come on, Matt, what're doing, asking her out on a date? Don't forget, I get to rape her first."

I pressed the barrel of the AK against the back of Gray Hair's head.

"Oh no you don't!," I said, "And Matt's not my type either. Listen up, because Mamma's not in a friendly mood right now."

It took less time than I thought. In the space of ten minutes, I relieved both of them of their weapons, cell phones, and keys to the van, found some rope, and hog-tied all three of them. Last but not least, I covered their mouths with duct tape. After a quick search of the cabin, I found Tina.

Tina was lying on one of the beds, looking as sick as a dog. She was pale, her lips were cracked, and she was curled up in a fetal position. She was so weak that the kidnappers hadn't even bothered to tie her up.

"Tina," I said, rushing to her side, "I'm here to help you. Everything's going to be all right."

She opened her eyes briefly and looked at me. Her expression was hollow. I had seen pictures from the end of World War II that showed prisoners being freed from the concentration camps. They had all been so weak from their ordeal that they could barely process that they were being set free. Tina had the same haunted look that the victims of the Holocaust had. The suffering from her narcotic withdraw was taking its toll on her big time.

I put an arm under her and helped her up. She was so weak she could barely stand. She put an arm around me and I started walking her to the door. It was slow going. I had a weak person by one arm and I held onto the AK with the other. It was awkward to say the least.

"Don't," she whispered, "Leave me. Save yourself, whoever you are."

"The name's Crystal Parker," I said, "And I don't leave people behind."

We made our way out the bedroom door and slowly towards the front door of the cabin. The kidnappers glared at us as we walked by. Looking at them in their hog-tied position with their mouths taped, I couldn't help but stick my tongue out at them as we made our way out the door. *This rescue has been brought to you courtesy of a pot of water*! No fancy James Bond gadgets, just a pot of water.

I helped Tina into the van. She climbed in and collapsed in the back seat. She needed medical treatment bad. As soon as we were out on the road,

I would call 9-1-1. There's no way she could last much longer without a doctor's care. As soon as she was settled, I got into the driver's seat, gunned the engine, and took off.

I peeled rubber backing away, quickly turned around, and started driving down the trail. The sun was setting in the horizon, making the road too dark to see. I switched on the headlights, and could see just up to a curve in the road. Keeping my eyes on the road, I picked up one of the cell phones I had taken, switched it on, and pressed 9-1-1. I held the phone to my ear. Nothing.

"Now what?" I muttered.

Glancing at the screen, I saw the words "NO SIGNAL". *Blast it!* That's right; in the mountains it was impossible to get a signal. Crud! Why is it we can put a man on the moon but we can't invent a cell phone that will work in the mountains?

"Tina," I said, "As soon as we get out of the mountains, I'm calling for help. We can't get a cell phone call out from here."

"Why bother?" she said, "I'm not worth it. I know Jesus saved my soul, but I'm not worth the risk. You should have just saved yourself. I'm just a lousy hooker."

"You were worth Jesus going to the cross for," I countered, "All people are precious in His sight, and that makes everyone worth taking a risk for. I do not bail out on people, my friend."

"Thanks," said Tina weakly.

"Save your strength," I said, "We'll stop at the first town we come to and get you in the hospital."

"A detective tried to get me into rehab," she said, "But something happened."

"We'll talk about that later," I said, "You just…"

Up ahead, I could see a pair of headlights coming towards us. I didn't know whether the people were friendly or not, but I didn't think it would be wise to take a chance. I had both feet flat on the floor as we raced down the road.

Then it happened. The headlights belonged to a long, black car. The driver suddenly spun around until his car was across both sides of the road, blocking our path. A passenger got out of the car, holding a rifle. *No, not them! Not now!*

Instantly, I slammed on the brakes and threw the van into reverse. I looked in the rear view mirror as we backed away, hearing gunshots. A crack suddenly appeared in the windshield. Then smoke started pouring from under the hood of the van.

Then two tires blew out.

"No!" I screamed, "*No, no, NO!*"

The van spun crazily. I fought the steering wheel, praying that I could regain control and make a getaway on flat tires. Then a third tire blew, and the van came to a total stop.

"Tina," I yelled, "We've got to run for it!"

I grabbed the AK and made my way back to Tina. She was moaning, and curled up in a fetal position. Blast it, she was cramping from the withdraw!

"Tina, come on," I begged, "You've got to help me here!"

The side door to the van suddenly burst open. I found myself facing two men in black suits holding truly wicked looking rifles, pointed right at us. With a sigh, I handed over the AK and stepped out of the van. Right behind the gunmen, I saw a familiar face that chilled me to the very marrow. He was dressed in a black suit and tie and looked about as friendly as a shark.

"Well, well, Miss Parker," said Chase, "I must give you an A for effort. If we hadn't been coming to the cabin just now, I might have missed you."

"Timing wasn't always my strong suit," I said through clenched teeth.

351

"But I really must insist that you stay for a while," said Chase, "I've got a little homecoming to prepare for, and I would truly hate for you to miss your own fiancée's party."

"I'm not really a party girl," I said sarcastically.

"Oh, but I'm sure *this* party will interest you greatly," said Chase.

I looked helplessly as one of Chase's goons lifted up Tina and slung her over his shoulder like a sack of potatoes. She groaned, but said nothing.

"That girl needs medical attention!" I shouted.

Chase laughed. "All in good time. You and Miss Stewart have to help me prepare for our little party. You see, Miss Parker, you and Tina are going to help me accomplish something that even Sir Arthur Conan Doyle wasn't able to accomplish when he was writing all of those Sherlock Holmes stories."

I swallowed. "What do you mean?"

"Very shortly," said Chase, "I intend to depart from this country. I'm getting way too much attention lately. But before I go, you and Miss Stewart are going to help me bring about the death of Sherlock Holmes."

CHAPTER TWENTY

Jeremy Winslow's journal [kept on flash drive]
By the time we got to Mr. and Mrs. Witherspoon's house in Durant, it was late. We had stopped at a convenient store and picked up some sandwiches en-route. I took the opportunity to call Shelly. She asked Jessica about a particular cabin. Jess remembered that her family spent several vacations camping in cabins in many places. She couldn't remember a particular one. She was hesitant about trying to force Chris' memory, but agreed that we might have no choice. We were literally up against the wall and out of options.

The Witherspoons lived in a modest, one story white house with green trim. Laurence Witherspoon was tall, with brownish-gray hair. His wife Helga was short, a little plump, and had brunet hair. They welcomed us into their home, looking like their world had caved in on them without mercy. Under the circumstances, I didn't wonder. They showed us into the living room, which was covered in wall-to-wall cardboard boxes. Chris and I removed our hats as we sat down on the sofa.

"Mrs. Witherspoon," said Chris, "Thank you for seeing us. We're sorry for your loss."

"Please excuse the mess," said Helga, "We've been so busy going through Amanda's things."

"We understand," said Chris, "and we want to apologize for intruding like this."

"If it will help nail the scum that...did that...to our baby," said Laurence, "that's all that counts."

Helga dabbed her eyes with a handkerchief. My heart ached for her. No parent should have to bury their children. It's supposed to be the other way around. It would be hard enough if Amanda had died in an accident or from an illness. But to literally be butchered by a maniac! No one deserves that kind of death, or that kind of grief. No one. I prayed that God would bring them comfort and peace.

"We tried so hard to convince her that what she was doing was dangerous," said Helga, "But she kept saying that she had everything under control...that she could handle it."

"When those other call girls were murdered," added Laurence, "we begged her to come back home. We pleaded with her, telling her that anybody that called her could be the killer. But she wouldn't listen. I keep thinking that if I had

354

tried harder…said something…maybe given it one last try…"

"I'm sure you did everything that there was to do," I said, "Mr. and Mrs. Witherspoon, I've talked to a lot of girls in the same boat as your Amanda. Nearly every time, they are convinced that they can handle whatever happens. Believe me, the only people who deserve to be blamed are the people who committed the murders. You have nothing to feel guilty about."

"Mr. and Mrs. Witherspoon," said Chris, "We have good reason to believe that Amanda accidentally came into possession of something that some notorious criminals want…something they were willing to kill for."

Laurence and Helga's eyes went wide. For the first time, they were grasping a possible reason for their daughter's death.

"We believe that all of the murders are tied into what Amanda found," added Chris, "And these criminals found out that Amanda had it."

"So that's what all of this is about," breathed Laurence, "It wasn't just some nut who likes to kill. She found out something that she shouldn't have."

"Yes," I put in, "And if we can find what she had, then something good will come from

Amanda's death, because it will help put some very dangerous people away for good."

Laurence and Helga looked at each other. Then they looked at us, a new determination in their faces.

"Mr. Holmes," said Laurence, "If this will bring meaning to our baby's death, then we'll do everything possible to help."

"We need to do it fast," said Chris, "These demented individuals are holding two other women hostage. We have until noon tomorrow to find them."

"One of the girls is sick from narcotic withdraw," I added, "And the other is a fellow detective...and she's Mr. Holmes' fiancée."

Helga swallowed. "Oh, my stars! I'll put the coffee on. What are we looking for?"

"Your daughter had something with a combination lock," said Chris, "And there was something that unlocked with a very tiny key."

I held up the tiny key we had found. Helga looked at the key. Then she burst into tears, fleeing from the room. Laurence looked sadly in the direction that Helga had fled, and shook his head.

"That key," explained Laurence, "goes to a girl's diary. Helga got it for her last birthday a few months back. She kept it, along with some jewelry, in a small fireproof safe."

"Would you happen to know where it is?" asked Chris anxiously.

Laurence nodded. "We cleaned out her apartment shortly after the murder. It's in one of these boxes over here."

Laurence got up and started moving boxes. He handed us box after box, and we sat them to the side. Finally, he came to a large box at the bottom of the stack. The box was taped up, and he slit the tape with his pocket knife. Opening the lid, he removed some ceramic figurines, and then pulled out a tiny, metal safe.

Chris pulled out the paper with the numbers on them and handed them to Laurence. Laurence twisted the knob according to the numbers, and opened the safe. There were several necklaces, sets of earrings, and a small, leather bound book. Laurence pulled out the book and handed it to me. Sure enough, the diary had a lock with a tiny keyhole. I inserted the tiny key and twisted it. Perfect! It opened.

Inside, where full pages should have been in the diary, we found that the pages had been cut away in the center. In the center of the hollowed out diary was a purple computer flash drive.

"Bingo, Watson," said Chris, "We've got it!"

"Thank goodness!" said Laurence, "But what in thunder is on it?"

"Some secrets that our foes believe are worth killing for," said Chris, "Please don't ask me to say any more right now. The entire tale will come out soon. But believe me, sir, your daughter did our country a great service by taking this computer disk. I'm not exaggerating, sir, when I say your daughter may have saved our country from ruin."

Laurence swallowed. "Then her death wasn't meaningless?"

Chris shook his head. "No it wasn't. I wish I could say more right now. But, with two other lives on the line…"

Laurence held up his hand. "I understand. You've got two other lives to save, including the woman you love. I just hope that someday the pain will go away. But when this is all over, please don't forget where we live. We'd like to properly thank you for bringing justice for our daughter."

We prayed with the Witherspoons before we left. Helga insisted on giving us some coffee for the road, and then we were on our way. I drove while Chris sat in the passenger seat, lost in thought.

"A purple flash drive," muttered Chris, "If we had gotten the color wrong on our decoy, it would have been a dead giveaway."

"Hopefully," I put in, "We'll have time to get some phony code written on our decoy. Moriarty is bound to check the disk out."

"A friend of mine will handle that end," said Chris, "His name's Justin, and he did me a good turn earlier. You and I, Watson, need to focus on figuring out where this cabin is Moriarty was discussing. If there *is* a cabin, it could be anywhere."

I swallowed. This was the moment I had dreaded, and now it was here. How would he react to the news that Chase was his brother? What would he do when he realized that his mortal enemy, who now had Crystal at his mercy, was a brother he couldn't even remember and who had faked his own death?

Lord, I prayed, *help me through this! Help me to tell the truth without driving him over the edge!*

"Holmes," I said, "I think I can help. I've something to tell you, but you're not going to like it."

Crystal Parker's journal [kept on memo pad]

Tina was dropped onto a bed like a sack of dirty laundry in the back bedroom of the cabin. She lay curled up in a ball, moaning. Chase looked at her without pity. His two goons looked bored.

"You've got to get her some medical attention," I said, "She's going to die!"

Chase shrugged. "Not my problem. I'll still have a lot of leverage with *you* as my hostage."

"She doesn't know anything," I said, "There's nothing she can do to hurt you!"

"If she doesn't know anything," said Chase, "Then she doesn't know anything that can *help* me, either. You're all the hostage I need to keep my dear brother right where I want him."

Tina was sweating furiously, moaning in agony. It was awful watching her suffer like this! It didn't matter if she had started taking drugs of her own free will. All I knew was that she was suffering terribly, and my heart broke for her. I once talked with a person trying to kick the drug habit, and she said it was a bear to do. The body craved the very poison that was killing the addict slowly, and made the body hurt like everything when it didn't get its fix. No wonder it was so hard for addicts to get clean and *stay* clean!

"Please," I begged, "You can't just let suffer like this!"

Chase smiled. "Very well. Mister Brown, please be kind enough to shoot Miss Stewart."

The overweight thug reached under his suit coat for his weapon. He took out a .45 with a silencer and aimed it straight at Tina.

"NO!" I shrieked, *"You can't! Please!"*

I threw myself over Tina's groaning form. I shut my eyes tightly, waiting for the shots that would end my life. *Lord,* I prayed, *please make it quick!*

Nothing happened. I opened my eyes and looked up. Chase and his goons were smiling like they had just heard the world's funniest joke.

"Now, Miss Parker," said Chase, *"You're* the one allowing the girl to suffer. I was going to put her out of her misery."

I stared at Chase, my eyes blazing with fury. Chase's only response was to smile. He was enjoying taunting me. Clearly he was a man who enjoyed inflicting pain on others. How in the *world* could Chris and Jessica be even remotely related to this monster?

"This is interesting," said Chase, "You actually care about a drug addicted hooker. Why?"

361

"No matter what mistakes she's made," I said, "She's a human being, and precious in God's sight. She's as important to God as a princess or a CEO of a multi-million dollar industry, because everyone is important to God. That makes her important to me."

Chase smiled. "You're just like your fiancée! You care too much for others no matter what they do. Did you know that on the night I set fire to our parents house, Chris actually tried to save our parents from the fire that consumed our house? It was stupid. They had abused us without mercy. You know they once even used a *soldering iron* on Chris' back, and he still couldn't let them die without trying to save them? He was always stupid that way."

"Actually," I responded, "Hearing that makes me more proud of him than I already was."

"That figures," said Chase, "But I'm prepared to offer you a deal, and I'm only going to say this once. Are you listening?"

I nodded.

"I'll give Miss Stewart some medical attention," he said, "But in return, you have to vow that you won't try to get away. As long as you don't try any more stunts, I'll give her the help she needs.

But, the first time you even *think* about running for it, Miss Stewart will be butchered just like all of the other prostitutes I had killed. And, I'll make you *watch*. Do we understand each other?"

"*Perfectly*," I snarled.

Jeremy Winslow's journal [kept on flash drive]

Chris looked at me curiously, his face perfectly framed between the earflaps of his deerstalker. His expression was a mixture of anticipation and fear.

"What I have to tell you isn't easy," I said cautiously.

"Is it about my earlier life?" asked Chris.

"No," I said, "But it is about Moriarty."

Chris' eyebrows narrowed. He studied my face, trying to read my thoughts by my expression.

"What do you know about Moriarty?" I asked, "I mean about who he is?"

Chris shrugged. "Earlier in the year, we began tracking him through a list of aliases. We know that he killed a man named Hugh West and assumed his identity after breaking out of a juvenile correction center. He is also known by the name Chase Anderson."

I swallowed, trying to form the words that I had to say.

"There's something else," I said slowly, "Something that may help us find him and the girls. It may help you remember the cabin, if there truly is a cabin."

"What is it, Watson?" snapped Chris, "Spit it out, man! We've hostages to rescue, and one of them is Crystal!"

"There's no easy way to say it, Holmes," I said, "But Moriarty is your *brother*!"

Chris' mouth hung open. The look on his face was a hard one to take. I had prayed for so long that he would remember the truth on his own without having to be told. How could he feel anything about me but utter betrayal for holding out such an important truth from him? In one sentence, I had probably lost my best friend. My hands held the steering wheel in a death grip as I struggled for the right way to explain everything.

"My *brother*?" said Chris slowly.

"Yes," I said, "I'm so sorry, Holmes, but it's true. I know we should have told you right away, but the doctors advised against it because of the gaps in your memory."

"My brother *Mycroft* is Moriarty?" asked Chris, "Mycroft has turned to crime…and now has my fiancée?"

"Mycroft…" I said slowly.

364

For just a second I didn't know what to say. Where in the world did he get the name Mycroft? Then it dawned on me. In Sir Arthur Conan Doyle's stories, Mycroft Holmes was the brother of Sherlock. In a couple of the stories, Mycroft played an important role in the cases that Sherlock was investigating. The thing was, Chris was accepting that Moriarty was his brother, but was filtering what he knew through his delusions. Since he still believed that he was Sherlock Holmes, his brother would naturally be Mycroft Holmes. But, confound it, would he be able to remember anything about a special cabin?

"It makes sense," muttered Chris, "Mycroft was always smarter than me, and I've always known that Moriarty was the most brilliant criminal I'd ever encountered. Somehow he must have gotten Chase Anderson's DNA and left it where it would be found in order to shift suspicion away from *him*. It's a brilliant move; I'm kicking myself for not seeing it earlier."

I absolutely didn't know what to say. Every truth he encountered was being filtered through his delusions. Would that *help* us to find the girls or *prevent* us from finding them? And if we did find them, would it be in time?

CHAPTER TWENTY-ONE

Jeremy Winslow's journal [kept on flash drive]
The rest of the drive was spent in silence. Chris leaned back in the passenger seat, totally absorbed in his own thoughts. He pulled his deerstalker over his eyes, and he held his fingertips directly under his chin. I knew he was trying desperately to remember any and all details from his past. For a brief moment, I pondered whether or not to tell him more...to actually tell him the truth of his identity.

But, would it be the wise thing to do? The last time Jessica tried to tell him the truth, he sunk into a temporary catatonic state of shock. If that happened now, it could sink any chance we had to find the girls.

In the end, I decided to hold my tongue. The risk was too great. Besides, every police officer in the state was also on the case searching for Crystal and Tina. Any moment we could get word from search and air rescue that they'd been found.

We stopped at the home of Chris' friend, Justin. Chris told me about Justin's rather...unique personality and the earlier visit he and Crystal had paid to him. His taste in decorating was somewhat...interesting in a *Twilight Zone* sort of way. He greeted us warmly at the door with a firm handshake. Quickly we told him our dilemma. When he learned that Crystal had been taken by the people we were after, he took a deep breath.

"What can I do to help?" he asked grimly.

Chris handed him the purple flash drive. "We need you to make a counterfeit program; one that will fool Crystal's kidnappers without doing the damage this disk is designed to do. And remember, we are under a *serious* time limit my friend."

Justin nodded grimly. "Consider it done."

While Justin worked, Chris switched on one of Justin's other computers. In seconds, he began pulling up topography maps of Oklahoma.

"Watson," said Chris, "Where in Oklahoma might a person find cabins?"

"The mountains," I replied, "Camp grounds...the Falls Creek church encampment."

Chris smiled. "Even if I ever went to Falls Creek myself, I can hardly picture Mycroft as ever setting foot in a church camp. Justin has plenty of computers. Set one up, and get some satellite pictures of some other camp grounds. I'll focus on the Arbuckle Mountains. You can look up some other campgrounds. Maybe between the two of us, we'll come up with something."

367

I nodded and selected one of the other computers. While it was warming up, I gave Shelly a quick call and brought her up to speed. Then I got down to serious business.

It was nine p.m. We had fifteen hours to find a needle in a state wide haystack.

Shelly Winslow's journal [kept in shorthand]

After Jeremy's call, I found Jessica surrounded by a stack of diaries and photo-albums taller than the stack I was working with. After hours of pouring through old family albums, Jessica still didn't have a clue about any special cabin that Chase could be hiding out in with Crystal and Tina. Even Tim was getting in on the action, looking through some scrapbooks.

"They're working on finding Crystal and Tina," I said, "and Jeremy has told Chris that Moriarty is his brother."

Jessica and Tim both inhaled.

"How did he take it?" asked Jess.

"Right now his main concern is finding the hostages," I answered, "He thinks his brother's real name is Mycroft Holmes, and that he got some of Chase Anderson's DNA to fool the police."

"In the stories," said Tim quickly, "Mycroft was Sherlock's smarter brother."

"Jess," I said, "Are you sure you don't remember *anything* about a cabin?"

Jess shook her head. She looked like a woman who was on the verge of falling to pieces. Tears were streaming down her face.

"*No*," said Jess, "We stayed at several cabins in several different camping areas when we were growing up. We vacationed in different *states*. I can't think of any one that stands out more than the others."

I told the both of them what I knew of the investigation, and how the boys were looking at satellite photos of different campgrounds.

"Chris is hoping that seeing some pictures will jar some memories," I said, "We need to pray harder than we've ever prayed before. We don't even know if there *is* a cabin! Chase could be setting Chris up to fail by feeding him a phony clue!"

Jessica hung her head in despair. Here we were, surrounded by memories—diaries, newspaper clippings, scrapbooks, the works—and we couldn't find *any* hint of what we were looking for.

"I'll text my Sunday School teacher," offered Tim, "He can have the whole class praying. For that matter, he can text the pastor and get the whole church in on it."

"Go for it," I replied.

I picked up an envelope stuffed filled with pictures. It showed the entire family at various times of the year—Christmas, Easter, summer vacation. I found a photograph of Jessica as a child at Halloween, dressed as Cinderella. The next Halloween photo was of Chris. I couldn't believe it---he was dressed as Sherlock Holmes.

"Even back then, he loved to play Sherlock Holmes," explained Jess, "So, it was only natural that he dressed the part on Halloween. He and Chase would play their own detective games for hours. They'd go off on their own to play their own version of *The Hound of the Baskervilles* and other Sherlock Holmes stories. Chase *always* preferred to play the part of Moriarty. I don't know why, but he loved to play the role of the villain."

"I guess those games trained him for what he's doing now," I said sadly.

I sat the picture down and picked up another. It showed all three of the children, sitting on a couch. It was interesting. None of them looked happy. If anything, they looked tense, like they were afraid to move.

Jess had told me several times that they had been abused as children. The tenseness I saw in the faces in this picture made me believe it. All three of them looked terrified of whoever had taken the picture. I shook my head sadly. How could anybody abuse children?

I sat the family picture aside. Then, on impulse, I picked up the one of Chris in his Sherlock Holmes outfit. A new thought struck me.

"Jess," I said, "Where did Chris and Chase play their Sherlock Holmes games?"

Jess shrugged. "Anywhere they could. I was never in on the games. It was a boy's thing, you know. When we were at home, they would play in our backyard or in their room. Sometimes they'd bring their stuff along and play when we took family vacations. Why?"

I thought furiously. "Did they play their games at the same cabins that you and your parents were staying when you went camping?"

Jess shook her head. "They'd always go down the camping trails on their own. Why?"

"Maybe something happened during one of their games," I speculated, "something out of the ordinary that made that one game different from the others. Jess, was there ever a time when the boys acted different after their games during a family campout? Can you think of *anything* different about one of their little games?"

Jess thought hard. I had to give her that. She was trying with all her might to think of anything that made one particular play adventure stand out. Whatever it was, it was something that Chase carried with him into adulthood.

"I'm trying, Shelly," said Jess, "Heaven help me, I'm trying! But whatever happened, the boys kept it to themselves and hid it well. I'm sorry!"

I sighed. "It's not your fault, Jess. If anything odd *did* happen once, they kept it secret and you have nothing to feel guilty about. I'll tell you what: make a list of every campground that you can remember staying at when you were a child, especially the ones you stayed at when the boys were playing their detective games. Maybe hearing the names of the campgrounds will jar Chris' memory."

"If there *was* a special cabin," said Jess gloomily.

"It's all we got," I said, "Hopefully, it will be enough."

Crystal Parker's journal [kept in a memo pad]

Tina Stewart lay on her bed, seeming more relaxed and calm. I'll say this for Chase, he could keep his end of a bargain when he chose. However, I hated his method of supplying treatment for Tina.

He helped her by giving her an injection of morphine, her drug of choice. Her fix satisfied, she could relax and feel less pain. Within minutes, she was relaxed and sleeping peacefully. At least, as peacefully as a person could when their wrists were chained to a bed.

I sat in a chair beside her bed. It was interesting. The doors and windows weren't even locked, although there were guards posted both outside the door and outside the cabin. Chase didn't bother having me chained or tied up.

Of course, he knew I wouldn't try to leave without Tina. My concern for her kept me bound to this cabin more than any chains or ropes could ever do. Chase couldn't have picked a more powerful incentive to keep me from trying to escape if he tried.

So, I just sat in the chair and watched Tina sleep. I was glad one of us could. By this time tomorrow night, both Chase and his goons would be in prison, or me and everyone I cared about would be dead.

It was not a cheerful thought. How I ached for this to be over! How I longed for us all to be free of the shadow that had hung over us for so long! I wanted to see these human monsters behind bars for the rest of their days. I wanted for Shelly,

Tim, and Gage to be able to go across town to the store or to school without having to have police protection. I wanted desperately to walk down the aisle in my wedding gown and see Chris' smiling face as I walked towards him and the preacher in our church.

I wanted my father to say that I was his daughter again! It was strange; I had actually come to accept that my father had disowned me for not continuing the family tradition of going into the military. I had given up years ago of ever seeing my parents again. But how I longed for things to be different! I wanted him to hug me, tell me I'm his daughter again, and for our family to be whole.

Please God, I begged, *let it happen! Let justice prevail! Let us be free of these monsters for good!*

There was a knock on the door, and suddenly it swung open. I couldn't believe it; Chase was coming into the room carrying a tray of sandwiches and a picture of water. A guard stood beside him, gun pointed towards me and Tina.

"A snack to eat at gunpoint," I said sarcastically, "No thanks, I'm not hungry."

Chase shrugged and sat the tray on the floor.

"Suit yourself," said Chase, "However,

374

tomorrow is going to be a very busy day. You'll want your strength."

I chuckled. "Like I'm supposed to trust that food isn't poisoned?"

Chase smiled. "Pick a sandwich. Any sandwich, and I'll eat it myself."

I looked at him, uncertain. After a few seconds hesitation, I pointed to a sandwich in the middle of the tray. Chase nodded, picked it up, and took a large bite. Then, he poured some water from the picture into a cup and drank it in one gulp.

"If I wanted to harm you," said Chase, "I wouldn't have to sneak poison into your food or drink. No, Crystal, I need you alive and alert when your white knight comes to rescue his damsel in distress and her doped up friend."

With a sigh, I picked up a sandwich of my own and started eating. Ham and Cheese. I'd had better sandwiches, but Chase was right about one thing: I needed to keep my strength up. I wanted to be strong enough to give him the face slapping of a lifetime.

Chase motioned for his guard to leave. The guard nodded and left, shutting the door behind him. Then, Chase pulled up a chair and sat across from me.

"What are you doing?" I asked, "It can't be that fascinating watching me eat a sandwich."

"I want to ask you a question," said Chase.

I arched my eyebrows. "I'm not telling you anything."

Chase smiled. "I don't mean information that would harm your friends. But, I'm curious about something."

"I've been curious, too," I replied, "I'm curious how anyone related to Jessica and Chris could have such a callous disregard for human life."

Chase opened his mouth, but said nothing. Apparently, I caught him off guard. So, he could be surprised by something. Good! That was something to keep in mind.

"What's your question?" I demanded.

"You're a puzzle to me, Miss Parker," he confessed, "It's easy to understand why my brother wants to apprehend me. Even though he remembers nothing about me, I am a criminal. As such, he naturally wants to see me behind bars. Likewise, Jeremy Winslow—Chris' 'Dr. Watson'—is a detective as well. The kidnapping of his family last year also gave him a very personal reason to want to put me in prison.

"But you, Miss Parker, are a puzzle. You know that Chris is a madman, and yet you love him.

376

You know he's going against a highly trained crime syndicate, and yet you willingly court that danger when it would be simpler to just walk away. Why is that?"

I studied Chase's face. I couldn't believe what the man was asking. Here he was, hounded by every police officer in the state, risking everything just for petty revenge and to make a few more dollars, and all he wanted to know why I was involved with his brother! Of course, who was I to understand how a sick mind works?

"You said it yourself, Chase," I replied, "I love your brother. Whether he ever regains his identity or not, I'll still love him. He's warm, decent, and cares about me. He's also the bravest man I ever met. I could never walk away from that."

"You risk everything simply out of *love*? I can't understand that."

I smiled sadly. "I didn't think you would."

Chase stood up and shrugged. He opened the door to leave, and then turned to face me once more.

"You better eat some more," said Chase, "Whether your fiancée figures out my little clue in time or not, those sandwiches are going to be your last meal."

He turned to go, shaking his head.

"Chase," I said suddenly, "Wait a second."

Chase paused and turned to face me.

"If this *is* my last meal," I said, "Could I have a paper to leave a last message for Chris? It'd be a comfort to have a way to say my final goodbyes."

Chase snorted. "Why should I do any favors for the people who helped hound me out of the country?"

I glared at him. "I thought you were recreating the last battle between Moriarty and Sherlock Holmes. Don't you remember how in the story, Moriarty allowed Holmes to write a final letter to Dr. Watson?"

Chase blinked in surprise. "So he did, so he did. Very well, I'll bring you something later."

The door shut behind him. I faced Tina, whose face was deathly pale. Between the withdraw pains and the ordeal of what we were going through, it was a wonder she was still functioning. She was trying to be calm, but her eyes showed the same terror I felt.

I would love to be able to say that I was totally fearless. But that would be a lie. I was terrified and shaking like a leaf, wondering what the next few hours would bring.

CHAPTER TWENTY-TWO

Jeremy Winslow's journal [kept on flash drive]
Satellite picture after satellite picture came across my computer screen. I found myself amazed at the sheer detail I could find of various cabins around Oklahoma. The close-up pictures of the cabins were of such detail that I could read the license plates on any cars and trucks parked outside the cabins. If only I could find the *right* cabin!

"Ten campgrounds down," I commented, "Probably a couple of hundred to go. Holmes, have you remembered *anything*?"

"I'm seeing the same images you are, Watson," fumed Chris, "And, so far, *nothing.*"

For the first time since I'd met him, I heard a trace of fear in his voice. We'd been looking at satellite images on the computer screen for hours, and not a one stirred an ounce of memory in his mind.

I could only imagine the terror he was fighting. Two lives depended on him remembering something from his childhood—one of whom was his own fiancée--and he couldn't remember anything.

"He wants that flash drive, Watson," said Chris, "To give it to him, I've got to be able to find him. But *where is he*? Blast it, if we're not in time, Crystal and Tina's deaths will be on my head!"

My heart went out to him. When Shelly and Tim were being held hostage, I died a thousand deaths in my mind while praying that I would be able to find them safe and sound. If they had been killed, I would have spent the rest of my days blaming myself for getting involved in a case involving the mob. No amount of reasoning would have convinced me otherwise. This was what Chris was facing now—the possibility of blaming himself for the rest of his life for the deaths of a material witness and of the woman he loved.

Justin continued to work hard on a counterfeit flash drive. His fingers flew over the keyboard faster than I would have dreamed possible. He had two windows open on his computer: one window showed the codes on the flash drive Chase wanted. The other showed the phony code that Justin was inventing as he moved along.

My watch beeped, causing me to jump. I saw an incoming call from Shelly and got it on the third ring. I went into the hallway to take the call.

"Hi, Sweetheart," I said, "Give me some good news."

"Chris and Chase used to play detective games when they were kids," said Shelly, "Chris played Holmes while Chase was Moriarty. Go figure."

"Did a cabin figure in their games?" I asked, "We're *desperate*, honey!"

"Yes," said Shelly, "but Jess doesn't know which one. They stayed at a lot of different campsites over the years, honey, and this was a boy's only game if you know what I mean. We think something happened during one of these games, but we don't know what or where. The boys would wander to other cabins and leave Jess with their parents. Jess is making a list of every place they went camping during the years they played their games."

I mind raced. It was nearly midnight. We had a total of twelve hours left to both have that counterfeit disk made and figure out where Chase was hiding. Justin was doing great on the code, but Chris and I was getting nowhere. Unless...

"Honey," I said, "There's something I want to check on. I'll call you back. Love you."

Chris was staring at his computer screen, silently begging the pictures on the screen to tell him something. I poured him his fifth cup of coffee for the night and carried it to him.

381

"You find anything?" I asked, handing him the cup.

"Yes," He said, "I've found that I'm still not seeing anything familiar."

I sipped on my own coffee and looked at him.

"Maybe we're going about this all wrong," I said, "I've got an idea."

"I like it already."

"We've spent the last few hours trying to get you to remember one specific cabin in the entire state," I said, "But what can you remember about your relationship with Mycroft himself?"

Chris blinked several times blankly. He stood up, looking past me at the living room window. I noticed for the first time that the windows were taped over with newspaper articles. Chris didn't seem to notice. He was looking at the windows without seeing them; his mind's eye was thinking about what I had just asked.

"Watson," he muttered, "My incompetence rivals that of Hendricks himself! Why didn't I think of that myself?"

"Considering that in the last twenty-four hours," I began, "A bullet has creased your skull, Crystal has been kidnapped, and you've learned that your own brother is responsible…"

"That's no excuse!" snapped Chris, "All the excuses in the world won't help if I don't piece together the only clue Mycroft has allowed me!"

Chris sat down, his fingertips pressed together under his chin, and stared at me.

"Mycroft was an interesting man," he began, "At least, what I can recall of him. He and I always seemed to have a rivalry that went a step beyond sibling rivalry. I remember we used to play games…detective games…"

I sat across from him. "That's good, Holmes, very good!"

"He always liked to play the criminal," continued Chris, "And he liked to see if he could outwit me."

"Sounds like he carried that into adulthood," I said.

Chris waved that thought off. "I remember something about paintings. There was something about paintings…but I just can't think… So much of my childhood is a blank."

"In some of his current crimes," I said, "He put hidden codes into some paintings he did."

Chris snapped his fingers and stood up. His eyes were wide, excited. He wasn't so much seeing the living room as he was the memories that were flooding back.

"Mycroft went from *playing* the criminals in our games," said Chris, "To actually committing crimes in real life. I seem to remember him selling drugs."

It was working! He was actually remembering some things about his brother. He was still as confused as ever about their true names, but he was starting to remember things!

"He was selling drugs," he repeated, "but he still had some sort of bizarre need to outsmart me. He invented codes and used them to put hints to his crimes in his paintings. Besides making money as a criminal, his chief goal was to invent a code that I couldn't crack."

Chris paced back and forth, looking from one window to the next. Then he looked at Justin, who was still typing away on the counterfeit code. Chris' look of excitement was replaced with one of pain.

Of course! No matter how successful Chris was at finding where Chase was hiding—and freeing Crystal and Tina—Chris still had to face the fact that his own brother was the mastermind responsible for the deaths of so many people. It had to hurt and it had to hurt badly. Putting myself in his place, if anyone in my family had been in on

384

kidnapping Shelly and Tim, it would haunt me forever. Chris took a sip of coffee and then turned to face me. His face was contorted in mental agony.

"I never realized the code in the painting was to real crimes," whispered Chris, "I thought it was another game. Then I went to find a book he had borrowed, and found the drugs in his room. That's when I knew it was no longer a game to him. I thought and thought about what to do. Then I confronted him."

"What did you do?"

Chris swallowed. "I went to Mycroft and told him what I knew. Then I begged him to stop. I told him that if he didn't, I would go to the police. That's when he told me that if I did, he would spend the rest of his days making me regret it."

Suddenly, Chris hurried back to his computer. His fingers started flying over the keyboard.

"Fool that I am, Watson!" he shouted, "I should have realized what he was telling me!"

"What do you mean?"

"The place where I confronted him! Watson, it was at a *cabin*! He's got Tina and Crystal at the cabin where I confronted him about his crimes as a teenager!"

I looked over his shoulder. "Where's the cabin at?"

"It's in the Arbuckle Mountains," said Chris, "It's right at Turner Falls. We were camping with our parents. I took him to another cabin further down the trail. It was deserted, and it was one cabin we used in our games. I took him there so we could talk away from our parents."

And to be away from Jessica, I thought to myself. *You wouldn't have wanted to involve her in this.*

Chris brought up a satellite image of the Arbuckle Mountains. We got a wonderful view of Turner Falls and the surrounding cliffs. Suddenly, Chris zoomed in on one particular cabin.

"There it is, Watson," whispered Chris, "It's still there! That's the cabin where I confronted Mycroft when we were teenagers."

I looked at the satellite pictures. They showed a typical log cabin out in the middle of the mountains. The cabin had a majestic view of Turner Falls, overlooking a steep cliff. A blue van and black Lincoln Town Car were outside the cabin. Chris zoomed in on the license plate for the Town Car: XTZ487.

"I knew satellite pictures could zoom in close," I muttered, "But this is something else."

Chris laughed. "If Tim were playing in his back yard with Rex, satellite pictures could get a good close-up of Rex's dog tag numbers."

I raised my eyebrows. "I don't know if I like that or not. But to find the girls and Mycroft, I'll put my right-to-privacy concerns aside."

"Here's the van license number," continued Chris, "LCA399. Let's run those plates, Watson. Justin, how is that flash drive coming?"

"I need a few more hours," said Justin, "But I'll have it for you well before your deadline."

I hacked into the police department computers and quickly had the lowdown on our two mysterious vehicles.

"The Lincoln," I said, "Is owned by a Charles Tate, from Norman. He was reported missing by his wife of forty years two days ago. According to Mrs. Tate, her husband went to their local *Dollar General* to pick up a few things, and never came home. She also stated that her husband never goes anywhere without telling her."

"Interesting," said Chris, "And I would be willing to bet that our missing Mr. Tate doesn't own a cabin in the mountains!"

"No bet," I replied, "And the van was stolen in Midwest City last week. The owner, Rebecca Lawrence, was found dead in a dumpster."

387

Justin looked up from his computer and frowned. "Hey, guys, with everything I'm hearing, you've got more than enough to call SWAT and to lead one humongous raid on that cabin right away."

"Crystal and Miss Stewart would be dead the second Mycroft sees his cabin surrounded," replied Chris, "No, my friend, Watson and I are going to stick to the timetable that Mycroft established. We know where they are. That's the main thing. We still have ten hours. That gives you time to finish your counterfeit code, and it gives Watson and I time to think of a nice dirty trick."

Detective Maria Lorenzo's journal

It's my opinion that Alexander Graham Bell needs to be dragged out into the streets and flogged. I mean, the man had no idea what he was turning loose on the world when he invented the telephone. If he had known about telemarketers, automated operators, and late night phone calls, he probably would have kept his opinions to himself.

I had dropped into bed from sheer exhaustion around midnight, and knew that I would have to be getting up at six. It's a mighty sad world when a detective's own car becomes a crime scene, especially when an important material witness is right out of the car while the detective is looking at another crime scene. The paperwork alone is a bear. The tongue lashings aren't fun either.

Hendricks raked me over the coals when he heard what happened. He had been less than pleased when his pet theory about the Stalker killings turned out to be way off the mark. He really handed me my head when he learned that I was doing whatever his least favorite private detective was telling me to do. Never mind how many times Anderson had been proven right. Hendricks still didn't like it.

After the eternal tongue lashing, I spent the rest of my day and evening seeing what stones I could turn over to find Crystal and Tina. All I turned up was a big fat zero. I prayed that Anderson and Winslow were having better luck when I crawled under the sheets.

I was just starting to get good and asleep when the phone rang. Muttering something about how God has a wicked sense of humor, I grabbed the phone. I vaguely recognized the voice of Winston Turner, one of the biggest tech geeks the police department has.

"Detective Lorenzo," said Turner, "Hi. I hope you weren't busy."

389

"No," I said sarcastically, "I was only getting some sleep. You know, when a person closes their eyes with their head on a pillow and dreams about whoever they have a crush on. It's what we poor, hardworking detectives get too little of."

"Good," said Turner, "You weren't busy."

I clenched my fist, wanting desperately to reach through the phone to throttle the man.

"I thought you might want to know," said Turner, "I finished examining that microchip that was pulled out of Detective Holmes…I mean, Anderson."

"I know who you mean," I said, "But we already figured it was a tracking device."

"That's just it," said Turner, "It *wasn't* a tracking device."

"Really?" I asked, "Then what was it?"

"It was a chip with a lot of weird word processing documents on it," said Turner, "The writing is in some language I don't know, but it looks like some bird dipped its feet in paint and went walking over some paper."

I sat up in bed. I already knew that Chase Anderson was into weird codes. It sounded like he had some info implanted in his brother, but why? Why go to all that trouble?

"Thanks, Winston," I said, "Anything else?"

"Yes," he said, "Be careful, Maria...I mean, detective. Anyone that has the pull to get doctors to implant microchips like this is no one to mess with. Be careful who you trust."

"I will," I promised, "Thanks, Winston."

After hanging up, I speed dialed Jeremy Winslow's number. With the kidnapping of Crystal and Tina, I knew they were still up and at it. Sure enough, he picked up on the second ring.

"It's Detective Lorenzo," I said, "Hi, I've got some news."

"So do I," said Jeremy, "But, ladies first."

Briefly, I told him about what Winston had discovered about that microchip. He listened intently.

"Interesting," he muttered, "When we get his codes deciphered, I bet the contents of that microchip will be *very* fascinating reading."

"I know what you mean," I said, "Now what was it that you guys found?"

"We know where they are," said Jeremy, "And we've got a plan."

Crystal Parker's journal [kept in a memo pad]

The sound of construction work greeted me shortly past dawn. I had lain on the floor beside

Tina's bed all night, scarcely closing my eyes. It would have taken a ton of sleeping pills to make me even *think* about sleeping. Instead, I spent my time praying. For hours, I poured my heart out to God about my fears, the state of Tina's soul, my desire for justice, and my love for Chris. Poor Chris! He had to be out of his mind with fear. I said an extra-long prayer for him.

At ten p.m., Chase interrupted my prayers. True to his word, he brought me some notebook paper. When he left, I snatched up the paper. For several minutes I stared at it, thinking. This could very well be my last communication ever with Chris, which made it my most important ever. With a sigh, I started to write.

"My darling Sherlock," I wrote, "If you're reading this letter, then know I am with Christ in heaven. Please, please my beloved, don't blame yourself. I know you did everything there was to do to find me in time. It's not your fault; the only people responsible for my death are the criminals who did the deed.

"I want you to know, Sherlock, that the time I've spent with you has been the happiest of my life. You're the first man to treat me like I was something special. You're certainly the first man who claimed that I was beautiful.

"Sherlock, darling, you showed me what it's like to be loved. For that, I am forever grateful. I only hope that I made you feel loved as well, because I have loved you with every ounce of my being. You're a great man, and a great detective. Thank you for the time we've had together.

"Look for a large memo pad, darling. I've written some notes in it about my last hours since my kidnapping.

"Farewell, darling. Again, don't you dare blame yourself. I'll be waiting for you in heaven, where we'll be together again.

"All my love,
Crystal"

I read the paper, folded it, and put it in my pocket. The sound of power tools interrupted my thoughts, and I ran to the window. The sun was just rising in the horizon, sending forth beautiful streaks of orange and yellow over the majestic mountains and Turner Falls. Under other circumstances, the scenery would be beautiful and peaceful. But at the moment, it looked like God might just be giving us one last look at earth's beauty before we died.

Off in the distance, overlooking the cliff, were some of Chase's men. They were working on

393

some kind of platform. I couldn't see any details, because they were obscured in the shadows. But, the platform they were building was tall and close to the edge of the cliff. While I couldn't make out the exact details, I got a vague impression of the shape of the platform.

Heaven help us!

I think they're building a gallows.

CHAPTER TWENTY-THREE

Shelly Winslow's journal [kept in shorthand]
    The call came at seven a.m. It was a Saturday, one of the few days I get to sleep in. For just a brief second, I was irritated. Then I saw Jeremy's number and remembered everything. I snatched up the phone instantly.

    "Hi, Sweetheart," I said, "Give me some wonderful news!"

    "We know where they are," said Jeremy.

    Relief washed over me in waves. "Thank you, Jesus!"

    "We've called Detective Lorenzo, and we're planning our strategy," said Jeremy, "We need a *lot* of prayer support right now. No matter how we do it, it's going to be dicey."

    "You've got it," I said, "And, honey?"

    "Yes, Gorgeous?"

    "I love you," I said, "You come back to us safe. Promise?"

    "I love you too," said Jeremy, "I promise. Lots of hugs and kisses."

    I swallowed. "I'll give you the smooch of a lifetime when I see you again."

    "That's *worth* keeping my promise! Keep those prayers coming."

    "You've got it," I said, "Bye."

"Bye."

I hung up the phone and sat up in bed. Tears were streaming down my face. I was proud of my husband, and scared to death for him. I was proud that he was playing a part in both a rescue operation and taking down the head of the mob. But I was terrified that something would go wrong. All it would take was one bullet, and I would lose the most wonderful man in the world. Maybe it was silly; I lived with that fear every day.

But I hadn't been this scared for him since 9/11. Jeremy didn't know it, but he wasn't the only one that still had nightmares about the horrors of that day; of the hours I had spent waiting for some word about whether he was dead or alive…and of screaming when I saw the towers collapse.

Now I would be waiting by the phone again. And this time, I would be waiting for word about my husband *and* about two of my best friends in the world.

Quickly, I got up out of bed and hurriedly dressed into some jeans and a long sleeved blouse. Then I went to wake up Tim and Jessica. We didn't have any warning about 9/11, but we certainly had some warning about the raid on the cabin. And that gave us some time to pray.

Jeremy Winslow's journal [7:15 a.m.]

The hours passed with all the speed of a turtle with a broken leg. Justin was agonizing over his counterfeit code, trying to make sure it was good enough to fool Chase without doing any real damage to the nation's computers. Finally, he declared the purple flash drive to be as ready as it could possibly be and handed it to Chris. Chris shoved the flash drive deep into the pocket of his cape-covered overcoat and shook Justin's hand warmly.

"I don't know how I'll ever repay you," said Chris.

"Just get those girls back safely," said Justin, "And let me know they're OK, Holmes."

Chris nodded and went back to studying every available map of the area surrounding the cabin. Whatever fears he felt was buried deep in the recesses of his brain. He had transformed himself from terrified fiancée who was afraid of failing the love of his life, to that of the Holmes of popular legend.

It had been uncanny to watch every trace of human emotion vanish from his face as he became totally absorbed in the problem at hand. I didn't know it was possible. His fears were replaced entirely with his devotion to bringing his plan to fruition. It was uncanny, and it might just help him survive his ordeal.

"We have to assume, Watson," he said, "that they have the roads coming in and out of the area watched. Mycroft will be waiting to see if I've obeyed his instructions to come alone."

"There's no way you're going to do that, by the way," I said firmly, "You know you can't trust him to go through with the exchange."

Chris flashed me a look. "Oh, you mean I can't trust the world's most ruthless criminal to keep his word? I never would have guessed that."

"Well, if the roads are being watched by his men," I said, "What does that leave us?"

Chris grinned and patted me on the back. "Watson, my friend, how are your skydiving skills?"

Shelly Winslow's journal [7:20 a.m.]

There was a sharp knock on the door. Jessica, Tim, and I looked up from our prayers. Gage was still sleeping peacefully on the blanket beside me. Rex had been curled up against Tim. At the knock, Rex trotted over to the door and sat at strict attention.

I walked to the door, scratched Rex's ear and looked through the peephole. I saw a white-haired man with a thick mustache standing outside my door. His slacks and white shirt were perfectly ironed and his shoes were neatly polished. A gray haired woman in a green pantsuit stood at his side.

"Who is it?" I asked through the locked door.

"General Walter Parker," said the man gruffly, "Crystal's father, and her mother.

I smiled and took the chain off the door. Opening the door for them, I welcomed them in and showed them to the living room. My phone rang, and I recognized the number as the father of one of the Baker Street Irregulars. I smiled and answered the call.

"Hey, Mrs. Winslow, it's Bubba," said the voice, "We saw the people go into the house. Is everything all right?"

"Yes," I said, "It's Crystal's parents. We're fine. And, thanks."

"Our pleasure. And we want you to know that we're praying for her safe return."

"So are we," I said, "I'll call back later. And thanks."

After ending the call, I saw my guests talking with Jessica. Chris had written to the Parkers weeks ago. He had hoped that they would reconcile their differences with Crystal and agree to come to the wedding. But, as far as I knew, they had never responded back. Mr. Parker frowned when he saw me approaching.

"I want you to know," said Walter, "That it wasn't *my* idea to come. This was all Emma's idea."

"Walter, *please*," said Emma.

"We need to be honest," Walter told her, "As far as I'm concerned, Crystal stopped being our daughter the day she chose to break the family tradition of a military career."

With a sigh, I turned to Tim. He wasn't at all happy to hear anybody talk about Crystal like this, especially her own father. He took an angry step forward.

Tim," I whispered, "You and Rex go see if there's anything good to watch in your room."

Tim nodded reluctantly and retreated to his room. Rex trotted at his heels.

"General Parker," I began, "With all due respect, this would be a really good time to put aside your personal differences with your daughter."

"I have no daughter," said Walter firmly, "My daughter would never have snubbed her nose for an honorable career just to marry some nut who thinks he's a fictional character."

Jessica stood up. Walking over to Walter, she held her index finger right under his nose, waving it as she spoke.

"Now you listen here," said Jessica, "My brother may have some mental issues, but he loves your daughter. Ever since he's met her, he's treated her like a fairy-tale princess! He's never talks harshly to her; he's so busy praising her he doesn't have *time* to speak harshly. He'd cut out his own tongue before saying an unkind word to Crystal, and he certainly doesn't have it in him to raise a hand to her in anger! Not every woman has it so lucky!"

"You better believe it," muttered Emma.

Walter turned to his wife, crimson red. "What do you mean by that?"

"Never mind!" snapped Emma. "You should apologize to Jessica for insulting her brother, Walter."

Walter sighed and rolled his eyes. "Sorry. I had no idea he was your brother."

"Apology accepted," said Jessica reluctantly, "But instead of talking about how wrong Crystal is in her choice of careers, you should be praying for her. She needs everyone's prayers right now."

Emma clutched her husband's arm. "What's wrong with Crystal?"

Slowly, hesitantly, we told them what Crystal was in the middle of. Emma's eyes widened in horror as we told her what we knew, and then she burst into tears. Walter's face, however, seemed to be chiseled in stone. I don't' know if he had it in him to show any tender emotion.

"I knew it," he muttered, "If she had listened to me and gone into the military, this would never have happened."

Emma turned to Walter, her eyes blazing. "Walter Brenan Parker, it's long past time that you get that boulder sized chip off your shoulders! If she *had* gone into your precious military, she could just as easily have been shot or killed by a suicide bomber!"

"It's my precious military that's responsible for the freedoms we have today," insisted Walter, "That's one thing that Crystal never understood."

I held up my hands. "That's enough! The only thing that matters right now is that Crystal and another young lady who's being held hostage come back safe and sound. If you both want to argue over who's right and who's wrong, you can do it elsewhere. But if you'd like to pray, we could sure use you. We need all the prayers we can get!"

"I'll stay and pray," said Emma, "*General Parker* can do what he wants."

Walter sighed. "I'll stay…and I'll pray."

Crystal Parker's journal [9:00 a.m.]

Nine o'clock. Three hours to go until the deadline. The sound of the power tools has yet to let up outside. I had long ago closed the blinds. Why would I want to watch people construct the instrument of what may be my execution?

Tina awoke an hour ago, and she is positively terrified. She's been curled up in a ball, her knees pressed against her chest, staring into space. I know how she feels. A part of me wants to be curled up in a little ball myself. A part of me wants to break down and cry an ocean of tears. But, I can't. I've got to help Tina through this time. I have no idea of how it's going to play out, but I've got to help her through it.

"I don't want to die," whispered Tina softly, "As horrible as my life has been, I still don't want to die!"

I walked over to the bed, sat down beside her, and put my arm around her shoulder. Her face was a pitiful mask of sheer terror. She looked up at me, and then she simply burst into tears.

"I want to go *home!*" she wailed, "I want to go back to my crummy apartment, lock the door, and never come out again!"

"Tina," I whispered, "I want you to listen to me. My fiancée and his partner are moving mountains to find us. I promise you they won't stop until they do."

"Your fiancée," said Tina, "He's the detective who thinks he's Sherlock Holmes?"

"Yes," I said, "And I've seen him do the most amazing things. He's solved crimes that have left a lot of other cops scratching their heads. And his partner is no slouch as a detective, either."

"His partner," repeated Tina, "Let me guess...he thinks he's Dr. Watson?"

"At least my *fiancée* thinks his partner is Watson," I said, "And I'm their partner at the agency, too. Let me tell you, when we sink our teeth into a mystery, we go at it like a bulldog takes to a bone."

"Even when the victim is nothing but a lousy hooker?"

I smiled. "When someone needs help, they need help. You're as important to us as a millionaire. Period. God says you're valuable and so do we."

404

Tina swallowed. "Another detective...Maria Lorenzo...she said pretty much the same thing. She helped me pray that Jesus would save my soul."

"Tina, that's awesome!" I said, "That's wonderful! Welcome to the family of God."

I gave her an extra hug.

"I just hope," she said, "That I get a chance to actually *live* for God now that I belong to Him. I know He's forgiven my sins, but I want the chance to do something with my life besides sell my body for sex before I see Him face to face. Is that silly, or what?"

"There's nothing at all silly about that," I said, "Let's pray about it right now."

We bowed our heads, and there in the middle of a crime boss' cabin, we prayed.

"Heavenly Father," I prayed, "We thank you that Tina is now a member of Your family. We thank you that we know that her name is written in Your Book of Life. We pray, heavenly Father, that you would help us.

"Lord Jesus, deliver us from the hand of our enemy. Show Chris and Jeremy how to find us, and give them success. Help us to trust in You, dear Jesus. Calm our nerves. Let Tina have a chance to show the world the change that is in her heart. Give me the chance to marry my fiancée, the man I love with all my heart. In Your Name I pray, amen."

"Amen," said Tina.

Jeremy Winslow's journal [9:30 a.m.]

Chris and I picked up Detective Lorenzo from her apartment at 9:00. Chris shared his plan with her, which left her questioning his sanity for thinking of it, and her own sanity for agreeing to it. But, with the clock against us big time, our options were slim and none, and Slim left last week.

By 9:30, we were at the airfield. It was a small airfield, used mostly for students learning to fly, skydivers, and cargo plane. Chris parked the car and led us to a cargo plane. It was an interesting plane, with the legend *STAR CRUISER ATLANTIS* in bold print stenciled across the door.

"Here we are," said Chris cheerfully, "All set and ready to go."

"Easy for you to say," I muttered, "You're *driving*. Lorenzo and I are the ones jumping out of a perfectly good airplane."

Chris chuckled and patted me on the back. "They're *expecting* me to drive up to give them the disk. They'd be asking questions if I *didn't* show. Besides, as long as you remember the most important rule of skydiving, you'll be safe."

"What's that?" I asked.

"If your parachute doesn't open," said Chris, "Just go back up to the plane and they'll give you another one."

"Remind me to kill you!" I growled.

In spite of herself, Lorenzo smiled. I, however, was far from smiling. I already had one bad experience skydiving and had vowed to never *ever* jump out of a plane unless it was crashing again.

I was even less comfortable when the door to the pilot's cabin opened and the pilot stepped out. The pilot was a small, slender woman wearing fighter goggles, had a dress that was a carbon copy of the dress Princess Leia wore in *Star Wars*, and was waving a toy light saber.

"Howdy guys," said the pilot, "The Star Cruiser Atlantis is ready to take off."

"Is she any relation to Justin, the King of Atlantis?" I whispered to Chris.

"She's his girlfriend, Ruth Garner," whispered Chris, "They met at a comic book convention two years ago."

"Let's go," said Ruth, "We need to be gone before Darth Vader and his goons show up."

"I am suddenly getting very sad," I said.

"Look," whispered Chris, "She's a certified

pilot, and I *am* trusting her to help us retrieve Crystal and Miss Stewart."

Lorenzo waved at Chris and climbed into the *Atlantis*. Reluctantly, I followed. The plane was loaded with several stacks of crates. Several were marked *medical supplies*. Several others, however, were unmarked. Lorenzo was already strapping on a parachute and having absolutely zero difficulties.

"So," I said casually, "You've skydived before?"

"It's my hobby," said Lorenzo, "I'm a charter member of a skydiving club in Oklahoma City."

"Like you don't get enough danger on the job?" I wondered.

"Oh," said Lorenzo, "I find skydiving relaxing. Haven't you ever skydived before?"

"Twice," I said, "Both times were emergency situations. The second time sort of killed my love for the sport."

"What happened?"

Picking up a parachute, I began to strap it on. It had been a while, but I still remembered what I was doing. It was sort of like riding a bicycle; some things you don't forget.

"What happened on that second time?" asked Lorenzo again.

408

"The parachute got tangled in the lines," I said, "It wouldn't open right. It was like bailing out of a plane with *no* parachute."

Lorenzo's face grew deadly serious. "What did you do?"

"Thankfully, my partner was able to maneuver his way towards me," I said, "I had to unharness myself from my useless pack and grab on to my partner all in the space of a few seconds. His chute opened perfectly, and I held onto him like a madman all the way down."

Lorenzo swallowed and made her way to a seat. I followed close behind.

"Ladies and gentlemen," said Ruth, "This is your captain speaking. We want to thank you for flying Atlantis Airlines. We are now leaving Space Station Nine and will be at our destination shortly."

"Has she been drug tested?" I whispered.

"I don't really *want* to know," whispered Lorenzo.

I settled down into my seat, trying desperately to calm my nerves. We had two lives on the line, and if anything went wrong, this whole plan could blow up in our faces. Glancing out the window, I could see the ground getting smaller and smaller below us. It was 9:45 a.m. A little over two hours to go.

CHAPTER TWENTY-FOUR

Sherlock Holmes' Casebook; 10:00 a.m.

After dropping Watson and Detective Lorenzo off at the airport, I instantly got back on the road. If all goes well, I'll be at the cabin with time to spare. Mentally, I knew I was as prepared as I could be. I had tried to think of every *possible* thing that could go wrong and tried to think of a solution. We had planned well, but there was always the chance that something would go wrong. Especially when dealing with my brother.

It had been hard to realize that I even *have* a brother, much less come to grips with the fact that he's really Moriarty. Actually, there's a lot that's hard to come to think about right now. It's been agony realizing that there's so much about my earlier life that is an absolute blank in my memory. I had sweated bullets thinking that my loss of memory was a sign of insanity and that it might lead to Crystal walking out on me. God had been kind when He gave me a woman as devoted as Crystal. I prayed that same mercy would lead to a safe homecoming for her as well as for Miss Stewart.

I still struggled to remember more about Mycroft. I remember nothing of Mycroft other than the fact that he used his great intellect for crime.

Were we ever close? Were we always at odds? I had no idea. I don't even remember what life was like with our parents or if I had any other siblings.

I had so many questions. I had no idea if I ever went to college or how I became a detective. Did I ever have a girlfriend before I met Crystal? Was I so absorbed in catching criminals that I never took time to date? How did I come to know Jesus? There was so much I didn't know; I only remembered enough about my relationship with Mycroft to find the cabin. But that was all right. Right now, getting Crystal and Tina back safely and putting Mycroft away for good was all I cared about.

After that, the only thing I cared about was my life with Crystal. Crystal...everything I had feared had come to pass. I had postponed proposing to her for so long because I was afraid that being close to me would endanger her. Now that day has arrived, and all I could do was pray that our plan would work.

One thing was certain. With my brother, he was bound to have some nasty surprises ready. Hopefully, I had a bigger surprise for him. If not, Miss Stewart and the woman I love more than life itself will die.

Jeremy Winslow's journal [10:30]

"Another few minutes and we'll be at the drop site," said Ruth.

Once we were airborne, Lorenzo and I made our way to the cockpit. I had to admit, Ruth was flying this plane like a pro. She was, to say the least, interesting. She was as obsessed with comics and science fiction as her boyfriend, and yet she was as talented at flying as Justin was with computers.

"I've got to hand it to you," I said, "You're an ace of a pilot. Justin should be proud of you."

"Thanks," said Ruth, "I met Justin at a comic book convention a few years ago. Then he hired me to fly emergency supplies as disaster relief after Hurricane Katrina, and we've been dating ever since."

"Is disaster relief the main flying you do?" asked Lorenzo.

"That covers about half of my flying," said Ruth, "The rest comes from people who want me to fly cargo and who want tours of famous areas. I've had people hire me to fly over famous battlefield sites of the Civil War. I even had one group hire me to fly over the old Alcatraz prison."

"Are there any jobs you *won't* accept?" I asked.

"I won't handle any cargo that's illegal," said Ruth, "And I did turn down one guy that wanted me to fly over a nudist camp. That boy was a real creep! I *have* handled some dangerous assignments, however. This Fall I've been commissioned to fly a group through the Bermuda Triangle for their vacation. There's room for you two to come along, if you'd like."

"Thanks but no thanks," I said, "Why would anyone pick the Bermuda Triangle for a vacation spot? I'm more the Hawaii type of guy, myself."

"They're trying to figure out what happened to the infamous Flight 19 squadron," answered Ruth.

"What was the Flight 19 squadron?" I asked, wishing instantly that I hadn't.

"Flight 19," Ruth explained, "was a squad of five TBM Avengers that took off from Florida on December 5, 1945. They were on a routine mission, and were never seen again."

"What happened to them?" asked Lorenzo.

Ruth shrugged. "It's still a mystery. All five planes vanished without a trace. No debris was ever found. They just up and disappeared in the area we call the Bermuda Triangle."

Lorenzo looked at me and blinked. I shrugged.

"A lot of people think it's a lot of bologna," said Ruth, "People say there's a logical explanation and that the Bermuda Triangle is a lot of guff. All I know is that an entire squadron of planes vanished without a trace; that much is documented. No oil slick or debris were ever found. And then, interestingly enough, a coastguard plane was sent out to look for them. The coastguard plane also vanished without a trace."

"Surely you jest," I said.

"Surely I don't," said Ruth, "I don't know why it happened. There *could* be a logical explanation, I don't know. I just know it's one of the weirdest mysteries of the sea, and this group wants to be the ones that figures it out."

"It'll make for some interesting reading if they do," said Lorenzo.

"You two better get ready," said Ruth, "Another ten minutes and we'll be at the drop site. Also, there's a few party favors in those crates you may want to take with you. I have the feeling that whatever you're walking into, it's going to be *quite* the party."

Crystal Parker's journal [10:45 a.m.]

My knees were aching from how long I had knelt beside the bed, praying. Tina was kneeling beside me, her eyes clenched shut. We had both poured our hearts out to the Lord, praying for both mercy and justice. Tina had at first insisted that she didn't know how to pray. But, when I told her that prayer was simply talking to God and listening to what He had to say, she took to it right away, weeping as she talked to Him.

After a time, there was a knock at the door. Before we could move, the door swung open. Chase walked in, followed by two of his armed gunmen. Chase was smirking arrogantly as he looked down at us.

"So, when all else fails, you pray," snickered Chase.

"Actually," I said, standing up, "Prayer is my first line of defense."

"It doesn't seem to be doing you any good now," said Chase.

"It's not over yet," I said firmly.

Chase shrugged and motioned for us to follow him. With no choice but to obey, we followed him out to the living room. Amazingly, the men I had hogtied were still lying on the floor, bound and gagged. Several of Chase's men lifted them up and dragged them to the door.

"You didn't untie them?" asked Tina.

415

Chase laughed. "They couldn't guard one sick drug addict and an unarmed woman in the kitchen. They're of no use to me anymore."

I shook my head sadly. Every one of them was seeing the price of failure. What could bind anyone to someone who would kill them for making a mistake? We watched as they were dragged by the shoulders out the door and dumped in a heap into the back of a pickup truck. Their eyes were wide with terror. With the duct tape over their mouths, they couldn't even plead for their lives. But, knowing Chase, it wouldn't do any good if they could.

"I know it's a little early," said Chase, "But, just in case my dear brother shows up early, I wanted everything to be in place. Come along, girls, it's just a little ways behind the cabin."

I glanced over at Tina. She was trembling, but making a show of being brave. I knew how she felt. My heart was hammering in my chest in fear, but there was no way I was going to let Chase see my terror. I wasn't about to give him the satisfaction.

Chase's men maneuvered their way behind us and prodded us forward with their rifles. Chase led the way, occasionally looking back towards us with a smirk. Looking around, I could see birds flying over the mountains. Off in the distance, we could see a dear running through the woods. We could hear the roar of Turner Falls. *If this is my last day on earth,* I thought grimly, *At least my last view will be of some gorgeous scenery.*

"This way, ladies," said Chase cheerfully.

We followed Chase along a dirt path behind the cabin. He led us away from the cabin down a trail leading towards the cliffs and Turner Falls. The roar of the waterfall intensified as we neared it. As we followed him, we could see a large structure before us. I shielded my eyes from the glare of the sun. I could make out a large shape in front of us, but couldn't make out what it was. The sun's reflection off of it was blinding. Whatever it was, it was the thing that Chase's men had spent all morning working on. He had had a full construction crew building the thing.

Then, as we approached it, I could finally see what it was. I stopped short, just ten yards from it, and couldn't make myself move another inch. My stomach sank down to my toes as I realized what he had in mind.

"No," I whispered softly, "No, you can't!"

Jeremy Winslow's journal [10:50 a.m.]

"We're over the drop zone," called Ruth.

Lorenzo and I nodded and walked over to the cargo door. Ruth had put the plane on autopilot and joined us.

"By the way, Ruth," I called, "Thanks for everything. Oh, and you can be proud of Justin. His computer work, along with your flying skills, has given us a fighting chance. Whatever happens, thanks."

"Just get those girls back safe," said Ruth.

Lorenzo and I stood ready as Ruth opened the door. The crates Ruth had mentioned had been filled with ammo belts and all sorts of goodies. I had a feeling we'd be needing all of the "party favors" we could get. We had strapped the ammo belts around our waists, donned helmets and gave Ruth a thumbs up sign. She said something to us, but whatever it was got drowned out by the sudden rush of air.

The air screamed as it rushed by us. Looking out the door, we could see the mountains over two miles below us. The color drained from my face as I saw just how far down the ground was. Lorenzo motioned for me to go. I tried. So help me, I tried. But I was frozen in place. My mind was telling me to jump, but my body refused to budge.

That was when I felt a pair of hands shoving me roughly out the cargo door. The world did a

418

crazy somersault as I tumbled head over heels out of the plane. A part of me wanted to scream. A part of me wanted to chew out Lorenzo good and proper. But no sound came out of my mouth.

After a few seconds, I got my bearings and stopped spinning out of control. I found myself laying out flat in a proper skydiving position. Above me, a perfectly good cargo plane was flying away. Far below me were the mountains, Turner Falls, and about two miles of empty space.

Looking to my right, I saw Detective Lorenzo. Her chute hadn't yet deployed, and she was looking at me, concerned. My look said it all: *When we get back, I WILL get even!* She looked at me, smiled, and waved. I frowned and shook my fist.

Lorenzo pulled on her cord. The parachute opened quickly and jerked her upwards. I pulled on my own cord. For just a moment I thought nothing was happening. My mind went instantly went into panic mode. Then I felt myself jerked upwards like a marionette being yanked upwards by a puppeteer.

Slowly, gently, we drifted towards the ground. The mountains came up to greet us, about four miles from Turner Falls. Lorenzo drifted to the ground and instantly started shedding her helmet and parachute.

419

I landed about a dozen yards from her. I followed her example and got myself out of my chute and helmet.

"Pretty good," said Lorenzo, "I'll have you joining our skydiving club in no time."

"Only when you teach pigs to fly," I shot back.

We rolled up and packed our chutes. Then we hid them in the bushes. Finally, I took out my compass and got our bearings.

"Turner Falls is due east of us," I said, "Judging from Chris' directions, we ought to be at the cabin with time to spare."

Lorenzo nodded and we started walking. We said nothing while we walked. We were too busy praying.

CHAPTER TWENTY-FIVE

Sherlock Holmes' Casebook [11:30 a.m.]

I'm getting close. The road is twisting up the mountain with more curves than my fiancée. Every inch of the way, I'm praying that I'm right about their location and that the girls are still alive. With every prayer came a vow that if Mycroft has harmed them in any way, he would seriously suffer.

By now, Watson and Detective Lorenzo should already be in position, or at least close to it. Coming by plane—even if they did have to skydive—they had to have made better time than I did. Coming the route they did, Mycroft's men could not possibly see them coming.

It was a pity that Lestrade isn't with us to bring Mycroft and his men down. He was with me at the beginning of the Crimson Dragons investigation. It would have been great for him to be here to take Mycroft, AKA Moriarty, into custody. Lestrade...

He had been a wonderful detective, and an even better friend. We butted heads more times than I could count, but he had been a true friend, a smart detective, and I had always had the greatest respect for him. For him to have discovered that his own father—a second generation detective in his family—had sold out to Moriarty had been a bitter blow. But, faced with the realization that he would have to testify against his father, he chose to commit suicide instead. It was another life that Mycroft would have to answer for.

The road dipped and turned. The trees on both sides of the road cast shadows, making the branches resemble long bony hands from the Grim Reaper himself. Along the way, I passed a few cabins. None, however, was the cabin I sought.

At last, at 11:42, I went around a bend and saw a tremendous view of Turner Falls in the distance. It was the cabin directly in front of me, however, that caught my attention. It was a small, ordinary cabin. Nothing about it would have attracted attention. The vehicles that Watson and I had seen on the satellite photos were still in front of the cabin, along with a couple of pickup trucks.

A dozen men wearing camouflage jackets and holding hunting rifles stood outside the cabin. Seeing my car approach, they dropped to their knees and aimed their guns right at me.

I put the car in park and stepped out, hands in the air. One of the men yelled into his walkie-talkie. Instantly, the door to the cabin opened and a man in a black leather jacket stepped onto the

422

porch. He was a little shorter than me and the arrogance on his face was unmistakable.

"Well, well," said Mycroft, "I see you're out of the hospital, brother."

"No thanks to your men putting me *in* the hospital, Mycroft," I said, scowling.

"'Mycroft'?" he repeated, blinking, "Oh, I get it."

"What you're going to *get* is a death sentence when you're caught," I said grimly.

Mycroft chuckled. "I think not, brother. In case you haven't noticed, everyone who has gone up against me has a way of suffering."

"Or people close to them," I snarled, "Like the time you kidnapped Watson's family. You *do* love to hold people's loved ones hostage, don't you?"

Mycroft shrugged. "It gets the job done."

I clenched my fists. I reminded myself that the time to confront my brother about the past would be later. Right now, there were other lives at stake. I stood still while Mycroft patted me down, removing my sidearm from its holster.

"Where's Crystal and Miss Stewart?" I demanded.

Mycroft laughed. "Oh, they're hanging around somewhere. Come on, I can't wait to show

423

you my little surprise."

He motioned for me to follow him. The gunmen came up behind me. I followed Mycroft, hating him for the smirk on his face. If it was the last thing I did in this life, I was going to remove the sneer from his face...

We came to a clearing, and I came to a sudden stop. There before me, at the very edge of the cliff, was a huge, solid steel platform. Twin chains ran up the length of the scaffolding, along a catwalk, and down the edge of the cliff about twenty feet. The chains led to a pair of large cages made of crisscrossed steel bars, dangling over the cliff about a thousand feet in the air. Far below at the bottom of the cliff was a shallow pool from the waterfalls and large rocks. Twin ladders led from the scaffold to the tops of the cages.

Inside one of the cages were three men. Then men were hogtied with lengths of rope and their mouths were covered in duct tape. Inside the other cage were the girls. One of the girls had to be Tina Stewart. She lay on the floor of the cage, her hands behind her back. The other girl was my darling Crystal. She was standing in the cage, her hands likewise behind her back, up against the back of the cage. Both their mouths were covered in duct tape.

424

"CRYSTAL," I shouted, "I'M HERE DARLING!!"

Crystal looked up. Her eyes were wide with sheer terror. My heart ached for me to be able to run to her, hold her, and show her that everything was going to be all right! Instead, I turned to Mycroft, my eyes blazing. Looking at the sneer on his face, it was all I could do to keep from picking Mycroft up and tossing him over the side of the cliff. But, somehow, I restrained myself. I had to focus on getting those girls out of that cage.

"Mycroft," I snarled, "You *will* regret this."

Mycroft yawned and stretched.

"I believe you have something for me," said Mycroft, smiling, "Something in the way of a computer disk."

"Do you think I'm stupid?" I snarled, "You think I'm going to trust you to let them go free unharmed once you have the disk? Free your prisoners and the disk is yours."

Mycroft looked at me, his face a mask of mock surprise. His eyes were wide in mock innocence.

"Sherlock, Sherlock, Sherlock," he said soothingly, "I believe you've made a terrible mistake. You are going to hand over the disk right this second, or this will happen to your lady love and her friend."

Mycroft pulled a tiny remote control from his jacket pocket. He pointed it towards the platform and pressed a button. Instantly, there was an explosion at the top of the catwalk. Before I could move, one of the chains along the catwalk snapped. The cage holding the three men was suddenly in free fall. It shot downwards, dragging the broken chain behind it, all the way to the bottom of the canyon, and crashed on the rocks below. I gapped at Mycroft. Crystal and Tina's terrified eyes were the size of saucers. His men stood unmoving.

"Oops," said Mycroft, "Butterfingers!"

"It's a stupid man who slaughters his own men!" I yelled, "The rest of you should take note. You could be the next ones in one of those cages!"

Mycroft chuckled. "An explosive just like the one I used to punish those idiots for failure is attached to the cage holding up the girls. The only difference is, it's on a timer instead of being controlled by my remote. There's no shutting it off, and anyone tampering with it will cause it to explode."

"If I give you the disk," I said, "How do I get them out of there?"

Mycroft dug into his pocket and pulled out a set of keys. He held it high in the air, making sure I could see it.

"Why do you think I installed ladders on that platform?" asked Mycroft, "Hand me the disk and I give you the keys. One key will unlock the door to the cage. The other ones will unlock their chains once you're in."

"By what stretch of the imagination do you believe I'll trust you to let us go once I give you this disk?" I demanded.

"Do you have a choice?" asked Mycroft, "The bomb will detonate in exactly...fifteen minutes and counting. Refuse to give me the disk, and I toss the key into the falls. Any questions?"

"None," I snarled.

With a sigh, I handed over the disk. One of them men opened a laptop computer and inserted the disk. Within seconds, we could see several columns of code filtering across the screen. I prayed that Justin's code had done the trick. For several seconds I held my breath. Then at last, Mycroft smiled.

"You've done well, brother," said Mycroft, "And here's your reward for a job well done."

Mycroft held the keys out to me. I reached out to take them, and then it happened. Mycroft

427

jerked his hand away just as I was about to take the keys. Before I could move, he tossed the keys up, out, and over the cliff. I stood, horrified, as I saw the keys drop all the way down into the falls. I glared back at Mycroft, who only laughed.

"You have twelve minutes and thirty seconds to pray for their souls," said Mycroft savagely.

At that moment, a small cylinder shaped object flew out from the bushes. It hit the ground and rolled towards Mycroft's men. A jet of white gas instantly started spraying out as another cylinder accompanied the first, spraying its own white gas.

"Tear gas!" shouted Mycroft.

Mycroft's men started gagging. They dropped their weapons and sank to their knees as the gas took effect. Mycroft looked in horror as his men rolled on the ground, gasping for air. That was when my fist shot out, having a close encounter with Mycroft's nose.

He sank to the ground, holding his nose as Jeremy and Lorenzo came running from their hiding place in the bushes. They had on gas masks and were holding Uzis. The men on the ground were in no position to put up a fight. While they were

428

gasping for air, Jeremy and Lorenzo were grabbing several pairs of plastic zip ties from their pockets. Instantly they knelt down by Mycroft and his men.

While they were tending to Mycroft and his men, I took off running. I made my way to the ladder positioned above the girls' cage, coughing and gagging from the effect of the gas as I ran. It was ten rungs down from the top of the ladder to the cage. I made it in four seconds. My first obstacle: the escape hatch on top of the cage was locked. I dug my Swiss Army Knife out of my belt pouch, selected a small screwdriver blade and started working on the lock.

"Hang on girls," I shouted, "I'm coming!"

The lock was a bear. If there was one thing I could say about my brother, it was that he always selected state of the art equipment. The bad thing was, it was eating up precious time while I picked my way through the lock. After several tense seconds, however, the lock slid open. Instantly, I tore open the hatch and dropped into the cage.

A young woman I had never met before was lying on the floor of the cage, her hands behind her back. That had to be Tina Stewart. She looked exhausted and terrified. Who could blame her? Turning her over, I saw she was wearing a set of

429

police handcuffs. I selected a different sized screwdriver and started working on the cuffs.

"Don't worry, girls," I said, "Watson and Detective Lorenzo have everything under control. You're going to enjoy seeing Mycroft and his men get what they deserve."

The police handcuffs were tricky. I was an expert at picking locks, but police handcuffs were hard even for a pro. One minute passed. Then two. Finally, I heard the tumblers click and the cuffs opened. I jerked her hands free of the cuffs, and she tore at the duct tape over her mouth.

"Go!" I ordered, "We'll be right behind you."

"Mr. Holmes," she cried, "There's something you need to know! It's...."

"Go!"

"But—"

"No time to argue," I shouted, "Go!"

I lifted Tina up until she could climb out of the hatch. She instantly started climbing up the ladder while I ripped the duct tape off of Crystal's mouth.

"Don't worry, darling," I said gently, "I'm here and I'm going to get you out."

"You can't," sobbed Crystal, "You don't understand..."

I looked behind her back and saw that her hands were firmly locked in a set of chains that were bolted to the back of the cage. It was a good thing I wasn't relying on shooting the locks. At that angle, there would be no way I could shoot the locks open without accidentally shooting Crystal herself. I studied the chains, looking for the keyhole.

There wasn't one. There was no keyhole for me to pick!

"Where's the keyhole?" I demanded.

Crystal was sobbing. "Moriarty had the lock welded shut before locking me in here. There's no lock for you to pick. There's no way to get me out!"

Jeremy Winslow's journal

I had to give Chris credit. When he came up with a plan, it was a good one. Once Lorenzo and I safely parachuted down into the mountains, we made our way up the back trails, apprehending some of Chase's men that were left standing guard along the trail. Then it was a simple matter to make our way to the bushes and wait for Chris' signal. It had been tempting to take out Chase and his men right away, but we needed to know what the setup was for Crystal and Tina.

Once we threw the tear gas, we knew it would be no trouble handcuffing Chase and his men with those zip ties. We had them all nice and giftwrapped in their zip ties within two minutes. Last but certainly not least was Chase himself. He looked like he wanted to make a run for it, but facing down two Uzis mad him reconsider.

"Well, Chase," I said, "Or should I say Moriarty? It's been a long time coming, but you're finally going to get what's coming to you. With all the evidence we have on you, it's going to be no trouble getting you the death penalty."

Incredibly, he smirked at me. "Maybe so, but my brother is going to die before I do. As a matter of fact, he's going to die in just a few minutes."

Lorenzo and I exchanged glances.

"Go see to him," said Lorenzo, "I can hold down the fort here. I was about to call for backup anyway."

I needed no further urging. I dashed towards the platform. Just as I reached the ladder, I saw a young woman that I guessed was Tina Stewart climbing up. I held out a hand and pulled her up to safety. She threw her arms around my shoulders and sobbed for several seconds.

432

"It's going to be all right," I said soothingly, "What's going on down there?"

Sobbing hysterically, Tina told me about how Chase had welded the keyhole to Crystal's chains shut. There was no way to get her out of that cage! Gently, I pushed Tina away and she ran towards Lorenzo. I pulled a small set of field glasses out of my ammo belt and gazed up at the explosive. Sure enough, I could see the motion detector attached to the bomb. Chase had told the truth; any tampering with the bomb would set it off.

I quickly climbed down the ladder to the top of the cage. Looking in, I could see Chris working on Crystal's chains.

"Holmes! What's going on?"

"My knife has a metal file on it," he shouted, "I'm filing through Crystal's chains."

"Hurry," I shouted, "You have two minutes left!"

"Sherlock," cried Crystal, "You don't have time! Forget about me! Save yourself!"

"Never!" snarled Chris.

"You could find someone a lot better than me," she pleaded.

"You're my life, Crystal," said Chris soothingly, "Either we both walk out of here alive, or we both die together!"

Tears were flowing down Crystal's face as Chris filed away on the chains. I glanced at my watch, and my heart leaped to my throat. He had one and a half minutes to get them both out of there.

"I've already looked at the bomb," I explained, "It's got motion detectors to set it off if I tamper with it. How can I help?"

"There's not enough room for us both to work down here," said Chris, "Even if you had your own file, you couldn't maneuver in here to work."

"Sherlock," cried Crystal, "Please, go. You haven't time!"

"I'm getting there," said Chris, "Honey, you just think of what you're going to look like in your wedding gown. You're going to be more beautiful than you already are."

"One minute, Holmes," I shouted, "Hurry!"

"I'm nearly through," said Chris, "Watson…"

"I'm staying, Holmes," I replied.

"You have a wife and two sons," said Chris, "Go, and that's an order!"

"I can't hear you over the filing," I replied, "Forty-five seconds. I hate to rush you…"

"*GOT IT!*" shouted Chris.

Crystal's hands jerked free. In a flash, Chris scooped her up in his arms. He lifted her high in

434

the air. I grabbed her hands and pulled her up. The moment she got to the top of the cage, she started up the ladder.

"Grab my hand, Holmes!" I shouted.

Chris jumped and I grabbed his hand. Gripping tightly with both hands, I yanked him upwards. Without a word, I pulled him until he reached the top of the cage. As he scrambled to his feet, I was climbing up the ladder. By now, Crystal had reached the safety of the cliff and was peering over anxiously. I reached the top of the ladder and climbed onto the ledge.

Then I heard the explosion. I looked up just in time to see the chain holding the cage snap from the force of the explosive. The cage and chain fell past me, missing me by about two inches. I looked down to see Chris. He was halfway up the ladder when the bomb went off. The cage was dropping rapidly, pulling the chain behind it.

The chain had missed me, but it didn't miss Chris. The thick chain slammed hard into Chris' chest. *He was knocked clear off the ladder!* Crystal screamed as Chris fell backwards. My eyes widened in horror as he fell. He tumbled backwards, flipping head over heels, arms scrambling madly, and there was nothing either of us could do to help.

435

Crystal continued to scream as Chris fell. He had made perhaps five of the ten rungs on the ladder when the chain hit him. As he fell, he frantically reached for something to grab.

He found it! His left hand gripped the last rung on the ladder. His body swung madly as his hand held that last rung in a death grip. Finally, he gained control of his body and grabbed the rung in both hands. About that time, the cage hit the bottom of the cliff with a great crash.

"Thank you, Jesus!" exclaimed Crystal.

"I'll be more thankful when I'm back on solid ground!" exclaimed Chris.

Two minutes later, Chris made it to the top of the cliff and we walked back to where Tina and Lorenzo were holding the prisoners at gunpoint. Tina looked like she wanted desperately to empty the gun into her tormentors. I could understand how she felt.

Chris looked at his brother with contempt. Chase's nose had stopped bleeding, but dried blood had matted directly under his nostrils. Looking at Chris, Chase shrugged.

"You may have won this round," said Chase, "But it's not over yet. As a matter of fact..."

Before he said another word, Chase jumped to his feet. Incredibly, his hands were free. I saw the severed zip ties around his wrist and a knife in his hand.

Spring loaded knife up his sleeve, I thought wildly, *why didn't I think of searching him?!*

In a flash, Chase was on Chris. Chris grabbed Chase's wrists, holding him at bay. Lorenzo, Crystal, and I had our guns ready, waiting for a clear shot. But Chris and Chase were twisting and turning, fighting over the knife. There was no way to fire without risking hitting Chris. Chris snapped Chase's wrist back and the knife clattered to the ground. Chase threw his full body weight against Chris, and he went down, pulling Chase with him. They rolled on the ground, while we kept our firearms ready, waiting for one good shot.

Chris pushed Chase away and was quickly on his feet. But Chase was close behind him. Chase gave Chris a wicked karate chop to the throat, and Chris let go of his brother, gagging. Chase pulled Chris around and punched him in the stomach. Chris doubled over, gasping for air.

Chase slammed Chris against the steel platform. Chris grunted and gave Chase a wicked punch to the gut. Chase crumpled to the ground, but not for long. He kicked Chris in the knee with all his might. Chris' knee gave out from under him, and he hit the ground.

Chase pulled himself to his feet, and pulled Chris up with him. He grabbed Chris by the shirt, and flipped him over his shoulder. It was with a start that I realized that their fight was taking them closer and closer to the edge of the cliff.

Life was about to imitate art, I thought wildly. In the Sherlock Holmes story *The Final Problem*, Holmes and Moriarty faced their final battle directly over a waterfall in Switzerland. It was widely believed that Holmes and Moriarty both went over the cliff to their deaths. It wasn't until three years later that public outrage over the supposed death of Sherlock Holmes, that the writer- --Sir Arthur Conan Doyle—explained that Holmes had faked his death in order to track down the assassin that was trying to kill him.

The only problem was that real life was not like a fictional story. Chris and Chase were in a knock-down-drag-out fight that was taking them back to the very cliff that Chris had just escaped from. If they both fell over, no amount of public pressure could ever bring Chris back from the dead.

"What'll we *do*?" demanded Crystal, "I'm trying, but I can't get a clear shot. They're both going to be killed!"

"Keep your eyes peeled," I said, "Keep praying for an opening."

Chris and Chase had reached the very edge of the cliff, punching and kicking each other every step of the way. Their arms were wrapped around each other in death grips, and neither was giving an inch.

"You're going over that cliff yet, *brother*!" snarled Chase.

Chris responded by bringing his right fist up and it had a close encounter with Chase's chin. Chase staggered, momentarily losing his grip. That was the moment Chris needed. Chris shoved Chase backwards. Chase screamed and clawed madly in the air. Then he fell backwards.

But he didn't fall far. Just as he fell back over the edge, Chris reached out and caught him by the wrist. For several seconds, Chase dangled dangerously in midair. Then, slowly, Chris hauled him back up. Instantly, we were at Chris' side, guns drawn. Chase looked at us, sighed, and stared down at the ground.

"*Now* it's over," said Chris, "all except for your trial and your execution."

Chase glared at his brother. Incredibly, a slow smile spread across his face.

"That's where you're wrong, Sherlock," said Chase coldly, "Arresting me is *not* the same as

439

convicting and executing me. This isn't over by a long shot. I will *not* die before you do, brother!"

Chase was still spouting threats as several police cars came into the campground and he was loaded into a squad car.

"How can anyone be so consumed with hatred?" wondered Lorenzo.

"It's all a matter of choice, detective," said Chris, "Both Mycroft and I shared the same parents. I chose to use my talents for the cause of justice, while Mycroft chose to prey on society as a parasite."

Crystal drew Chris close and gave him a long, lingering kiss. When their lips parted, she looked up at her fiancée with eyes that glowed with love.

"Thank you, darling," said Crystal, "You're the most wonderful man in the world."

"I'm not nearly as wonderful as *you*," said Chris.

Lorenzo smiled. "I guess you're going to do some serious celebration now that Moriarty—or whatever you want to call him—is in custody."

"In a way," said Chris, "But a part of me doesn't feel good about it. Mycroft could have done so much good for society. Instead his whole life was one terrible, tragic waste."

CHAPTER TWENTY-SIX

Jeremy Winslow's journal [kept on flash drive]
Crystal raised her glass of punch high in a toast. Me, Shelly, Chris, Lorenzo, Tim, and Jessica followed suit. On the evening after the arrests, we met together in the office of Sherlock Holmes and company for a celebration. A friend of Lorenzo's catered it with everything from sandwiches, chips, cake, coffee, and punch. Tim was more interested in the cake than anything else, although Shelly made sure that he got some nutritious food in his system before diving into the cake.

"To the capture of Moriarty," said Crystal.

"Here, here," said Chris.

"And to the people who made it all possible," said Lorenzo, "Without you guys staying with the case in spite of overwhelming odds, it never would have happened."

"I certainly wouldn't be here if they hadn't," said Crystal.

"And my life wouldn't be worth living if I lost you," said Chris.

Crystal kissed Chris while Tim made gagging noises. We all laughed at that.

"What happens now?" asked Jessica.

"The D.A. will go over every scrap of evidence there is against Moriarty," explained

Lorenzo, "It'll take some time to sort through it all. It may be a year before the trial even *starts*. But make no mistake, there's enough evidence to convict a hundred men. Moriarty and his gang will never see the light of day again. Probably, they'll all get a death sentence."

"At least it's all over," said Shelly, "No more going into hiding."

"There is one more thing to take care of before we can officially say it's over," said Jessica, "One *very* important item of business."

"Really?" said Chris, "What's that?"

Jessica said nothing. She simply walked over to my desk, reached down, and pulled out a black, metal file box. It was the same file box that Chris had once kept the documents establishing his identity as Christopher Anderson; the box he had vowed to open once Moriarty was captured. All of those documents were gone now, destroyed by Chris and Jessica's brother. I had no idea what she had in mind, but whatever it was, she was dead serious.

"You have a promise to keep, Sherlock Holmes," said Jessica, "And I'm not letting you put it off one more second."

Chris smiled. "All of the case files I kept in there were destroyed days ago by Moriarty."

442

"True," said Crystal, "But there were some other copies to be found elsewhere. Open it up, darling."

Shelly leaned over close to me. "There were enough photographs and newspaper clippings in their mother's scrapbooks to fill up his file box."

I smiled as Chris placed the file box on his desk. I had thought that any chance of this moment was gone for good once Jessica and Chris' house had been broken into by Moriarty's men. However, God intended otherwise. Crystal leaned close to Chris with her hand on his shoulder as he opened the box and began pulling out papers. He first pulled up a photo of himself in his police officer's uniform.

"Ah yes," said Chris, "Here's a photo I took during the case of the giant rat of Sumatra. The paperwork on that should be in here somewhere."

Shelly and I looked at each other. Then we looked at Jessica; the smile was fading from her face. She looked anxiously at her brother as he pulled out a photograph of himself in a tuxedo. In the picture, he was standing next to a woman in a wedding gown that could only be his late wife Tabitha.

Chris frowned. "That's from the case of Lord Abernathy of the club foot and his abominable

443

wife. They had turned their mansion into a literal house of horrors. I barely escaped out of the deathtraps in their home with my life."

Tears were streaming down Jessica's face. For years she had lived with the hope that whenever Chris studied the pictures and documents in his file box he would remember his true identity. But it wasn't happening! His mind's eye wouldn't allow him to see the truth that was standing right in front of him!

NOW what do we do? I wondered. I glanced over at Crystal. She was shedding more than a few tears herself and was doing her best to hide it from Chris. Chris, meanwhile, pulled out a copy of his marriage license from his wedding to Tabitha.

"This document," said Chris, "Is from the case of the aluminum crutch. A sniper's rifle was hidden inside the crutch. If I remember right, it's one of the cases that first put me on the trail of Moriarty, I mean Mycroft. What a treasure trove we have here! Thank you, guys; this is really starting to help clear away at least *some* of the mental fog from my memory!"

This was too much for Jessica. She fled the room, sobbing. Crystal fled after her, holding her hands to her mouth. Shelly, Tim, and Lorenzo crowded around me as Chris pulled out a copy of Grace's birth certificate.

"This, Watson," said Chris, excited, "is a newspaper clipping concerning the case of James Philamore, who walked from his driveway back into his house to get his umbrella and was never seen again. What a time I had with that one!"

Crystal Parker's journal [kept on her tablet]
I caught up with Jessica, who was sitting on the steps beside the elevator. She held a handkerchief to her face, sobbing. I sat down beside her and put an arm around her shoulder. For nearly a minute, she cried into her handkerchief.

"I thought he would snap out of it!" sobbed Jessica, "I thought at last he was about to have his identity back! The doctors said that seeing the pictures might bring him back to reality."

"I'm sorry," I said simply.

"I don't understand it!" she continued, "He sees the pictures, but his mind is seeing something else! He can read all those clues to solve his blasted mysteries, but when it's something relating to who he really is, his mind won't let him see it!"

"Maybe his mind's not ready," I said, "Remember how you once told me that there's no guarantees with his sanity?"

"Yes," said Jessica sadly, "I also said he might *never* get his sanity back. He's substituting false memories for real ones, Crystal. I don't know if he'll ever get past that."

I thought about that for a minute. She was right. Chris' true identity might be lost for good. He might be locked in his Sherlock Holmes identity for the rest of his life.

"Jessica," I said, "I can't begin to imagine what it's like for you. He's your brother and he doesn't even recognize you. I can't begin to know how much you're hurting. But you've always got a friend in me...and in Shelly, Jeremy, and detective Lorenzo."

Jessica swallowed. "I want to live long enough to see him recognize me. Is that selfish, Crystal?"

I shook my head. "No way. I'd feel the same way if I were in your shoes. At least Chris calls me by my real name instead of a fictional character. I also promise that none of us are giving up on him. We're never going to give up looking for a way to help him find his way back to reality."

Jessica looked at me gratefully. "You have no idea how glad I am to know that Chris has a woman like you willing to stand by him in spite of everything."

I smiled. "Chris is a wonderful man. No matter what name he uses, he's the most wonderful man I've ever known and I can't wait to try to be a good wife for him. Hopefully, within a few years you'll have some nieces and nephews to spoil."

Jessica smiled warmly. "I'm already looking forward to it. Crystal, you're going to make a terrific wife and mother!"

"From your lips to God's ears," I smiled.

The office door opened and Detective Lorenzo walked over to us. Her face was a mask of great, great concern.

"Are you two all right?" asked Lorenzo.

Jessica nodded. "I guess so. I have to say this isn't what I'd hoped for, but Chris is still alive. As long as he's alive, there's hope."

Lorenzo nodded. "That's right. In the Bible, Abraham and Sarah had to wait over *twenty years* for their baby to be born. Chris knows he's had memory problems. He's also seeing the faces of his late wife and daughter in his mind, even if he can't remember them."

"True," I said, "And you're right, Jess. As long as there's life, there's hope."

"We're working on getting Chris' personal records back," said Lorenzo, "And Chase is behind bars. True, we still have to give him his day in court

447

and convict him, but he *is* under arrest. That alone is worth celebrating."

Jessica smiled. "You're right! I should be grateful for what I've got!"

"There's something else to be grateful for," said Lorenzo, "I just got a call from Tina Stewart. She's settled in at the New Hope Drug Rehab. She is determined to kick the drug habit and to *stay* off the drugs. She's getting some good, Christian counseling. She's also looking at taking some classes to get a real job. There'll be no more prostitution for her."

"Praise God!" I exclaimed.

Jessica sighed. "There's still some good coming out of all this after all. I guess I'll just have to face the fact that God's got a plan for Chris that—for now, at least—still involves him thinking he's Sherlock Holmes."

"True," I said, "But don't give up hope. We'll find the right way to help him find his way back yet. Now, let's get back. I want to see if I can con my fiancée into telling me where we're going for the honeymoon!"

CHAPTER TWENTY-SEVEN

Jeremy Winslow's journal [kept on flash drive]

In the weeks following Chase's arrest, the case against him became all but a slam dunk for the D.A. The deciphering of his code book revealed names of everybody connected with the Crimson Dragons, including several prominent politicians. The flash drive containing the virus Chase had designed was turned over to the D.A. with the intention that the code would be destroyed after the trial.

The microchip that had been implanted in Chris' skull turned out to have the numbers for several offshore bank accounts which, all together, totaled over ten *billion* dollars. The information had been kept in encrypted codes that, thanks to Shelly uncovering the secrets of the codes, the DA was able to use as evidence. Had Chase succeeded, he would have relocated to the Bahamas as the world's richest man.

The microchip also revealed every one of Chase's hideouts. This led to a multitude of arrests and a truck load of evidence that closed the books on several unsolved cases. A multitude of offshore bank accounts gave a good indication of how Chase had financed his operations. Chase must have thought it was a great joke that information to his money and hideouts would be in a microchip inside the skull of his mortal enemy; a microchip he could access with a computer at any time.

Tina Stewart was succeeding splendidly at getting off the drugs and *staying* off them. The news that her mother ended up getting beaten to death by one of her "clients" made Tina even more determined than she already was to get her life straightened out. The last we heard from her, she was acing every class that she was taking and looking forward to whatever God had in store for her.

The day of November 10th finally arrived. The church was packed. Besides friends and family, several people that Chris had helped over the last six years showed up to see what was turning out to be the wedding of the year. The sanctuary was decked out in purple and gold. The pianist was playing the most romantic love songs ever written. And Chris stood before a mirror trying in vain to tie his bow tie.

"Blasted tie!" he growled, "Whoever invented ties should be *hanged* with his own invention! I'm tempted to go *without* it."

Chuckling, I picked up the tie and approached Chris with it. Sure enough, the main

450

reason he couldn't tie the tie was because of how badly his hands were shaking.

"Sherlock Holmes," I said, "You are not—I repeat, *not*—going to your wedding without a tie. It just isn't done; a tux isn't a tux without a bow tie."

"Watson," he said with a forced calm, "I will be just as married whether I'm wearing a tie or not."

"Tell that to your bride," I said, "She'll use a *lot* more words to tell you why you need a tie than I will. Fair warning."

Chris sighed. "Fine. Help me with the thing, though. I'm shaking like a leaf on a windy day."

I laughed and made Chris raise his chin. Tying his tie, I couldn't help but laugh some more. He looked down at me and frowned. I made him raise his head again.

"I fail to see the humor, my friend," growled Chris.

"Come *on*, Sherlock," I said, "You must see the irony. I've seen you pick locks, rescue people in cages above a cliff, hack into top secret computers using equipment you invented yourself, diffuse land mines, and solve mysteries that leave most detectives scratching their heads. But you can't tie a tie."

451

After a few moments, with Chris fussing every step of the way, I got the tie to his tux looking perfect.

"There," I said.

"*Finally*," he said, and sank into a chair.

In the background, we could hear the pianist playing some general love songs. People were being seated in the church, and now all we had to do was wait for the pastor's signal.

"You know, Watson," said Chris finally, "I want to thank you again for how you've stood by me all this time. Your own family was endangered more than once by my brother, and a lot of people wouldn't have stuck by me like you've done. And thank you for sticking with Crystal and me when we were in that cage."

"We're friends, partners," I said, "I wouldn't dream of doing anything *but* staying the course with you. There are reasons why detectives consider their partners to be brothers. I'm just glad to see the day when Moriarty—or whatever name you want to call him by—is behind bars. I'm doubly glad to see the day that you and Crystal get married."

Chris laughed. "You and me both! But tell me, as a husband, why I'm more nervous now than when I'm facing a gun battle with gangsters!"

It was my turn to laugh. "Holmes, this is a big step! You and Crystal are going to be building a new life together! It's different from going out on a date and then going to separate homes, my friend. On *my* wedding day, I was wondering if I could be a decent husband, a good lover to my wife, and a good father to our future children."

Chris swallowed. "My thoughts are going in very similar directions, my friend."

I patted my friend on the shoulder. "Holmes, I have a feeling you're going to do great. Just remember the two little words that can help keep peace and harmony in the home."

Chris blinked. "*Two* words? I thought it was *three* words; you know, the words 'I love you'."

"No, Holmes," I grinned, "This is different. The two words that can keep a husband in good graces with his wife are the words 'yes, dear'. A husband who wants tranquility in the home says those words a lot. And if I want Shelly to know I said that, I'll tell her myself."

Chris laughed. It was good to see him smile and laugh. He was more relaxed than I'd ever known him. Having Chase behind bars awaiting trial had lifted a huge burden off his shoulders, as it had for all of us. No longer were we forced to live with police guarding our homes. Chris no longer had to worry about his loved ones suffer because of his investigation. Those days were gone. Now Chris could enjoy life and just focus on being happy with his bride.

The only fly in the ointment was that Chris still hadn't gotten his memory back. It had been a bitter blow when Chris looked at the pictures and documents in his file box and he *still* couldn't remember anything. He didn't even see the pictures for what they really were. Poor Jessica still has to accept Chris not recognizing her as his sister. She's coping, but it hurts her deeply. The only thing I can figure is that his mind just isn't ready to face the truth.

I still believed the day would come when Chris *would* regain his identity. It was just going to be a gradual process. He knew that he had gaps in his memory; that was progress. He also knew that Chase was his brother. The rest was just going to be one gradual step at a time. For the moment, he just wanted to enjoy a new life with Crystal, and I didn't blame him one bit.

"I visited my brother in jail yesterday," said Chris suddenly.

I blinked. "You have *got* to be kidding!"

454

Chris shook his head. "I wanted to tell him that I forgive him."

"You actually *forgive* that monster after all he's done?"

"God commands us to forgive," said Chris, "So, with His help, I do. Remember, Watson, forgiving someone doesn't mean you condone their actions. It's never easy, but to live in obedience to God, I *have* to forgive him. Look, I want Mycroft to pay for his crimes on earth, but I don't want him to die lost in his sins. We should never want *anyone* to die lost in their sins, no matter what they've done."

I smiled and nodded. Chris was right. Yet it was hard. I had to admit, I hadn't even *thought* about the issue of needing to forgive Chase and his men. After all, the man had put my best friend through the wringer and it resulted in his going mad.

He had my own family kidnapped, and I personally had been nearly killed on several occasions. I had been too busy being happy that it was all over to even think about forgiveness. But Chris was right. God commanded us to forgive others, and I would need to ask His help in being able to. There was no way I could do all this on my own. The good thing was that God never *intends* for us to do it on our own! He's there to help us, and He's always there to help us when we want to obey Him.

"What was his reaction when he saw you?" I asked.

"I couldn't repeat his words here in church," said Chris, "When he saw me, he spent a lot of time warning me that I may have won *this* round, but he wasn't out of the game yet. Every sentence he said was peppered with language that would do justice to a sailor."

"So he told you that your ordeal with him isn't over," I said.

Chris nodded. "Basically, yes. I'm sure you recall his words on that cliff when he told us that *arresting* him was not the same as *convicting* and *executing* him. In short, he told me not to expect there to actually be a trial."

I grinned. "He wouldn't be the first criminal to boast that he would bust out of jail before the trial ever started."

"True," said Chris, "But remember who we're dealing with, my friend. I've given strict instructions on jail security and who should and shouldn't have contact with Mycroft. It's going to take a good long time before the trial is even ready to begin, and we can't afford to take any chances. I'll just be glad when the trial is done."

456

"That day will come," I said, "It'll take some time, but it will happen."

"Speaking of time," said Chris, "Isn't it time for the wedding to start? I'm ready to change Crystal's last name to Holmes. I wish they'd call us in there to get started. You just be ready to hand me that wedding ring."

I looked blankly at Chris. I stuffed both hands into my pockets and came out with empty hands.

"Uh, Holmes," I said, "I don't know how to tell you…but there's a hole in my pocket. I think I…I think I, uh… lost the ring."

"*WHAT?!*" roared Chris.

"Sorry," I said, "It's got to be somewhere between here and my house. But, it's a pretty big hole in this pocket. We'll just have to delay the wedding until I find it."

Chris' face was interesting. I didn't know a man could turn purple and green at the same time. Then, with a smile, I pulled the ring box out of my coat pocket and showed him that the ring was still safe and sound inside.

"Watson," he said grimly, "Remind me to kill you!"

"That was payback for making me go skydiving," I said grinning.

457

The door opened and Reverend Marshal, a young bearded pastor of forty, stepped inside.

"Gentlemen," he said, "It's five minutes before the ceremony. We can go to the altar."

"Sorry, Reverend," I said, "I think Holmes has chickened out and is about to call off the wedding."

"Actually," said Chris, "I was about to tell the Reverend that he needs to plan your funeral service. There's ten million comedians out of work and you're trying to be funny! Let's go, wise guy!"

Crystal Parker's journal [kept on her tablet]

I'm nearly as scared as I was when I was dangling over the cliff. Almost, but not quite. For the millionth time, I looked at myself in the mirror. The dress was perfect, the veil was wonderful, and I had done what I could with my hair. Now if only I had lost those last few pounds that I had promised myself I would lose!!!! Shelly looks great in her long, purple dress. She keeps telling me that I look great, but the mirror tells me otherwise.

"Honestly, Crystal," said Shelly, "You look *fabulous.*"

"But it's my *wedding day*," I cried, "and I want everything to be perfect!"

"It *is*, and it will," said Shelly, "You'll see. When you march down that aisle in five minutes, your man is going to be totally captivated when he sees you!"

My face went so pale that I was the same shade of white as my dress.

"Five *minutes*," I said, "It's only five minutes? But there's so much I have left to do..."

Shelly chuckled. "The only thing left to do is to walk down that aisle and say your vows. In less than an hour, you're going to be married to the man of your dreams. Look, I was as nervous as you when I married Jeremy. But, afterwards, I realized that everything I was scared about was just in my head. The important thing is that we were married."

"You're right," I said, rolling my eyes, "I've just been looking forward to this for so long, I'm as nervous as a cat in a dog pound."

"I've noticed," said Shelly, "But, trust me, it's going to be great! Then, later, you're going to look back and wonder why on earth you were so nervous."

"Maybe," I said, "But right now, my mind is going in about a trillion different directions. Will the pastor remember to announce as Mr. and Mrs. *Holmes* instead of Anderson? He does know about Chris' mental state, but..."

"He's been reminded," promised Shelly, "Jeremy's talked to him about that more than once."

"And when I throw the bouquet," I continued, "I want Jessica where she'll be the one to catch it. And…"

"Don't worry," said Shelly, "Just focus on that man waiting for you at the end of the aisle."

"I just wish my parents were here," I said, "I want Mom out there and I want Dad to walk me down the aisle! I mean, I'm grateful for Jessica giving me away, but it's not the same."

Shelly frowned. When I had heard that my parents had actually visited Shelly and prayed with her and Jessica during my kidnapping, I thought that they were going to come around. But they left town without even seeing me once they learned I was safe.

Chris had called them several times after Chase's capture. But, as far as I knew, Dad was still holding his grudge. I hated it. Until our falling out, I had always been known as Daddy's little girl. I had always dreamed of the day he would give me away to my Prince Charming, and now that would never be.

"Crystal," said Shelly, "I know you want your family here, and I hate that they're not. But, right now you just need to think about the man that's waiting for you at the other end of the aisle."

I nodded. "You're right, Shelly. I can't think of anything now except---"

There was a knock at the door. Shelly opened it, and my mouth was hanging open. My parents were standing there before me in the doorway!

With a squeal, I ran to them and threw my arms around them. They put their arms around me and held me tight. Mom was crying and Dad was telling me how much he loved me. I started crying, and for a moment I was worried about what my tears were doing to my makeup. Then I realized that, at that moment, I couldn't care less about my makeup. My parents were here, and that's all that mattered.

"Didn't Chris tell you?" asked Shelly, "Your parents agreed to be here the first time he called them after Chase was arrested."

"I *knew* Chris was the world's most wonderful man!" I whispered.

Dad looked at me; *really* looked at me. He looked at me like I was a piece of fine China that might break if he held me wrong.

"When we heard what that maniac tried to do to you," whispered Dad, "We were terrified. We

461

were ashamed that we almost lost you and my stubbornness would have prevented us from telling you how much we love you…and how proud we are of you."

"Thank you, Dad," I said weakly.

"And when we learned from *Shelly*," put in Mom, "That your groom went to such incredible lengths to get you back safely, we knew that we couldn't ask for a better man to marry our daughter. Any man that's willing to die for you is a man I'm *proud* to call my son-in-law!"

"I agree," said Dad, "Shelly gave us every detail of how Chris saved you."

I looked at Shelly. She smiled and waved at me, all innocent. Then Dad was hugging me, and it felt wonderful.

"Chris wanted this to be a surprise," whispered Shelly, "as a sort of wedding present."

"He couldn't give me a better wedding present if he gave me the Hope Diamond!" I said.

Dad smiled. "Forgive an old fool for his stubbornness. Is it too late for your old man to walk his *little girl* down the aisle?"

My lips quivered. "No it isn't. I would love for you to. Thank you, Daddy."

I looked at Shelly. She was shedding a few tears of her own.

An usher led Mom away to be seated. Then the wedding march started. Wiping my eyes, I decided that my makeup was indeed going to be a mess. But, that was all right. My heart hammered in my chest as, one by one, the bridesmaids went into the sanctuary. Then Shelly, as the matron of honor, went in.

Then it was my turn. Dad took my arm and we went in. All of our friends were there; Jessica was holding Gage and Tim was beside her, the Baker Street Irregulars and their parents were there, Justin and Ruth were there, Maria Lorenzo, everybody. There, at the far end of the auditorium, was Chris. He looked magnificent in his tux and his face lit up as he saw me. For just an instant, he glanced at my father, nodded, and then looked back at me. My darling's face glowed with joy.

I had no idea what our future held. I had no idea if Chris would ever get his memory back or if Chase really would succeed in causing us future grief. But, I knew that Chris and I had a future together, and that was what counted the most.

The pianist played louder at the wedding march. The packed church stood to their feet. Then, with my father's arm locked in mine, we started walking down the aisle.

A NOTE FROM THE AUTHOR

One of the beautiful things about the Bible is that promises us that God welcomes every prodigal into His Kingdom that repents of their sin and accepts Christ as their personal Lord and Savior. No matter what that sin is—even murder—that sin can be forgiven if the sinner will just repent and put their trust in Jesus.

The Voynich Manuscript--which was alluded to when Chris, Crystal, and the rest of the team was trying to decipher Chase's code—actually exists. Written in the 15th or 16th century, it was acquired by book seller Wilfred Voynich in 1912. It now resides in Yale University, and is known as the most mysterious manuscript in the world. Many consider it to be a rather ingenious code, although its purpose is still the subject of debate today. Having seen pictures of pages from the manuscript online, I can understand why there is a lot of mystery as to the meaning of the manuscript! An excellent website for those interested in seeing the actual manuscript is www.voynich.nu.

Many of the conspiracy theories that Justin, the "King of Atlantis", alluded to are actually a part of conspiracy theory folklore. The Philadelphia Experiment, Hanger 18, the Men in Black, etc. are all the subject of debate and believed by many to actually exist. The author does neither advocates nor ridicules such theories. They are simply presented in this novel as legends that some do believe in.

The disappearance of Flight 19 actually happened. Many attribute the disappearance of the entire squadron of Flight 19 and the coast guard search plane that vanished to the Bermuda Triangle. Others attribute the disappearances to more natural reasons. The cause for the disappearances continues to be the source of debate.

The crimes of Jack the Ripper, alas, are all too true. The books and theories as to the identity of Jack the Ripper and the motive for the crimes would fill an entire library. An excellent source material for those interested in the crimes of Jack the Ripper is "Jack the Ripper—the Final Solution" by Stephen Knight (copyright 1976 by Treasure Press). This book provided valuable insights into the facts of the Ripper case as well as some interesting theories.

The Sherlock Holmes cases that Chris mentioned in Chapter 28—such as the case of the giant rat and the case of the aluminum crutch— when he opened the file box are the names of cases that Sir Arthur Conan Doyle referred to in his stories. These were cases that Holmes decided were too sensational to make public and were said to be kept in an old file box belonging to Watson.

One of the questions I am most often asked about the Alias Sherlock Holmes series is just how many books will be in the series. At this time, God has not revealed that to me. The series began with God directing me to begin the series, and I will continue the series as long as God allows me to. I have been truly humbled by the positive response the series has gotten as to people enjoying the Bible truths presented in each book and their actual concern for the welfare for the heroes in the series.

At this time, I am doing research for the next installment in the series. While it is too soon to reveal much in the way of the plot, I can say the next book will address some issues that law enforcement has faced in today's times. It will also mark a new chapter in the lives of Chris and Crystal as they adjust to actually being married and tries to make the life together they have long wanted.

As for the future of Chase Anderson and whether or not he will play an important role in future novels, it is true that he is behind bars. But the trial hasn't happened yet...

Thank you, dear reader, for your continued support in the series.

---Rev. Russell Baker